S0-AUX-849

Governments across the globe ducked for cover. Long-drilled and partly prepared, millions of RUS urbanites sealed themselves into subway tunnels, then slid blast-and-firestorm-proof hatches into place to ride out the blast-furnace interval. Most Americans were asleep, and in any case had only the sketchiest notion of adequate shelter. A few city dwellers—the smaller the city, the better their chances—sped beyond their suburbs before freeway arterials became clots of blood and machinery.

The American public had by turns ignored and ridiculed its Cassandras, who had all warned against our increasing tendency to crowd into our cities. We had always found some solution to our problems, often at the last minute. Firmly anchored in most Americans was the tacit certainty that, even to the problem of nuclear war against population centers, there must be a uniquely American solution; we would find it.

The solution was sudden death. A hundred million Americans found it.

SYSTEMIC SHOCK

Ace Science Fiction Books by Dean Ing

ANASAZI
PULLING THROUGH
SOFT TARGETS
SYSTEMIC SHOCK

SYSTEMIC SHOCK

DEAN ING

ACE SCIENCE FICTION BOOKS
NEW YORK

All characters in this book are fictitious.
Any resemblance to actual persons, living or dead,
is purely coincidental.

SYSTEMIC SHOCK

An Ace Science Fiction Book/published by arrangement with
the author

PRINTING HISTORY
Ace edition / June 1981
Ace Science Fiction edition, third printing / October 1986

All rights reserved.
Copyright © 1981 by Dean Ing.
Cover art by Alexander.
This book may not be reproduced in whole or in part,
by mimeograph or any other means, without permission.
For information address: The Berkley Publishing Group,
200 Madison Avenue, New York, New York 10016.

ISBN: 0-441-79383-5

Ace Science Fiction Books are published by The Berkley Publishing Group,
200 Madison Avenue, New York, New York 10016.
PRINTED IN THE UNITED STATES OF AMERICA

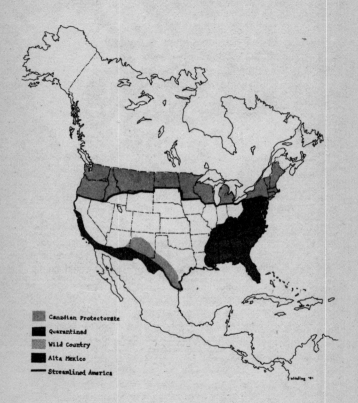

Canadian Protectorate
Quarantined
Wild Country
Alta Mexico
Streamlined America

Neutral

SinoInd or
Pro-SinoInd

Allies or Pro-Allies

Windling '81

For Diana and Vicki

PART I: VICTIMS

Chapter 1

In early August of 1996 the Atlantic states baked like some vast piecrust under a paralyzing heat wave. It moved scoutmaster Purvis Little, in Raleigh, to plan the Smoky Mountain pack trip that would save a few lives. It also moved the President of the United States to his retreat in the Shenandoah hills.

The weather relented on the evening of Friday, the ninth. Young Ted Quantrill hardly noticed, racing home after his troop meeting in Raleigh, because he knew he'd have to politick for that pack trip. The President noticed it still less; despite the air conditioning in his hoverchopper, a tiara of sweat beaded his balding head. The bulletin that had drawn him back to Washington suggested complications in the sharp new rise of foreign oil prices; a rise that in itself further impeded his race for reelection against Utah's Senator Yale Collier. The President considered Yale Collier a charismatic fool. Ted Quantrill's parents thought the same of scoutmaster Little. In any event, a modest proportion of fools would survive the next week, while some of their critics would die.

Chapter 2

Through twenty years and three administrations, pundits
in American government had watched helplessly as the
Socialist Party of China wooed lubricious favors from the
Middle East. Every few years some think-tank would an-
nounce that global addiction to oil was on the wane, thanks to
this or that alternative energy source. Just as regularly, the
thinkers went into the tank. Fusion was still an elusive
technique. New fission plants had been banned in the UN
General Assembly after the pandemic of fear that peaked in
1994. Loss of coolant (Alabama, '87), outgassing (Wales,
'91), partial meltdown (Karachi, '93), and accidental scatter
of confined radioactive waste (Honshu, '89; Connecticut,
Shantung, '94) had taken only a few hundred lives—far
fewer than, say, offshore oil rigs had taken.

But the fission boojum had scared the bejeezus out of
voters from Reykjavik to Christchurch, and even autocrats
reluctantly agreed to decommission some of their reactors. It
was not that fission plants no longer existed, but they were
fewer while power requirements grew.

If the million-plus deaths from the Birmingham and Minsk
bombs of '85 added to the clamor against fission plants, that
connection was hard to find. A million deliberate killings
was human nature acceptable to the public, while a few
hundred accidental killings composed a goad toward reform.
Industrialized nations rushed to develop clean power sources.
Meanwhile, they continued to burn petroleum.

Direct solar conversion, wind-driven generators, and alternative chemical fuels plugged part of the energy gap,
while the price of energy made conservationists of most
Americans. Still, fossil fuel remained a favored energy
source: storable, compact, simple. While developing one's
own oil resources, one was wise to import as much as
practicable. So said the Chinese; so said we all. As early as
1979 China's ruling party, the SPC, served notice of its intent

to anyone who might be paying attention. The SPC's official news agency, Xinhua, said:

> Nearly 160 Moslem mosques of the autonomous Ningxia Hui region of Northwest China are being reopened . . . after damage to varying degrees in the past few years. The mosques are under repair with government funds, including the famed Yinchuan edifice and a Tonxin mosque known to be 800 years old.

And again:

> The Koran, the sacred book of Islam, is now being retranslated into Chinese . . .

Though riddled with dissent on many topics, the Associated Islamic Republics was quick to imply devout thanks to China for her turnabout. The SPC could pivot as effortlessly on oil as anybody, with better coordination than the reconstituted, ham-fisted Russian Union of Soviets.

The abortive NATO-USSR conflict of 1985 has been chronicled elsewhere by Hackett, *et al*. Doubtless it won the popular title of World War Three on the basis of the nuclear exchange that swapped Birmingham in England for Minsk in Byelorussia before the collapse of the USSR. The newer and smaller RUS retained the frozen mineral wealth of Siberia; had lost nothing directly to China. But the lands lost to the RUS were all in the temperate zone where grain—and Islam—could be grown, and even exported.

No war, or any other movement, could be considered truly worldwide if it did not directly involve the two billion residents of China and India. Between 1985 and 1996, China's heavy industry expanded with Chinese supertugs towing icebergs to (ex-Saudi) Arabian shores, bringing desalinization equipment to rival Israel's and aiding the transformation of desert wastes. If a few million Chinese suffered from lack of that equipment in 1995, the SPC could wax philosophical

so long as those old Japanese-built oil tankers kept sliding
into ports near Peking.

China did not lack oil but what she had, she proposed to
keep while importing more from reluctant Mexicans and
willing Arabs. India was not rich in oil; but she was well-
positioned to obtain it easily from Islamic friends.

All this, Americans knew. What had alarmed the State
Department a week previously was the first of a series of
urgent communiques from Mikhail Talbukhin, the RUS ambassador. The Supreme Council of the RUS had decided that
Talbukhin should share a maddening discovery with us:
recent price hikes on Arab oil were by no means uniform.

The Russians had voice-printed tapes to prove it. China
and India were obtaining massive kickbacks, and had done so
for years. Somehow, under the noses of US and RUS spy
satellites, the SinoInd powers were obtaining *twice* as much
Middle-East oil as we had thought.

At first the notion of smuggled oil seemed wildly unlikely,
but State Department people agreed that the evidence was
convincing. The President addressed the question, What Do
We Do About It? He did not address it quickly enough for
RUS leaders, who saw that something was done about it the
following Tuesday.

On Tuesday, August 6, a tremendous explosion had been
noted by a US satellite over India's coastal state of Gujarat. It
was no coincidence that Gujarat lay directly across the Arabian Sea from the source of India's, and China's, oil. Within
hours the United States had stood accused, on the evidence of
Indian ordnance experts, of sabotaging a huge Indian water
conduit. The RUS backed US denials; not merely because
Russians had in fact done the job themselves, but for a much
better reason. The RUS craved Western support against the
unreconstructed socialists next door.

By Thursday, August 8, alliances had crystallized in the
UN. Every active unit of the National Guard went on standby
alert.

Chapter 3

Ted Quantrill had given up hope of shouldering a
backpack until his father, an active reservist, took a hard look
at his orders on a Thursday evening. The following day, Ted
was en route to the high Appalachian Trail. On that day the
boy assumed his own argument—the trek would be his fif-
teenth birthday present—had caused the change of heart.
Only later did Ted Quantrill begin to suspect the truth.

Chapter 4

From satellite and local report, it was obvious that the
Gujarat disaster was more than the loss of a water conduit.
Whole square kilometers were ablaze in an area known for its
experimental cotton production by Indians with Chinese ad-
visors. But cotton did not burn this way; and even if it did,
China would not have risen to such monolithic fury over a
trifling setback to an ally's agribiz. The blaze and the fury
might be appropriate if both were rooted in oil. Not a few
thousand gallons of it, but a few million.

Ranked fourth behind Arabia, the RUS, and Mexico in her
known reserves of oil, China could have been providing
India's supply, and this scenario was studied. But China
exported significant quantities of the stuff only to Japan.
With its expertise in shipbuilding and manufacture of preci-
sion equipment, Japan slowly forged her co-prosperity link
with China, and shared the cyclopean fuel supply. Some of
China's imported oil came from Mexico and Venezuela and
some, for the sake of appearance, came in tankers from the
Middle East. American satellites yielded an estimate, based

on a nosecount of tankers through the Strait of Hormuz, that China was buying a third of her oil from Arabs.

But no satellite had penetrated the bottom of the Arabian Sea. No research vessel had identified the progress of a stunning Chinese engineering project which, using an acid-hydraulic process, quietly tunneled a meters-broad pipeline under the continental shelf from Arabia to Gujarat on the western plain of India. It was known that China had invested in a scheme to run water conduits from the Himalayas to western India. What no one had suspected was that the conduit was double-barreled. Water ran toward the southwest. Oil ran toward the northeast, then on to China herself. No wonder, then, that China had exploded so many nuclear devices under the Tibetan plateau; the resulting cavities were being filled with oil pumped from the AIR crescent. It was an immense undertaking, yet it required no technical break-throughs. Its strength lay primarily in its secrecy.

With one well-placed demolition device just upline from a pumping station, the RUS severed water and oil conduits. Automatic cutoffs could not prevent the immediate loss of fifty thousand barrels of crude oil, which gravity-flowed from its conduit and spread atop the water as it burned. The RUS had well and truly blown the cover of the SinoInd conduit. Now, everybody's fat would sizzle in that fire.

Chapter 5

The train clung to its monorail and hummed an electric song as it fled in a lateral arc from Raleigh past Winston-Salem. The scoutmaster, Little, was too busy controlling sixteen of his charges to worry about the seventeenth. The Quantrill boy lazed alone by a window, one hand cupped to his ear, watching an unusual volume of traffic stream near their track that overhung the highway median strip. As always, most highway traffic was cargo; some old diesels, mostly short-haul electrics. But today a surprising number of private cars shared the freeway.

Bustling down the aisle, Purvis Little promised himself to confiscate the Quantrill radio, which defied Little's orders on a pack trip.

Ray Kenney flopped into the seat next to Ted, jabbed an obscene finger in Little's direction. "Old fart," he muttered; "took my translator. Said we were only looking for the dirty words."

Quietly, without stirring: "Weren't you?"

"If I'm gonna learn the language, I gotta know 'em all," Ray said, innocence spread across the pinched features.

Ted smiled at the tacit admission. What Ray lacked in muscle and coordination, he made up by honing his tongue. If words were muscle, Ray Kenney could outrun the monorail.

Ray leaned toward his friend, pretended to stare at the traffic, and whispered. "Got a fiver? Wayne's gonna buy some joints in Asheville. If you want in, I can fix it."

Ted considered the idea. A few tokes by the underaged on a weed in a sleeping bag was nothing new, a token rebellion to relieve chafing under Little's authority. But Wayne Atkinson, their only Eagle scout, seldom did favors without three hidden reasons for them. Atkinson probably had the joints already. "I'll pass, Ray. Thanks anyway."

"Scared?" Ray caught the cool glance from Ted Quantrill's mint-green eyes. The scar over Ted's nose and the sturdy limbs furthered the impression that Ted did not yield easily to fear. He might, however, yield to a claim of it. "Wayne isn't scared. He's cool, he never gets caught."

"But you do; you're not Little's pride and joy."

"If I had merit badges coming out of my ass like Wayne does," Ray began, and then jerked around.

There was no way to tell how many seconds Little had been standing behind them. Ray braced his knees against the seat ahead, thrust his hands between his thighs, slumped and stared at nothing.

"I'll take that radio, Quantrill," said the scoutmaster after waiting long enough to make Ray Kenney sweat. He took the

radio, slipped it into his shirt pocket, pursed his zealot lips.
"Was it reggae jazz, or polluting your mind with a porn
station?"

Not sullen, but weary: "Just a newscast, Mr. Little."

"Oh, no doubt," said Little, suddenly favoring Ray Kenney with a we-know-better smirk. "How will we ever explain your sudden interest in current events, Quantrill?"

Little turned away expecting no answer. He was halfway
to his seat when Ted replied, "No mystery, Mr. Little. My
father's in the Reserve, flies patrol from Key West to Norfolk. And there's a big tanker gone off the Florida coast."

Little frowned. "Sunk, you say?"

"Just gone; disappeared." Ted's shrug implied, *you tell
me, you've got the radio*.

"Get your gear together, boys," Little called. "Asheville
is the next stop." Then he hurried to his seat, fumbled in his
shirt pocket, and cupped one hand to his ear.

Ted Quantrill was wrong; a compelling mystery *was* un-
folding in the Florida Strait sea lanes. The tanker *Cambio
Justo*, under Panamanian registry, had last been reported off
Long Key, lumbering north toward Hampton Roads with a
quarter-million deadweight tons of Mexican crude oil in her
guts. The *Cambio Justo* could hardly run aground in four-
hundred-fathom straits. She could not just fly away, nor
could she evade satellite surveillance while she thrummed
over the surface of a calm sea. But she could always sink.

Two hours after the *Cambio Justo* vanished, a sinking was
everybody's best guess, and as far as it went that guess was
dead accurate. What no newsman had guessed yet was that
she had not sunk very far.

Chapter 6

The interurban coach disgorged Little's brood in
Cherokee. From there to Newfound Gap they invested an old
diesel bus with their high spirits. At the Tennessee border

they reached the old Appalachian Trail, streamed off the bus, watched the vehicle drone up a switchback and out of sight. The bright orange paint and the acrid stink of diesel exhaust bespoke a familiar world that, for a few of them, vanished with the bus as completely as had the *Cambio Justo*—and for the same reasons.

"Wait up," Ray Kenney puffed as the youths ambled down the trail under a canopy of oak, hemlock and pine. He pulled a light windbreaker from his pack, zipped it over slender limbs as Ted Quantrill sniffed the sweet tang of conifers in the mountain air.

"Move it, Kenney," a voice commanded from behind. Wayne Atkinson, the oldest of the boys, enjoyed a number of advantages in Little's troop. Wayne wouldn't have said just what they were; not *couldn't*, but *wouldn't*. His rearguard position was one of responsibility, which Wayne accepted because it also carried great authority. Below average height for his age, he was strongly built, fresh-faced, button-bright and sixteen. Wayne Atkinson gave the impression that he was younger, which enhanced his image to adults. The biggest members of the troop, Joey Cameron and Tom Schell, accepted Wayne's intellectual leadership without qualm and, because they could look down on the top of his head, without fear. Among themselves, the smaller boys called him 'Torquemada'.

Ray was already shrugging his backpack into place when the last of the others eased past on the narrow trail and Atkinson got within jostling distance. Lazily, self-assured: "If your ass is on the trail at sundown, I get to kick it." He followed this promise with a push and Ray, stumbling, trotted forward.

Atkinson reached toward Ted Quantrill with a glance, let his arm drop again, motioned Ted ahead. Ted moved off, trotting after Ray, leaving Atkinson to ponder the moment. Quantrill's part-time job at the swimming pool had toned his body, added some muscle, subtracted some humility. Sooner or later that kind of insolence could infect others, even little twits like Ray Kenney, unless stern measures were taken. Wayne considered the possibilities, pleased with his posi-

tion, able to see the others ahead who could not see him. It
would be necessary to enlist Joey and Tom, just to be sure;
and they could provoke the Quantrill kid by using his little pal
Kenney as bait. All this required isolation from Purvis Little,
who would sooner accept the word of his Eagle scout than
that of God Almighty. Wayne's roles at award ceremonies
reflected glory on his scoutmaster, and God had never seen
fit to do much of that.

To give Little his due, he took his duties seriously and
imagined that he was wise. He called rest stops whenever
Thad Young faltered. The spindly Thad, long on courage but
short on wind, made every march a metaphor of the public
education system: everyone proceeded at the pace of the
slowest.

The summer sun had disappeared below Thunderhead
Mountain, far to their west, before Little reached their
campsite near a sparkling creek. The National Park Service
still kept some areas pristine; no plumbing, no cabins. The
more experienced youths erected their igloo tents quickly to
escape the cutting edge of an evening breeze, then emerged
again, grumbling, in aid of the fumble-fingered.

Tom Schell slapped good-naturedly at Ted's hand. "Take
it easy with that stiffener rod," he said, helping guide it
through a tube in the tent fabric. "It's carbon filament. Bust
it and it's hell to repair."

"Thanks. It's brand-new; an advance birthday present,"
Ted replied, imitating Schell's deft handiwork.

The Schell hands were still for a moment. "If you have a
birthday up here, I don't wanta know about it."

Ted thought about that. "Aw, birthday hazing is kind of
fun."

"Not if Wayne's got it in for you. Look: you've got your
friends and I have mine, Teddy. If you're smart, you won't
talk about birthdays until we're back in Raleigh."

"How do I get outa this chickenshit outfit," Ted grinned
as they pulled the tent fabric taut. No answer beyond a smile.
Tom Schell flipped his version of the scout salute from one
buttock and wandered off to help elsewhere, leaving Ted to

pound anchor stakes. Ray had forgotten the stakes, sidling toward the big campfire site where Little was talking with the strangers.

When he finished, Ted fluffed his mummybag into the sheltering hemisphere of fabric. He found Ray with the others, who by now had abandoned their weiner roast to listen to the tall stranger and to gawk wistfully at his two stalwart daughters. "We'll sleep on the trail if we have to," the man was saying. "We're taking the first ride back toward Huntsville, Mr. Little. I hope it's still there tomorrow."

"We've got a radio too." Purvis Little did not try to hide his irritation. "I heard all about that tanker. I'm sure it has nothing to do with that mess in India and even if it did, you're only scaring the boys."

A murmur of denial swelled around him; no young male liked to let his visceral butterflies flutter before young females. The stranger said, "*I'm* scared," in a shaky basso, "and I'd like to see all of us go back together. If there's to be a war, we should be with our families."

"Good luck on the trail," Little replied, his hands urging the man and his silent daughters toward the path. Then he added, with insight rare for him: "If there's another war, those families would be better off here than in Huntsville, or any other big city."

The older scouts were plainly disappointed to see the girls striding from sight in the afterlight. "What the heck was that all about," Ted asked.

"Beats me," said Thad Young. "What's an escalation syndrome?"

"It's when one government tries to hit back at another one," Ray said, "and hits too hard."

"Like Torquemada Atkinson," Thad guessed.

Ray, following Ted back to their tent: "Naw. That's annihilation." Pleased with his definitions, Ray Kenney did not realize that the first was genesis of the second.

Chapter 7

The RUS vessel *Purukhaut Tuzhauliye* nosed into the
Arctic Ocean, two days out of the Yenisey Gulf, early Satur-
day morning with nearly two hundred thousand tons of heavy
Siberian crude scheduled for the White Sea and Archangelsk.
That was by Russian reckoning; the Chinese had scheduled
her up the escalator.

The *P. Tuzhauliye*'s cargo had been extracted from beneath treacherously shifting, half-frozen peat in the oil fields
near Dudinka and, by Siberian standards, was precious stuff.
The ship's captain conned her carefully through the Kara Sea
shallows, quickened her diesels south of Novaya Zemlya
Island, neared the dropoff of the continental shelf where,
many fathoms deep, something huge and hostile lay waiting.

Chapter 8

Eight o'clock in the morning, or almost any other time, off
Novaya Zemlya was broad daylight in August. Transmuted
to a campsite near Clingman's Dome in the Smoky Mountains, that same instant was illuminated only by dying embers
of a showy, wasteful Friday night campfire. While Wayne
Atkinson outlined the sport he proposed the following day
with the help of Joey and Tom, a 'Bulgarian' radioman's
assistant on the *P. Tuzhauliye* received a signal through his
microwave unit.

Wayne did not bother to tell his confederates that hazing
Ray Kenney might bring on violence with Ted Quantrill. The
radioman's assistant had not told anyone his secrets, either.
One, that he had been raised an Albanian, scornful of Russians; two, that he had emplaced explosives with remote
detonators on every communication device he could find

aboard ship, including sonar; and three, that he was one of Peking's many agents in place. The Albanian mole had been in place for over a year. Wayne Atkinson had been enjoying the sleep of the innocent for only a few minutes when, a continent and an ocean beyond, the Albanian paused at his breakfast in the ship's mess.

After a moment the man checked his watch, decided against filling his belly because of the icy water he expected to feel soon, sought his exposure gear, then paid attention to his receiver again. He encoded a signal on his watch while standing in the shadow of the broad fo'c'sle, estimating his chances of surviving the wake of 50,000 horsepower screws after a free leap of ten meters from deck to salt water.

From widely-spaced points down the length of the four-block-long tanker came sounds, hardly more than echoes, of muffled detonations. The Albanian eased himself over the rail, inhaled deeply, and leaped out as far as adrenaline could carry him.

The Albanian heard faint alarm hoots over the splash of his own struggle and the hissing passage of the *P. Tuzhauliye,* braced himself to enter the great vessel's wake, then felt a series of thudding impacts through the water. More alarms were going off aboard ship, which began to settle visibly as gigantic bubbles burst around her.

In itself, the ship's wake would not have been fatal. The Albanian resurfaced, pulled the 'D' ring on his flotation device, then felt it ripped from his benumbed hands by an enormous eddy—the kind of eddy that might accompany the sudden sinking of four square city blocks. The inflating raft fled in the direction of the *P. Tuzhauliye's* radar mast which was rapidly submerging and, as the Albanian gasped, he rolled and strangled on ice brine. He was not as lucky as the Grenadan agent on the *Cambio Justo,* who had been picked up alive by a small submarine tug.

Concrete ships were well-known to westerners. But the first oil tankers had been Chinese junks and so were the first submersibles expressly designed to steal a supertanker intact. For all their burgeoning industry, the Chinese owed much to friendly Japanese shipbuilders. Early semisubmersible drill

rigs such as the *Aleutian Key,* designed in New Orleans, had
been built by the Japanese a full generation before. Even the
details of omnithrustor propulsion, long a feature of seagoing
drill rigs, were employed. Indeed, the Chinese craft had been
perfected while transporting oil from wellheads in the East
China Sea. Enormous turbine-driven concrete caissons fitted
with half-acre suction pads on hydraulic rams, the Chinese
submersibles were capable of changing from strongly negative to positive buoyancy in seconds. Or vice-versa. Like the
Great Wall and SinoInd pipeline, these craft were both vast
and conceptually simple. The most complicated detail was
sliding the filmy half-kilometer plastic condom over the
submersible and its prey by means of small submarine tugs.
No oil slick traced the passage of the drowned tanker as she
was borne under polar ice to her final resting place on the
shallow undersea Yermak Plateau, sixteen hundred klicks
distant.

Though the *P. Tuzhauliye* was never found, the *Cambio
Justo* would be located four years hence near Matanzas,
Cuba. In both cases, the Chinese saw to it that the tanker was
soon minus her crude oil, and plus a great deal of salt water.

Chapter 9

Purvis Little finished gnawing a breakfast chickenbone
and began on a cuticle. Ted Quantrill's radio finished its
newscast as the scoutmaster turned to his Eagle scout. "First
time I've ever been sorry I didn't bring a transceiver. Maybe
I'd best hike to the Ranger Station and call some of the
parents."

"I'll hold the fort here," said Wayne Atkinson. *And make
war on some of our little Indians,* he added to himself.

Thad Young took his skillet from the coals and wandered
from Little's vicinity spooning Stroganoff. In common with
most twelve-year-olds, Thad had bizarre notions about

breakfast. He listened to Ted and Ray argue the demerits of ashes in their omelet, then remembered the morning newscast and pointed his spoon at Ray. "What's a measured reprisal?"

Blink. "Uhh—exactly two litres of shit in Atkinson's hat," Ray said. "I dunno, Thad; where'd you hear it?"

"Oh, the President's afraid the Russians won't make a measured reprisal. What're you laughing about, Teddy, it's your radio they're listening to."

Ted jogged Ray's shoulder in rough endorsement of the joke, then turned serious. "I think it's about that missing tanker; a lot of politics in the air. My dad'll find the tanker, wait and see."

"In the Arctic? This is another one," Thad said, with a roll of his eyes. "Mr. Little is gonna hike out and see about it. Or somethin'," he added, consigning all adult motives to limbo.

The warble of Little's whistle convened the troop a few minutes later. Nothing to worry about, said Little, looking worried; but while he visited the ranger station, the troop would be in Wayne Atkinson's care. There were to be no excursions far from camp, and—a hesitation—their gear should be packed in case they had to move to another site.

"I'll bet," said Ray as they watched Little's head bob from sight. "A tenner says we're going home."

"Knock it off, Kenney," from the gangling Joey Cameron. Joey, no great mental specimen, hewed to one cardinal principle: he worshipped authority. Joey enforced his religion whenever possible.

Ray again: "Betcha I'm right. We won't even get to swim in the pond."

"I'll *throw* you in if you don't strike that tent and pack up." With that, Joey swept his brogan toward a tent stake. They all heard the *snap* as the stiffener rod broke near the stake.

Ted came to his feet with an anguished, "Cameron, you klutz! That's my—"

Joey Cameron caught Ted off-balance with a big hand on his breastbone, pushed the smaller youth who fell backward over a log. "That's your tough luck," he said. He had intended neither the injury nor the insult, had acted on impulse. But Joey patterned his behavior on Wayne's. Contrition was somehow a weakness to be avoided.

"We can fix it," Ray said quickly, fearful that Ted might come up swinging. He extended his hand to his friend, watched Joey back away with long careful strides, managed to deflect Ted from anger as they studied instructions and ferrules in the mending kit.

In half an hour the rod was repaired, their gear repacked in backpacks. Robbie and Tim Calhoun, thirteen-year-old twins, aided in rigging a polymer line between trees so that packs could be hung above the range of marauding ants. Robbie nodded, satisfied. "Now let's take a swim. Joey can be lifeguard."

"Who'll guard *his* life," Ted muttered, half in jest.

Ray patted the air. "Forget it, Teddy. You're like the damn' Russians, trying to make a war out of an accident."

"And you're like the damn' UN, trying to get me to do nothing and hiding it with big words." The Calhoun twins stood listening, mystified.

"You mean like 'measured reprisal'? Just remember to measure Joey Cameron first, Teddy. He's a klick high and a year older."

"So?" Next Thursday I'll be a year older too."

"You'll be a few days older, just like everybody else. Come on, let's see how deep the pond is."

The pond had been dammed a century before; local flat stones fitted by long-dead hands of pioneers. Descendants of those folk still lived nearby in the valleys, with the help of legislation in Tennessee and North Carolina. Sites in Utah, Idaho and Oregon were also set aside for people who kept the old ways; living anachronisms who spun their own cloth, cured their own meat, distilled their own whiskey. There were still other repositories of ancient crafts and ethics in the north among the Amish, in the west among separatists from Mormonism, and in the southwest among latino Catholics, Amerinds, and just plain ornery Texans. City-bred in Raleigh, Ted Quantrill knew little about the back-country ways in his own region and next to nothing about those beyond it. Late Saturday morning, he only knew the sun felt good on his back as he spread himself to dry on moss-crusted stones after his swim.

Gabe Hooker was a boy who went along. He was roughly Ted's age and size, with the special talent for being agreeable. Across the pond, affable Gabe basked in the momentary favor of Wayne Atkinson. He heard Wayne suggest a cleanup project for the tenderfeet back at the campsite, and found himself selected as leader of the cleanup. Gabe rounded up the neophytes and went along.

Ted Quantrill's first intuition came with the silence, and the repeated soughing gasp that punctuated it. He opened one eye, surveyed an apparently empty pond, half-dozed again. He enjoyed the breeze tingly-cool on naked arms; lay catsmug and mindless as a stone in celebration of idleness. During the early part of the summer Ted had worked halfdays at a Raleigh pool, checking filters and diving for lost objects, scrubbing concrete and learning to catnap. And losing baby fat, and gaining inches in height. Unnoticed to himself, Ted was emerging from the cocoon of boyhood. Wayne Atkinson had noticed it—which explains why he was drowning Ray Kenney.

Again the quiet cough, a wheezing word through water. Ted opened the eye again, moved his head very slightly. Twenty meters away was Tom Schell, legs dangling from the lip of mossy stones into deep water at the dam. Tom frowned down at Joey Cameron, neck-deep in water, and at Atkinson whose muscular left arm encircled a log. Wayne's right arm, and both of Joey's, were busy.

"Let him up a minute," Tom urged quietly. "He's swallowed water twice."

"You afraid pissant Quantrill will hear?" Atkinson sneered at Tom Schell, hauled something to the surface, let it burble.

"You *want* him to?" Tom glanced quickly at Ted, saw no movement.

Wayne and Joey glanced too. "Who cares," Wayne said, caring a great deal. The Kenney kid had allowed himself to

be drawn into the game, duck and be ducked, and had
realized too late that Wayne had vicious ideas about its
outcome. "You're the little shit that gave me that nickname,
aren't you?"

No answer. Schell, reaching out: "Enough's enough,
Wayne."

Joey saw his leader nod, wrestled a limply-moving mass to
the lip of the dam. Ted Quantrill recognized the face of Ray
Kenney as it drooled water.

Flashes of successive thought rapid-fired through Ted's
mind. Purvis Little: no help there. Ray was coughing and
gagging as Schell dragged him from the water. Schell,
Cameron and Atkinson had deliberately set the stage with
only one witness, or at least Atkinson had, and none of them
doubted that they could overpower Ray and Ted together.
Quantrill went to a crouch inhaling deeply, quietly, hyper-
ventilating as he ran on silent feet. Joey saw him then, yelled
an alarm in time for Wayne Atkinson to turn.

Quantrill was unsure of the murky bottom and chose to
leap feet-first. He chose to plant one foot where Joey's solar
plexus should be, and made his next choice in grabbing the
handiest piece of Atkinson. It happened to be the sleek blond
hair.

Ted's inertia carried him past them and his tactical instinct
made him slide behind Atkinson as he gripped and shook the
blond mop underwater. He hammered at the face with his
free hand, knew from the sodden impacts that his fist caused
little damage, released his grip, thrust away and surfaced.

Atkinson emerged facing Joey Cameron, dodged a round-
house swing by his friend. "It's me, you fucker," he sput-
tered, and whirled to find Ted.

Their quarry made his eyes wide, began to swim backward into deeper water bearing all the stigmata of terror.
Even Joey Cameron was not tall enough to stand on the
bottom farther out.

A brave scenario occurred to Mr. Little's pride. "Stay put,
this 'un's mine," said Atkinson, who was a fair swimmer.

Ted continued his inhale-exhale cycles; noted that Ray

Kenney was trying to sit up as Joey climbed onto the dam. Dirty water hid his legs as Ted drew them up to his chest, still simulating a poor backstroke, mimicking mortal fear of the older youth. Atkinson swam in a fast crawl, grinned, paused to enjoy the moment as he reached for Ted Quantrill's hair. The doubled blow of Quantrill's heels onto his shoulder and sternum knocked him nearly unconscious.

Wayne blanched, shook a mist of pain from his eyes. "For that," he began, then realized that Quantrill had used the double kick to start a backward somersault. Wayne kicked hard, encountered nothing, then felt himself again dragged backward by his hair. He managed to gargle Joey's name before being hauled under, inhaling more water than air as he gasped. His thighs were scissored by another's, his right hand cruelly twisted by another's, his world a light-and-shadow swirl of horror until his groping left hand found another's locked in his hair. Then Atkinson's head was free, but both arms were now pinioned by another's, and in his spinning choking confusion he tried to breathe. It was not a very smart move.

When Quantrill felt his struggling burden grow spastic, less patterned in its panic, he released it and treaded water calmly as Atkinson, sobbing, floundered toward shore. Joey Cameron thought about loyalty instead of terrain and stalked Quantrill across the pond. Here the silt was unroiled. Joey could see the stones on the bottom. He did not see the one Quantrill was holding until it crashed under his chin, and from that instant his vision improved remarkably. He saw that a fist with a rock in it beats a long advantage in reach, and he saw the futility of swinging on someone you cannot find when your eyes are swollen shut and your opponent waits to slash like a barracuda.

Throughout the fight, Quantrill coupled his terrible slashing fury with utter silence as he mastered the urge to weep in rage, and with an increasing clarity of purpose. The cries and sobs that drew younger boys back to the pond issued from older throats than his. By the time Ted Quantrill chased a galloping blood-streaming Joey Cameron to shore, he was dimly aware that he had done several things right; things that were new to him but that seemed very old and appropriate.

Item: let the other guy make all the noise. You know how he's taking it, and your silence rattles him.

Item: make the other guy fight your fight in a setting you choose.

Item: one enemy at a time, please.

Item: don't expect help from weak friends.

Item: don't expect thanks, either. Your friends may not see it the way you do.

Tom Schell qualified for a merit badge in first aid that day; would have qualified for another if they gave them for diplomacy. Tom listened to the wound-licking growls of Atkinson and Cameron, kept his own counsel, and found Ted nursing skinned knuckles at the pond. "You won't get a date with Eve Simpson for that dumb stunt," he said, invoking the name of a buxom teen-aged holovision star. "Wayne was just teaching Ray a lesson. When Little gets back he's gonna be plain pissed off."

"Let him take it out on Wayne. I did," Quantrill smiled.

This kid is all wire and ice water, thought Schell, staring at Quantrill as if seeing him for the first time. The chill down his back only aggravated Schell. "Su-u-ure. And why'd you tell the twins about your goddam birthday? They passed it along. A word to the wise, Teddy." Tom Schell shook his head as though superior to all that had happened, as though he had not lent tacit support to the worst of it.

Ted nodded, attended to his knuckles and the pursuit of new thoughts. He was in the process of realizing that each of them—Wayne, Joey, Tom, Ted—thought himself more sinned against than sinning. It never occurred to Ted to view the hapless Ray Kenney as a sinner; that for an individual or a nation, placing oneself in a helpless position against known danger might be an evil that generates its own punishment.

Chapter 10

The scoutmaster felt reassured by his calls to Raleigh, and by the phrasing of media releases over the Quantrill radio. The emergency session of the UN, he was sure, would do the job. Purvis Little had never heard of I. F. Stone, whose legendary journalistic accuracy grew from a realist's premise: "All governments are liars; nothing they say should be believed."

Little's first act on returning to camp was to call his own emergency session. He blew three short blasts on his whistle, saw the bandages on Joey Cameron's face, then glanced at his Eagle. "Good to see you practicing first aid with Joey," he began. "I need to talk with my patrol leaders."

"Practice hell," Atkinson said, regarding his splinted left middle finger. Then he remembered to smile. Regardless of the facts, Little always favored the one who was smiling.

"Language," Little tutted; "settle down, now." He draped an avuncular arm over Wayne's shoulder, raised his voice over the hubbub as other scouts surrounded him. "I've got good news, boys. Despite some rumors among our—" he sought the gazes of Ted and Ray, "—young worrywarts, we're not going home. I've talked with some parents, and they're confident that our country is not about to make war on China or Atlantis or Venus."

As every boy knew from holovision, the Venus probes had returned with wondrous samples from the shrouded planet. Mineral specimens suggested only a form of primitive quasilife there, and holo comics had extracted all available humor from the notion of intelligence on Venus. Dutiful laughter spread from the patrol leaders.

Little went on to warn his scouts against further worrisome talk about the outside world, and ended by announcing that he'd found a berry thicket not far from camp. Wayne Atkinson bided his time. When the patrols were out of sight searching for berries, he doubled back to find his scoutmaster. Somewhat later he brought Schell and Cameron back, and later still the rest of the troop straggled back with their booty. By then, Purvis Little understood the hostilities in his world roughly as well, and with roughly the same amount of bias, as India understood her problems after her secret session with her Chinese allies.

Chapter 11

The President sat back in his chair to give an impression of ease as he regarded the image on his holoscreen. The transmission link to the American embassy in Moscow was only as good as its security, and he worried about that. "You haven't answered the question," he said to the image, then glanced toward the Secretary of State who sat near him.

"Mr. President, Mr. Secretary," said the American ambassador from half a world away, and hesitated, "—I can only say I *believe* that the RUS will be patient. I'm convinced they really did pick up faint signatures of Chinese tugs under polar ice—or at least they think they did. But they've assured me they will take no unilateral action as long as there's a shred of doubt."

"What they really doubt," rumbled the Secretary of State, "is the motive for our patience. Isn't that it?"

"With all due respect, Mr. Secretary," said the ambassador, unwilling but staunch, "that's it. The RUS isn't so concerned about its own view as about that of the Chinese and Indians. What if *they* think we're lacking in resolution?"

"They might make a terrible mistake," said the President. "We have conveyed that to Peking, of course. You're aware the Chinese are serious about offering 'acts of God' as the explanation for the sinkings or whatever the hell they were?"

"Divine retribution for the Gujarat thing? I can't believe it, no sir," said the ambassador.

"Neither do they, obviously," said the Secretary of State. "But the SPC must think that position might be useful if taken seriously by a lot of Judeo-Christian Americans. And that could weaken us from the inside. Guilt enfeebles the sword arm," he said with a thin smile.

"Pity there aren't many Christians in the SPC," said the ambassador.

While it may have been a pity, all three men knew it had been no accident. While the Socialist Party of China carefully nurtured its mosques, its Central Committee regulated the churches and synagogues on the mainland; and those were in major cities where Judeo-Christian worship could be watched easily. The Buddhist and Neo-Confucianist ethics of Chinese intellectuals depended strongly, as they had for centuries, on the concept of shame—to the virtual exclusion of guilt. Proper behavior in China was reinforced not by one's internal fear of wrongdoing, but by one's fear of being caught at it. The Japanese found it easy to deal with the difference; Islamic countries found it almost as easy. On the other hand, most western Russians, particularly since their post-collapse rapprochment with the west, were still molded from the cradle by basically Christian traditions of Godhead, and of guilt. In this dichotomy of basic motives, the Russian Union of Soviets was like the western world, sharing an ethic that looked inward for strength.

In China however, the individual was not the basic societal unit, but only a piece of one. China was hoping to exploit our notions of guilt as a weakness. RUS leaders were regaining tight control over Russian media, the better to exclude such disturbing ideas as the Chinese suggestion that God had taken two tankers in punishment for Gujarat. But Americans were free to choose their messages, and some would focus on the Chinese message in all honesty. Our President knew all too well that assumed guilt might be laid at the feet of his administration in the form of blame—especially by religious fundamentalists who had heard Senator Collier speak.

"Damn the SPC," the President muttered aloud, "*and* our guilt-hoarding Christians."

"Not for attribution," said the Secretary with quick humor.

"Just those who aren't reasonable," said the President in irritation. "You know who I mean."

They knew, and changed the topic to guess at reprisals the RUS might select for the loss of the *P. Tuzhauliye*. The ambassador and the Secretary quite properly stuck to the foreign issue; the domestic issue looked even bleaker. Every media survey pointed to the growing strength of the coalitions behind Senator Yale Collier of Utah.

It was not that the President was, as Collier hinted, godless; it was just that Collier was so spectacularly Godly. The Church of Jesus Christ of the Latter-Day Saints had no better exemplar of Mormonism than the best-known of its Council of Apostles, the organ-voiced Yale Collier. Educated at Brigham Young University, trained as a young missionary in Belgium, seasoned in argument on the Senate floor, Collier kept his farmboy accent and exuded a sense of destined greatness. He was also one of the best verbal counterpunchers on anybody's campaign trail.

In June the President had made a passing reference to Collier as a fundamentalist. Collier had tickled millions of holo watchers by his droll objection. He presumed, with a shake of the great head, that the President knew the term 'fundamentalist', among Mormons, meant 'polygamist'. The Senator had taken only one wife, his handsome mate Eugenia. Perhaps, Collier added waggishly, a man without children found it difficult to believe that a single union could be blessed with eleven children, but such was the case. He, Yale Collier, humbly awaited an apology.

By this stroke, Collier implied that the President was either ignorant of religious terms or casual about the truth; and stressed his own status as a virile family man; *and* left room for comparison between a once-married man who had eleven kids and a twice-married man who had none. The nation's holo pundits had played the potency jokes threadbare until July.

For example: one satirist noted that the Collier union was in better shape than the national union. The current administration was cursed with two issues, while the Colliers were blessed with eleven.

One major political issue revolved around relations with the Russian Union of Soviets. The liberal administration favored stronger ties with the RUS, still the largest geographic entity on the globe though it had lost the monolithic control it had once exerted over the southern, strongly Islamic, border states. The RUS was currently getting American help toward its goal of making each state in its union self-sufficient in energy resources.

The conservatives under Collier were quick to point out that the US, with its hodgepodge energy programs, could not afford to help make Russians stronger—again!—than we were. A healthy RUS, they argued, was a threat to a fading America. The blossoming SinoInd romance was too obvious a threat for dispute.

Thus, for its Presidential campaign, conservatives linked the foreign issue to the domestic issue of energy programs. For a dozen years America had annually spent billions on fusion research, to be met largely by frustration as most avenues of study terminated in blind alleys. Physicists believed that clean, safe fusion power might yet be practicable, if research programs were expansive enough. But progress was slow at best. One by one, members of Congress yielded to the cries of a public that was paying higher taxes for its energy programs without a downturn in the costs of electricity, fuel, travel. Fusion research funds, pared in 1994, were cut to the bone in 1995. The administration protested: "You can't expect stronger progress from a weakened program."

"Fiirst give us tax relief," the electorate seemed to be saying, "and other progress second. We can wait for more tokamaks and the other fusion mumbo-jumbo—and don't mention fission to us again."

By this topsy-turvy expectation, the American public further delayed their fusion panacea, and found alliance in a coalition between big business and conservative religious groups. Big business, as always, felt galled by taxation. Besides, as long as energy could be kept expensive to the consumer while industry got it cheaply by tax relief, one could make a profit selling an endless array of windmills, solar panels, storage batteries, and alcohol stills to two hundred and fifty million Americans. This view accorded well with groups that—with some justification—yearned for an earlier time. Fundamentalists tended to favor a still that yielded grain alcohol from corn in a process one controlled at home, over an electric outlet that drew power from a distant turbine/alternator in a process one couldn't understand at all. Besides, you couldn't drink electricity . . .

Gradually, Americans were reviving a general opinion that muscle power was more ethical than machine power; that simplicity was next to Godliness. The tenets of Mormonism, outwardly simple in its absolutes and its demands that each Mormon household be as independent as possible, became more attractive. One out of every twenty-five Americans was now an LDS member—ten million Latter-Day Saints. They comprised a heaven-sent bloc of patriots, and a hell of a bloc of votes. Privately, the Secretary of State suspected that the country might prosper under a Mormon President. In a liberal democracy, the administration usually bowed to its citizens. In an honest-to-God theocracy the administration bowed only to revelation from Above.

Chapter 12

Quantrill was scouring his messkit after supper on Saturday when Tom Schell, without elaborating, told him he was wanted by the scoutmaster. Ted paused long enough to slip on his traditional kerchief, plodded through the dusk with a naive sense of mission in his soul. He felt sure that Little wanted to hear the truth until he entered Little's tent, saw the smugness in Wayne Atkinson's face.

"Sit down, Quantrill," said Little. It was either the best or the worst of signs; for minor discipline, you stood at attention. "What I have to say here is very painful for me."

Ted didn't understand for a moment. "I'm not happy about it either, Mr. Little. When I saw that Ray was unconscious, I just—"

"Don't make it worse by lies," Little cut him off wearily. "I've had the whole story from my patrol leaders, Quantrill. They were all witnesses, and they agree in every detail."

Tom Schell would not meet Quantrill's glance, though Atkinson and Cameron were more than happy to. Ted, angrily: "Do they all agree they'd nearly drowned Ray Kenney?"

"I'm sure Ray Kenney would say anything you told him to," sighed Little, and went on to describe a fictional scene as though he had seen it. Ray, running from a harmless splashing by a good-natured Eagle scout; Wayne, alone, brutally attacked from behind; Joey, trying to reason with the vicious Quantrill after Wayne's aloof departure; Ted Quantrill, hurling stones from shore at the innocent Joey. "It was the most unworthy conduct I have ever encountered in all my years of scouting," Little finished.

"You didn't encounter it at all, Mr. Little," Ted flashed. Anger made him speak too fast, the words running together. "It didn't even happen."

Little swayed his head as if dodging a bad smell. "Oh, Quantrill, look at the lads! I'm sure you'd like to think none of it happened. You may even need—psychological help—to face it," said Little, leaning forward to brush Ted's shoulder with a pitying hand. "But we can't have that sort of violence—mental imbalance—in a scout troop, Quantrill." Almost whispering, nodding earnestly: "It all happened, son. But we can't let it ever happen again. The best thing I can do is to let you resign from the troop on your own accord.

Wouldn't that be easiest for you? For all of us?"

A sensation of enervating prickly heat passed from the base of Ted Quantrill's skull down his limbs as he let Little's words sink in. Fairness, he saw, was something you gave but should never expect to receive. In the half-light of the single chemlamp he noted the simple deluded self-justification on Joey Cameron's face, the effort to hide exultation on Wayne Atkinson's part. Tom Schell fidgeted silently, staring upward. Ted showed them his palms. "What else can I do, Mr. Little? You wouldn't believe me or Ray. Maybe I *should* resign. Then I won't have to watch Torquemada Atkinson hit on my friends."

"You're the hitter, Quantrill," Joey spat.

Quantrill's head turned with the slow steadiness of a gun turret. "And don't you ever forget it," he said carefully, staring past Joey's broken nose into the half-closed eyes.

Purvis Little jerked his head toward a movement at the tent flap. "Go away, Thad; this doesn't concern you, son."

"Durn right it does," sniffled Thad, pushing his small body into the opening. Behind him, Ted saw, other boys were gathered in the near-darkness. "We been listening, Mr. Little."

A wave-off with both hands from Little: "Shame on you boys! Go on, now—"

"Shame on *them*," Thad blubbered, pointing an unsteady finger at the patrol leaders. He ducked his head as if fearful of a blow but, now helplessly crying, he rushed on: "I seen part of it today an' Teddy's right, those bastids is liars, you don't know diddly *squat* about what happened—what those big guys been doing all along!"

A chorus of agreement as others streamed into the tent, some crying in release of long-pent frustrations.

Little had to shout for order, but he got it. Thad disabused him of some errors, and Ray's version was similar. The Calhoun twins, Gabe Hooker, even the shy Vardis Lane all clamored to list old injuries; reasons why the nickname 'Torquemada' had stuck. The sum of it shed little glory and

less credibility on Wayne Atkinson, who still hoped to bra-
zen his way out.

Finally, Little turned openmouthed toward his patrol leaders, awed by his own suspicions. Joey saw Wayne's steady
glare of denial and aped it until—''Wayne lied, Mr. Little,''
Tom Schell said quietly. He did not bother to add that he had
endorsed every syllable. Maybe no one would notice.

''That's right,'' said Joey. If Tom was flexible, Joey could
be flexible.

''I see,'' said Purvis Little; and the glance he turned on
Ted Quantrill brimmed with hatred. Holding himself carefully in check: ''I misjudged you, Quantrill—and some
others, too. Forget what I said, but now I have to talk to my
patrol leaders and,'' between gritted teeth, ''the rest of you
please, *please* get out.''

Chapter 13

The murmur of voices from Little's tent was distant,
carrying only sad phatic overtones. Ted, quarreling internally with new unwelcome wisdom, thought Ray Kenney
asleep until Ray said, ''I'm glad we got you out of that.''

''After you got me into it? The least you could do—but
thanks.'' It had not escaped Ted that his friend had asked for
gratitude without once giving it.

''We kept you from getting booted out,'' Ray insisted.

''Getting out anyway, soon as we get home.''

''You can't; you're our leader.''

Silence. Ted Quantrill knew that he could lead; knew also
that he did not want followers.

Ray, through a yawn: ''Things'll be different now that
Little understands what happened.''

''He doesn't. He never will,'' Ted replied, and discouraged further talk. Ted knew that with one hostile glance, Purvis Little had given him a valuable discovery: most people will hate you for identifying their illusions.

The lesson was worth remembering; the whole day was memorable. Ted Quantrill wondered why he felt no elation, why he wished he were alone so that he could cry, why it was that he felt like crying. He had not yet learned that new wisdom is a loss of innocence, nor that weeping might be appropriate at childhood's end.

Chapter 14

While Quantrill slept in Tennessee, savants in Peking and New Delhi gauged America's response. Once, India would have looked to Moscow for counsel and arms, but no more. The RUS had been forced to cut foreign aid, and to yield more autonomy to the predominantly Islamic peoples of her southern flanks from Lake Baikal to the Black Sea. One sign of her troubles, as the RUS well knew, was the damnable *tariqat*.

Tariqats, Moslem secret societies, were flourishing in the 1980's while Russian-speaking USSR bureaucrats sweated to modernize Azerbaijan, Uzbekistan, sprawling Kazakhstan, reluctant Afghanistan. The tariqat was a far older tradition than Marxism, more staunchly rooted, in some ways harsher in its discipline. And Allah met His payrolls: despairing RUS bureaucrats joked that their earthly rewards could not match baklavah in the sky. No wonder that first the USSR, then the RUS, became alarmed as tariqats flourished in the Islamic RUS republics. The tariqat was a broad covert means to reject Russianization, and RUS moslems embraced it. Moscow knew her underbelly was soft on Islam, and worried about ties between its tariqats and the AIR next door.

Directly to the south of the RUS lay the Associated Islamic

Republics, in a vast crescent from Morocco to Iran, abutting India which was still officially the world's largest democratic nation; unofficially a polyglot nation in the process of trading chaos for Islam.

Since the 1960's, pundits had been predicting that India '. . . can't keep this up much longer.' Some observers meant her overpopulation; India's women, a miracle of dreadful fecundity, steadily produced mouths that could not be fed, much less find employment. Some referred to India's acceptance of fourteen official languages. Still others indicated India's rejection of western ties while fumbling away her parliamentary democracy.

Underlying India's manifold ills was the central fact that, until recent years, three-quarters of her citizens espoused caste restrictions in some form of Hinduism. But recently, tens of millions of *harijans*—untouchables scorned by ruling castes—had become literate, and at that point began an accelerating conversion to Islam urged on by India's already prominent Moslem minority. One might almost suggest certain parallels between the fast-rising conservative religious movements of the two most populous democratic nations on earth. By 1988 the Reformed Jan'ta party, a coalition of reform groups, was led by Moslems. Amid these delicate adjustments came the River War with Pakistan.

Moslem Pakistan had several times struggled to produce a democracy, falling back on martial law each time. Thanks to her draconian rule she lost her eastern half to India in 1971, and when India annexed Bangladesh she welcomed more Moslems into parliament. Still devoutly Moslem, still incapable of sustaining a democracy, still wrangling with India and fumbling with nuclear energy, Pakistan existed largely with western aid until 1988, when she lost the River War.

The Sutlej River cascades from Himalayan headwaters, crossing India's Punjab before entering Pakistan. Pakistan was well into her project to irrigate fallow land with Sutlej water when India, with desert property of her own, began to divert too much of the Sutlej. Pakistan protested. India borrowed a smile from Buddha. And while debate smouldered in

the UN, Pakistan's agribiz choked on dust. Pakistan gathered
her American tanks and RUS Kalashnikovs, and struck.

Twenty days later, Pakistan was only a memory. If India
was poor in fertilizer, it was because a full one-third of her
national budget was spent on arms. As her exports of steel,
cement, and machinery mushroomed, so did her imports of
French helicopters. Profits from her new shipyards funded
her navy. Pakistan had suicidally attacked a nation whose
one prosperity lay in arms, a growing giant with growing
power.

India overflew Sukkur and Karachi in two waves. The first
was a horde of small choppers firing minicannon and homing
missiles; the second was a wave of larger choppers transporting whole infantry companies. Pakistan surrendered, obtained recognition as the State of Sulaiman, and was instantly
absorbed by India as educated Moslems everywhere gave
thanks. It was thought possible that India had deliberately
provoked the River War. Perhaps 'possible' was too weak a
word.

Now, in 1996, the fifty million Moslems of Sulaiman
formed a gentle buffer as India's border with the AIR crescent. India was now one-third Moslem; her Hindu majority
found it easier to accommodate Islam every day.

In capitals from Moscow to Washington—with a studied
pause in Brussels, the real nerve center of common-market
Europe—one glance at a map could bring cold sweat. The
Islamic co-prosperity sphere ran from Gibraltar to Indonesia;
and now that China had made her peace with Islam and
forged links to Japan, the still-floundering RUS might be
excused for fearing herself savaged by COMECON, the
Asiatic common market. It was well-known that India had
taken Chinese aid to build her 'irrigation' conduits near the
old Pakistani border. But the RUS had only now discovered
that China was irrigating her subterranean tanks with oil via
the new conduit.

The RUS sabotage, then, was a ploy to reveal SinoInd
duplicity, while interrupting it, using American hardware so
that retaliation might be delayed and, when it came, less

tightly-focused on a RUS barely able to defend its huge perimeter since 1985. Surely the RUS never expected the reprisal to spread across the globe as World War Four.

So much for expectation. India's furious militants scanned American foreign and domestic crises, judged despite Peking's counsel that Washington's response to the tanker reprisal was one of weakness, and made a terrible mistake.

Chapter 15

Ted Quantrill surged up from his mummy bag, mumbling, then fully awake as Ray Kenney continued to shake him. "Ah, jeez, I thought we'd settled all that last night," he said. "*What* shit's in the fan?"

Ray's eyes were haunted. "On your radio," he said. "Everybody's at Little's tent; come on!" With that Ray ducked out, leaving Quantrill to translate as he would.

In jeans and sneakers, Quantrill plodded to Little's tent. He could hear his radio before he arrived; saw in Purvis Little's face a bleakness deeper than ever before.

". . . in Trincomalee fear that the Indian assault group has subdued the leased US base on Sri Lanka. From New Delhi comes a warning that captured American personnel will be held hostage against any loss of Indian lives. This, unless American cruise missiles are turned back from their present course toward New Delhi.

"A report just in—did you check this, Curt?—A report from UPI confirms the Xinhua announcement that a Chinese *jing ya* satellite is monitoring a wave of cruise missiles proceeding south from a RUS base near Magnitogorsk, near the Urals. Black Star agency denies the Chinese allegation of widespread destruction at the RUS launch complex, but admits several booster launches aborted by saboteurs firing hand-held missiles.

"Meanwhile, sources in Washington remain silent after the early-morning White House statement aired earlier. In the words of Press Secretary Newhouse, 'A measured reprisal, a demonstration of American determination designed to halt the unprovoked Indian aggression in Sri Lanka, is now underway from elements of our Seventh Fleet in the Arabian Sea. The President has asked me to stress that this demonstration is against Indian property, and not against the blameless Indian people. For the duration of this emergency, all military reserve personnel are ordered to report immediately to their units; all leaves are cancelled. We pray God that the modest American response will terminate this rash military adventure by India.'

"We have no more word on that report of general mobilization in the SinoInd countries. Stay tuned. Now this."

A syrupy baritone began. "Tired, listless, logy this summer? Don't be downcast on dog-days, ask your pharmacist—" Click.

Purvis Little drew a shaking hand from Quantrill's radio, saw that it *was* shaking, clasped his hands together and stared past them at his feet. "I don't know. I just—don't—know."

"My mother's in the reserve. Will she be gone when I get home?" This from Thad.

Tom Schell: "Indian bastards! We'll show 'em."

Wayne Atkinson: "Indians and Chinese *both*? And since when are Russians our allies?"

Ray Kenney: "I want to go home—"

A chorus tuned up, its most prominent word being 'home'. Without a word, Little began to strike camp, ignoring the narrowed eyes of a watchful Wayne Atkinson. Slowly at first, then with haste that bordered on panic, the troop repacked.

Quantrill tarried to help Thad stuff his pack, saw Atkinson take up his rearguard position, smiled reassuringly as Thad watched them stumble out of sight at a half-trot. "They aren't waiting, Teddy! What're they doing?"

"I don't know; *they* don't know. Don't worry, Thad, the trail's still there."

Thad shouldered his pack, tried a tremulous smile. "If we hurry, we can catch up and listen to your radio."

"If we hang back, we still can," Quantrill said. He held up his hand, and Thad saw that Quantrill had quietly stolen his radio back. They headed for the trail, switching frequencies, making no effort to catch the others. Long before he reached the trailhead and the rest of the troop, Quantrill knew the target of the Allied US/RUS reprisal.

Chapter 16

India's Uttar Pradesh region lay between New Delhi and Nepal, fed by Himalayan silts, feeding much of India from her huge grain fields on either side of the upper Ganges. Kanpur was more than a railhead: it was the nexus of mountainous wheat surpluses on which India depended. During last-second attempts to flee in half-light over New Delhi's hopelessly choked thoroughfares in a chopper, the co-pilot called back to Prime Minister Casimiro: "Hostiles still twenty minutes from us—"

Punjabi State Minister Mukkerji, trading frowns with Casimiro: "Impossible! Can cruise missiles hover?"

Casimiro licked dry lips, lurched forward as his stomach lurched upward, fought his innards and grabbed for the headset. "Here, give me that thing . . ." Two minutes later, after a near-mutiny by the pilot, Casimiro's chopper was swinging back toward the parliament complex. The old US cruise missiles could not hover, but could and did change course near Jaipur, hurtling eastward fifty meters above Indian soil toward her brobdingnagian breadbasket at near-sonic velocity. New Delhi, then, was not the American target, and nuclear weapons were not the threat. In hurried parley with General Kirpal, Casimiro and the available cabinet ministers deduced much from scattered reports filter-

ing into their blastproof—though it was feared, not
firestorm-proof—digs near Parliament.

I. F. Stone was right, of course; the Americans had lied in
saying the cruise missiles had come from a Seventh Fleet
Shangri-La. The birds had approached as parasites carried by
US bombers from Diego Garcia Island to the Arabian Sea,
then launched in their long dog-leg, to put the fear of a
Christian God in New Delhi before dashing their brains out
against Uttar Pradesh granaries.

Of the seventy-two cruise missiles launched by the
Strategic Air Command, sixty-four carried conventional
high explosives. The other eight carried aerosol-dispersed
chemical poison as lethal as botulism toxin, with special
loiter programs to distribute the stuff over what was left of the
granaries after the earlybirds had strewn them across the
landscape. Seventy-two conventional weapons are far too
few to munch all the wheat in Kanpur's vicinity, even grant-
ing pinpoint accuracy and complete mission success—which
it was not. Six missiles succumbed to natural ills en route,
three were actually downed by Indian-manned Mirage fighters in an insane treetop rabbit-chase, and five missiles missed
their targets. But following the fifty-eight bull's-eyes saun-
tered over all eight of the dispersant drones, pumping out
cargoes of poison that contaminated exposed wheat and the
outsides of many granaries still untouched by explosives.

Then came the RUS cruise missiles, fleeing zero-length
launchers from Magnitogorsk. There had been no agreement
with Washington; but there had been a RUS recon satellite
tracking the US birds, and a volte-face correction in the RUS
robot flight path so that, wherever US birds roosted, RUS
birds would also. This blatant me-too ploy by Moscow was
based on the computer-derived conclusion that only an instant alliance with the Americans could possibly deter China,
who alone had the technology and the will to evaporate
supertankers, from moving onto RUS soil while the US was
embroiled with India. All sixty of the RUS cruise missiles
were tipped with conventional explosives. A handful of them
hit Kanpur. The rest exploded against granaries, bridges, and
a rail depot.

This was good shooting, but bad tactics. India's first conclusion was that she must scrap all the wheat stockpiled within ten klicks of reported contamination, meaning roughly a third of her Uttar Pradesh supply. Her second was that the US/RUS strikes, instead of killing a million Indians outright, had doomed many millions to slow starvation unless India accepted mortifying ceasefire terms for American grain.

The American terms, hastily sketched in by pill-popping diplomats in Washington, were not inhuman; but they did specify an American presence on Indian soil. It was undemocratic, it was Judeo-Christian. It would be humiliating to India's leaders in the sight of Islamics everywhere.

India's third conclusion sprang from reports by tariqat members in Tazhikistan, warning of RUS troops moving into a region that adjoined both China and India. The report was false; had been generated in Peking and released among Tazhiks for a purpose which would, in time, become all too scrutable.

While Washington, Brussels, and Moscow sought some way to engage in meaningful dialogue with Peking and Riyadh as a conduit for calm negotiation with New Delhi, India's war-horse Kirpal was already coordinating a SinoInd reply to the US terms. This coincided perfectly with China's plans: she alone, except for the RUS themselves, knew just how inflated were the population figures across the enormous breadth of Siberia, and just how much RUS oil was being drawn from Siberian wellheads.

Chapter 17

"I absolutely forbid it," Purvis Little shouted toward the sedan that rolled away toward Asheville. Gabe Hooker did not look back. Wayne Atkinson jabbed a scornful finger skyward from the car.

Tom Schell sat on a guard rail at roadside in the dusk.
"Face it, Mr. Little, the bus isn't coming on a Sunday.
Maybe hitching rides is better; what if there's no bus tomor-
row?"

"Safety in numbers," Little said testily. "And I'm still
responsible for your safety. It's a long way back to Raleigh,
boys." The scoutmaster moved nearer to the group that
lounged on packs around the Quantrill boy, listening to the
radio which Quantrill had flatly refused to surrender again.
Not that it mattered much; on AM or FM, only a few stations
were broadcasting and all said the same things. The federal
freeze order had stabilized wages and prices while outlining
consumer rationing; Russians were championing the US
cause; Indian wheat had been the target of our 'bloodless'
demonstration; Peking was silent; stay tuned.

Presently Quantrill pocketed his radio. "Too dark for the
solar cells; I'll save the batteries for later," he apologized,
then raised his voice. "Mr. Little, should we set up camp and
eat?"

It gave them something to do. A few vehicles passed, most
at high speed. Propane stoves soon glowed under panniers of
tea. None of the boys seemed hungry. Those who felt like
weeping crept off to do it alone, so it was bedtime before
Little realized that four more of his scouts had hiked off to
hitch rides to the east.

Ray Kenney's mummy bag was deployed next to Quantrill's. Both of the boys were still awake when the late
bulletins came, and both listened with breathless awe until
the highway blockage bulletins began to repeat. "How're we
gonna get to Raleigh now?" Ray whispered.

"The question is, will it still be there?" Quantrill regretted
his reply but felt curiously detached from Raleigh. His father
was on active duty; his mother had left to spend a week with
kinfolk in Danville; his little sister had died two years ago.
Quantrill thought of his upstairs room with its soccer posters,
the pylons he used to fly his formula racers in the room, his
hidden trove of pornflick cassettes, his suspended model of
the Venus lab. It all seemed priceless to his childhood,
valueless to his future.

Quantrill framed several replies to Ray Kenney, heard the boy weeping hoarsely, and realized that he was as likely to make things worse as to improve them. He recalled something his father had said once: "Talk is cheap, but silence is just about free." The smile of reminiscence was still on his face when Quantrill began to snore.

Once in the night, Quantrill waked for a moment; puzzled at the heavenly—hellish—display overhead. A meteor-bright line scrawled a curve, winking regularly before a final yellowish flash. The line disappeared almost instantly. Halfway across the sky a tiny star flared, then winked out just as abruptly. Quantrill thought sleepily of Perseid showers; failed to note that meteorites do not maneuver; rolled over and slept. Thus he did not see the awesome streaks that laced the night sky later when space junk began to plummet into the stratosphere.

Chapter 18

The series of launches near Ining, in northwest Sinkiang, were too suspiciously spaced and too numerous to ignore. The RUS passed its data on by coded link with a US synchronous satellite thirty-six thousand klicks above the Pacific. Almost certainly the Americans were monitoring the launches anyway, in addition to the SinoInd subs known to be nearing Scotland, Australia, the US eastern seaboard and elsewhere.

We were monitoring. Our Air Defense Command computer complex, in nanoseconds, offered the 0.858 probability that the Chinese were aiming a stab for our eyes in the sky. Red telephones were in use and fingers were near buttons. All that remained was for any one of those Chinese devices to achieve low orbit, then 'jink' suddenly to higher orbit in a classic pop-up intercept. ADC scrambled the F-23's equipped with Vought AA-Sat (anti-antisatellite) systems from England, California, and Queensland. It was still possible that the Chinese were flinging up *saanzi*, 'umbrella', surveillance satellites, and not one of Vought's dreadnaughts must slip its leash unless a Chinese vehicle initiated the maneuver that would assure an intercept path with a US satellite.

No human presence could have kept track of so many satellites, from lunar-orbit Ellfive study projects to the synchronous-orbit Comsats to the nineteen-thousand-klick Navstar navigation devices and barely orbital research facilities. ADC's computer watched it all with ease, simultaneously keeping tabs on existing RUS, Chinese, and other satellites.

On one end of a hotline, Col. Robin LoBianco jumped. "Jink, Mr. President! It's targeted against a RUS *Molniya*."

From the other end: "That's not our war, Robin. I'm watching the display."

"Yessir. Russkis will be mad as—*jink*! Shit, it's a Demitasse, I have seven jinks! Against ours . . ."

"Fire the Moonkillers, Robin. *That's* our war."

Chapter 19

China had hoped to conceal the extent of her A-Sat weapons, the most sophisticated being her *Jin ji*, 'urgent', system. We had specs on it, a multiple independently-targetable antisatellite weapon cluster; hence a MITAS, hence a Q-clearance word, Demitasse. We had bragged on our Vought AA-Sat systems, which deployed interceptors on rocket boost as first-stage launch vehicles. The F-23's followed programmed pop-up maneuvers before releasing their solid-propellant missiles, which then would seek warheads such as Demitasse in pinpoint intercept. What we had not bragged about was our Moonkillers.

Though offensive armament had been prohibited by treaty

on US satellites, defensive weapons had been installed. Satellites with sufficient energy storage were furnished with lasers capable of holing three-centimeter titanium plate. Heat dissipation in the system was so crucial that only five or six laser bursts could be rapidly fired at an approaching enemy. It was, of course, line-of-sight—but it could zap you from almost any orbital distance.

Satellites without surplus electric energy storage used something less elegant. It was a curious version of an idea used by Germans, then in our old SPRINT rockets. Solid propellant rockets are so simple and storable that a five-stage hypervelocity bird could be depended upon after years of storage. The entire weapon fitted into a cylinder fifteen cm. wide, seven meters long. The most deceptive feature was the propellant and chamber walls, so flexible with thermal protection that the cylinder could be curled into a hoop which passed as a segmented toroidal pressure vessel. It was a pressure vessel, all right . . .

The automated drill was 'uncurl; aim; fire.' Four stages of the weapon were straightforward boosters; the fifth carried a shaped charge that shotgunned a cloud of metal confetti, and the average 'burnt velocity' of those pellets relative to their launcher was on the order of 8,000 meters/sec, perhaps double that figure relative to an onrushing target.

Altogether, some fifty American satellites had been fitted—some retrofitted—with laser or shotgun defenses. Taken together with their control modules they composed the Moonkiller system. The name was an obvious conceit, since they would not have stopped a sizeable asteroid; but in the early hours of Monday, 12 August 1996, they made expensive colanders out of forty-two Demitasse warheads.

RUS satellite defenses, Moonkillers and Vought AA-Sats accounted for most of the other Demitasse weapons but, in an hour-long display of orbital pyrotechnics watched by uncounted millions, some of those warheads obliterated their targets. Particularly galling to the US Navy was the loss of fully half of its laser translators. American subs, equipped with extremely sensitive detectors, had for years depended on communications via blue-green satellite laser that penetrated hundreds of meters into ocean depths. If you were on-station, you got the flashes.

In a small Extremely Low Frequency radio facility near Eau Claire, Wisconsin, Lt. (JG) Boren Mills whirled from his console. ''ELF grid test program to standby, Chief,'' he said, remembering to speak far down in his throat. Mills had been jerked from reserve status in grad school at Annenberg less than thirty hours before, to this Godforsaken tunnel in cheese country, but Mills was—had been—the kind of grad student who seldom forgot to employ the communication theory work he read. It had already earned him one promotion.

''At your mark, sir,'' said the balding chief, prompting him.

''Uh—yes, at my mark: mark.'' Mills touched fingertips to his headset, gnawed his lip, caught himself at it, forced his personal display to read *calm*.

''Running, sir. Should I test the time-sharing translators again? I can't believe anybody wants to use the ELF grid as main trunk transceivers.''

Mills saw a red-code flash on the display, studied it a moment, muttered, ''Jesus Christ on Quaaludes,'' then remembered the chief's query. ''Test them again; all possible speed, Chief. We're losing laser translators over the Pacific and Arctic.'' The ELF radio grid, though it lay across thousands of square klicks of dairyland and had cost an immense fortune, was a distant second choice to orbital laser methods. The message rate of extremely low-frequency radio was, by definition, extremely low. But it was not as vulnerable as an orbital translator either, as Mills was learning.

In moments the chief completed his software tasks, glanced at the new weekend warrior who, though green as a NavSat's eye, was shaping up damned fast on short notice. The chief judged Mills's age as twenty-seven, putting it three years on the long side because of the jaygee, the widow's peak high on a forehead that never sweated, and the hard brown eyes that never wavered. Slim, erect, with a strong nose and graceful movements, Boren Mills could surrogate maturity better than most. The voice was soft, almost a caress, when he wasn't working at it. The chief had seen lots worse. Mills might be one of the Navy's braintrust brats, but he knew how to do a job. The chief eased over to see past Mills's shoulder, and gulped at what he saw.

"Stay at your post or go on report," Mills snapped, then spoke softly into his throat mike as the chief leaped back to his post. "With enough power, you may be able to get Arctic coverage from echo soda module, I say again echo soda. That's an awfully shallow angle to penetrate that deep in sea water, but it's your lasers, Commander. I'm just an elf . . . Affirm; grid test programs running and green, we're ready when you are."

Mills turned the level, heavy-browed stare on the chief. "Pull the test programs, ready ELF grid for main-trunk use at-my-mark-*mark*! Chief, we're losing more orbital modules; too many bogies are getting through."

The chief took a deep breath. "Sir, last time we really tried this grid for main trunk we caused a brown-out in Eau Claire, got charged with witching milk from cattle, and had downtime here you wouldn't believe."

Mills listened again to his headset, saw verification at his console. "ELF grid to main trunk, logged and confirmed," he said softly, watching the display as he typed. "Chief, I want a man on every auxiliary power unit and I want your hangar queens running."

"We don't call 'em that, Sir, we—"

"We are at war, Chief, tell me another time. I don't give a fat rat's ass if every cow in Wisconsin gives condensed milk and farmers freeze in the dark; we are at this moment the Navy's first-line comm net and if any part of the grid goes down *it will not be this one*. There are SinoInd subs launching God knows what right now. You think they're propaganda leaflets?"

"Nossir. But I notice we seem to be getting a lot of comm from orbit."

"Not enough of it from the Navy. And it's Navy that's got to bag those subs."

The chief scanned his console, nodded to himself, mopped his face. "I'll set up four-hour watches. What should I tell the ratings?"

"Tell them I want no surprises."

"I mean about the A-Sat attack, Sir."

A pause. Then, "Tell them the SinoInd effort to sweep our satellites away has been repulsed. Failed. Defeated."

The chief brightened. "Aye, Sir."

Boren Mills permitted himself an almost silent snort at the ease with which men could be manipulated. Statistically, the SinoInd attack *was* a failure. But it had been a tactical success. Our hunter-killer teams would suffer delays in coordination. Allied bases in Germany, South Africa, Australia, the Seychelles, and Scotland were to take loads of fast-dispersing nerve gas launched from SinoInd subs offshore. Even these ghastly weapons implied a certain restraint; a hope on the part of Peking that US/RUS strategists would follow her lead in avoiding nuclear weapons and attacks on mainland centers.

But China could not dissuade India from repeating her one-two punch which had overwhelmed Pakistan. Once India's closest ally, the RUS had rained cruise missiles with poor discrimination onto Kanpur; and the RUS presence among Afghans was a chronic thorn in Islamic flesh. Two waves of Indian choppers formed near Peshawar and essayed a blitzkrieg liberation war on Afghan soil. The immediate gains, they felt, could be bargained away after the cease-fire that must surely follow China's sweep of Allied satellites.

RUS patrol craft spotted the first wave of assault choppers using side-looking radar that scanned valleys in the towering Hindu Kush range. Indian choppers, though limited in speed and range, were almost equal to the task of dodging the grid of particle-beam projectors that flared from hardened mountain sites. Almost, but not quite. Offense and defense cancelled, leaving the way clear for the Indian troop choppers. The RUS then drew its defensive curtain.

The curtain bomb, a megaton-yield nuclear device, was the culmination of two generations of research into directional-effect neutron bombs. Properly oriented, delivered by unmanned vertols to various altitudes, a curtain lanced its deadly radiation in a tight conic pattern that was lethal a hundred klicks from the detonation site. Since the RUS detonated her devices in a wavering line from Qandahar to Kabul—territory of a tribute state, if not precisely RUS soil—she did not expect this tactic to be considered as a nuclear attack on foreign soil. The fallout, blast, and thermal effects would be largely confined to Afghan regions.

But thousands of India's first-line assault troops perished in the actinic glare of curtain bombs, and by the political definitions that led her into Afghanistan she did not consider that to be RUS soil. China did not know how closely her enemies were linked and interpreted the neutron curtain as an Allied willingness to tempt Armageddon. Within an hour, the full panoply of SinoInd nuclear, chemical, and bacteriological weapons was committed.

The first strategic exchange had favored our side, with the survival of a few US/RUS satellites while the SinoInds had only orbital debris. But both China and India had placed much of their air power on submersibles, some with skyhook choppers to provide midair retrieval for aircraft that could not land vertically.

Both the US and the RUS had spent tens of billions on surface craft, enormous nuclear-powered floating airfields that were too easy to find, too vulnerable to nukes. SinoInd attack subs, with data provided by drones and buoy translators, fired their missiles without surfacing and moved off at flank speed to make second strikes as necessary.

The SinoInd air-launched ballistic missiles were easier to spot, and many were creamed by the tremendous wealth of defensive fire from our carriers and missile frigates. But our carriers were such potent offensive platforms that the SinoInds threw everything at them at once. For every

US/RUS carrier in the Indian Ocean, at least one nuke got within a thousand meters or so; and that was all it took. We lost a carrier in the Mediterranean; we lost one each in the Atlantic and Pacific.

Chastened, stunned by the terrible algebra of One Nuke = One Carrier, our surviving flattops raced for anchorages inside bays with sub nets, with steep mountains nearby, and there were few such places available. The best that could be said was that twenty per cent of the aircraft on our carriers managed to get aloft in search of an enemy, and a place to land.

Governments across the globe ducked for cover. Long-drilled and partly prepared, millions of RUS urbanites sealed themselves into subway tunnels, then slid blast-and-firestorm-proof hatches into place to ride out the blast-furnace interval. Most Americans were asleep and, in any case, had only the sketchiest notion of adequate shelter. When the Emergency Broadcast System went into operation, most American stations ceased transmission while the rest broadcast belated warnings. Many Americans had never heard the term ''crisis relocation'' until the past day or so, but it was obviously a weasel-phrase for ''evacuation''. A few city dwellers—the smaller the city, the better their chances—sped beyond their suburbs before freeway arterials became clots of blood and machinery.

The American public had by turns ignored and ridiculed its cassandras; city planners, ecologists, demographers, sociologists, immigrants, who had all warned against our increasing tendency to crowd into our cities. Social stress, failure of essential services, and warfare were only a few of the spectres we had granted a passing glance. We had always found some solution to our problems, though; often at the last moment. Firmly anchored in most Americans was the tacit certainty that, even to the problem of nuclear war against population centers, there must be a uniquely American solution; we would find it.

The solution was sudden death. A hundred million Americans found it.

Chapter 20

The Civil Defense merit badge had not been popular with
Purvis Little, but Tom Schell's parents had insisted. "What
we really need," Tom sighed, "is a better map."

Robbie Calhoun: "Maybe Tim has his cartography manual," with a nod toward his twin.

As Tim Calhoun dug feverishly into his pack, Ted Quantrill flogged his own memory. Never very active in collecting
merit badges, he did not at first conclude they had done him
much good. Woodwork? Cycling? Aviation? First aid?
Weather? *Weather*! "Most of the continental United States
lies between thirty and forty-five degrees; and in these, uh,
longitudes, prevailing winds are west to east."

"Latitudes," Tim corrected him, flipping through a dog-
eared pamphlet.

Little regarded Quantrill with interest. "What in the world
are you talking about?"

"Meteorology, Mr. Little. Merit badge stuff; I either
remember it word-for-word, or not at all."

"Durn if you do," Tim insisted, stabbing at the open
pamphlet. "Latitude is the word."

"So I blew it," said Quantrill; 'the important word is
west-to-east.''

"That's a phrase," said Ray Kenney.

"Stop bickering," Little snapped. A dozen times during
the hour since they'd waked, he had seen senseless quarrels
flare this way—once in a fistfight. Little did some things
right, and keeping the boys busy until the bus arrived was one
of those things. "Tim, I want an 'X' over every place that's
been—hit." He did not want to say 'annihilated by a nuclear
weapon'. Not yet. Not even if the Knoxville and Charlotte
stations both said so.

Slowly, Tim marked through Raleigh; then Wilmington,
Huntsville, Little Rock, Charleston on his regional map.

"Anybody know where Tullahoma is?"

"Couple hundred klicks west of us," said Quantrill, and could not keep from adding, childishly, "—some cartographer you are."

"What does it matter, Quantrill?" Little said quickly.

"No matter—unless you're east of it; downwind. Like we are."

Tom Schell recalled his civil defense study and nodded. "If we head for town now, we might find a deep shelter in time. Mr. Little, it's been twenty minutes since the last car zoomed past here. I'm gonna hitch the next one and you guys can all rot here if you want to."

Little studied the pinched faces around him, saw Thad Young guarding the radio from shadows that diminished its pathetic output to silence. "Thad, anything more about Asheville?"

"Just that the highways are all clogged. Some looting," said the boy, his ear near the speaker.

"Safety in numbers," Little muttered for the dozenth time, then raised his voice. "Boys, I want you to march single-file behind me. If we can get to Cherokee, we can find a way to Asheville."

Five minutes later the troop had settled into a good pace eastward, just off the left shoulder facing traffic, most with packs though Ray and Thad had discarded theirs. "Yeah, I'll share my sleeping bag if we have to," Quantrill said to Ray, then made an effort at levity. "But one little fart and you're outside lookin' in."

Tom Schell, at the rear, walked just behind. "But that's all he is," Tom laughed.

"You're supposed to be flagging cars, not ganging up on me," Ray replied.

"So show me a car," Tom said. None had passed since they began their march. He clapped a good-natured hand on Quantrill's shoulder: "Anyhow, Teddy's a gang all by himself. Take it from an expert."

Quantrill turned to smile at Schell, saw the vehicle behind

them swerve into sight before he heard it. "I never thanked you for—hey, here comes one!"

The vintage motor home teetered on the curve before its rear duals found purchase, then picked up speed on the downslope. Quantrill saw the lone driver, realized that the vehicle could hold them all, stepped into the near lane and waved his arms hard. Ahead of them, the others were reacting the same way. Tom must have realized that the driver had no intention of slowing; made a gallant gesture by stepping almost into the vehicle's path, facing it, arms up and out.

The driver slammed at his brakes just long enough to provoke a slide, then corrected desperately as the motor home straddled the center stripe. Tom Schell gasped, "*Ah, God,*" before the left front fender impacted his chest at high speed, the sickening sound of his imploding ribcage half lost in the roar of the diesel.

The body of Tom Schell hurtled a full forty meters, pacing the motor home and nearly parallel to it before colliding with an oak, five meters up in its foliage. The driver fought the wheel through the next bend, tires squalling, and continued.

Not one of the survivors moved until the body slid, supple as a bag of empty clothing, from tree to gravel where it lay, jerking. Then something in Purvis Little cried out, not in grief but for retribution. Reaching down for a stone, sprinting ludicrously after the motor home, the scoutmaster howled his impotence without words.

Quantrill raced to within a few paces of the victim, saw Ray Kenney speed past him in pursuit of the others, stopped in revulsion at what he saw. Quantrill bit his lip, knelt at the roadside to think while steadfastly refusing to stare again into the dead eyes. In the distance he could hear the cries of a mindless mob, now all but lost in Smoky Mountain stillness.

It was much easier to hear your radio estimate megadeaths than to see and hear and smell and—Quantrill swallowed against a sourness in the back of his mouth—taste a single death. Big hearty Tom Schell: one moment a mixed bag of vices and companionable virtues, the next a flaccid bag of

skin leaking away into imperturbable gravel, one eye winking as though it had all been a grotesque joke. But the dirt
would soak up Tom's blood without qualm or shudder.
Lucky dirt; you die for it, and it doesn't give a damn.

And how many had died during the few seconds since Tom
froze at the center stripe? The question flashed into Quantrill's mind, held him mesmerized. New York-San
Antonio-Colorado Springs-New Orleans, on and on, endlessly. Multiply Tom Schell a million times; ten million. It
was suddenly as though Tom had died yesterday, or the day
before. It was all a long time and many deaths ago, his mind
soothed. Just don't look back for a refresher course.

Slowly, Quantrill took his radio from its sunny lashing
atop his pack. After several minutes he stiffened, thinking
hard on the outcomes of bacteriological weapons west of
Winston-Salem and a flat prohibition against travel westward
on US 40. So Asheville was not to be spared after all; and
while fallout might be lethal, it diminished with time. Germ
warfare, he decided, might not—and it was harder to hide
from, and to counter.

Two hundred klicks west was a towering mushroom over
what had once been a military research facility. To the east
was home, under another such cloud—and microbes were
there too. Quantrill repositioned his radio, shrugged his pack
higher on his shoulders, and turned his back on home.

Chapter 21

The US/RUS attack was full of glitches, and there was no
hope of catching the enemy by surprise. But while the tunnels
under Dairen, Tsingtao and Canton resounded with survivors
streaming toward the countryside, fleet installations adjoining these cities were wiped from existence. Karachi, Bom-
bay, Madras, Calcutta were no better prepared than Ameri-

can seaports and suffered as many casualties as Oakland, Honolulu, San Diego, Norfolk.

The extended Chinese presence to leased bases in Albania, Cuba, and AIR countries brought a hard-won lesson to her friends as we pounded her sub pens at Durres, Bengazi and Manzanillo. Highland marines stormed a secret supply depot on the Irish coast, took its comm center intact, and lured three SinoInd subs to offshore rendezvous where two of the craft were captured. The third, a small two-hundred-ton experimental job, evidently was shaped very like a whale. Sonar traces suggested that its power plant was unconventional and, British Naval Intelligence inferred from its pygmy dimensions, must have been launched from some vast tender; a hiveship. Pygmy subs simply could not carry enough fuel for extended pelagic cruise unless nuclear-powered.

These tentative conclusions were not reached for some days because the British had very little hard evidence to work from. The pygmy sub had gone down in deep water, scuttled in a half-dozen blasts aft on the pressure hull that took all but one of its dozen crew members to the bottom.

The surviving crewman yielded little under normal interrogation. He was particularly careful in his choice of words when asked about his craft's induction system, and could not hide his educated diction well enough to pass as an ordinary seaman.

Under modest drug-induced hypnosis, the crewman revealed that he was a mechanical engineer entrusted with the little sub's Snorkel and exhaust systems. He knew approximately zip about its engine; only that steam was its exhaust. The British hypothesized about sponson tanks with hydride fuels, and forwarded their findings to US Naval Intelligence. It seemed an odd way to push a sub around, but it was after all an experimental model. Ninety per cent of everything, the Admiralty quoted, was crud. Few analysts entertained suspicions that this was part of the other ten per cent.

Tiny Israel, still a nation surrounded by implacable foes except for moderate Turkey, felt an increasing squeeze as most AIR countries embargoed petroleum and high-grade

ore to her shores. Under the circumstances, visitors thought it
bizarre that Israel's internal transportation system would
grow so dependent on air cushion vehicles that, even with the
most effective ACV skirts, still used a third more fuel than
wheeled vehicles and many times more than electric trains.
Israel's Ministry of Transportation pointed out that an ACV
did not require expensive roadbeds, and that her synthetic
fuel industry was expanding on a crash basis. From Elat to
Acre, Israel's noisy ACV transports levitated centimeters off
the sand and left dust-tails in their wakes, until the night of
Monday, 12 August 1996.

Chapter 22

Yakob ben Arbel swept a hand over his bald head, gazed
out the window across Tel Aviv rooftops, glanced again at
the note and sighed. "Bones, page twenty-one, line fifteen. I
gather the *jehad* is already in motion. You are certain it said
'bones'?"

"How could I *not* check it twice," shrugged Irina
Konolev. "And it'll barely be dark at nine-fifteen. We
haven't a snowball's chance in the Negev of pulling this off
without being spotted."

"Speaking of the Negev, our settlements along the eastern
wadis are low on fuel. We must get every spare liter we can to
them from Beersheba. We have," he checked his chronograph, "four hours, Irina. I hope the Knesset knows what it is
about, this time."

"I'll take our records to Netanya for you, unless you want
them," she said. The Ministry of Transportation would be a
nightmare of conflicting priorities without a copy of records
up to the moment.

"You know better than that. My unit will not be back by
the time you leave Netanya." A grin: "I shall probably be

safer than you. Oh! Call my wife, tell her to keep the TV on and the kids within earshot.''

Irina stepped nearer, planted a kiss under his mustache. ''That's because you're a better colonel than you are a bureaucrat,'' she said. ''Want your uniform pressed?''

She was nearly out the door before he stopped laughing long enough to say, ''It will have worse than wrinkles on it before this night is done. And for the love of Jahweh do not forget the wadi fuel.'' Then he began checking records on operational readiness of vehicles in the Hazor-Shemona region. For the next four hours, ben Arbel knew he must forget everything but his role as a ministry subchief, and see that every possible drop of fuel was available without alerting AIR moles that something was in the wind. However well or badly he performed, the balance of the job would be in other hands by twenty-one hours, fifteen minutes.

At nine-fifteen PM he would be changing; by nine-twenty, racing to the McDonnell vertols hidden north of Ramla. The vertols were so new that even the US Airlift Command had not received many; so ingeniously modified that each could eject fifty airborne troops like cartridges and pick up more troop pods without stopping.

Yakob ben Arbel smiled. It was fortunate that the United States had continued its tradition of sharing its latest weaponry with Israel through the twists and turns of re-formed (if that was the word) Russians and Marxist Moslems. It almost seemed a shame that Israel, with her sophisticated electronic R & D, could not afford to share her biggest breakthrough with the Americans. Later, perhaps; not yet. The entire future existence of the US did not depend, as Israel's did, on a weapon that had never been battle-fledged and could not directly harm a soul.

Ben Arbel inferred rightly; agents of the Mossad had monitored the countdown in Riyadh and Cairo as the AIR set in motion their machinery for *jehad*; holy war on Israel. While Saudis ruled Arabia and Sadat lived on in Egypt, Israel could hope for something less than eventual apocalypse. Since the quasi-Marxist coups and the formation of the AIR,

only uncertainty as to RUS and American responses had kept
the jehad on the back burners.

Without any question whatever, the combined AIR forces
could inundate all Israel in a month of hand-to-hand fighting,
or pulverize her in a day if nukes were employed. Once,
Israel had intercepted such messages in time to act first; twice
she had responded quickly enough to survive without advance warning. This time she would need, not only advance
warning—and she had that much already—but a monumen-
tal series of deceptions on a scale unmatched in human
history, and all with split-second timing.

The jehad, beginning with nuclear-tipped air strikes from
desert bases in Iraq and Arabia just before dawn, would be
followed by mop-up bombardments from missile-carrying
Egyptian and Libyan frigates. Because Allah was merciful
there would be no troop thrusts into Israel's debris until the
radioactive wasteland had 'cooled' enough for selected
motorized infantry advances. It might take a month, but the
AIR could wait. They had waited and prayed for years
toward this moment, a time when US/RUS and European
eyes were focused on their own survival. Their prayers
would be answered, imsh'Allah, on the morrow.

At nine-fifteen PM, Israel's television and radio stations
broadcast a bulletin to the effect that the bones of the pa-
triarch Joseph had been positively identified. Some stations
carried the item with a tongue-in-cheek waggishness—
'what, again?'—but all carried it. Because Israelis, even
those with deep-cover civil defense jobs, are as fallible as
anybody, stations swamped with telephone calls found it
necessary to repeat that the bones were indeed those of
Joseph. The ensuing uproar down the length of Israel was
immediate; citizens spread the salient news from house to
house. By ten PM, darkness hid the dust of the first cargo
ACV to thrumm west from Hazeva, loaded to its rubbery
skirts with the only cargo Israel considered indispensable.

Monitors in the Sinai and elsewhere informed AIR leaders
of the activity, but nothing was done with the information.
The Jews, it was felt, were only making genocide easier.

Of the one hundred thousand ACV's that massed along the
Plain of Sharon between Tel Aviv and Haifa from midnight
to three AM, only a few thousand had needed to traverse
much more than two hundred klicks of sand. Last-minute
maintenance and refueling proceeded with less than the expected attrition rate, thanks to people like Irina Konolev, her
mind and fingers flying as she allocated fuel and personnel
from her portable computer terminal in Netanya.

Fleetingly, Irina thought of her plain-featured, stolid boss,
the family man with the big laugh who was also the colonel
with the big responsibility. She hoped he would still be
laughing at dawn; she would not have been surprised to learn
that Colonel ben Arbel lay in a personnel pod as his vertol
flashed over wavetops of the Red Sea. She might have
grinned, had she known that the knot of McDonnells had
passed muster at the enemy IFF query near Tiran by flaw-
lessly surrogating an Indian Air Force response. Ben Arbel,
in the second wave of vertols, arced inland south of Yanbu
while the first wave was converging on another target to the
south. The targets were wholly insignificant from a strict
military point of view; but as political prizes they were
crucial.

At three-oh-three AM, a series of temblors was recorded in
the shallow Mediterranean southwest of Beirut. Lebanon and
Syria braced for tidal waves that would not come, because
the temblors had been initiated by sonic generators in rock far
below the seabed ooze. On Cyprus, now an island province
of Turkey, the wave could be seen approaching on radar. It
was very high, and it stretched to the horizon. Cypriots from
Limassol to Cape Greco were wakened and warned to abandon the southern coastline. Cyprus had felt tidal waves before; everyone knew that even a low wave could become
huge as it mounted island shallows. Cypriot radar was watching something that wasn't there; one operational mode of
Israel's most secret weapon, a microwave ghost that could
make radar strain at gnats while swallowing camels.

The face of the wave approached Cyprus behind the ghost
image at two hundred klicks per hour. It was composed of the

fastest fifty thousand Israeli ACV's in close formation, followed at whatever speed they could muster by the remaining
transports. The wave did not break against Cyprus's beaches;
much of it continued inland for some distance before settling
to disgorge literally millions of passengers—most of Israel's
population. Israel had given technical aid to Turkey in return
for a secret promise that Cyprus would accept refugees, but
the Turks had been given no details on just how that exodus
might occur.

The code phrase for the operation was entirely appropriate, for the Old Testament specified the precious cargo
which Moses had taken when leaving Egypt. The bones of
Joseph had formalized one Exodus, and now they had pre-
cipitated another.

Before the human tidal wave settled, AIR military leaders
were arguing furiously with the civilian *majlis* commanding
them. It was too late, they railed; the first wave of fighter-
bombers was almost airborne; the frigates were off Port Said
and Libyan captains might not be willing to honor an abort
signal.

But Islam's spiritual leaders knew the Marxist veneer over
their people was barely epidermal. In their bones, devout
Moslems might reject their leaders, perhaps question their
own devotion, once they saw on television that Medina,
Mecca, and Q'om were suffering unspeakable defilements
before being turned into radioactive craters.

As one Knesset member put it: "Given the certainty that
we've taken the *Masjid Al Haram* and might let the world
watch on TV while we cover the Ka'aba with pigskin, I think
they'd be willing to defer doomsday. Think about it: once the
Holy of Holies has been blown into the ionosphere, a Moslem would have to pray in all directions."

The point was well-taken by top-level *majlis* of the AIR. If
Israelis would permit frequent inspection to verify the Jewish
claim that no harm had yet come to the shrines of Mohammed
and Khomeini, the majlis would cancel the attack on Israel's
abandoned soil. The abandonment had not been complete
enough to give the majlis hope that Moslem squatters could

infiltrate the place. Sedom and Nazareth and Haifa still rang
with the clangor of Israel's business, but now a business run
exclusively by warriors of both sexes. In the matter of her
vulnerable citizens, Israel had cleared her decks for action.
The AIR saw it as a stalemate, though Israel could still lose
on Cyprus. The jehad would have to wait . . .

Chapter 23

Our Atlantic coast sunrise was a many-splendored thing on
Monday, thanks to micron-sized hunks of Cape Cod and
Bethesda and Cocoa Beach that floated in countless quadril-
lions toward the dawn. Not many people admired it. Most
survivors were too busy retching, or wondering how to filter
death-laden air once they figured out a way to pump it into
their rural root cellars. Or tallying candy bars and drinkables
against the headcount in a few mass transit tunnels. Or
cursing our lack of Civil Defense which, like charity, begins
at home. Or . . . but the list was worse than endless; it was
pointless. Unlike Moscow and Kiev, American cities had not
spent the funds to preserve flesh and blood under firestorms
fifty klicks in diameter that consumed every ignitable scrap
aboveground.

Raised to kindling temperature by nuclear airbursts, trees
and plastic façades contributed to monstrous updrafts that
sucked air from suburbs; which grew to two-hundred-klick
winds roaring across urban structures at a thousand degrees
Celsius, mercifully asphyxiating millions before incinerating
their remains. As citizens of Tokyo and Dresden had learned
by 1945, the immediate danger was firestorm.

Toward the midwest, Americans fared better. Here we
were less centralized, with more rural homes dependent on
their own solar power, more homeowners who knew how to
cannibalize a car's electrical system and to jury-rig a bellows

air-pump with cardboard and tape. Here were fewer prime targets, more well-stocked pantries.

The Pacific coast was a patchwork; rubble from San Diego to Santa Barbara, emulating the Boston-to-Norfolk devastation, and an unchanged, achingly lovely stillness from Point Arena to Arcata where Chinese fallout had not yet reached.

Least affected of the American homeland on Monday was the intermountain region from the Sierra-Cascades to the great plains. Albuquerque and the Pueblo-Denver strip were smouldering hulks, of course. The MX sites in Nevada and south of Minot had taken cannonades of nuclear thunder. But the MX called for ground-burst bombs. Though anything downwind of a ground-pounder would be heavily hit by fallout, the firestorm effects were enormously less. There was nothing much to burn in Nevada, and Dakota corn was largely spared. Thanks to a cunning variation on the MX theme, the submerged portable MX modules were also intact. Apparently it had never occurred to SinoInd strategists that a Trident launch system might work handily in Lake Sakakawea.

At the bottom line, as Israelis on Cyprus knew, lay the survival of the population. In our intermountain region, folks near Twin Falls, Winnemucca, Green River, and Holbrook wept and prayed for their urban relatives; and while they prayed, they worked. Prayer and honest labor characterized these people more than most, particularly among members of the Church of Jesus Christ of the Latter-Day Saints— Mormons.

It should have surprised no one that paralysis of the body politic might leave one limb functioning if it were insulated against systemic shock. If you put aside the arguable features of Mormon theocracy—the *fact* of theocracy, women's rights, resurgent polygamy, the identification of Amerinds as lost tribes of Israel,—you could focus on the more secular facts of Mormonism. They scorned drugs, including nicotine and alcohol; they swelled their ranks with as much missionary zeal as any Moslem, and they strengthened their church with tithes. They were studious. They voted as a bloc.

Each of these factors was a survival factor, though not obviously so. The most obvious survival factor was the one which Mormons had taken for a century as an article of faith without demanding an explicit reason: stored provisions.

Every good Mormon knew from the cradle that he was expected to maintain a year's supply of necessities for every family member against some unspecified calamity. Mormon temples maintained stocks of provisions. A year's supply of raw wheat was not expensive, and its consumption meant that one must be able to grind flour and bake bread. The drying of fruit, vegetables, and meat allowed storage at room temperature with no chemical additives more injurious than a bit of salt and sulfur.

Mormons had such a long Darwinian leg up on their gentile neighbors (to a Mormon, all unbelievers including Jews were gentiles) that, by the 1980's, the church found it wise to downplay the stored provisions. Faced with a general disaster, a Mormon might choose to share his stored wealth with an improvident gentile—but no longer advertised his foresight because he did not want that sharing at gunpoint. Devout, self-sufficient, indecently healthy, many of the more liberal Mormons had moved to cities by 1990. Most of those perished. The more conservative Mormons, and the excommunicated zealots of splinter groups, tended to remain in the sprawling intermountain American west; and most of those were alive on Monday, 12 August 1996, the day that would become known as Dead Day.

Chapter 24

At first, Quantrill thought the pickup would ghost past him to disappear down the mountain as two others had done, on Tuesday morning. It was a green '95 Chevy hybrid with the inflatable popup camper deck that melded, when stowed, into an efficient kammback. Then he saw it ease onto the shoulder and ran to open the right-hand door. "Got room for my pack?" He was already shucking it.

"What if I said 'no'?" She saw him hesitate, then chuckled. "I'm kidding. Room between us, or push it through the hole," the woman said, aiming a gloved thumb at the orifice behind her.

Quantrill tried to smile as the Chevy coasted downhill, glanced again at the driver. His first impression had been of a tanned little old lady, sun-crinkles at the corners of her eyes, wrinkles running down her throat into the open-necked work shirt. But the lines on the throat were sinew, and the chuckle hummed with vitality. He revised her age at under forty, saw that her own gaze mixed shrewdness and curiosity.

"Where'd you spend the night? You look hungry," she said.

"A cave in the bluffs back there. I have some sausage and granola. Afraid to drink the water."

"Smart boy. Got a canteen? Fill it from mine there," she pointed at an insulated jug. "Actually a Halazone tab is all you'd need. With this fiendish high-pressure area, not much fallout is moving our way. My name's Abby Drummond. Headed for Gatlinburg?"

"I guess," he shrugged, topping off his canteen. "Anywhere there's shelter, ma'am."

She drove in silence, the tire-whine loud because the diesel was not running and she was recharging her batteries on steep downslopes. At length she said, "I'll let you off at the Gatlinburg turnoff. I'm going to detour south of Knoxville."

Quantrill nodded, wondering if the woman regretted giving him the lift. Well, she wasn't very big. A woman alone . . .

Abby Drummond slowed at the turnoff, then drove a hundred meters past an abandoned sedan and stopped. Quantrill shouldered his pack, waved, walked fifty paces before he heard the voices. He turned, then removed his pack again with hurried stealth.

Two men, heavily dressed as city folk will for an outing,

had materialized from the roadside. One stood on the Chevy's front bumper, a prospector's pick waving before the woman's eyes. The other was opening the passenger door. Quantrill could hear them talking, did not need to know what was said. His decision seemed the most natural thing in the world, and changed him forever.

He took the canteen, scanning the brush for a handy weapon, slipped as near as he dared. If he rushed the men, the last fifteen meters would be in the open. Since they stood at right angles, he felt sure that one of them would spot him. He found a stone the size of his fist, let himself breathe deeply, then tossed the stone high in the air.

Quantrill was moving before the stone hit the ground on the driver's side. The pick-wielder jerked around, but the man with one foot in the cab did not move. Quantrill ran as quietly as he could but saw Mr. Pick, hearing quick footfalls, whirl back on uncertain footing. The sodden *thunkk* of the full canteen against the man's temple carried all of Quantrill's speed plus the length of his arm and canteen strap, and Quantrill's inertia carried him behind the man on an oblique course before he could stop.

The little pick glanced off the Chevy's plastic hood, the man spinning half around before collapsing. He groveled to hands and knees, vented a long moan, then fell face-first in the dirt.

Quantrill backed away, swinging the canteen like a bolo to threaten the second man until he saw that the man's attention was riveted on Abby Drummond, and his hands were now in the air. "Okay, okay," he was chattering, "people make mistakes. What about my buddy, sounds like the boy bashed his head in." But he was stepping backward now, staring at the short ugly revolver in Abby's hand.

Quantrill snatched up the pick, saw that the felled man was breathing heavily, and resisted a vicious impulse as he moved to the open door. Then, as though he had always known such things, he stopped. He was nearing the talker, whose flickering gaze seemed to suggest some quick judgment. It was very simple: Quantrill had been about to obstruct the woman's field of fire. The man was preparing to act.

Quantrill backed off, said "Wait," in a more peremptory way than he intended, retrieved his pack, trotted far down the road ahead of the Chevy. Then he waved it toward him.

Abby Drummond accelerated quickly away and did not entirely stop as Quantrill tumbled into the passenger seat again. A hundred meters back, one man stood helplessly watching them while the second was reeling up to a sitting position.

"Could've been worse," she said. "You'd best drop your canteen out the window. Could be contaminated now. In fact, you and I are taking chances with each other as it is. I've come from Spartanburg."

Quantrill did not understand and said so, discarding his canteen with reluctance. "I've been camping up here since Friday," he said. "If it has fallout on it, so do I."

"Not fallout; microbes. Those men were out of fuel, and were running from the same thing we are—whether you know it or not, ah, what's your name?"

"Ted Quantrill, ma'am."

"I called you a boy, and so did that poor devil back there. We were wrong, Ted. You may be only sixteen or so, but—"

"Fifteen, almost."

"Man enough for me back there, Ted. Call me 'Abby'; looks like we'll be together awhile, if you're up to it. Frankly, I'm glad to have a man along. I gather you weren't headed home."

Quantrill spent the next twenty minutes telling his tale as Abby guided them toward foothills and the outskirts of Maryville, Tennessee. He did not tell her about Tom Schell: least said, soonest forgotten. She seemed to know which side roads to take and, if she was faking her knowledge of their predicament, he decided it was a damned convincing fake. "Anyway," he finished his account, "if I catch anything, you'll have to give it to me."

Abby chuckled again, saw that he had intended no double-entendre, and slapped the steering wheel as she laughed outright. "I'll see what I can do," she said in arch innocence. "But seriously, I think we got out in time. If we didn't, we'll know by tomorrow, I guess. We probably shouldn't mix with other people for a day or two. The only ethical thing to do, wouldn't you say?"

"You're 'way ahead of me," he said. "Jeez, I don't even know where we're going."

She told him.

"*Oak* Ridge? Shit-fire, I mean, uh—"

"Whatever turns you on," she said easily.

"I mean wouldn't that be a prime target?"

"It's just a museum now, Ted; the Union Carbide people ran out of funds years ago. I work there in the summers. My best friend there is Jane Osborne; believe you me, Janie knows the tunnels as well as anybody. Most people don't even know about 'em. Not at the museum, but—well, you'll see. Uh-oh."

Quantrill saw why she was slowing. Just ahead lay a bridge, barricaded so that only one car could pass. Four men in khaki, all with riot guns, stood guard. "We can't fight those guys," he muttered.

"Deputies, I'll bet. Act sleepy, I'll do the talking," she said, and rolled down the window as she stopped.

The spokesman was middle-aged, kindly, firm. No traffic from the east, he said. "Official cars only."

"But I'm from Oak Ridge," Abby said. "I *am* an official." She selected a card from her bulging wallet as she invoked the phrase with resounding dignity. "The American Museum of Atomic Energy. I only came down to pick up my son here, and bring him back."

"Back from where," the man said, no longer so kindly, but jerking his eyes toward Quantrill as he returned the card.

"What's the name of that silly mountain we just left, hon," she asked, looking brightly at Ted. "Poor dear, he's been up there only one night alone and so tired he can hardly move. Teddy, answer mother."

"Uh—Clingman's," he said, and rubbed his eyes. "We aren't home yet." It was a complaint; almost a whine.

"Soon. Go back to sleep."

A second man, silent until now, had been listening. His age and wedding ring suggested that he might have a family of his own. "Lady, you had to be crazy to let the boy go camping alone at a time like this. How many anthrax victims has he rubbed up against since yesterday, and why didn't your husband come along?"

"The Lord took my husband, sir," she said softly. "And left me only the boy. I promised he could have his little adventure; and Teddy was complaining that he didn't meet anybody up there. I didn't think God would take him away from me when he's all I have—except for my official duties. I do have those; and I'm late." Not quite a protest.

The older man, ruminatively: "Those are Georgia plates on your car."

Without hesitation: "Georgia plates are cheap, and a widow has to make ends meet. Chief Lawrence in Oak Ridge knows that."

"I reckon he does," the younger man laughed, and turned to his companion. "Look, Sam, they aren't really from across the Smokies—and she *is* an official. And they haven't had a chance to catch anything. Whaddaya say?"

The older man exhaled slowly, then stood aside. "What was the name of your police chief again?"

Already rolling, the diesel now warming up to take its share of the load: "Calvin Lawrence," Abby said, "even if I didn't vote for him."

The man smiled, waved her on, waved again as the Chevy eased onto the bridge. She waved back, then rolled up the window and heaved a sigh of record proportions. "We're a good team," she said.

Quantrill: "You're a great team all by yourself. I almost believed you myself, mom."

"Mom your ass," she squealed, and backhanded his shoulder lightly. "I'm thirty-four years old, fella. In the right clothes I could pass as your hotsy."

"I think you could pass for any damn' thing you wanted to."

"And why not? I didn't tell you what my profession is, nine months a year."

Slyly: "Does it involve lying to deputies a lot?"

"By God, but you're getting cocky! What I do, is cause the willing suspension of disbelief."

"I believe it," he said quickly.

"You have some good lines, inside *and* out," she winked. "Anyway,—I teach drama at a junior college."

"You really a widow?"

"Of the grass variety. Twice. I like macho men, but I don't like to be directed, I like to direct." She glanced at him again, laughed again. "Mom your ass," she repeated, laughing.

When she laughed, Abby Drummond seemed more like thirty than forty. Quantrill decided the tan and the strong muscular lines had led him astray, then reflected that she could be almost any age. All that play-acting might let her be anything she liked. To anybody. Suddenly he was aware of the first stirrings of an erection. "You and that deputy both mentioned anthrax," he said quickly. "Tell me about it; I thought it was a cattle disease."

Chapter 25

Abby Drummond had felt secure in Spartanburg until (she told Quantrill) Monday night after she snapped off her holo set and spent an hour reading De Kruif, the *Britannica*, and other snippets from her small library. Anthrax was one of the few diseases with an epizootic potential that included not only cattle but swine, sheep, horses, domestic pets—and the domesticator as well. Isolated by Koch in 1876 and fought with Pasteur's vaccine in 1881, anthrax in its original form was well-known.

If breathed, anthrax spores caused pulmonary infection

that advanced within days to lethal hemoptysis—
hemorrhagic pneumonia. Human victims might tremble and
fight for breath before the convulsions and the bloody froth at
the mouth, or they might just succumb quickly and quietly.

Introduced into a skin abrasion, *B. anthracis* produced a
large carbuncle with an ugly necrotic center which soon fed
ravenous microbes into the bloodstream where, without
prompt treatment, septicemia led to meningitis and usually
death. Ingested, the bug was just as deadly. Consumption of
anthrax-killed beef was not a very popular form of suicide,
but a little dab would do you.

Toxoids, proteins produced from the bacterial toxins,
could provide immunity. Antibiotics might halt the progress
of the disease. If there was one optimistic note to be struck in
this dirge, it was that recovery from anthrax usually meant
permanent immunity.

On the other hand were four murderous fingers. Anthrax
was so contagious that a corpse could infect the living. Onset
of the disease led to death so quickly that treatment often
came too late. The bacillus reverted to spores that could lie in
lethal wait for a host, sometimes for years in open fields.
Finally there came the fact that, within hours after Indian
craft dispersed the disease, the Surgeon General's office
announced that a new, more virulent and invasive strain of
the bacillus was involved.

The defunct USSR, in 1980, had succeeded too well in
developing a modified *B. anthracis* in one of its bacteriological warfare centers near Sverdlovsk. And had failed misera-
bly to contain it, resulting in the now-famed Sverdlovsk scare
that killed scores of citizens and further curtailed the supply
of local beef while Tass News Agency denied the obvious.
Sverdlovsk had been lucky; the distribution of its anthrax had
been meagre, accidental, and vigorously fought. Unlike the
farmlands of the southeastern US in 1996.

The SinoInd delivery system took a multiplex approach to
the problem of vectoring the disease. To start with, paranthrax spores were much smaller than those of the original
bacilli; a cubic centimeter of them could be dispersed fifty

times more widely for the same effect, because they multiplied faster. The dispersal method was by sub-launched Indian cruise missiles, fat capacious cargo drones that flew a leisurely mach 0.7 from the Mexican Gulf toward Virginia, voiding trails of deadly paranthrax spores as they passed over agrarian centers. Macon, High Point, and Roanoke typified the targets.

Though American epidemiologists did not yet know it, pulmonary paranthrax spread fast because still-ambulatory victims spread the microbes in their exhalations. As active bacilli or after sporulation on contact with air, the disease was literally designed to spread into the countryside.

The region west of the Appalachians had been spared immediate effects of paranthrax because the Pensacola bomb did not arrive until two flights of old Marine Sea Harriers scrambled from there, following sonar contacts to the surfaced Indian subs in the Gulf. In the brief engagement, one sub dived after launching five of its fat birds. Our Harriers shot down three of them; the other two spread death.

The second sub was caught with its panels down as it readied the first of its missiles intended for Mississippi, Tennessee, and Kentucky. Despite direct hits on its deck pods with One-eye missiles, the sub might have escaped but for the act for which Marine Captain Darryl Tunbridge won his Medal of Honor. Tunbridge, a flight instructor whose Harrier was equipped with depth charges, used the hover mode of his sturdy old Harrier as he watched tracers climb past his wing. He marveled at the valiant Indian gunner's mate who manned the quad one-cm. antiaircraft guns while his own decks were awash; did not pause to wonder at his own risk as he overtook the diving sub at fifty knots, hanging almost dead overhead, feeling the shudder of one-cm. slugs in his fuel tanks, dropping his depth charges while virtually scraping the sub's squat conning tower. The Harrier faltered as the sub's bow, impelled by two mighty blasts, rose from the water.

Captain Tunbridge's honor was posthumous, but that sub would never launch a missile from her permanent rest at 330 fathoms.

We soon realized our debt to the Pensacola Harriers. We needed more time to discover just how virulently effective were the two cruise missiles that got through. Had the disease spread from farmlands toward agrarian centers, we could have organized teams to distribute penicillin, chlortetracycline, erythromycin. Once those centers were fighting for their lives while evacuees fled to spread the epidemic, there was little hope for the nearby farmlands. There was not enough disinfectant on earth to cleanse ten thousand square klicks of grass.

"I think I got out of Spartanburg in time," Abby sighed. "First symptom is usually skin itch, followed by open sores that don't hurt much, with swelling. The fever and pains in the joints don't begin 'til later."

"Lordy; makes me itch just to think about it."

She lent him a vexed glance. "Do tell," she said, and scratched herself. "Hand me the Clorox."

He watched her dampen a face tissue, dab it to cuticles; imitated her; stowed the jug of bleach. "This all we can do?"

"Until we can get antibiotics. This may not do much good but from what I've read, it's a start. The things I couldn't find at my apartment were antibiotics and thirty-eight cartridges."

"Oh well; six shots are more'n you need," he said.

"You don't get it, Ted. I don't have even one."

Long pause. "You faced those bastards down with an empty gun?"

"*Now* you got it," she smiled; winked.

Chapter 26

Jane Osborne's two-bedroom bungalow lay on the outskirts of Oak Ridge near the museum. She did not answer Abby's calls. They saw a neighbor peering from a shuttered window. He refused to answer their hails. They decided against going into the house until after their self-imposed quarantine. But in the detached garage was Abby's storage and, "I've got medicine and an old TV in there," she explained. They wrestled with musty cartons in the garage. The garage lights worked, and Abby immediately plugged the Chevy's recharger into a garage socket. Abby's penicillin was long outdated, but they shared the half-dozen tabs.

Without cable connections, they had only two available TV channels, curiously flat without holovision. They learned that Memphis and Tullahoma fallout did not yet seriously threaten the Oak Ridge area, though local background count had risen as particles drifted down from the stratospheric jetstream. There were no pictures of gutted cities; the news was vague and optimistic. An old public service announcement illustrated how a basement room could be protected against modest fallout by taping cracks, blocking windows with books, and shoveling dirt shin-deep onto the floor above.

"Jane's house doesn't lend itself very well to that," Abby judged, lighting a candle amid spectacular sunset reflections. "We'll be better off in the tunnels. I'm sure Jane can get you in with us."

They elected to eat the canned food in the garage. It was Quantrill who realized that a sparing rinse in bleach, followed by a soaping and rinse from a garden hose, might disinfect them externally. They soaked their clothes as well, rinsing them outdoors in darkness, joking about the effects of bleach to decoy their attention from their mutual and necessary nudity.

But jokes were not equal to the dimly-outlined grace of Abby Drummond. He held the hose as she rinsed her dark shoulder-length hair and erred in thinking that her eyes were closed. He saw the gentle curve of her buttocks, the faint pendulous sway of foam-flecked teats, the effulgent gleam of water on her thighs, and turned slightly away from Abby as his desire had its usual effect. In silhouette, his erection was now a gravity-defying flag.

She wrung her hair dry, squatting, as he turned the stream
of water on himself. It wasn't exactly a cold shower, but
. . . "I've been thinking," she said, and took the hose and
soap from him. "We've done a lot for each other in the past
twelve hours. Let's not stop now."

She began to lather the small of his back, both of them
squatting in the grass, and gradually her hand scrubbed to the
back of his thighs. Quantrill held his breath until his ears
popped, mesmerized by the soft huskiness of her voice and
the progress of that bar of soap. "We could both be sick, or
worse, in a week," she continued. And continued. Now he
was breathing quickly, a sense of warmth flooding his loins,
rising up the back of his neck. For a moment, Quantrill
imagined that his ears must be glowing in the dark. *At least*
his ears.

"Hey; you don't know what you're doing," he breathed.

"I know exactly what I'm doing," she insisted, purring it.
"I'm making sure you're nice and clean. And when you're
all good and soapy, you can help me clean where I can't do it
alone."

"I think you'd better not," he said after a moment.

She paused. "If you really and truly don't want me to,"
she said.

His laugh was embarrassed, frank, sorrowful: "God no,
Abby, but in another minute I won't have anything left to,
ah, soap you with."

Again the hand, now both hands, sleekly caressing his
belly as she wriggled beneath him. She manipulated him, let
him feel the warm accepting cleft that pulsed at the exact tip
of his body, resumed rubbing him, now cupping his buttocks. "You take your time, lover," she said, "and scrub me
out good."

When he felt some control return Quantrill eased downward, pressed into her carefully, felt her move to accommodate him with small sounds of pleasure. He stopped again,
his control ebbing.

"Think of yourself as the rotorooter man," she said,
understanding better than he, "doing an unpleasant job. Or

just think about something else—but not for very long," she teased. Presently her own breathing quickened and, as he gently swept strands of damp hair from her face, she moved against him in repeated sinuous thrusts.

At last she lay still, stroking his ribcage as he moved above her. "Penny for your thoughts," she whispered.

Gruffly: "Wondering—if the—neighbors—can see," he said. "You?"

Insinuating: "Wondering if you know I've already come."

The heat in his loins was suddenly a fever. "Liar."

"Truth. Yes," she crooned, then in vehemence, sensing his urgency, "oh yes; absolutely, please yes," she said, empathizing the synaptic explosions that thundered down the halls of his mind.

For perhaps a minute they lay communicating their satisfaction with grunts of pleasure, brief kisses that said more about reassurance than of lust. Then she gave his backside a playful slap. "Now you'll have to scrub me outside," she said. "There are chiggers in this damn' grass."

Chapter 27

Later, when Quantrill offered to open a jar of mint jelly for her, Abby made the first reference to their earlier delights on the grass outside. "I can cope," she snapped, wrenching the lid loose. "Why do southern men still think sex makes a weakling of a woman?"

"Never thought about it," he shrugged, watching the TV.

"Think about it," she growled, tasting the jelly, watching the set of his jaw as he refused a taste. "Oh, hell, you were just trying to help, Ted. I'm on edge." She laid a hand on his shoulder as she asked softly, "Was I your first, um, experience? Wait; forgive me, don't answer that."

"First one that was like they say it's supposed to be," he said, "and don't tell me whether to answer you, and don't forget it was your idea! And even if I was klutzy I'm not one damn' bit sorry. You want me to go now?"

He stared toward the ancient TV, which was running a plea for voluntary induction. In its wisdom the Department of Defense trusted in the blonde charms of wide-eyed Eve Simpson, the child star whose cleavage was no longer childish, whose buxom bogus innocence permitted just enough jiggle to enslave the daydreams of youthful—and many not so youthful—males. Little Evie moistened her lips to croon her fascination with 'our boys in uniform'.

Abby Drummond realized that young Quantrill might soon be wearing a uniform. She stepped toward the TV, paused. "May I?"

Quantrill nodded. She snapped off the set, sat on a box facing him, placed the jelly between her thighs in subtle symbolism, asked permission again as she took his hands.

At first he glanced over her shoulder, then into the dark; anywhere but into her face as she said, "I take too much for granted. And I'm a shitty dancer because I like to lead, and I'm sensitive as hell about the big-strong-man syndrome. So I've sent you some rejection signals I didn't mean.

"You may have tears in your eyes, and you may not have a lot of experience, but the best men start that way, lover. At everything. You're being forced to become a man faster than anybody should, and it's going to get a lot worse before it gets better. Have you ever seen anyone die?"

After a moment he met her eyes. "No," he lied.

"Neither have I, but we will. Lots of them, maybe. I'm having a hard time dealing with you because I see you as needing an older person's advice, *and* as being a man who usually does things right the first time. So I act as though there were two of you. I'll work on that. If you don't want any of teacher's advice, tell me now and I'll do my Goddamnedest to quit. But don't ask me to forget you're a man, mister. You are altogether too good at making love to a woman."

"Why the hell," he sighed with the faintest of smiles, "is that last thing so important to me?"

"I don't know, Ted. Maybe advertising has given it more importance than it deserves. But with the bod you have, and the tenderness you show me,—well, don't you worry about it, luv. Hell, I'm giving advice again!"

His smile now more confident: "Don't stop, Abby. Things're going too fast for me and I don't have anybody else to trust. In fact, I wonder if I should trust anybody's advice a hundred per cent."

"You're a natural," she grinned back at him. "Trust your instinct a lot, because it's dead-center. For example, it told you not to trust anything too much. It was right. I saw how you willed yourself to be a child today at that road-block, on the spur of the instant. I think you're a born actor; not all great actors are long on brains but they have great timing and they have terrific instincts. Come to think of it, the smartest actors know how to hide half their brains so they don't scare other people off. If I have any advice on how you'll survive best, it's just to act like a kid and hide half your brains."

"From everybody?"

She saw the direction of his inquiry. "Not quite; you'd die of loneliness. Your instinct will tell you who you can open up to." She placed a middle finger in the mint jelly, placed a tiny smear of it on her lower lip, licked the finger clean, smiling all the while. "No, not quite everybody. Now you take *me*," she said, leaned forward, transferred the sticky smudge to his own lips.

Quantrill did not have to be told twice.

Chapter 28

Wednesday morning, Quantrill was awakened by roving hands for the first time in his life and learned that there was something better than merely breakfast in bed. He fluffed out

their bedrolls later while Abby opened canned fruit, and
wondered aloud whether Jane Osborne was coming home.
"It'd be nice to take a shower in the house," he said.

"I'm going to take a chance on us," she said, and after
using bleach on her hands she went into the house. She
returned while Quantrill watched the TV. "Recorded message at the museum," she said. "It's now a crisis relocation
center and it's full. Taking no messages at the, har, har,
moment—maybe a year-long moment. That's not like Ellis;
something tells me the museum directorship is in new
hands," she went on, more to herself than to him.

"Let's take a shower and then go find out."

"Oh; forgot to tell you. No more water pressure. We'd
better drain that hose for drinking water. There'll be more in
the hot water tank and the tank behind the toilet."

Abby found her old watercouch folded away and, with
Quantrill's help, half-filled it in a rear niche of the Chevy.
The hundred liters of water would last them two weeks, she
said. They used the toilet water for its customary purpose, a
single flush serving them both.

Of still more importance was the penicillin they found in
Jane Osborne's medicine trove. Abby admitted she had acted
from unreasoning fear in swallowing her tabs the day before,
and convinced Quantrill that he should not begin to take his
fresh ones unless he developed definite symptoms. She was
telephoning fruitlessly to find a source of radiation meters
when the TV and hall light winked off.

"Well, that's all the omen I need," she said grimly, and
after locking the house they drove through eerily silent streets
to the museum.

"Boy, I never saw a museum like that before," Quantrill
muttered at the gate. The cyclone fence was strung on heavy
pipe, an obvious jury rig blocking the drive to the foremost
building. He spied other structures in the distance.

"You said it," Abby replied, peering at the rump end of a
cargo van that faced away from them in the drive, twenty
meters inside the gate. Concrete blocks had been stacked
chest-high in a vee that protected the van, and bullet holes

pocked the metal panels that showed. She fumbled for her wallet, murmured, "Just be your boyish self," and stepped from the Chevy.

The voice that issued from the van was a shocking study in contrasts, warmly feminine but powered at the hundred decibel level. It would have been audible a kilometer away. "PLEASE DO NOT ATTEMPT TO ENTER THIS CRISIS RELOCATION CENTER. THE CENTER IS CROWDED FAR BEYOND CAPACITY, AND THESE PREMISES ARE UNDER MARTIAL LAW. YOU ARE UNDER SURVEILLANCE BY HEAVILY ARMED OFFICERS. TRESPASSERS WILL BE SHOT WITHOUT FURTHER WARNING. THANK YOU FOR YOUR PATIENCE."

Waving her identification, Abby called out, "I work here! Abigail Drummond, grounds maintenance records; I'm sure my supervisor will be glad to see me."

"PLEASE DO NOT ATTEMPT TO ENTER THIS CRISIS RELOCATION CENTER," the voice began again, and repeated its stentorian message. Abby plugged fingers into ears and waited until the bullhorn thanked her again for her patience.

"I am vitally needed here," she shouted. "May I speak to Mr. Ellis, or Miz Osborne, please?"

"PLEASE DO NOT—," the bullhorn replied, fell silent, then said in crisp male tones, "YOU IN THE CAMPER! GET OUT AND STAND IN FRONT, LEAN FORWARD, BOTH HANDS ON THE HOOD."

Quantrill did as he was told, prickles of fear and anticipation on his spine. From the tail of his eye he saw an armed man approach the gate from the van. The man said nothing, only thrust a pocket comm set through the gate slit to Abby.

Her talk with the new administration was short and not particularly sweet. Perry Ellis was in custody; Jane Osborne would verify the stranger's identity when she returned from a work detail; and what made a grounds keeper think she was vital to the center?

Abby's reply was a brilliant bit of temporizing. The center would need expert maintenance of its grounds equipment for latrine trenches and protective earth ramps, and someone to coordinate it with the computer. She and her cousin, Ted Quantrill, could operate heavy equipment and the diagnostic machines that made breakdowns few and far between. She and her cousin would wait in the camper for Ms. Osborne's return.

Sliding back into the Chevy's cab, they rolled up the windows and exchanged a quick handsqueeze. "I hope you know how to operate heavy equipment, 'cause I can't even drive. You sure you want to go in there?"

Drumming fingertips on the doorsill: "All I know is, a lot of people can stay alive there. It used to be a center for civil defense studies. I suspect they aren't overcrowded, and they don't intend to be. Ellis in custody, hm? It takes a decision from the Governor to initiate martial law, Ted, and we haven't heard anything about that. I think it's a scam—but a damned effective one. Once we get inside we're going to be like prison inmates. But we can still stick together. It's got all the advantages of organization, and all the disadvantages too."

A swatch of Ray Kenney's sarcasm, invented to spite a scout leader, popped into Quantrill's head. "Every hour is a sixty-minute asskiss," he quoted.

"It beats radiation poisoning," she said. "If you know a better place to go, tell me."

Until that moment Quantrill had thought of himself as an uncomplicated risk-taker; the sort of loner who would always gamble against long odds rather than submit to regimentation. Suddenly and with startling clarity he saw that, when the risk was not a bloody nose but life itself, he could be downright conservative. "I'll go with you," he said, adding with sudden concern, "if they'll let me."

"Why wouldn't they? Gorgeous young specimen like you," she grinned. She learned why they wouldn't, five minutes later.

Without preamble the bullhorn crackled: "ABIGAIL DRUMMOND, YOU ARE VERIFIED AS A SEASONAL EMPLOYEE. YOUR SKILLS ARE USEFUL, IF NOT VI-

TAL. IF YOU'RE AN IMPOSTOR YOU WILL BE SHOT, LADY, DON'T THINK WE WON'T. SEND YOUR COUSIN AWAY; WE ALREADY HAVE TOO MANY MEN."

Abby and Quantrill exchanged a long stare. Abby got out of the Chevy, called toward the van: "I'll drive him back to town."

After a long pause the bullhorn said, "GOOD DECISION."

Cursing, Abby drove back toward town. "Already have too many men, do they? I don't like the sound of that. And they have my personnel records so they know my age and what I look like. Now where do we go?"

Quantrill stroked her hair. "I go away, and you go in there."

"You're kidding. I'd be petrified in there if you weren't with me. Janie's the fainting type; no help in a tight spot."

They passed an all-hours market. Behind a shattered glass front they could see a man cradling a deer rifle. "At least I'll have a few days' food," he went on as if he hadn't heard. "If you don't like it there it should be easy to get out."

"That's an idea," she said, and turned onto a secondary road, talking quickly. Minutes later she drove the Chevy off the road toward a copse of wilting trees and coasted to a stop. "Just past here is the perimeter fence, Ted. They may have sentries, but we have eyes, too. There's a drainage ditch from the maintenance shops that'd hide me almost to the fence. We could set up rendezvous, say at dark, and toss some blankets over the barbed wire to get you in. You could hide for weeks in the tunnels, maybe mix with the others. Or we could get me out, depending how it looks inside."

They spent a half-hour going over alternatives. Whether it took Abby a half-day or three days to make rendezvous, they were faced with the fact that Quantrill could not drive. Their last half-hour was spent teaching him, a cram session that left them both irritable.

"At least you're not slamming the brakes anymore," she said as he drove, overcorrecting, toward the gate. "Wait.

Stop here and turn around, Ted; sure as hell they'll demand
the Chevy as an entrance fee. I'll walk from here.''

Sweating with concentration, Quantrill got the vehicle
pointed back toward town. "Abby," he said as she slid out.
She paused, managed a wan smile. "Abby, I never said I
love you, did I?''

Airily, misunderstanding: "I'd never ask you to tell such a
whopper for a one-night stand, Ted. Cheers.'' She turned
away.

In the distance the bullhorn was blustering. Quantrill ignored it. "But it's not a lie,'' he shouted, protesting.

"Don't say it, Ted,'' she said, not turning. "It wouldn't
help.''

He watched her retreat, holding herself unnaturally erect,
and realized that she was compensating for simple terror. He
drove away quickly, aware that in another moment he would
have called her back in panic. Whatever happened, he told
himself, at least Abby had reached her sanctuary.

Quantrill took two wrong turns before finding the bungalow, let himself in with Abby's key, assured himself that
the telephone line was still active even without house current.
It had been Abby's idea that she might be able to phone him.
He spent an hour taping seams in Abby's bedroom, stacking
books and magazines against the outside wall, listening to his
radio quantify the gradual rise in radiation in the area. He
found a certain satisfaction in anger over their decision, the
night before, to sleep in the garage. It would have been so
much better, infinitely more voluptuous, to writhe with Abby
between sheets. On impulse he pulled back her coverlet,
thrust his face against her pillow; inhaled. It did not smell of
her presence, but mustily of her absence.

Quantrill did not understand how much the human organism is sexually provoked by sudden social change. He
knew only an enormous need, and lying in Abby's bed his
daydream led him to assuage that need. He felt guilty afterward, as always—but felt relieved as well.

Sundown found Quantrill piling blankets on the Chevy's
seat. This time he ran over only a few curbs and took only one

wrong turn before parking the little camper near their rendezvous point. He had moved stealthily on foot into the grove of small trees, was estimating where he could most easily drive up to the chain-link fence, when he first heard the delta approaching.

It came as a faint hiss, then a whirr, then the susurrus of ten billion sopranos whispering in the dusk. When he finally looked to the west the thing was nearly overhead. The yellow delta slid down its invisible glidepath like a sharply defined cloud, rocking very slightly in warm evening breezes, a rigid polymer-skinned dirigible the length of two football fields, powered by external multiblade propellers. Quantrill had seen the fat spade-shaped cargo craft many times, but always at great distance. Even with its elevons canted and its engine pods gimbaling for thrust vector control, a delta did not look like a steerable craft; certainly not like one that could winch sixty thousand kilos of cargo into its belly and skate away into the sky at the speed of a fast monorail.

A trapezoid of lights flickered across the meadow inside the museum perimeter, making Quantrill squint. It seemed to throw the drainage ditch into deeper shadow. The ponderous delicacy of the delta's mooring held Quantrill's attention for long minutes. Finally anchored by rigid struts, the great helium-filled airship stilled its propellers. The air-cushion cargo pallet rose to meet the section of shell that scissored down with cargo. Quantrill could hear faint shouts of the handlers five hundred meters away and wondered if the commotion would help Abby.

A part of him hoped that Abby would want out, for whatever reason; he did not want to go over that fence. Yet if Abby said to come, he would do it. When had she made a poor decision?

He would not know the answer for many hours.

Chapter 29

While Quantrill roved the perimeter in search of sentries, peering through the last light of a blood and saffron dusk, Eve Simpson catalogued her new hardships among California's Channel Islands. "They promised me," she said, scowling in the late sun as she jogged along the beach, "*promised* me I'd be playing that civil defense bit against a war hero. So what do I get? A vapid nit without a ribbon!"

Trundling beside little Evie in a gold cart, her male secretary made an entry in his portable 'corder and judged that it was time for his hourly demur. "Evie dear, they don't have any new heroes available just yet. He *did* look the part. And my goodness, what a voice!"

"Resonance I'll give him," Eve puffed. "Brains, I couldn't find. The next hapless ass NBN fobs off on me who blows a dozen takes because his labile memory isn't up to three lines of dialogue, welllll," she said ominously, and fought to recover her breathing rhythm. As much as she despised jogging, Eve loathed dieting more.

Bruce, her secretary, knew why the National Broadcasting Network paid him so well: given enough provocation, NBN's most prized teen sexpot could discover a blinding migraine that might hold up shooting schedules for days. It wouldn't be such a bitch of a job, he admitted to himself, if little Evie were your standard model seventeen-year-old Hollywood centerfold—which is to say, trained to be utterly disinterested in anything beyond immediate appearances. But Eve Simpson was distinctly abnormal, he gloomed, noting the rivers of perspiration that trickled down her spine to be absorbed by the velour stretched across those famous buns. In ten years she might be pudgy. Right now she was a morsel men—most men, he smiled to himself—craved. Until they fetched up against the inner Evie. A mind swift and incisive as a weasel's bite, a tongue she wielded like a broken bottle. A clever gay fellow could feast like a pilot fish on gutted egos, cruising near the jaws of Eve Simpson.

Eve slowed to a walk as the beach curled toward the east, then turned away from rocky prominences and began to retrace her path. "You're watching the rad counter, I hope," she said. "The Lompoc and Santa Barbara fallout pattern could shift on us."

"We're clean as puppy teeth," he said and snickered, waving a negligent palm at the glass-ported concrete dome just under their skyline. "I'll bet there's a batch of vice-presidents gnawing their cuticles to ribbons up there, watching you and worrying enough for all of us." He steered around a pile of kelp, giggled. "If the wind changed we'd hear them from here; they'd have a feces hemorrhage."

"Bruce, you wouldn't say 'shit' if you had a mouthful," she accused, lengthening her stride as she called back. "Did you ever wonder if there were such a thing as being too socialized?"

"Oh, Gohhhd, Evie's a sociologist again," he moaned.

"At least you can pronounce it," she shot back. "Oh: see if I have a schedule conflict between my dialect tutor and blocking out the scenes for my Friday 'cast. And have wardrobe magic up some bra straps that don't slice me in three," she added.

It was pure hell to make do on a desert island, she thought. Well, not exactly a desert. Eve slowed to a walk again, noting the similarities between the familiar scrub oak and cactus of Catalina, and her present location on Santa Cruz Island. She knew the history of Santa Cruz from the Caire settlements through the Stanton purchase, its off-limits status, and the far-sighted lease arrangements NBN had worked out with the Bureau of Public Information. Knowing the dichotomy between news broadcasts and the actual progress of the war, little Evie thought of it as the Bureau of Public Disinformation. Invasion defenses by civil defense organizations in Los Angeles, indeed! *What* organization? *What* Los Angeles?

For that matter, what civil defense? Eve's media theory

tutor, a Southern Cal professor named Kelsey with connections at AP and UPI, was already squirreling away a collection of news items which, by the process of wartime censorship, had become non-news. One day it might become ten pages in a learned journal; meanwhile it was grist for Eve's formidable mill.

News: patriotic Americans over eighteen years of age were swamping induction centers.

Non-news: it didn't take many people to swamp induction centers that for the moment had no means to ship inductees, or training centers for them. When the military machinery got in gear, sixteen-year-olds might feel the draft.

News: a coordinated counterattack by US/RUS orbital weapons had won the first great battle in near space. We alone had orbital spies.

Non-news: the RUS moonbase was now only a collection of desperate people in a few leaking domes, unable to mount another launch and without hope of survival if another bevy of nukes came their way.

News: an estimated twenty per cent of China's population, and twenty-five per cent of India's, had perished.

Non-news: so had a full forty per cent of ours. Centralization had provided the good life. Too much centralization had obliterated it.

News: survivors in all US coastal areas were girding themselves for invasion, clearing debris from vital thoroughfares, cheerful in their faith in flag, mom, and apple pie.

Non-news: that piece of news was a lie. Survivors in most coastal regions were scrabbling for existence after less than a week. Any transportation that depended on rails or macadam was in thick yogurt, though beltline throughways around a few cities had survived beyond Dead Day. Moms were dying, apples were radioactive, and east of the Alleghenies the flag carried paranthrax.

News: crisis relocation centers were getting supplies from

federal stores by secret means in a coordinated
mutual-aid effort. The few isolated cases of local
satrapy would be documented and punished.

Non-news: it would be hard to keep the role of the delta
dirigibles a secret for long, and few of the centers
showed much interest in anything beyond their own
survival. Some were dispensing antibiotics and
broadcasting survival tips oriented toward keeping
their gates clear of more evacuees.

News: The Church of Jesus Christ of the Latter-Day Saints
urged Americans to turn to prayer and good works; to
accept this judgment of God with a firm resolve to
emulate the Godly as a path to survival.

Non-news: Catholics, Jews, Unitarians and athiests
wanted equal time. It was not difficult to infer a
connection between different ratios of survival between faiths, and different amount of Godliness.
What *was* difficult, to gentiles, was explaining away
the fact that Mormon temples were responding hero-
ically with food and medical help to anyone standing
in the queues outside.

Eve Simpson had already absorbed an undergraduate's
knowledge of media and information processing. She knew
that word of mouth was still the best advertising, and that a
convincing demonstration was the spoon that filled mouths
with the right words. It occurred to Eve that Senator Collier
of Utah was a convincing demonstrator with the right words
and, under these circumstances, the right background. B.A.,
J.D., and LDS. His Presidential candidacy might be a
foregone conclusion if the latest rumor were true.

She had heard it while on Stage Three, one of the concrete
domes of the hush-hush complex they called Sound Stage
West. The complex had been built into the mountain over-
looking the secluded valley of Santa Cruz Island so that
news, non-news, and rumor could all receive their 'proper'
processing in an emergency. The President, it was rumored,
was not safely tucked into a maximum-security hole, nor was
the Vice President. The stream of messages issued by the

White House press secretary only purported to come from the top. The rumor dealt with a brace of impact nukes and one of the provisioned caverns of Virginia's once-lovely Shenandoah Valley. If it was true—real non-news—then the Speaker of the House was now President of the United States.

Eve found the rumor worrisome. "Give me that towel," she said suddenly, and mopped herself as she climbed aboard the golf cart. "Put this thing in overdrive or something, Brucie; I want back inside."

"You've got time," he soothed.

"Have I? If our government goes belly-up, Bruce, the only thing left to glue this country together will be media. Tell me honestly: do you think Sound Stage West could take a direct hit?"

"So they say," he replied, intent on conning the vehicle. "Since three of NBN's top shareholders and a senator are here with their hotsies and luggage, I tend to believe it."

The big titties bounced with Eve's laughter. "Why is it that fags have all the brains," she gurgled rhetorically. Bruce merely smiled. He knew how to field a left-handed compliment, however poorly tossed.

Chapter 30

By nine PM Eve had finished her stint for NBN, a rack of lamb, a half-hour mimicking the lilting lingo of South Afrikaners for the government's impending plea to African neutrals, and a quick scan of Medler's *Games Governments Play*. It was a curiosity and a commonplace that, for all her media experience and theory, Eve had never actually watched a news broadcast during its taping. Now, cloistered with five hundred others in an effort to maintain a 'business-as-usual' impression to holo viewers, Eve found herself in closer quarters. She needed merely to traverse a tunnel to emerge in the wings of NBN's Nightly News set. The item on the Amur crossing, she realized, was several hours old even though it was datelined on Thursday morning, RUS time.

In Eau Claire, Wisconsin, the Nightly News tape aired at midnight. Lieutenant Boren Mills had been awake for twenty hours; he damned the discomfort of his contact lenses, switching to bifocals in the privacy of his room in the Bachelor Officers' Quarters. His attention was only half on the holo because Mills already knew of the SinoInd invasion of the Amur region.

". . . Shortly before dawn, this Thursday morning," said a young man in clipped British diction. In the distance sprawled mountains; a river glinted not far away, partly hidden by massive concrete apartment complexes of a typical small RUS city. At ten klicks' distance no flames were visible, but smoke roiled from rooftops. Mills guessed it must be Khabarovsk.

But the newsman continued, "Elements of the Chinese Third Army crossed the Amur River here, at Blagoveshchensk. Amphibious trucks towed primitive rafts filled with soldiers, protected by mortar fire. The Chinese met stiff resistance here and at Khabarovsk; but in several places along the six hundred kilometer front, CPA troops have driven thirty kilometers or more into RUS territory.

"The civilian population has been evacuated. The civil defense cadre of Blagoveshchensk remained behind and is inflicting heavy casualties on the advancing Chinese People's Army. A RUS spokesman has assured this correspondent that the CPA cannot hope to consolidate these temporary gains. He says the Chinese are using outmoded equipment that probably can't withstand modern RUS weapons expected soon from Vladivostok.

"But this morning, the CPA took portions of the old trans-Siberian railway north of the Amur. So, at high noon in Siberia, the CPA boasts an invasion and a vital rail link. The question is: can they keep either of them moving? In Blagoveshchensk, I'm Peter Westwood for the BBC."

Mills was wide awake now. As the news turned to Cana-

da's entry into the western rank of warring nations, he
cudgeled his memory for the Vladivostok messages that had
passed through his ELF channels. The RUS port city, within
artillery distance of China, had taken such a nuclear shellack-
ing that even its submarine pen entrances near Artem had
collapsed. There was no longer any point in sending US subs
there for repair or provisioning. Mills made a silent wager
that China had more than an old rail link in mind. Strongly
gifted with visual memory, he recalled that the Chinese thrust
was generally northeastward. By driving to the Sea of
Okhotsk they would also cut the big new Baikal-Amur
railway—a truly crucial artery through Siberia which had
cost twice as much as our Alaska pipeline.

Oil, iron, coal, even diamonds passed from Siberia to the
coast on the new artery and if it were slashed, much of Siberia
might bleed to death. Yes, Mills decided, the RUS was in
damned big trouble if SinoInd forces could push a spearhead
to the Okhotsk Sea. And if the RUS was posturing about help
from devastated Vladivostok, that posture would fool no
one—that is, no one but surviving Americans who found
their media more believable each year.

Boren Mills had guessed already that Canada was ready to
throw in with the good guys, even with her growing mistrust
toward the fumbling RUS colossus that owned more Arctic
resources and techniques than Canada herself. Mills did not
care what Canada did, so long as she did *not* permit the US
Navy to install the new ELF grid at Barnes Icecap on Baffin
Island. The grid could be laid there cheaply and quickly,
could be easily hidden there; but already, as a very junior and
very efficient officer, Mills knew that he could give odds on
his being posted there. Baffin Island! Mills groaned to himself and, as NBN turned to the siege of Guantanamo, began
to snore.

Chapter 31

"Turn the durn thing off, Liza," growled the weather-beaten man on the pallet. "It's just wastin' power, and I can do without hearin' why the Mexes are neutral." The hand he waved toward the old portable TV was a ghastly contrast to the rest of his wiry body. The fingers were so grossly swollen by blisters that the hand seemed a cluster of long pinkish grapes. Wayland Grange had not yet lost much of the sparse straight hair on his head, but swarthy skin already was peeling from his forearms. He closed his eyes, held his breath, lay back and faced the ageless stalactites overhead.

Louise Grange nodded to eleven-year-old Sandy, who snapped off the set. "You ought not to take off that cold compress, Daddy," she rebuked her husband softly.

"Ain't the hand that hurts," he grunted, now staring into the gloom of a cavern lit by a single candle that kept his wife's coffee warm. "Tryin' not to lose my supper." His stomach muscles knotted again; he felt the cool damp rag caress his forehead, recognized the loving touch as his daughter's. Like her father, Sandy wasn't long on talk. But her soothing hands were quick and sure, and the girl always seemed to know where it hurt without being told. "Must be half-past twelve," he managed to say. "Time you was asleep, sprat."

"Daddy's right, Sandy," said Louise, nodding toward the pile of quilts and supplies they had carried from the scorched Blazer. "Make you a nice pallet, hon."

"Can I write in my journal?" Sandy's few words, moth-flutter soft as usual, managed to carry both acquiescence and pleading without a hint of protest.

"Just for a minute," her mother warned, redirecting a stray wisp of graying blonde hair that had escaped the bun at her nape. Louise and Wayland Grange exchanged eyebrow lifts, signals that passed for smiles in the laconic little family.

Sandy's journal was one of life's little mysteries. Wayland had once teased his wife about a traveling book salesman because, as he put it, "You and me together couldn't read our way through a deck of cigarette papers."

Sandy's school near Sonora, Texas, may not have had carrels or video classes, but it had something, for sure. Even if Sandy did not read much, even if her spelling was no-holds-barred after she'd missed a year with that lung infection, the sprat had filled more than one spiral binder with words. No one but Sandy had ever read those words. No one in the family had ever mentioned the possibility, despite curiosity that was a mixture of pride and concern. The Granges were that kind of family.

For minutes the silence of the cavern was broken only by the skritch of pencil and sounds of breathing. Across the great sweep of Edwards Plateau in southwest Texas were dozens of known caverns and many more undiscovered. Wayland had guessed that hundreds of others, folks who had spent their lives among the sand-strewn washes and sere rangeland of Sutton County, would emerge safely from their favorite hideyholes when the time came. Their own cavern was no match for Longhorn or Carlsbad, but Wayland had first made love to Louise on the cool sand of its long-dry streambed. It was their retreat; secret, inviting when temperatures soared and locusts buzz-sawed in the mesquite. Some men longed for tropical beaches. Wayland Grange would have given you three Waikikis and a Boca Paila for their inviolate, unnamed grotto south of Sonora. As long as a man had to die someplace, it might as well be where he had loved living the most.

Low, so Sandy would not overhear: "Daddy, we got to find you some help. I'll try the ceebee after the child is asleep."

"Now where you think help's comin' from, Liza? Sure God, none's comin' from San Angelo." He tried to chuckle. He would never know how he found his way, drunked up like that, to the state four-wheel-drive Blazer and then south from San Angelo to Sonora. The air base had taken a twenty megaton airburst just far enough away from the research station at San Angelo that the grain silo had withstood the blast. It had been Wayland's luck that he and Doug Weller had killed a liter of mezcal in the silo, waiting for Aggie researchers to doctor the packets of grain for experimental animals at the Sonora breeding farm. Wayland had been lying just inside the concrete silo arch, all but his forearms protected from direct rays of furious radiation, when it happened.

He hadn't even heard it, didn't feel the earth heave, did not stagger to his feet until seven hours after the great blast that turned San Angelo to a disaster area. Too small and laterally spread to support a genuine firestorm, the little city might not die. But neither would it be able to help a man who had rushed to put his family a hundred klicks away in a cavern.

"We got all we needed out of San Angelo," Louise whispered, spreading the cool cloth on his brow. "I thought sure you was gone, Daddy. It was just God's mercy."

"That and hundred mile-a-hour overdrive. Liza, don't you let nobody take that Blazer. It's my regular state vehicle. You tell 'em I still need it to check on the animals on the range."

"Poor things," she said, thinking of the swine, the fowl, the cattle still penned near Sonora. "How about them still penned up?"

"All I hope is that they bust out. They're bred to live on Edwards Plateau—better'n they did when my great-granddaddy first come. Specially the hogs. Peccary ain't in it with them big boogers. One of them Aggie boys told me once a ol' boar can put on enough fat to armor him against a bomb."

"Pity you ain't a fat old boar."

"I done enough rootin' in my time," he said. "And you gave me the only litter I ever wanted."

"Hush, don't talk like that, Wayland." When she used his given name, she was worried. "You talk like an old man."

A long silence before he whispered, "Liza, I ain't gonna *be* a ol' man. I'm spewin' outa both ends and I got chorizo sausages for fingers, and I can't hardly whip a newborn foal, let alone lift one. We got to think on the notion that you and the sprat'll be on your own pretty soon.''

"Hush. The Lord will provide," she said, louder than she had intended. "We got food for two weeks here, and good water back in the cave."

"And you *stick* here," he insisted, still whispering. "If I don't make it, don't tell nobody. Make out that I'm nosin' around Sutton County like always, and get the Blazer serviced for me if you can. You done it before."

"When you were bombed on that Mexican rotgut," she sniffed.

"Don't start in, Liza. I prob'ly won't do it no more."

Quickly: "Yes you will, and bad as it tastes I'll do it with you."

"What would the sprat think," he marveled, and laughed almost silently until another stomach cramp intervened.

"She'd think we're crazy together, and she wouldn't be far wrong. Now you get some sleep," she said, nestling beside him, hoping that her presence would lead him to slumber.

Sandys jurnal   Aug. 14 Wens.
I never knew my dady had this cave. All day and night the same temperture, its spooky but neat. I like it. Mom drove us in the truck. She drives like the d-v-l was right behind, maybe he is. I prayed he wont get u.s. I mean the U.S. ha ha. But mom says God came thru with my dady and watches over us. I believe it. t.v. says we and rushians are winning. I wish I had my doll.

Chapter 32

Quantrill waited for Abby Drummond until long after his hope had evaporated with the last of a plutonium-enhanced sunset. He gave thanks for the Chevy's silent electrics and retraced his way to the bungalow, shoring up his spirits with a reminder that he had vital new information. Sentries moved in twos, and from their voices the same pair came past at roughly half-hourly intervals. He assumed they were armed and wondered if, given a gun, he had the guts to fire on them.

The next day he returned with an ornate brass spyglass from Jane Osborne's mantel, studying the delta dirigible that still surged listlessly on its mounts a half-kilometer from his cover. For a cargo vessel highly touted for its efficiency, the delta was certainly taking its time. Not once did he note the date: August 15, his birthday.

By Friday, Quantrill was half-crazed with waiting. The radio warned locals to stay indoors except for the most necessary outings and gave conflicting reports of a Chinese invasion that threatened a major RUS supply line in Siberia. Britain declared war on the SinoInd powers, as had Canada and, in accord with the ANZUS pact, Australia and New Zealand. Indonesia and Southeast Asian countries favored the SinoInd axis, in concert with other Islamic states. All Africa was neutral toward the major combatants, though its Mediterranean countries were poised to pounce on Israel. Most of southern Africa favored the US/RUS allies; so did some west equatorials. The young fragmented African republics trebled their border patrols in fear of neighbors while warning Axis and Allies away. Africa had reeled under foreign invaders too many times to trust either faction.

Quantrill gave up trying to visualize the alignments, feeling blind without televised graphics or even a tutor terminal. It was clear to him that Europe seemed solidly pro-Allies, and that the new Marxist countries of Latin America feared official ties with the SinoInds. Things would work out, he thought: the media were very specific on that point.

He rechecked his equipment again Friday evening before his rendezvous. He could eat from his pack for days though water might be a problem if Abby had to hide him. He had the fence-straddling blankets and the short ladder from the garage; first-aid supplies; and a frighteningly sharp little cleaver from the kitchen. He eased the Chevy into shadow before the sun touched the horizon.

He had already watched the sentries pass, wondering why the big yellow delta was still moored, when her faint whistle reached him. He had forgotten the whistle would be their signal; found it almost impossible to whistle back; scurried to the fence heedless of danger as he managed his whistled response, peering hard into the high grass.

"Ted?" Abby's voice, strained of its vitality. "Ted?"

"Abby! I can't see you," he called.

"Just as well. I didn't make it, lover. Listen—"

"Finally you did," he said, between a sob and a laugh.

"Shut up and listen." She coughed, spat, tried again. "It's worse than I thought. Paramilitary types own this place." Cough. "They have radio and satellite uplinks, little rocket launchers, the works. Only problem is, they use us like we were property. Nobody gets in or out on pain of death. They give you ID, and you get shot if you can't produce it. You wouldn't last, Ted."

"Abby, the sentries won't be back for ten minutes. I can have you over the wire right away. Promise; I *promise*, honey! When I say the word, you make a run for it."

More coughs, and something else. Then a pause. "Run for it, huh? I can't, I'm—tired, lover." More quickly, still curiously lacklustre in spirit: "I've decided to stay. Just came to tell you thanks, and don't bother. I'd—probably end up turning you in. You don't know me, Ted; I'm really a moral coward."

In something near panic, he virtually shouted: "I'm coming in!"

"If you do I'll—stand up and scream." Cough. "I mean it." Pause. "Thanks for the memory and all that crap, Ted. You come in here and I'm your enemy." Cough, then a despairing laugh: "We have too many men here already." Then something like a clearing of her throat.

Quantrill's mind rebounded from her rejection. When you're tired, he thought, you lose heart. But Abby sounded both tired and determined. "I love you, Abby." It was not what he had intended to say.

"You're a snot-nosed kid," she said. "You've let your-self get tied to a piece of ass, captured like that delta over there. Pity you can't hitch a ride west on it."

"Why couldn't we?"

"It's a hostage. Tied down with glass cable." Cough. "Look, I'm going back, kid. I don't need you and I took a chance getting out here. Do yourself a favor: screw off."

"Abby, don't throw me away," he pleaded. Tears gleamed on his cheeks.

Cough; clearing of her throat, then words tightly strung as on wires: "Fuck off, kid. I won't answer again."

He saw a movement in the grass ten meters from the ditch. He did not see the sentries, but knew they would soon be in sight. She made no further response to his pleas and, gal-vanized by a masochistic urge to see her once more, he made his way to the tallest of nearby trees.

The sun's afterglow at his back, Quantrill strained to locate his lover and tormentor from his perch high in the tree. Then he saw her crawling toward the ditch. She was in a coverall, face down, dragging her legs. A dark stain had spread from above her waist to her thighs. Twice she paused, racked by coughs that she fought against. Once she spat, and in the bronze afterlight he could see that it was dark with blood. His mouth was open to shout when he realized that the sentries were approaching.

Abby must have heard them too. She lay full-length, hands pressed over her mouth. Quantrill suddenly saw himself as an obvious large bulk which he could not entirely hide behind the tree trunk. He could not climb down unobtrusively, dared not drop, was motionless with anticipation and fear.

The men, hardly beyond their teens, talked as they paced the perimeter, carrying stubby carbines in unmilitary fash-ion. ". . . don't give a shit what they say," the taller one was griping; "I bet these goddam coveralls aren't much protection in the open. I bet—"

"Hold it!" The other grasped his arm, swung his carbine up and stared into the grass away from Quantrill.

"Just a dog barking," said the tall one.

"I know a cough when I—there," he exulted. For all her best efforts to muffle it, Abby's spasm came again. The stocky youth swept his arm around to suggest a flanking maneuver. Quantrill heard safeties clicking off. Both men moved away from him, closing in on the prone Abby, and Quantrill could not make himself move.

She played dead. "Told you I hit somebody out here 'while ago," the tall one crowed as they stood over the motionless form. "Turn him over, Al."

The stocky Al toed at Abby's ribcage, then pressed hard and sprang back at her thin scream of pain. "It's a cunt," he shouted.

"Work detail," she moaned; "I was on work detail!" Now she sobbed, trying to roll over, jerking with agony. "Help me—"

"Sheeeit," said Al.

"Why'n't you call when we come up, then," asked the other.

"She's the one got outa the shops today," Al concluded. "They won't like knowin' you only managed to wing 'er." They talked louder as Abby's sobs increased, her pleas only a noise to be overcome.

The tall one nodded, stepped up close and readied his own carbine. "I can fix that; it don't make much noise."

"Naw, you'd leave powder burns. More questions," said Al. "C'mon."

They left Abby, walking backward, and Quantrill developed an instant's scenario in which he would reach her, somehow get her over the fence during the next half-hour, then to a doctor. He gasped when Al, playing out his own fanciful game, snapped the carbine up and fired a burst from ten meters.

Abby Drummond screamed only once; louder than the hissing muffled staccato of gunfire, not loud enough to be heard across the meadow. Her body rolled with the impacts, came to a final rest in the relaxation of death. ''That's how you do it,'' Al snickered, patting his carbine. ''Let's get a move on, Wally. We'll report at the end of the shift like it wasn't nothin' to be excited about.''

Wally followed Al, looking back at their victim. ''You're just plain bad-ass,'' he said admiringly as they swaggered off.

Chapter 33

When Quantrill's shock and fear turned to rage, he was able to control his body enough to climb down from the tree. Now he knew that Abby had paid twice for trying to make the rendezvous, realized her desperate valor in repulsing him; saw the pitiless logic that had compelled her. He did not see his own frozen helpless apartheid as survival, but instead as plain cowardice. He refused to dwell on the moment of her death. That had happened a long time ago; what mattered now was the immediate future. He could drive the Chevy, but where? Local fallout was a long-term worry. His most pressing worry now was one he had nurtured from early childhood.

In the interplay between Quantrill's intellect and his will crowded a hierarchy of motives. His intellect would not have risked death for revenge, or for personal gain, or for the sheer hell of it. Very well then: his will offered the motive most effective on youths of the south and southwest: the stinging goad of the white feather. He had stood by and watched inert while horrors had been inflicted. Only direct action would set things right.

Quantrill had not yet developed the subtlety to seek the roots of corruption; he sought only to prune its branches. At some point between self-accusation and his return from the Chevy he had become a killer. He had no revolver, no experience, truly no white-hot anger. He had more lethal weapons: unshakable resolve and a talent for improvising.

He filled the big water jug from the Chevy's camper stove tank, filled the half-liter squeeze bottle from that, tested its range. He chose a small tree near the fence and, with his collapsible camp saw, cut it more than halfway through. The lights from the delta mooring dispelled the night just enough for him to recognize the two forms that passed once more before he was ready.

He heaved the contents of the jug through the fence, wiped his hands dry on grass, lay down in the shrubbery near enough to touch the fence links. Now his muscle tone was that of a young cat lying in wait. He would remain still until his quarry passed so that the first glimmer of his revenge would not be seen.

The two sentries were not talking, merely plodding their path, as they stepped onto damp matted grass. "Whatthefuck is this," said Wally, stopping, his words masking the rasp of Quantrill's stove lighter.

Al did not answer in words, but in a howl as the stove fuel ignited, a line of flame racing through the fence and along the path underfoot. Quantrill was already spraying more fuel from his squeeze bottle onto Al's head and shoulders, his target illuminated by the blazing grass.

Wally jumped to one side. He might have saved himself had he not stood petrified in astonishment as Al flailed and slapped at his blazing hair. He never saw the stream of fluid that played up his back, barely had time to feel its volatile wetness before he too was a lambent torch in the night.

Quantrill did not wait to see how thorough was his handiwork but raced to his campsaw and, aided by the light of a growing grass fire, made a dozen feverish passes through the sawcut in ten seconds. The tree cracked like a rifle. Quantrill tossed his saw over the fence, hurled his pack over after it, then scrambled up the leaning tree trunk and rode it as it fell across the barbed wire.

By now the meadow was ablaze, doubtless a beacon to many eyes. Quantrill did not realize yet that the flames were high enough to hide his next moves, and opted for the saw instead of his cleaver. The tall Wally was whimpering, trying with dull single-mindedness to get out of the remnant of his coverall. Quantrill's flying kick caught him in the groin, sent him sprawling. With one foot in the tall man's chest, Quantrill needed only a single pass with the saw.

Al was another matter. "I can't see, can't see ohjeez," he mewled as Quantrill found the carbine. The man was stumbling away from the heat waves, falling, running again, still on fire, and Quantrill made a lightning decision. Al—what was left of him—might be a better diversion alive than dead. Quantrill grabbed his pack, ran in a crouch to something that lay spread-eagled near the drainage ditch.

He dragged the thing into the ditch with him, took an interminable thirty seconds to gets its sticky coverall off, found that it fitted him better than it had someone else. Two minutes after the first flame had kindled Quantrill was sprinting in the ditch toward the maintenance shops wearing a coverall, pack slung over one arm, a carbine and a camp saw in the other hand.

A man raced by without seeing him, yelling. Quantrill saw elongated shadows bobbing near and dived headlong on dry gravel. As he scrambled to his feet, snatching at a carbine he had never fired, an older man saw him, tossed him a blanket. "Go on, you sumbitch," the man shouted, "fight that fire with the rest of us!" Then the man was running, arms full of blankets, while more men ran by. No women; somehow that figured.

Quantrill grabbed the carbine, paused only long enough to conceal the plastic-sheathed cleaver in the coverall pocket at his shin before surging up from the ditch. Not thirty meters away was the near edge of the delta moorage, its lights searingly brilliant. He gaped incredulous at the great vessel now splashed with reflected firelight, and then at the man who was hacking at a polymer-wrapped cable as Quantrill approached. The man saw him and the carbine in the same instant, raised his hands in supplication.

The man was dressed in a yellow flight suit; clearly not one of the men who should be guarding the delta. "Scrub the mission," he called softly, not taking his eyes from Quantrill. In the meadow, other men were yelling orders, queries, obscenities.

"We're not armed," said a second man, rising from a crouch behind the second of the four mooring struts. In his eyes, Quantrill saw a calm smoking anger.

With a clarity bright as mooring lights, Quantrill knew that once their guard had become a fireman the delta's crew was trying, under cover of the confusion, to free their huge craft. "Can you shoot this thing?"

The man nearest him stammered, shrugged. "I used to."

Without a word, Quantrill skated the carbine toward him, fumbled the cleaver from his coverall, attacked the cable. It was glass rope; enormous tensile strength, yet so poor in shear strength that it could be cut by a patient man with a penknife. Quantrill was not patient. The cleaver bit deeply and fast.

The gangling man with the carbine took the cleaver and handed the carbine back as Quantrill stood up, the glass cable parted at his feet. "You got the right uniform," the man said, dashing to a rear strut. "So stand like a guard. Safety's off, buddy, all you do is aim and squeeze the trigger plate. Stand in the middle of that platform," he continued, puffing as he hacked through the polymer sheath of the glass cable. At the other rear corner, the second man was laughing insanely as he worked with shears.

Quantrill heard voices above him, dared not glance up. He heard brief whines and thunks of machinery, a call for 'full emergency buoyancy' which seemed to have no effect, and then saw the yellow-clad pair running up the struts using handhold cavities.

"No countdown; *lift*!" A voice echoed through the yawing hull above Quantrill. No one had warned him to sit down, and the pneumatic anti-inertial rams in the struts had thrust the great delta three meters into the air before Quantrill realized why he felt as if he had stepped into a fast-rising elevator.

The struts scissored, the platform began to rise into the

delta's belly, and still there was no sound of propellers. It occurred to Quantrill that they might rise completely out of sight unnoticed, and then a vagrant breeze struck the leviathan hull, and without its gimbaled engines it responded like any balloon with control surfaces.

Quantrill's horizon tilted. He swallowed his heart, grabbed at a cargo pallet tiedown ring with both hands. The carbine began to slide, but he pinned it with his leg. The delta slowly pendulumed back and Quantrill saw that his lower legs had tripped limit switches that, in turn, prevented the platform from seating into the hull.

Now the mooring platform was fifty meters below but now, too, came a bright series of blinks from beyond the mooring lights and a drumming through the hull. Then more blinks from another source, and impacts Quantrill could feel through the hatch floor. Looping an arm through a pallet mount, he groped for the carbine, brought it to his shoulder, aimed in the general direction of the flashes.

His first burst sent a dozen rounds earthward in a hammering hiss that, if not on target, at least quelled the firing from below. His second burst was longer, sweeping the mooring pad; two of the lights flashed out, sparks blooming like fireworks. The Stirling engine nacelles of the delta began to thrum now, slowly at first, with a steady rhythmic beat, the propellers whispering strongly now, a breeze fanning Quantrill as he saw the flash of the rocket launcher from near one of the buildings.

Wherever the projectile went, it did not strike the delta. Quantrill emptied the long double-clip in answering fire and saw a man fly backward like a flung doll. Then, with great care, he pulled himself into a fetal position and risked a look around as the cargo hatch thudded against its seals. Two men, the same two who had attacked the glass cables, slapped manual hatch locks into place, and then the taller one approached Quantrill in a sailor's rolling walk. "Welcome aboard," he said grinning, offering his hand and then, taking his first hard look at Quantrill, shouted: "Good God, cap'n; it's a kid!"

Chapter 34

Quantrill insisted that he had not been hit; that the blood was someone else's, though he did not expand on that. Not until he had removed the coverall and started to don a yellow flight suit did he feel the dull ache in his left calf. "He took a slug through the muscle; looks like a clean hole," said a crewman.

"Why doesn't it hurt more," Quantrill asked, limping down a narrow corridor to a faintly-lit room.

"It will," the man predicted. "Take this towel and stretch out. Co-cap'n Bly's our paramedic, I'll get him soon as we're at cruise altitude." He started to duck out of the room as Quantrill gazed at the swollen discoloration where the slug had exited his flesh. "You have any idea where we're going?"

"We had a stop scheduled at Hot Springs, but cap'n doesn't want a repeat of this. We're headed home for weapons refitting."

"Where's home?"

"College Station, Texas. If you got any Texas Aggie jokes, pal, better jettison 'em now," he grinned. "We'd like you to be a *live* hero."

The flood of self-redemption, and of awareness that he had been shot, washed over Quantrill in successive waves. He fainted.

Chapter 35

Sandys jurnal Aug. 16 Fri.
My dady had mom drive us to aggie pens today. Turkys are real dumb, most were dead and pecked up. We let the long

horns .go, the rushian bores had dug under the ciclone fence. Boy they must be woppers the hole was big as a tumblweed. My dady says its just as well. He dont want to deal with them d-v-ls, there smarter than some folks he knows. Mom and me helped my dady, he cant use his hands, says there better but I think thats a fib. Got fewl for truck. A man says aggie stashion here will do goverment work on ant racks. Boy that must be a sight but why bild ant racks? Mistery!! Man says fallout worse next 2 days so back we go to the hole. I dont like it so much now, it has long deep cracks and I hear things squeek back there. My dady is all tuckered, I wish I was bigger so he coud lean on me.

Chapter 36

As the delta neared the Mississippi River, isotope-enhanced RUS curtain bombs carved away two CPA spearheads south of the *Khrebet Dzhagdy,* the Dzhagdy mountain range. Once again the swath of destruction fried animal tissue through armor and, thanks to isotope enhancement, this time the land would lie fallow for over a year before it could be safely traversed. It was essential that a curtain bomb be physically aimed and sequenced with others. Given a few hours preparation, and despite the fact that they condemned half a division of their own rearguard to death as well, RUS munitions specialists were able to detonate a chain of devices that sterilized a strip of their own embattled soil for hundreds of klicks. It was truly a demilitarized no-man's land, and a jubilant Tass dubbed it the Wall of Lenin. Tacticians on all sides were quick to see that such a device, far from an ultimate weapon, generally was best employed in open country or down the length of a valley. The sizzling stream of neutrons could not zap an infantry squad through a mountain, though their escape might be problematic.

Taras Zenkovitch, the burly Ukrainian field marshal in the
Amur heights, watched a split-screen monitor that simul-
taneously showed spy-eye views of the western Amur basin
and the Irkutsk region around Lake Baikal. "Were I Chang
Wei," he rumbled into his scrambler circuit to the Supreme
Council room deep in the Urals, "I would be mobilizing at
Ulan Bator for a strike toward *Ozero* Baikal. Were I Minister
Konieff," he added, "I would have our ski troops dug in
above those Mongol passes in the next twenty-four hours."
Thanks to a glitch in the system, Zenkovitch had no video to
the war room half a continent away.

Chairman Oleg Konieff's reply lanced out of the mumble
of several voices: "Ski troops in August, Marshal Zenkovitch?"

"They will need skis before Chang is through testing us
there."

"Indeed. Have you less concern for their movement from
Sinkiang into Kirghiz and Kazakhstan?"

"With the shoulder-fired weapons we furnish the
Kazakhs, I would say Chang is the one who will have the
greater concern," Zenkovitch replied. "If the Afghans had
been as well supplied against us in 1980, our gunships and
personnel carriers would have availed us little."

It was a gamble to trust the southern Islamic republics
which had once been member states of the USSR, but so far it
was paying off. The doughty Turkic-speaking Kazakhs and
Kirghiz valued their nomadic traditions more than progress.
A mounted, befurred Kazakh with a self-guided SSM at his
shoulder comprised a wicked welcome for an Indian gun-
ship. RUS leaders were beginning to hope that buffer republics were more economical than tributary states.

"The SinoInds will suffer far more attrition than we, along
the southwestern border," Konieff agreed. "Our situation
south of Baikal may be more serious—*if* the Chinese still
hope to take the new railway."

"We will know that by the efforts they make to destroy
it," said Zenkovitch. "Will they send conventional air
strikes, or nuke the Ust' Kut and Kumora railyards?"

Another voice; Zenkovitch guessed it was Suslov, the dour Georgian marshal. "You seem to take the loss of our rail link for granted."

"We have known it was vulnerable. We can only sell it dearly and," he tried rough optimism, "hope the sale is not transacted."

Konieff, the crucial connection between the RUS Army high command and the all-powerful Supreme Council, headed off this clash of generals with, "Can our troops move beyond those passes to Ulan Bator?"

"I could have two divisions in Mongolia in sixty hours," Suslov rasped. "But they would only draw more Chinese into a region that must be defended man against man. Far more efficient to strike directly into Sinkiang, as I outlined in my summary."

Murmurs of agreement, with no grave dissent. RUS supply lines were much better to the Kazakhstan-Sinkiang border, and the Kazakhs—more or less friendly—were not expected to resist RUS troops moving toward China.

"And where do you stand on the defense of Irkutsk?"

"I concur with Zenkovitch," said Suslov, "with division HQ supporting a brigade of mountain troops in the passes north of Ulan Bator. No more than a brigade at the moment; we do not want to overstate our preparations there."

When Suslov and Zenkovitch agreed, it was a marriage of exigency and monolithic far-sightedness: fox and hedgehog. Konieff expected agreement from the Supreme Council and said as much.

In another war room near Yangku, Minister of Defense Chang Wei mused over a battle map with strategists of the CPA; the Chinese People's Army. The relief map might have seemed anachronistic with Chang, at forty-three the most vigorous leader of the CPA since Lin Piao during the historic Long March. Yet the solidity of the map lent an air of realism somehow lacking in video displays. Chang's heavy-lidded eyes were cool, but the pulse at his temple was prominent. When he spoke now, the chiefs of staff knew he addressed rotund Jung Hsia, Marshal of the 3rd CPA. "The flatlands and marshes of the Amur were a bitter lesson, compatriots. We would have done better to strike from Ulan Bator.''

Jung swallowed audibly. Wu Shih, a Jung disciple who was quick to see an implication, took the apologist's role. ''The Amur spearhead was a courageous blow, esteemed Chang. With more hovercraft, the 3rd Army might have reached the Dzhagdy Chain before the counterblow fell.'' The Dzhagdy range was the last natural barrier to the Okhotsk Sea. Once into those recesses, the CPA troops could have lived through the Wall of Lenin. ''We all accepted the risk; must we not accept its consequences?''

As Chang replied he removed small counters from the map, bitterly aware of their symbolism. ''Three front-line divisions are a costly consequence,'' he said, and glanced almost shyly at the small colorless man who had so far said nothing. ''Fortunately, I am assured, Minister Cha can extract a greater toll from the enemy.''

Cha Tsuni, Vice Minister of Health, gave a barely perceptible nod. A microbiologist and by far the least-known of CPA weaponeers, Cha was accorded special status. Few outside his laboratories in Tsinghai province knew exactly what he was doing. Cha adopted the serenity of a mandarin, the oral grace of a poet. Somehow this mannered image did not seem incongruous as he outlined his plan for mass destruction.

''The RUS would not be surprised,'' he began, placing his palm over the map's flat Mongolian expanse, ''to find our mongol clients defecting as we expand our air bases in the Gobi Desert. They have had the same problem,'' he added with the barest of sarcasms. ''They probably would welcome such a general defection, a migration to safety among the Buryat people—something like a pincers surrounding Lake Baikal.

''It is possible that such an exodus would be turned back by force, but the RUS needs laborers and, for the moment, can feed them. Now, esteemed comrades, I ask you what would happen if it should be discovered that refugees had spread smallpox into the Baikal region?''

The response was immediate consternation save Chang, who had already heard the arguments. Once eradicated from the globe except for laboratory strains, smallpox could be spread easily by immunized carriers. When CPA infantry advanced into the epidemic, they would be protected by vaccination. Such a weapon could be countered within a few months, of course, but by that time the Irkutsk region would be in Chinese hands. So would the Baikal-Amur railway, and by a lightning thrust northward China could cut the Russian Union of Soviets in two. The natural resources of Siberia could then be at SinoInd disposal, and an armistice might be quickly arranged with RUS leaders whose troops might not advance into an epidemic. Time enough, after that, to deal with America and the other allies. American concentration into urban clots had made it easy to diminish its gross national product a hundredfold. Under such circumstances,— and always assuming that Canada would not prove too meddlesome—an encroachment on the US might prove interesting.

Jung Hsia: "And why did we not use this tactic earlier?"

"Because we did not know what similar weapons the enemy might use in retaliation," Chang supplied. "But paranthrax is sweeping the eastern portion of the United States to such effect that we should be able to make the RUS see reason. They have not, hence probably will not, use germ warfare on this continent. In other words, after one quick success we might obtain a pan-Asian moratorium on biological weapons."

"A dangerous presumption," said Wu. "And the others?"

"Americans are more vulnerable than we, and less advanced in the precise tailoring of microbes," Cha smiled. "Even with their delivery systems, they could not destroy us as easily with microbes as we could destroy them. Besides: it was India, not we, who spread paranthrax on them. We have already expressed regrets, by suitable channels, to the Americans about that."

Jung stared at his relief map and sighed. "How quickly the

tactics become a simple matter of ethnocide.''

"I think not," Chang replied smoothly. "The US/RUS allies will surely see, and soon, that the statistics of genocide favor us. It will not be long before atmospheric contamination has risen so high that the RUS and US will be begging one another not to drop another nuclear device anywhere on the globe.''

"Curtailing their own special advantage," Wu put in.

"Exactly. As I have already told you," Chang added obliquely, "our own, ah, delivery system is well underway in Szechuan. Only China is so experienced in coordinating thousands of small industrial centers. Only we know just how many small factories are contributing to the devices. Not even Casimiro must discover it in India; there is no way to maintain a secret that is shared by five hundred members of a democratic Parliament.''

There had already been one leak from the Lok Sabha, India's lower house of Parliament, on the Florida invasion. This was only a minor irritant in the Yangku war room, for neither the invaders nor their delivery system were importantly Chinese.

Chapter 37

Quantrill quickly discovered, on awakening Sunday morning, that Texas A & M was more than a football team in east Texas. It was a research center and a military training university as well, with far-flung research stations. He was slower to realize that he was becoming an honorary Texan as the story of his Oak Ridge exploit flashed across the sprawling high-tech campus.

He was scanned, anesthetized, treated, and fitted with a padded thigh crutch before breakfast. Over steak and eggs, in talk with his rescuers, he realized that an entire regimental combat team had been en route to recover the delta *Norway* when, driven by his own internal demon, Quantrill appeared under the craft. Yes, he'd started the grass fire; no one asked why. Yes, he'd been scared witless when he had nearly slid from the cargo platform. He saw no point in wondering aloud why he had felt such an insulating calm before and after that moment. Quantrill had never studied differential response to stress, never wondered why a few people in every generation are predisposed by their glands to become gunfighters, stuntpeople, circus aerialists.

Then David Chartrand, the civilian captain of the *Norway*, sprang the good news and the bad news. The captain's own son had vanished with the Air Force Academy, and this youngster refreshed older, better memories for the reflective Chartrand. "I could name millionaires who want this thing, Ted: it's a delta pass. Anywhere a delta goes in this country, you can go," he grinned, handing Quantrill a coded plastic card. "Not just the *Norway* but the *Kukon,* the *Nobile,* and the rest. Just don't show it around too much; you could get mugged for it. And when you've finished your eggs, I want to introduce you to the country."

The egg-laden fork stopped in midair. "To the what?"

Now the bad news: "The whole country, son. Some people from ABC and CBS want you on a newscast."

There was absolutely no point in his chewing the rest of those eggs, Quantrill decided, because there was no possible way he could swallow them. He had been videotaped once at school; had found it harrowing. Almost, he wished himself back on that swaying cargo platform.

Still, he went with Chartrand and the tall, gum-chewing cargomaster, Bernie Grey. Emerging from the pneumatic pod that had shushed them cross-campus underground, Quantrill tried to smile back at a dozen people who scurried about with lights, cameras, coffee. His smile faded as he recognized ABC's Juliet Bixby and Hal Kraft of CBS. Both were familiar media faces, and Quantrill thought his breakfast insecure.

Bernie Grey, slender-muscled and long-haired, volun-

teered for the first setup interview. It was Bernie who had
first mistaken Quantrill for an enemy. Bernie struck out with
the fair Juliet, but seemed unabashed. Chartrand, unfailingly
polite, minimized his role and heaped credit on Quantrill.

The youngster in the yellow flight suit, a romantic figure
with his limp and his external thigh crutch gleaming in the
light, provided that rarity of the moment: an attractive man-
child, a diffident and inspirational model. Bixby and Kraft
did not share Quantrill's worry; if the kid broke down or had
an erection on camera, well, that's what editing was for. Ted
Quantrill was now public property; he just hadn't been completely processed yet.

Thanks to sensitive cameras, Quantrill was spared the
ferocious heat of earlier media victims. He sweated all the
same, perched on a stool as he had been told, the injured leg
stretched out as if by necessity. The last part of the interview
was transcribed as follows.

Q: How did you know the *Norway* had been hijacked,
   Ted?

A: Rumor around Oak Ridge.

Q: You're not from Tennessee, though.

A: From Raleigh. In North Carolina, ma'am. (SUD-
   DENLY ANIMATED) I'd sure like to know if my
   parents are okay. Dad is Captain Hurley Quantrill
   and mother's Janine Quantrill.

Q: We can check on it. Who brought you to Oak Ridge?

A: Ab—about a dozen people. Rides. You know . . .

Q: Captain Chartrand says you had a scout uniform on
   beneath your coverall when you came aboard.

A: (NOD)

Q: Tell us about it in your own words, Ted.

A: I, uh, had a scout uniform on beneath my coverall. Uh,
   when I came aboard.

Q: Um-hmm. Now tell us what it's like to rescue a delta.

A: Felt pretty good, sir.

Q: There are some fellows your age who would give
   anything to serve our country as you've done, Ted.
   What do you have to say to them?

A: (SHRUG)

Q: I'll put it another way. Ted Quantrill, what have you learned from your Oak Ridge experience?

A: Kill the sonofabitch. Uh, I'm sorry. I have to go.

Kraft and Bixby waved cheerful goodbyes as Quantrill limped away to find friends in yellow flight suits. By the time the tape was massaged into news, fifteen-year-old Ted Quantrill would be edited into a model scout. Like all media professionals, the interviewers shared an easy cynicism about the moments that would remain non-news.

Juliet Bixby studied her rival over her coffee cup. "That last question of yours was a heller, Kraft."

"News to me. I couldn't open him up at all."

"Oh, but you did." Shuddering: "Once when I was about five, I got separated from my parents at the San Diego zoo. I sat down in a quiet place, just waiting for them to catch up, and I kept having this funny feeling. And then I looked over my shoulder. Right on the other side of the bars from me was the biggest, cold-heartedest-looking Bengal tiger I have ever seen. Just looking down at me, like you'd study a chocolate drop. Well, that was how the kid looked, right at the last. No anger or remorse, Kraft—just cold competence."

"Christ, how you dramatize! Anyhow, he'll be only tonight's hero, Bix. Tomorrow he'll be forgotten."

"Maybe," said the famous Bixby contralto, "but not by me. You'll never catch me stepping between that little fucker and *any*thing he really wants."

Chapter 38

The full extent of the logistics problem faced by the US in late August of 1996 was only dimly visible to any fifteen-year-old—and scarcely less so to the Quartermaster General. During the next week, while the *Norway*'s gondola grew small projectile ports like pimples, Quantrill learned to pay less attention to holovision and more to what was happening around him. Holo charts, for instance, showed only a series of paranthrax hotspots east of the Alleghenies. Late summer harvests were supposedly a success with decontamination procedures and, admittedly, a new standard of acceptable contaminants. Yet Quantrill knew that the National Guard was now prohibiting any traffic across the Mississippi River because, after convincing medics that he no longer needed a thigh crutch, he served on the *Norway*'s overnight flight which supplied intrusion detectors to troops on the west bank. And the short-range missile pods under the *Norway*'s gondola suggested a breakdown of law and order. He inferred more about the scope of immunology when Bernie Grey told him what the *Norway* would deliver halfway across Texas to an A & M—"Aggie'—research station in Sonora.

Quantrill was learning to polymer-bond glass rope to a shackle fitting at the time. "Twelve *thousand* hamsters?" He squinted at Bernie's long horse-face, suspecting a joke.

"Plus life-support stuff, plus breedin' cages. And if you don't lay that shackle down, pard, the exotherm's gonna zap your fingers."

Quantrill did as he was told, saw a faint swirl of vapor from the aperture where the glass rope fitted, resumed his train of thought. "I thought Sonora was in Mexico."

"Bite your tongue," Bernie glowered, and winked. "We're still a little edgy about bein' confused with Mexico." He went on to explain that Sonora, Texas, was suitably isolated for immunological work, with natural caves and facilities for researchers dating back many years. "There's Aggie research stations all over. I grant there ain't much to see but you're welcome to come cuss it with me." Bernie held the shackle fitting by the rope; nodded.

"Bernie, where'd you learn your trade?"

"Rice University." Sigh: "Gone with the rest of Houston, I reckon. I was a basketball jock, but they had good courses in Aerospace structures. I got along."

"Personal question; okay?"

"Flog it by me."

"Why does everybody in Texas talk like old cowboy movies?"

Bernie Grey threw his head back and guffawed, then mimed a mystified fool. "Beats hell outa me, Ted." Sobering, still amused: "We don't *all* do it, and I don't do it all the time. You can't run a high-tech cargo system with cowpoke's lingo. Call it a linguistic badge; it tells folks you won't have no truck with eastern shuck."

Quantrill found himself smiling for the first time in a week. "But it *is* a shuck. Isn't it?"

"Yup. One you could stand to learn if you're here long. Just don't pile it on too deep 'til you learn how to spread it. And don't feel obliged. It ain't your fault if you can't carry the tune."

Quantrill followed Bernie to the great dome where deltas underwent refitting, watched the rope terminal pass a tensile test, listened while his friend rhapsodized on the favorite topic of Texans: Texas. Despite the leveling influence of media, a state the size of Texas had plenty of room for subcultures. A Beaumont Cajun's dialect might be barely intelligible to an Odessa roughneck unless one of them had traveled a bit. Geography had something to do with it, but much of it was a matter of choice. Only half joking, Bernie argued that air conditioning had nearly destroyed the urban Texan's identity, his acceptance of occasional hard times and determination to survive them with good humor.

"Wouldn't be a bit surprised," said Bernie, "if the war brought back the old frontier in some parts. There's fellers in Fort Stockton still packin' Colts to use on rattlers and roadsigns. And the weather drives the sissies out; in Sonora the sun'll melt the fillin's outa your teeth."

Quantrill assumed a slightly bowlegged slouch. "Purely makes a feller mean, don't it?"

Bernie cocked his head, fighting a grin, and nodded. "Too many sharps and flats, pard, but you got a good ear for bullshit. You'll do," he added, letting the grin come, ruffling Quantrill's hair. "Now let's get this shackle on the

Norway. We'll be liftin' about three ayem; put us over
Sonora by breakfast.''

Quantrill groaned. ''Doesn't anything start in broad daylight?''

''You bet it does.'' Lowering his voice as they passed an
Aggie undergrad in the tunnel, Bernie continued. ''Cap'n
says we shot down an Indian photorecon job near Lake
Charles today. You can bet it didn't fly from New Delhi.''

''Mexico? Jeez, I thought they were on our side.''

''They were 'til they joined OPEC and didn't need us
anymore. If you know any history, you can't blame 'em. But
cap'n thinks that recon ship came from somewhere off the
gulf coast. If there's more,—well, we'd be sugar candy for
some fuckin' Injun on a long sortie. So we're goin' tonight.
We don't make much of a signature for night fighters.''

''Boy, that's a weird idea,'' Quantrill said.

''What?''

''One of those guys shooting us down.''

''Weird ain't exactly how I'd put it.''

''It is if you think about it. Here we go again: cowboys and
Indians.''

Bernie Grey paused with his hand on a mooring strut of the
Norway; shook his head. ''I swan if this kid ain't one for the
books.'' In mock dejection, he climbed into the airship.

Quantrill followed, now familiar with the handholds, and
let the radiation monitor read him. Campus klaxons had
whonnnnked their warnings only once during their stay at
College Station; ground winds from the Austin area, someone said. But the campus background count was rising, as it
had nearly everywhere else, and the few who traveled
aboveground usually did so under wraps or in electrabouts.

Quantrill waited while Bernie used the airhose, a jury rig
with filtered air and fans to vent the dust overboard. Then he
played the hose on himself, returned to the monitor. ''Now I
see why captain Chartrand insists we get a burr haircut,'' he
said.

''It's that or a shower cap,'' Bernie shrugged, ''or fried
brains over the long haul. Shoot, you just *try* and park a

Texan under a shower cap! Instead, we're all gonna look like Army recruits. But better that than *be* one," he laughed.

Quantrill had seen the inductees, some of them looking no older than he, doing close-order drill in the hangar and gym. He felt no shame that he was one of fortune's few; by now he was accepted as an apprentice by the *Norway*'s usual eight-man crew, and was learning how to laugh again. Some things he worried about: he still had learned nothing about either of his parents. Some things he refused to think about. His will commanded that it was better to focus on a sense of belonging than on the hopeless sense of all that he had lost.

Shortly before three a.m. on Saturday morning, the *Norway*, her cargo of supplies and small live animals distributed by Bernie Grey for optimum trim, slid up over the Brazos River in a northerly arc to bypass the Austin desolation. Quantrill had been slapped on the shoulder by the cap'n, called 'son'; told that he would awaken over Edwards Plateau. His freshly-cut hair and an innocent anticipation had kept him awake for an hour, savoring the voyage like a child. But he was asleep on his aircouch when the *Norway* lifted.

Chapter 39

From six thousand meters, the dry ravines serrating Edwards Plateau were thrown into sharp relief by the dawn sun. Slender, sure-fingered Blythe Rogers, inevitably nicknamed 'co-cap'n Bly', pointed out salient features to the alert green-eyed youth who leaned over Rogers's shoulder. "Sometimes you see deer under those low cliffs," he said. "More likely along the Llano River ahead to portside, which isn't much of a river but wherever you see pecan trees fifty meters high, there's water and game—"

Quantrill's arm shot out, pointing at a ridge to starboard. "What's that?"

Rogers squinted, staring past the outstretched finger. Far below, a dark speck raced into the ridge shadow at an unlikely pace. "Must be a stray calf—but Gawd, he's traveling!" Without speaking, Chartrand gestured at the display, then studied his instrument panel again. "Why not," Rogers asked himself aloud, and flicked on the image enhancer.

By now they were almost over the animal and Rogers swept the ridge at low magnification. Briefly then, their quarry could be seen standing motionless. Rogers increased the magnification.

"God a'mighty," Rogers breathed, before they slid past the ridge. "Cap'n, did you see that peccary?"

A nod. "Glad I could see it from up here—only that was no peccary, Bly."

"You ever see tusks like that on a cow?"

Chartrand smiled and shook his head. "No, and I never saw a peccary the size of a Shetland pony. Gentlemen, you have just met an Aggie russian boar. Damn' if I know what it's doing out of the Aggie pens, but they were breeding some there. Working on a big low-aggression strain. I just hope that one's had his lobotomy, or whatever it takes."

Quantrill felt a prickling along his arms. The beast had been clear on the display for only a moment; huge shoulders innocent of fat, sharply ridged back tapering to muscular haunches, tiny hooves. But more awesome than the upward-curving tusks that flanked the snout like ivory goalposts was the fact that the great animal stood on hind legs, ears pricked forward over the demonic visage. The boar leaned against the canyon wall as if deliberately trying to blend into shadow. Quantrill asked, "Are they smart?"

"Beat you at checkers, I'm told," Chartrand said, flicking toggles as he spoke. "I'm getting the substation beacon, Ted; time for you to get aft. We'll moor in ten minutes."

Quantrill saw the distant gleam of window reflections on the horizon, tiny rectangular masses in a depression, trees that suggested a town. He scurried back to his station and buckled up. A delta crewman learned very soon that the big airships waddled and yawed as they lost headway. More than one veteran crewman had needed his barfbag.

The *Norway*'s automated snubber gear engaged minutes later as Quantrill, peering from a clear bubble, watched mooring struts scissor down and out. The prop shrouds gimbaled to produce lateral thrust and, with distinct thuds, the struts found their tapered sockets. The coloratura whisper of propellers died; faint whooshes of pneumatic interlocks; then Quantrill was unbuckling to help Bernie Grey at the cargo hatch. The *Norway* had brought her vital cargo to the Aggie station with her usual efficiency and quietude.

Quantrill scampered down a strut, tasting the aroma of Edwards Plateau, confident of his movements in the airship that was now *his* ship. It seemed indestructible as a bridge pillar, and Quantrill had no slightest inkling that he would never lift in the *Norway* again.

Chapter 40

David Chartrand was so preoccupied with his work that he did not monitor the special channel which updated other Air Defense Identification Zone limitations on civilian aircraft. The ADIZ display would have been his only hint that something big was breaking in the Mexican Gulf early Saturday.

The Navy's ELF grid in Wisconsin had been hamstrung for hours after a nerve center sustained burrow-bombs emplaced by a suicidal Libyan squad infiltrating from Canada. Three naval ratings had perished, five more ratings and an officer had been wounded. It was therefore hit-or-miss for a coordinated defense against the Indian wave of saturation sorties.

In a convoluted irony, the Indian attack aircraft had been developed from older craft furnished by the late USSR,

which had copied earlier British STOL designs. Never intended to land on anything smaller than a carrier, the
swing-wing jets were boosted from subs in the gulf. With
luck they would be recovered by skyhook choppers or, fail-
ing that, would ditch at rendezvous points after their low-
level passes at selected targets. The boosters permitted external fuel tanks and wavetop loitering while the squadrons
formed south of the hundred-fathom line.

Three squadrons of twelve attack craft then streaked north
and west, saving afterburner fuel for the moment of slash-
and-run. From Warner Robins in Georgia to the anchorage at
Corpus Christi, the SinoInd swingwings swept in with little
warning to deliver their single ground-pounder nukes, deliberately chosen as 'dirty' bombs. Most of the targets were
suspected induction centers—which explains why sleepy
little San Marcos, a college town between Austin and San
Antonio, rated such lethal attention.

Because the flight paths of the attack aircraft were north-
westward, US interceptors in Georgia and Florida were
forced to chase, rather than intercept, the intruders. Air
Defense Command interceptors from Alabama to Texas
scrambled in time to engage the enemy. They saved Tus-
caloosa, Lake Charles, and College Station among others,
but they also found that the Indian STOLs had minicannon.
They did not find Ranjit Khan in time to save San Marcos.
What happened there was an act of randomness, or of God.
Or of Puck. In any event, India did not greatly care for San
Marcos or for the other sortie targets. What she cared very
much about was the decoying of American air cover from
Florida—and in that, she succeeded handsomely. The
troop-carrying ACV's needed only an hour to cross the strait
from Cuba, and neared Florida across a front longer than the
Florida keys. We dared not nuke them; the wind was toward
our defenders. But we reduced Cuban installations to slag the
next day.

The invasion troops were led by Cubans, whose Kremlin
connection had evaporated with the end of foreign aid. With
the Cubans were well-trained Punjabis, Tamils, Gujaratis.

And with every Indian came fifty Nicaraguans, Guatemalans, Chileans anxious to avenge their ideological father, the martyred Fidel. The two thousand Indians were present chiefly to maintain the hardware. The hundred thousand latinos hungered for booty. They had not been told that paranthrax was already creeping down the Florida peninsula. Perhaps they would not have cared much.

Ranjit Khan sortied past the Texas coast up the Guadalupe River with an early sun over his shoulder, jerking his eyes from horizon to viewscreen comparator. His electronic package was relatively unsophisticated but Ranjit's comparator found Gonzales, Texas, and after that it was a simple matter to cram fuel into the afterburners for his dash to San Marcos. The town was not very large. Ranjit needed only to arm his hundred-kiloton weapon, jettison it while crossing San Marcos at Mach 1.5, and delay his banked turn while the drogue chute deposited his ground-pounder. But when Ranjit flicked at the armament switch, the pig-humping thing popped out of the console! Ranjit swore, reached under the edge of the console; his crew chief was going to catch hell.

Ranjit Khan felt several wires but could not see them. With the control stick between his knees he fumbled for the switch, saw it bobbing behind the hole in the console, leaned forward again and felt the aircraft respond as he nudged the stick.

Cold sweat gushed from Ranjit's forehead as he hauled back on the stick and the steeple of some Christian mosque, or whatever they were called, flashed by. In his rearview he saw twinkling myriads of glass fragments burst from office buildings in his thunderous wake. He had bombed San Marcos—but only with his machwave, very much too low for a proper pass.

Ranjit thought he could reinsert the Allah-accursed switch and arm his weapon, given a few minutes at loiter speed with his wings extended. He must relax, take his time, melt the ice in his guts and make a return pass. The Indian pilot throttled back and activated his wing hydraulics; began a long circle at fuel-hoarding speed. He was too intent on his console repair to notice the blip closing from behind on his sweep radar.

Goliad, Texas, did not have an air force—and then again, it did. It had an absolutely gorgeous, positively ancient F-51, the Golid Chapter of the Confederate Air Force. The CAF was a joke crafted by experts, and parts of that joke tended to be hazardous. Hank Curran was his own mechanic, his own man, and he was sixty-nine years old. He had flown a Mustang in Korea almost half a century before, and later while other Texans invested in bigger tractors Hank was looking for a toy. A bubble-canopied, Allison-engined, six-gunned, four-hundred-and-fifty-mile-an-hour toy. He found one with clipped tips and NASA scoops in Chino, California, in 1972 and by now he had replaced every piston and control cable. The scoops were replaced, wingtips added. Hank's paint job even had the black-and-white invasion stripes—but this was a different invasion.

The day everyone called Dead Day had been a lively day in the hangar at Goliad. Hank Curran invested the time installing one air-cooled and thoroughly illegal fifty-calibre machine gun in the 'Stang's starboard wing. He had never really expected to use it, but other pilots in the CAF had swapped him the metal links and over a hundred rounds of hopefully-live ammo; actually, it was all API, the armor-piercing incendiary rounds that had once been inserted at intervals in an ammo belt. Ever since, Hank had slept with one ear open for that air raid klaxon. Goliad even had one of those, linked to Port Lavaca's.

Early Saturday morning the klaxon made Hank spill his coffee. Nothing but sheer valiant CAF cupidity made him tear the screen door off as he ran for his Ford. He had the chocks away from the 'Stang's wheels and the engine oil temp up off the peg when Ranjit Khan's STOL thundered across the shoreline at Port Lavaca. Hank's canopy was sealing as he saw a hundred knots come up on his airspeed indicator; eleven minutes' worth of radar warning had been plenty for the Confederate Air Force.

Hank figured the bogie would come in low. He himself went high, the Allison rejoicing. He also figured his chances of being shot down by our own interceptors were about fifty-fifty, give or take a bit. At the moment, Hank did not give a shit. He believed what the holo told him; did not fully appreciate that San Antonio had been flattened to her beltline. San 'Tone was the great cradle of US military aviation. Hank Curran would protect its grave.

When the bogie wailed by him near Gonzales, its after-burners rocketing pink in the early light, Hank thought at first it was an old Marine Tomcat. Then he saw it bobble, stray low, dip, and correct in a beeline for San Marcos. No friendly pilot on earth would make a mach-plus pass over Gonzales at treetop level. And then Hank recognized the silhouette. He shoved the throttle to the firewall and hoped he could keep the rice-pickin' bastard in sight. He had no radar, no access to military scrambler circuits, and no hope of catching an air-craft of twice his speed.

Unless the bogie slowed down.

Hank had manually, dangerously, charged his fifty be-cause he had no automatic equipment. He knew that if it fired, it might fire all over hell and half of Texas because he had not boresighted or adjusted the gun; and every round would be a tracer, telling the sumbitch he was on the 'wanted' list. But Hank knew how to slide the stick over, easing the pedals, to let his aerial gun platform walk its fiery dotted line of tracers to a target. The problem was, the goddam bogie purely disappeared west of San Marcos as its afterburners winked out. Then he saw a sunglint on wings, the STOL rising up almost to Hank's own altitude at breathtaking speed, and again came the glint. The bogie began a great loitering arc that just might bring it around in a circle. Hank thanked Heaven he was not showing a contrail, kept himself high in the sun, and wished his eyes were younger.

Ranjit Khan's oval pattern took him two minutes, and by that time he knew he must pull the switch and its mount down, past the wiring bundle, to snap the miserable thing. He also knew that he would have to ground the switch body against the console or some other part of the STOL's airframe to complete the circuit. Unless the 'arm' signal was sent, he could not jettison his weapon either. So much for emergency refitting; Ranjit was not very keen on ditching at any speed whatever with the equivalent of a hundred thousand tons of explosive in the canister slung under his belly.

The offending item came into sight with one final tug; Ranjit nosed his aircraft down, set a visual heading for San Marcos, snapped the switch to 'arm' position and reached to ground it against the console plate. One way or another, he was about to do his bit for Asian democracy. And *still* Ranjit did not check his radar display.

The F-51 bored in from the southeast, her Allison singing like Valkyries, Hank Curran drymouthed as the enemy came within range. He would get only this one pass, and he had a slight advantage in altitude and a good angle on the bastard. Then the STOL's wings began to scimitar, its nose dropping as it gained speed, and Hank figured he'd been seen. He pressed the studs on his control stick, waiting that vital split-second to see where his tracers were stitching away before he maneuvered.

The worst possible thing happened, Hank thought—incorrectly. The recoil hammered his airframe, crabbing the entire aircraft very slightly so that Hank's tracer burst was not only far ahead of the Indian STOL but above it, too. If he hadn't been seen before, he sure-God had announced himself now.

Ranjit saw mach-three fireflies arc across ahead of him, knew instantly which quarter they had come from. He hit the afterburners, banked to the north,—and ran into Hank's last few rounds of API, lobbed in desperate seven-league trajectory after the fleeing jet.

Ranjit's aircraft had only one battery, the backup unit having been removed for this mission in the interest of fuel economy. It only takes one fifty caliber slug to decant one battery, zizzing through the bottom of the device to leave two clean holes. A second slug toured the engine accessory pack, damaging the alternator. By the time Ranjit was fifteen thousand meters up, he had lost sight of San Marcos and all interest in it; found that he had no electrical power for instruments or switches. He still had pneumatics and manual systems, so he could still fire his nose cannon.

The trouble was, there was nothing to shoot at and he could no longer be sure whether he had actually armed and dropped his nuclear bomb. He had seen no flash light the sky. His instruments certainly were not going to tell him. Ranjit raged and pounded against the arm of his ejection seat as he streaked over Kerrville on a westerly bearing. He armed his cannon, fired four rounds. Someone was going to regret this debacle. Ultimately, he thought, that someone might well be himself; but that was what paradise was for, to welcome warriors downed in holy battle. Ranjit Khan peered below in search of his own personal jehad.

The F-51 had been too long past redline on her tach, and Hank Curran gnawed the whiskers on his underlip as he tapped on the oil pressure gauge. A Mustang didn't deadstick worth a damn and he didn't want to do a gear-up in a plowed field. He decided to try the airstrip at Kyle. He might wind up in something worse than a field if anybody ever found out he'd been boring holes in the sky with tracer bullets like an old fool. But Hank had only been trying to protect his country, and just maybe that friggin' Hindu or Chinaman had cut and run for it because of him. He would never know whether his now-stuttering, vibrating old beauty had made any difference in anybody's life but his; he would like to think maybe it had.

Maybe it had.

Hank Curran ran out of runway and folded a wing within earshot of San Marcos, where five thousand inductees were in basic training. Ranjit Khan, with one eye on his chronograph, was estimating his remaining fuel and wondering whether he could get to Mexico. He was clearly not going to get another crack at San Marcos even if he could find it. He opted for Mexico; banked, then saw the buttercup-yellow gleam of a delta dirigible far ahead. It was motionless, moored near a group of long white buildings. It made the biggest, brightest target Ranjit Khan had ever seen.

Chapter 41

". . . like Vietnam all over again if the Cubans can hide
in the Everglades," Bernie Grey puffed, steering the air-
cushion pallet of supplies into the depot. Almost the first
thing they had heard in greeting was news of the Florida
invasion, only minutes old. A handful of maroon-coveralled
Aggie personnel were on hand; most had flocked to the
Caverns of Sonora, with most of the townsfolk.

Quantrill slid the pallet onto the floor. "I'd rather they hid
than have 'em take over. Uh—this the last load?"

"Yup. Le's find some breakfast, ol' buddy." Their footfalls echoes through the depot building, Bernie glancing at
his note 'corder. "Cap'n wants to get to Monahans by noon
to pick up some—" Quantrill never learned what Monahans
had to offer; the klaxon's hoot penetrated the building and,
before they could spring to the exit, the *Norway* had already
unlocked her struts. "Air raid," Bernie screamed, vaulting
onto the cargo platform with an olympian leap. "Find a
hideyhole, Ted!"

Already the airship was underway, the inertial bounce of
the struts carrying her too high for Quantrill to reach. His first
reaction was anger that the cargomaster hadn't helped him
get aboard. Then he saw Bernie's elaborated arm sweep, a
warning to get away, and realized that a lighter-than-air craft
was a much more vulnerable place than a ditch or culvert. To
Quantrill, an air raid meant a nuclear blast. He saw two men
galloping toward a concrete grain silo and chased after them.
He was the only one in yellow flight togs; was to learn that the
entire regular crew of the *Norway* had made it aboard. His
backpack was still aboard, too.

The great airship whispered southward where, Chartrand
knew, the shallow canyon of Devil's River might suffice as a

foxhole for a delta. A nuclear shock wave, catching the *Norway* moored, would utterly shred the great craft's filament-and-polymer body, but Chartrand imagined that either Sonora or the Aggie station was the target.

"I want every man in shock harness," Chartrand said on the intercom. "We're probably going to scrape some of our hide off."

The cargomaster: "Cap'n, should you fire our little birds? Hate to have 'em going off under us if we hit—"

"Sweet shit, here he comes!" Blythe Rogers, his display a split-screen with overlapping views, had obeyed the radar and was scanning the northeast quadrant for the blip. Unbidden, he threw the visual display onto Chartrand's monitor. Computer-enhanced visuals lent an unreal aspect to the monitor, the colors too sharp, too bright. And the arrowing enemy STOL growing too large as yellow lights burst from its nose. "The motherlover's gunning for *us*," Rogers shouted in amazement.

They had been airborne for scarcely two minutes; the arroyo still distant. Chartrand hauled the huge vessel into a shallow climbing turn, felt the faint tremors as three explosive mini-cannon projectiles found their marks. A line of small explosions racketed across the packed earth of Edwards Plateau and then the Indian STOL had passed, wings extended, banking for another pass.

Ranjit Khan knew he had made a mistake, loitering in on the enormous shovel-shaped mass of airship in an effort to get a certain kill; but he had not realized it could bumble away so quickly. Ranjit had seen sparkles of bright polymer and wispy structure splash from the delta's hull and knew that he had drawn blood. Ranjit was an educated man; knew that dirigibles had considerable space between their great gossamer buoyancy bags. But Indian dirigibles were filled with hydrogen, and Ranjit had expected to fly over a fireball. He throttled back, realizing that the airship pilot would require him to maneuver at great waste of his remaining fuel if the damned thing could squat in the shallow canyon to the south.

Ranjit was no fool. This time he would make a head-on pass, slowing to the snail's pace of an STOL as he forced the gasbag to turn or die. In the canyon it could not maneuver. So thought Ranjit Khan.

"We're losing pressure in Cell Five," Rogers said. "Can't tell how big the leak, but big enough."

Calm, quick: "Deploy two series of patches." Rogers flipped the protective cover from buttons, keyed an instruction.

The helium cell material was a ripstop fabric thinner than a wastrel's excuse, but it could be punctured rather easily. For in-flight repair, a delta boasted tiny subsystems on the floor of each cell; gadgets that actually blew bubbles. The skin of a bubble was a white polymer that turned from slick to sticky, then chitinous, as it encountered oxygen. Yet, for such a bubble to maintain neutral buoyancy in helium, it could have only one substance inflating it: hydrogen.

The bubbles migrated toward a leak so that they deployed to a puncture, popped, stuck and hardened in the hole, and usually plugged the leak, a white spot on the cell's black surface, easy to find and fix. But two dozen lemon-sized bubbles could not patch the rents in Cell Five. Chartrand found the *Norway* settling stern-first, and ordered more patches while he adjusted the elevons further. Then he called for more helium. "If I can get some sky under this bitch, gentlemen, abandon ship. Consider it an order," he said, still calm, watching his orientation display as the *Norway* slid over the lip of the canyon barely meters above the scrub. Even if he could maintain altitude, it would not be enough to let a chute open.

"We've got those twenty-two's, cap'n," Bernie Grey said.

"If you get a shot, take it," said Chartrand. Texas A & M had given them no heavy machine guns, but ROTC classes used weapons scaled down from twin-fifties for use against target drones. The twins fired twenty-two caliber slugs, four hundred rounds a minute. They would have been useful at

Oak Ridge, but against an Indian STOL?

Ranjit was having problems. He had felt one surge of fuel pumps, knew that his fuel plenums were nearly empty. He could make another pass and then horse the aircraft up and southward, ejecting a thousand meters or so before the craft began to drop. He might still walk to Mexico. He throttled back still more, practically gliding at a speed of three hundred klicks. The yellow delta had touched, tail-first, onto rocky alkali flats and even if it tried to turn, he could rake the gossamer brute with cannon. This time he could not miss.

Nor could Chartrand. He saw the line of alkali puffs stutter toward him from the approaching bird of prey. As the *Norway*'s struts swung down to absorb the airship's inertia, Chartrand made ready to trip their pneumatics. She would be tail-heavy, her prop shrouds were aimed ju-u-ust right, and she had something more potent than a pair of twenty-two's slung against her belly.

Ranjit saw his cannon rounds march up the arroyo to his target. There was no question of missing now.

The *Norway* flopped slowly, then rebounded with her pneumatics, actually rose fifty meters like a broaching whale, nose proud. The aft end of the gondola spurted long tongues of fire.

Ranjit saw the enemy's maneuver and started to smile. Turning upward rather than sideways was a surprise, but his cannon were boring through the great ship, end-to-end. As he began the smile, he also commanded his hand to put the STOL into a steep bank, the better to reach an optimum cruise altitude. But neither the smile nor the bank ever really occurred. Tiny spots before Ranjit's eyes grew from gnats to fencepoles in a second, and of the twelve little missiles Chartrand had fired shotgun-fashion dead ahead, eleven shrieked past.

The twelfth passed into Ranjit's portside air intake, detonating against the duct wall adjacent to his remaining fuel.

David Chartrand saw the deadly fireflower blossom, become hunks of wing and impeller and ejection pod, and then

it was a shower of metal and plastic, almost as big as the
Norway as they engulfed one another thirty meters above
Devil's River Canyon.

Sandys jurnal Aug. 24 Sat.

*Holo says sinowinds envaded Florida, one sure envaded
Texas. I heard the boooom in the hole, mom and me went
to see. It was up the drywash, well realy it was clean acrost
it. Mom woudnt let me go close to the delta stuff. Those
poor men, poor soles, mom said. I found a napsack, a
finger, some litle bullets and a dress of ribbons tied to a
heavy iron can. Well I gess its a dress. I rolled it all into a
gully. Coudnt lift the can. It must be forein, the words
arent ours. My dady doesnt talk much wont let me see his
hands. He jokes its a secret. Hes still wore out from letting
the animals go last week. I wish my dady didnt smell bad.*

Chapter 42

A grain elevator, Quantrill found, could be almost as deep
below ground level as it was high. So insulated were the
tunnel occupants that they knew nothing of the *Norway*'s fate
until many hours later. No one at Aggie Station noticed the
smoke to the south. The youth in the yellow flight suit was
recognized from a week-old holocast; seemed willing
enough to move cargoes around Aggie Station while he
waited for the delta to return. Still confident that he would
scramble aboard his airship after a day or so, and exhausted
after relocating thousands of terrified hamsters, Quantrill fell
instantly asleep in the staff quarters.

Dr. Catherine Palma damned her comm link with College
Station that night as the three-note signal interrupted her
work a hundred meters from Quantrill. It wasn't tough
enough setting up a four-level paranthrax barrier with a few
lay people before competent lab personnel arrived. No, she

also had to second-guess the radiation counters, treat contusions, and play administrator. Palma stored her console display, queried the comm link, and swore again; the Red Cross had finally come through for the green-eyed kid.

Cathy Palma pushed herself away from the desk feeling all of her fifty-one years; trudged to the staff dorm. She found Quantrill naked, his covers kicked away in sleep, the dull gleam of synthoderm over a wound in one leg. She stood beside him for a long time, thinking that those muscular youthful limbs had taken their last indolent tan; wondering if she would ever see her own daughter again. Cathy Junior would have liked this boy, but of course he was much too young.

He stirred then, and Palma silently made her way back to her office. Though she had not entertained sexual thoughts about the boy, she felt a twinge of the voyeur's guilt. Time enough to talk with him the next day. Thank God, she thought, for objectivity.

When she returned to her office she was met by one of the Sonora field men with news of the *Norway* disaster. Palma spent the next two hours at her comm link trying to bridge the supply gap which the delta's loss represented. She did not think of the youth again until the next morning.

Sunday morning was like any other morning for Palma. A hectic scramble to rejuggle tasks; a radioed promise to use two valuable hours finding and treating one of the field men who, from the sound of it, had taken a massive radiation dose and could not be moved; and ah, yes, the Quantrill boy.

She checked her pocket, then took her coffee across the half-deserted little cafeteria. He was alone, studying her face as she neared him.

"It's about my parents," he said. No barely-submerged hysteria there, but no hope either. And no wasted amenities.

She slid into a chair, willing him to play the man. "I'm Dr. Catherine Palma, Mr. Quantrill. I've heard about you. Yes," she went on levelly, "I've just had word from—whoever finds out such things. You can't always believe what you hear.'' Step One: give the poor devil a hint by manner and innuendo.

He looked away, as though to find some new exit from the room. ''That news about the *Norway*: we have to believe that, don't we?''

Toying with her cup: ''Yes, we sent a team out last night as soon as I heard. Apparently an enemy jet and our delta collided. No survivors. I'm sorry, Mr. Quantrill, I knew some of those men too.''

''I was starting to think of the *Norway* as home. Even left my scout uniform and backpack in her. Now—look, could I find some other clothes besides these?'' He looked down at the bright yellow uniform, his eyes dry, distant.

''There must be some Aggie coveralls—''

''No,'' he said quickly. ''Just—just plain old clothes.'' Her gaze was interrogative. He shrugged into her silence, added, ''I'll work for you, Dr. Palma. But I don't want to *join* anything I like. That hasn't worked out very well.''

After a long thoughtful pause, Palma said, ''I suppose it does sharpen one's sense of loss. But you have to make alliances with something, Quant—may I call you Ted?''

A nod. ''I don't have to make 'em with things I love, Doc. And I might like it here. I'm not making that sound very smart, am I?''

''Look, Ted, sometimes a long sleep and then some hard work can do wonders.'' She pulled the vial from her pocket, set it before him. ''Why don't you wash those down with water and hit the sack? It's not much, but it's all I can do.'' She had almost added that if he were older, they might have gotten drunk together. But her responsibility, not his age, was the barrier.

''Maybe I will. Thanks.'' He put the vial into his pocket.

Almost angrily she said, ''Don't you want to know what I found out?''

''About my folks? You've already told me. They're dead, aren't they? One, or both?''

It was curiously difficult for her to say it: ''Both. Your father was—in action.'' She couldn't say 'killed'. ''Your mother was admitted to a clinic in Durham, North Carolina, and I'm afraid paranthrax swept the place." More softly: "Do you know what we're doing here?"

"An antidote for it. Chartrand said that'd make this place a target if word got out."

"We don't call it an antidote, but you have the idea. Does it make you feel better to know you're helping destroy the thing that destroyed your home?"

"You want the truth, Doc?"

She sighed and stood up. "No thanks. There's too much of that going around." His response was a smile, peer to peer, and that was somehow unsettling from a fifteen-year-old. "Not that you asked me, Quantrill, but don't cut yourself off from humanity. We all need somebody, now and then."

"To dump on?"

"If you have to put it that way; yes."

"Who do *you* have, Doc?"

"I have the little fellows like the ones I gave you. Mostly so I can get enough sleep to keep going. And why am I telling you that," she laughed. Palma had good teeth.

"You needed somebody to dump on." His humor was so mordant, so subdued she nearly missed it. This youngster already played the man too well; perhaps that was the trouble.

"Fair enough," she said. "We take what we can get. See me when you feel better; right now I have to make a house call," she ended with a private cynicism and walked away quickly, dismayed at her prevision of a future full of children grown old too soon.

Sandys jurnal Aug 25 Sun.

We got a dr. here, she looked like she coud use one herself. She stuck things in my dady. They made me go outside but I heard some and worked it out my ownself. I dont see how a plate could be so small you coud have them in your blood. Mistery!! But thats why my dady is sick but now its just a matter of time, my dady doesnt have many platelets left. I prayed God to take away the rest of the bad platelets to make my dady well again.

The delta *Santos-Dumont*, hastily rescheduled to Sonora, brought vital personnel as well as supplies. Cathy Palma, sworn in as a Captain in the Preventive Medicine Division of the Army Medical Department, assumed her lessened duties with undisguised relief. Palma was on good terms with the civilian staff. Since the Army needed a smooth interface with the locals, the graying Palma found herself functioning as a one-woman clinical service. The crisis relocation center in the big Caverns of Sonora had its own clinic; the town itself was almost deserted.

On Thursday she sought out young Quantrill and handed him a small polypaper bag. "I thought you might need this to keep your nose clean—or whatever," she said, grinning.

He dutifully opened the bag, shook out the freshly-laundered square of bright cloth, and rewarded Palma with an open smile. "I give up, Doc; where'd you find it?" He was holding his scout neckerchief, with familiar snags now neatly mended.

She told him of the local people who could not be persuaded to leave their own small underground lairs; of a man who had retreated to a cave like some wounded animal, and was unquestionably dying there; of the little blonde girl who had presented the doctor with a new treasure she had found near the *Norway*'s crash site.

Palma had instantly realized that a scout neckerchief from the *Norway* could only belong to one person. "You have to realize that the Grange family isn't the kind that takes charity, Ted. Little Sandy paid me for easing her father's pain in the only coin she had."

"She had more," Quantrill guessed. "This was in my pack; I bet the little bugger found the whole thing. It's okay, Doc, she's welcome to it."

This was Quantrill's first sign of interest in anything since their first meeting. Others could move cargo—and this youngster seemed determined to retreat into himself. He hadn't even approached the *Santos-Dumont* during her brief moorage. "Quantrill, I need a strong back and a driver, and with that gimpy leg you're the one we can spare the most,'' she spoke the half-lie gruffly. "I'm requisitioning you."

"I don't drive worth a damn."

"You will," she promised. That was the day Quantrill first left Aggie Station with Palma. At her insistence he wore a white lab coat; quickly mastered the four-wheel-drive van, more slowly became an asset in Palma's mercy rounds. There were advantages, she decided, in a strong youth who seemed unmoved by the sight of suffering.

For the first few days Palma used her new assistant sparingly, leaving him in the depot area at times. Soon she was sending him alone on errands to towns like Eldorado, Junction, and Ozona in the filter-conditioned van. She noted without comment that he was picking up the local dialect. Perhaps it would soon be time to introduce him to people whose troubles were more immediate than his own.

Sandys jurnal Sep. 2 Mon.

Mom got new kemlamp. I got musquite from the drywash, we bilt a fire sinse my dady is always cold. He dont want us to touch him even to take him out in the sun. I bet I coud do it myself he doesnt way hardly any more than I do. When I kissed him tonite I thout why if my dady is so good does he smell so bad. His breth smells like his arms do, they have this watery stuff in the sores. His hair is coming out. He made me get a mirrer and he took a look and said if he had a dog with a face like that hed shave its a-s and make it walk backwards ha ha. He says more d-ms and h-lls than I ever heard. Its alrite God, at least hes awake again.

The emergency call from Salida Ranch came at one of the few times when Palma was near enough to make such a remote house call. Salida, a sheep ranch near the Llano River, was Quantrill's first experience at taking a four-wheeler over such rough terrain. By now he was nearly as adept as Palma at following the map display and found the faded clapboard house with its sheds, pens, and drunkenly-leaning barn a half-hour from the highway.

Palma walked through old ruts to the house, Quantrill

carrying her medical bag. A gaunt woman, her skin sun-creased like cured sharkskin, welcomed them with a gap-toothed smile. When Quantrill saw her husband, he wondered what she had to smile about; the man's lower leg was a gory mess.

"You're lucky, Mr. Willard," Palma said as she cleaned the worst wound, a gash in the wiry leg that might have been made by a cleaver. "These tendons will repair themselves if you'll give them a chance. Where were you standing when the boar came at you?"

"Standin' hell, I was ten feet up a mesquite," Willard said, his voice husky with exhaustion. "I knowed that devil was takin' my lambs, I seen his tracks for a week now. But when I throwed down on him with the thirty-thirty he was in heavy brush. Gawd but he was big!"

"I didn't know they ate sheep," Quantrill said.

"I didn't know they clumb trees," said Willard, "but you can tell them peabrains at Aggie Station they've crossed a Russian boar with a sure-'nough squirrel." It had not been a sow, he insisted. "A boar with the devil's own corkscrew."

Palma: "Did you get him?"

Willard: "Well, I *hit* him. Then he rushed me. If he hadn't'a been so heavy that branch would'a held him, and I wouldn't'a been here now. Hon, show the doc what he done to my brush gun."

Mrs. Willard produced an old lever-action carbine, holding it by the tip of its short barrel. Its stock was splintered and gouged, with bright scars in the blued metal of the receiver. And the rank odor suggested that the boar had anointed the gun.

"I'm gettin' me an automatic scattergun," Willard said, "and them Aggie fruitcakes can pay for it."

Quantrill typed Palma's instructions on a pocket printer as she finished dressing the leg; passed the copy to her. Palma repeated everything orally before yielding the copy to the taciturn Mrs. Willard, then paused outside the little house. "If he tries to work, Mrs. Willard, it may fester, and you'll have to get him to town. Can you cope out here alone?"

The leathery face was placid. "If need be. It's a visitation, Doctor. That boar's the devil's sign, just like the rest of the war. If I have to cope by sacrificin' lambs, so be it."

Palma bit back an acid reply. "You may be right about offering meat," she said finally. "Do you have poison?"

"For Ba'al? He'd get us, sure."

Palma and Quantrill exchanged glances; said nothing. Jouncing back toward the highway, Quantrill could contain his opinion no longer. "That poor old woman is plain gaga," he said.

"She's probably younger than I am," said Palma in jocose warning, "and you'll hear lots stranger ideas. Religious fundamentalists tend to think of the war as a judgment. I must say," she laughed gently, "a bunch of Russian boars loose on the land makes a very likely-seeming link with the powers of darkness."

"No more than paranthrax or fallout."

"Hm. Maybe, but a boar has the devil's own face—speaking metaphorically, you understand! And the hooves, and—did you know that a big boar's penis is ridged as though it were threaded? Don't laugh, Ted; that's what Willard meant by the corkscrew. The same sort of thing that was once said of Satan.

"Stop looking at me that way, you fool, I don't believe a word of it. But when you can hang three or four coincidences together, you get—well, you get Ba'al. The Biblical false lord. I suppose it's logical, in Mrs. Willard's eyes, to sacrifice to whatever god makes his presence felt the most. And maybe it'll keep that big devil away from the pens at night."

Palma ignored Quantrill's lifted brow at her repetition of the word, 'devil'. He persisted: "Maybe Willard should've used a silver bullet."

"Maybe—if that bullet were as big as your fist. You wouldn't expect to stop a Kodiak bear with a little thirty-thirty. Those animals that escaped from the Aggie pens were truly enormous; bigger by far than the Asiatic strain that reached over two hundred and fifty kilos; I've seen them. No, what Willard needed was an elephant gun and lots of intelli-

gence. I'm afraid guns are much more effective on humans
than on game of equal size.''

Sandys jurnal Sept. 3 Tus.

Mom and me found a store on Delrio road today. It was
oful. 2 men and 1 woman dead, looked like sombody shot
up the place with a 22. All the licker was gone. We took
cans of stuff. Cured ham, medisin, you name it me and
mom got it. Mom says it wasnt swiping, I gess it isnt if you
have to. When we got back I heard my dady from outside. I
never heard my dady like that. Mom made me stay out but I
can work the c b and tried to call the dr. and coudnt. I felt
so scared I was strong. I drug the stuff I found into my cave
by the other hole, you know the one I call the side door.
Mom says taking stuff from dead folks isnt swiping but I
prayed God to forgive me.

Chapter 43

On Wednesday, Quantrill drove Palma to the Caverns of
Sonora where, for the first time, he saw an effective relocation center. Laughing, chattering as though on a peacetime
outing, hundreds of citizens exercised briefly on the surface,
then returned below to be replaced by others. A few people
labored to erect windmill towers, building a complex of
twelve-volt lighting systems cannibalized from some of the
many cars parked nearby.

Palma's requisition was quickly filled from the makeshift
pharmacy near the cavern entrance. "In another week," said
Cathy Palma, leading Quantrill toward the surface by a
winding stair, "most of these people will be back home.
Unless the SinoInds hit us again, or we get a duster." A dust
storm, she added, would sweep up settled fallout, would
make topside breathing hazardous for a day or so even though
most of the ionizing radiation had decayed to bearable levels.

Quantrill squinted in the sunlight, moved to their van. "What was the stuff you picked up here?"

"Some drugs; opiates I'd hoped we wouldn't need, but the chelates didn't do the job." She coded the display as Quantrill drove along blacktop. "We've got another stop in the canyon a few klicks away. I told you about the Grange family; very tenacious in their ways, right or wrong. I'm afraid we're going to lose Wayland Grange, but he doesn't want the little girl to know that. So you keep her topside while I'm in their cave."

Quantrill found his orders easy to follow. The cave entrance was well-hidden in a tributary arroyo, and he would not have seen it but for the staunch little blonde figure in the pink dress, waving as they drew near. "Sandy, this is my helper. Why don't you show him the view," Palma said, indicating the broken countryside.

The girl nodded, her eyes large, solemn with surprise. She was small for an eleven-year-old, almost stocky, with scabs on both knees. She had not yet lost her baby fat, but her arms and legs hinted that she would develop a milkmaid's sturdiness. The little face was that of a worried angel, cheeks pink as her cotton dress, growing pinker yet as Quantrill extended his hand. The memory of another little blonde girl surfaced for an instant, was thrust vigorously back into the recesses of his mind. Endless mourning had not been a feature of the Quantrill family.

"Didn't expect company," she said, so softly he barely heard. She looked down at her feet, sockless in jogging shoes, as she offered her dirt-smeared hand.

Quantrill intuited her shyness in the handshake, resisted an impulse to hug the kid, realized he towered over her. He sat on a stone outcrop. "I'm Ted. I've got a bad leg," he said, "so take it easy on me."

It was the right tack. Soon she was guiding him by the hand, pointing to distant wreckage which had been winnowed for human remains, growing more animated as she showed him the places where she played outside. "Do you still play, Ted?"

He grinned. "When I get the chance, Sandy. But I'm no good at 'tag' right now. Give me another week."

"It's a deal," she chortled, then grew serious. "When my daddy gets well I'll show you the cave. What's the matter, don't you like caves?"

His face had betrayed him. "Uh, sure. Just got a twinge from my leg. I saw the Caverns of Sonora this morning."

Pride showed in Sandy's, "Pooh, they're nothin'. My daddy and mom don't know how big ours is. But I do. If I had a real good friend, I might show her what I found. Or him," faintly.

Charmed by her artless transparency, Quantrill hinted that he knew what she'd found, gradually leading her to guess that the backpack was his.

She caught her lower lip in her teeth, faltering, "I didn't mean to swipe your knapsack, I mean,—"

"We call it a backpack, and you didn't swipe it. It's yours, Sandy. From me to you. Okay?"

"Okay." Studied silence. Then, "I found some other stuff too. One thing like a big dress of ribbons but I think it's a parachute on a big heavy can. Is that yours, too?"

Supposing her singular treasure was a chute flare, Quantrill shook his head. "Finders keepers, Sandy. Just don't fiddle with the can. It might be dangerous," he said in understatement far beyond his comprehension. "A girl pretty as you could make a terrific dress from a chute. Maybe not as nice as the dress you're wearing," he finished, affecting not to notice the holes and smudges in the pink fabric.

"Aw, this ol' thing," she murmured, and covered her embarrassment by asking how his pack came to be in the delta. Quantrill spun a tale of his journey in the *Norway*, recognizing that the girl hungered for heroes, willing to present himself as such for a child in need. He did not perceive, as Palma did, that the friendship might be therapy for him as well.

In an hour, Quantrill and Sandy Grange were talking as equals, punning, exchanging riddles. Palma's call brought them back to the present; but before advancing to meet

Sandy's hollow-faced mother, Quantrill promised the girl he would return. Once more shy in the presence of the doctor, Sandy excused herself and, with a final wave, ducked from sight to seek her father.

"You'll have to tell Sandy soon," Palma said to Louise Grange.

"Wayland won't have it," was the sorrowing reply. "Better to have it sudden than have the child like I am, day and night."

"The relocation center has room," said Palma obliquely, "when it's over. And I'll do whatever I can; you know that."

"We'll make do," said the woman, and straightened her shoulders. "Just like when Sandy was sick and out of school."

Quantrill did not have to be told that their presence was an added burden on Louise Grange's composure. He started the van quickly and, with Palma's permission, illegally patched a video newscast into their dashboard display as he drove.

The news was increasingly an animated production. In Florida, Axis troops had advanced as far as the Everglades, where a small army of civilian 'swamp rats' was taking a heavy toll of invaders. Fort Myers and Miami suburbs were holding, thanks to a fleet of 'Frisbee' drones, the first solid evidence that RUS weapons would be expended for the benefit of Americans.

The disclike Frisbee, remotely deployed, three meters in diameter, squatted or floated inert until its sensors located a moving target. Frisbees did not discriminate friend from foe, but swarmed up briefly to discharge small particle-beam bursts while jittering in midair between obstacles. A hundred Frisbees made a fine defensive line against infantry or lightly armored vehicles—and so long as they held a line, neither invaders nor defenders were wise to enter the area. The only large moving thing a Frisbee disdained to zap was another Frisbee.

A truce was being negotiated between Israel and the AIR, with mediation by the UN, among rumors that all Israel might relocate with assistance provided by the Islamics. The

site of New Israel was open to conjecture, but it was understood that the site would not be lands presently occupied by
Moslems. With this understanding, Turkey trod a tightrope
between her NATO Allies and her AIR neighbors.

Scattered commando raids, an undeclared war of limited
reprisals, had been launched by European Allies and leased
SinoInd bases in North Africa. Thus far, they had used no
nuclear or biological weapons—perhaps because France, a
reluctant ally of the US/RUS cause, had her own credible
nuclear deterrent and an old grudge against some Africans.

Now relocated in Swiss bunkers, the UN continued its
pleas against further use of genocidal weapons. One encouraging sign was the bombing of China's flood-control
dams by high-flying RUS hive bombers, using guided bombs
with conventional explosives. Since the RUS was still exchanging sporadic nuke strikes with India, the non-nuclear
bombs suggested a RUS willingness to consider a nuclear
moratorium—as long as it was mutual. RUS marksmen were
obviously ready for conventional war, to judge from their
success in turning back the 'migration' from Mongolia. China's plans for a smallpox epidemic had depended on live
carriers, and few of those got through before the ploy was
discovered. RUS Frisbees finished the job; smallpox vaccine
developed a brief popularity south of Lake Baikal.

Canada's missile launches had been almost entirely defensive MITVs, intercepting SinoInd birds in polar trajectory.
So effective was Canada's umbrella that she had lost only
Edmonton, Toronto, Montreal, and Ottawa among her larger
cities. The same shower of MITVs that saved Vancouver had
also saved Seattle, Portland, and Boise—for the time being.
Canada's new capital was rumored to be somewhere near
Winnipeg; nations were suddenly vague about their business
addresses.

Somehow the newscast managed to convey a smooth
transition to a new President of the United States without
dwelling on classified details on the death of the previous
incumbent. Official bulletins now came from White House
Central, an unnamed site almost certainly west of the Missis-

sippi. Only once did the title, 'President Hyatt' identify the ex-Speaker of the House. It was easy to infer that the system, not the man, counted most. The system was apparently healthy, had not gone into shock, was even now gearing for national elections while it trained millions of inductees for a systemic defense.

The newscast ended with a personal message from Eve Simpson, whose hologramed convexities adorned barracks walls across the nation. Little Evie still innocently adored her boys in uniform and proved it with blown kisses.

"Did you notice," asked Palma as she killed the display, "they're not telling us where all of Evie's boys are going?"

Quantrill turned into Aggie Station with a shrug. "Florida, I thought. That's where we need defense most, isn't it?"

Negative headshake. "Paranthrax will become a natural barrier until we lick it from here. No, Ted; our boys won't be training to fight there. For our west coast, maybe—but I'm guessing they'll be heading for an overseas offensive. Don't ask me how or where."

"It's about time," he said, slowing the van.

"If you like being cannon-fodder," she snapped. "Anybody on an offensive in Asia is just asking for it. Don't even think about it, Ted. Think about little Sandy Grange back there; *that*'s what we have to defend." Palma took her bag, stalked away.

Quantrill watched the angry set of Palma's shoulders, reflecting that some people were natural defenders—Dr. Catherine Palma, for instance. And that some might find their niche only on offense—himself, for instance.

Sandys jurnal Sep. 4 Wens.
The dr. came again she brout the nicest boy. I promised to show him the real cave. Ted told me a long fib about how the napsack was his and he was on the delta once. Why woud he make up such a wopper unless he likes me? He said I was pretty. Boy what a b s artist! Teds real old, at least 15. I tell you whos pretty jurnal, he is!! He limps. He brushd aginst me once, boy,howdy I got trembly scared but I liked it. OK it was me brushd him. No fibs to you jurnal.

Have to stop now my dady has been asleep sinse the dr.
left, that must mean hes better. Mom is asleep but sobing
what will we do what will we do. I know what we will do.
As soon as those platelets are gone my dady and me will
build more rooms in a place I found way back in my big
cave. I bet mom is pregnet and I bet I know why.

Chapter 44

There was no precise moment when Quantrill could say he
began to follow the global war news. He avoided friendships
at Aggie Station with a distant politeness. He was drawn to
the day-room holo set in the evenings, to books when he was
idle during the day. He read Armstrong's *Grey Wolf* and
judged that in every era there might be need for a pitiless,
iron-willed Kemal Ataturk. From Pratt's *The Battles That
Changed History* he learned that most bloody mass engagements end with, at best, expensive victories by exhausted
victors. He decided, after Tinnin's *The Hit Team*, that greater
victories are won when a small accurate concentration of
intense force is thrust against an enemy's nerve center—as a
single bullet might topple a mighty strategist and send an
empire into shock.

He found himself still shockable the day he detoured on an
errand to the relocation center. He'd found a child's plastic
tea set, bartered a lapel dosimeter for it, and kept it hidden
until he trailed old tire marks to the grotto where the Grange
family maintained its miserable existence. The Grange vehicle was gone. He wondered if they, like others who had
chosen separate shelters, had moved nearer town.

But Sandy met him at the entrance. He saw traces of tears
in the patina of dust on her cheeks, saw her sunburst of
delight as, silently, he pulled the tea set from behind him.
"It's loooooovely," she cooed, hugging it to her breast.

"Don't tell mom if you swiped it, she'll be back from a swap meet soon."

He swore it had been a legitimate purchase, his heart full of her reflected joy. She beckoned to him then, and for the first time he eased into the little cavern. Wire-strung blankets defined the room.

The smell was overpowering. A man lay in the single patch of sunlight, only his face showing over hand-stitched quilts. Skin stretched tightly over his white fleshless face, eyes sunken, no hair—not even eyebrows—to relieve his skeletal appearance. The eyes snapped open; the lips formed words. Quantrill wondered how the girl could steel herself to kneel so near the stench of corruption; to smile into the face of death. Quantrill shifted position to hide his shudder.

"It's the boy I met the other day," Sandy murmured brightly. "He brought me a tea set." She watched the gray lips, then nodded. "We'll go outside before mom gets back, daddy."

As soon as possible, Quantrill moved outside and reveled in the clean dry air, admitted that he might have time for a mock tea party. "I snuck away; don't you tell," he said in an effort at the local dialect. "Have to get back right soon."

They were sipping cups full of air when Louise Grange drove up, her eyes darting from one to the other. "What's happened? Is Doctor Palma here?"

"No'm," Quantrill said sheepishly, and indicated the tea set. "I promised Sandy I'd pay her a visit. Thought she might like this."

Louise Grange placed her hand over her shallow breast, sighed, found a smile for him. "That's—awful nice of you."

"I'm gonna show him where I play, mom," Sandy began.

"Not in the hole, child! You didn't go inside, boy?"

Quantrill saw the almost infinitesimal headshake from Sandy. "Uh—well, we were going to."

"Not today, I'm afraid," said the woman. "It ain't fit for company. It pains me not to be a good neighbor, but—" She wrung thin hands together, beseeching him to understand without words.

"Time I was going anyhow," he said, and smiled. He waved to the girl as he put the van in motion. As long as she was visible in the rearview, he could see Sandy waving. He saw that his hands were clenched on the steering wheel, and cursed sickness. And friendship.

Sandys jurnal Sep 9 Mon.

Ted came again today, brout me a real tea set for my hope chest. Ive hid it here with my kemlamp in church. Well I call it church. The rocks in my cave are like carvd trees, they make it look like the bigest church in the world. You can get here from the hole by swimming. My dady would have a hissy fit if he knew how I found out but he coudnt spank me I wish he coud. Mom and my dady talk a lot. She takes notes and he has to wisper things over sinse her crying drouns him out. Im sorry Im getting this page wet. Im waiting for my dady to get better like he says he will. Mom says you have to beleive God will make my dady well. There must be a airshaft from the hole to my church sinse I just heard somthing like like moms voise but it sounded more like a booger. I will stop for now and go see.

Sandys jurnal Sep. 10 Tus.

god is a dam lie.

Chapter 45

The Libyan burrow-bombs may have played hell with the ELF grid, thought Boren Mills, but the concussion had blown him off the Baffin Island listings. Mills and others recovered in a spacious modern hospital in Thunder Bay, just across Lake Superior from the US, and Mills was secretly amused to learn that he now qualified for a foreign service medal. He complained of blurred vision for a week after his eyesight returned to normal, certain that the longer his recu-

peration, the more likely he would be posted to a reasonable
duty station. In his own mind Mills was not malingering. He
was studying the war's progress, the better to discover how
he might get himself posted to some spot where he would be
most effective. Boren Mills had been victimized by an explosion, and knew that he would never be effective in battle.

Thanks to attrition in the Navy, Mills became a full
lieutenant upon his return to active duty. His foreign service
and purple heart ribbons lent dash to his uniform. A new
sparkle invaded his eyes the day they spied a classified
bulletin on Israel's new gift to the US.

The Ghost Armada, as it was dubbed, had brought Israelis
safely to Cyprus by fooling every extant electronic device.
Though chafing at the delay, America was glad to have the
new system which could throw false blips on enemy acquisi-
tion radar while it kept genuine bogies off the scopes. Mills
indulged in a brief brainstorm, concluding that Israel's
weapon was nothing like the old Stealth program which had
been leaked by the US for political purposes a generation
before. The Ghost Armada would have to focus on the
sensors, not on the target to be sensed. Its application for US
purposes would require the best possible protection. Anybody remotely connected with the program would be non-
expendable, pampered, defended.

Lieutenant Boren Mills spent two days on his letter, up-
dating and modifying his own assessment of his special
talents. The self-assessment always formed part of the core
of a computer's file on anyone. If he was not identified by a
records search as a man ideally suited to help develop a
remote-coding microwave system, Boren Mills would be
sadly mistaken.

Boren Mills made fewer mistakes than most.

SPL order 251, 23 SEP 96 E X T R A C T

PARA 16. FOL NAM NAV OFCR is REL from ASG
W/PREV duty STN EFF this date and W/REP for PPTY
ASG to Kikepa STN, Niihau NAV FAC ASAP by MIL
TRANS Priority A RPT A to ARR NLT 1 OCT 96 Kikepa
STN, Niihau . . .

Permanent party posting to Kikepa Point was not quite
what Mills had in mind. He considered a relapse, researched
the island of Niihau, then concluded that he would be as
secure there as anywhere. Certainly a posting to a naval
research facility on a privately-owned island in the Hawaiian
chain was better than Baffin Island. If you were going to live
one step from the end of the world, it might as well be the
warm tropical end.

Mills could have been on a military transport the next day,
but wisely spent his next four days in a transient BOQ
cramming his head and his personal floppy cassettes with
everything he could learn on remote electronic query and
input modules. He was a very quick study; by the time he
landed on Oahu for the Niihau hovercraft, Lieutenant Boren
Mills would bear some surface similarity to the experience
profile he had claimed to the Navy's central computer.

His only worry was the seclusion of Niihau. There would
be no large population there, no finishing schools or sophisticated high schools with their breathtaking arrays of pre-
collegiate beauties. Mills's sexual preferences were kinky
only in the narrowness of the age group he preferred, i.e.,
early post-Lolita. Physical ripening, that first delectable
flowering of maturity, fascinated Mills; captured his lusts.
He did not maltreat or embitter the girls he knew; preferred,
in fact, a sixteen-year-old who already knew her way around.
There had been plenty of those in the cities, Mills reflected;
but it might be different at Kikepa Point.

He would cope somehow. As he packed, Mills was smiling on the inside. His posting to the Naval R & D facility
suggested that he was already on the way to success. In a
trivial way, he had already proven that he could remotely
stuff an electronic system with balderdash.

Chapter 46

Just when the optimists were clearing their throats to gloat over the 'modest' levels of global fallout, the second paroxysm of nukes came in October. The first group emerged from the sand seas of eastern Libya to take out Schwyz (an error; it was meant for Zurich), Lucerne, Berne, Lausanne, Zurich (if at first you don't succeed . . .), and in a shocker, Rome. It amounted to a simple refusal by Libya to take any more guff from the UN, from which she had withdrawn. Libya did not know whether she was united with Syria at the moment, or not. Syria said not. Libya's ruling junta, more willing than their venerated Khaddafi to follow bombast with bombs, unilaterally chose to break through the stalemate with Israel. Other countries of the AIR might permit the UN to mediate the newly vexed Jewish Question, but not Libya. To her junta it seemed clear that Christians and Jews had turned the UN into one enormous Swiss-based conspiracy. *Ergo,* Switzerland *delenda est.*

Libya did not target Cyprus or Israel itself, convinced that the Jewish Ghost Armada would somehow deflect her medium-range missiles harmlessly. Libya did not have enough Indian nukes to waste a single one.

Within a day, Libya's Mediterranean coast was a beach of radioactive glass, her junta atomized, her southern borders invaded by neighboring Chad, her existence as a political entity erased by a rain of missiles from a still-functioning Europe.

Strategists on all sides blanched, then, when missiles streaked up from a site near Ras Lanuf on the Libyan coast two days later. No one had suspected that Libya had a nuclear second-strike capability, let alone a delivery system that could reach the port cities of Guatemala, Nicaragua, Panama, Cuba.

It seemed to Latin-American Marxists almost as if a mad-

dened Libya, in her death throes, had responded on behalf of
the US in retaliation for the Florida invasion. But the US
submarine-based Trident missiles threw many smaller
warheads, and did not throw them so far. SinoInd leaders
insisted that the Libyan second-strike had really been a Yan-
qui stroke, but no one could prove it. No one except the crew
of the USS *Kamehameha*, whose Mediterranean armament
included eight Tridents of extended range with warheads that
did not fit the known Trident signatures. The Tridents had
emerged from very near Libyan soil. Flummoxed by American use of Israel's new weapon, every electronic watcher
pinpointed the launch site fifteen klicks inland. Latin American governments took the body blows as a probable hint by
an injured colossus that no further unfriendly acts would be
tolerated. If any fresh SinoInd troops entered Florida, they'd
better not speak Spanish.

As if to prove they were as capable as anyone of further
contaminating the globe, Chinese subs launched waves of
nukes against RUS industrial centers in Western Siberia, and
US centers in Colorado and Wyoming. In both cases, fossil
fuels were the targets. The RUS machine still depended on
petroleum, though America had made headway in converting
western shale and coal into fuel. Too many of the warheads
got through, and some were ground-pounders.

The immediate US/RUS answer was nuclear, chiefly from
subs that pounded SinoInd oil reserves in Rajasthan and
Sinkiang. As if in afterthought, a flurry of RUS warheads
detonated underwater in Japan's inland sea north of Kyushu,
where shoreline debris eventually proved that Chinese submersibles had been hiding there. Japan's leaders could hardly
have been ignorant of the Chinese presence, as Japanese
media were quick to allege. The Japanese dead numbered
only in thousands, chiefly from inundations by great waves.
But the inland sea was squarely between Hiroshima and
Nagasaki; and Japan was virtually one great urban clot.
Thereafter, Japan took her neutrality seriously.

The delayed US/RUS response began quietly in places like
Vorkuta, San Marcos, Izhevsk, Klamath Falls: basic training

sites. Green US troops began their passage through Ontario to Hudson Bay. Canada had developed her submersible cargo fleet to carry ore and petroleum under pack ice through a wintry Northwest Passage, but with round-the-clock refitting the sluggish vessels soon carried troops past Peary Land and Spitzbergen to Archangelsk. It was hoped that lurking SinoInd attack vessels could be decoyed by surface applications of the Ghost Armada. Meanwhile, so many US/RUS all-weather stealth aircraft were spanning the Bering Strait that visual-contact air engagements with SinoInd swing-wings were becoming the rule there.

Chapter 47

It had been over a month since Cathy Palma had ridden with Quantrill to the Grange cave. They'd found the entrance dynamited, the survivors gone without trace. The single wooden cross that stood in the rubble had been carefully carved:

Wayland F. Grange 1955-1996

For a time, Quantrill hoped Louise and Sandy Grange would turn up in Sonora, or among the thousands in the relocation center. Then in early October, Grange's Blazer was found abandoned and stripped, evidently by one of the religious zealot groups that seemed to be flowering as suddenly as desert plants. Quantrill accepted the news without comment.

Soon afterward came the flurry of second strikes that sent survivors back underground for weeks. Quantrill read more and watched the holo. And avoided emotional ties more than ever, though Palma had urged him to enroll in the relocation center school, hoping that he would respond to others his own age.

"Look," he said once to the exasperated Palma; "my

strategy is to learn from the library terminal. Geometry, inorganic chem, military history. It's all I have time for, and you said yourself I shouldn't go outside again for another week.''

"You think we can't run an immunology program without you, Ted? Don't flatter yourself.'' She saw the dull anger in his face. "You've done a lot; nobody denies that. But just between us, they're already in Phase Three in the labs. We're licking the bug! Believe me, Aggie Station can spare one cargo handler. And I can spare you if it means finishing your education.'' She did not add, *and rejoining your peers*.

"Between you and the holo, I'm getting what I want,'' he said stonily, and changed the subject. "For one thing, I'd like you to help me cut through all the crap I'm getting on the news about local guerrilla gangs. They sound like crazies to me, but you don't see anybody on the news really saying that. I need somebody to brief me, not bullshit me.''

Palma did not like his increasing use of military terms: *strategy, briefing, guerrilla* came easily to him these days. "Now's as good a time as any,'' she sighed.

He took his time phrasing the question, a legacy from taking courses via library holo terminals. "Are they Mormons?''

"No!'' Her knee-jerk response surprised Palma herself. She chuckled, peered guiltily at Quantrill, then back to her work. "Well, actually some of them think they are. I could make the same claim, Ted. I was raised LDS, but after my husband began trying to be a closet polygamist I backslid to a jack-Mormon, and then—'' Shrug. "No, you can't be a Mormon and deny the tenets of the Apostles. Or the revelations of the modern Prophets. But a lot of people have their own revelations, and these days a lot of those are nightmarish. That can be a strong divisive force if it happens to a particularly devout man.''

"Or woman.''

"All males may become priests, even blacks,'' she said. She added with a trace of bitterness, "Females can never attain priesthood. Honor, veneration, service, yes; priesthood, no. You wouldn't believe the underclothes a Mormon woman's supposed to have, and I won't burden you with *that*. If a woman complains too much, she's put on a sort of probation—'disfellowship', they call it. Nice, hm? Or they just excommunicate you. I didn't wait for that final rejection.''

"Maybe I shouldn't be asking you—"

"Ask away, whatthehell," she said as if sealing some internal bargain.

"Why do they raid other people? I thought Mormons had food and stuff all socked away."

She silenced the labeler, fixed him with a firm gaze. "They do. I repeat, these guerrillas aren't true Mormons. Of course they take terrible chances driving like maniacs through fallout, and some of them will be sorry. Some of them are just banditti, out for loot, but some honestly think they're bringing the gospel. The cars they steal, the churches they burn, are all part of their saintly splinter-group zeal to stamp out heretics. And there are in-betweeners who aren't above collecting some riches on the way to Heaven. Reminds me a little of the devout conquistadors of the Sixteenth Century.''

As the labeler began ticking away again, Quantrill put some other labels—political labels from newscasts—together. "Let me guess; a heretic is anybody who doesn't wear a Collier button.''

'' 'Pull through with Collier','' she quoted the campaign slogan. "Collier's a good man, for my money; he publicly disavows the cults, but they may intimidate a lot of people from the polls. You can't expect police to control them all. I'm inclined to think Governor Street is fighting an uphill battle, even here in his own home state.''

The ex-Governor of Texas was also an ex-Major General, whose current position as Undersecretary of State bolstered his claim as potential commander-in-chief of a besieged country. But fairly or not, James Street was saddled and hagridden by blame for a war which had come while his party was in power.

"At least all the networks seem to like Street," Quantrill said.

"Of course they do; they don't like censorship, and an LDS Apostle in White House Central will lean in that direction."

"Who needs holovision? Seems to me if you read the Book of Mormon, you know what's gonna happen anyway."

She smiled at what she imagined was a joke. He read her expression, then pulled a thin faxed pamphlet no bigger than a wallet card from his pocket. She glanced at its cover. "Um. The Church of God In Revealed Context, eh? Yes, they're one of the biggest splinters in the backside of the LDS. Not as violent as some."

"Just tell me if that's really from the Book of Mormon, Palma. The centerfold. Read it," he urged.

Wherefore it is an abridgement of the record of the people of Nephi:

1 Nephi, 17.

He raiseth up a righteous nation, and destroyeth the nations of the wicked. And he did straiten them in the wilderness with his rod; for they hardened their hearts, even as ye have; and the Lord straitened them because of their iniquity. He sent fiery flying serpents among them; the day must surely come that they must be destroyed, save a few only, who shall be led away into captivity. Ye have seen an angel, and he spake unto you; yea, ye have heard his voice from time to time; and he hath spoken unto you in a still small voice, but ye were past feeling, that ye could not feel his words; wherefore, he has spoken unto you like unto the voice of thunder, which did cause the earth to shake as if it were to divide asunder. For God had commanded me that I should build a ship.

"It's disjunct, as I recall," said Palma.

"Junk, hell. Destroying nations with fiery flying serpents is a pretty close description, I'd say. The only thing that doesn't follow is that explanation where they tell you the ship is a ship of state. No kidding, Palma; is it, or isn't it,—"

"DISJUNCT," she said loudly to silence him, "means

separated; disjointed. I don't remember the whole Book of Nephi, but I do know the special wackiness of the Church of God In Revealed Context. They do numerology mumbo-jumbo, like numbering phrases and reading off those that are prime numbers, or something equally arbitrary. And sometimes they come up with passages that fit when they were never intended to. This particular cult doesn't invent any new text—I think. They just combine pieces of what's already there—usually in order, but that piece about building a ship might be pages away.''

He mulled this over. ''I guess it'd be easy to check.''

''Yes, but few gentiles do—and Revealed Contexters play strictly by their own rules, so even if their compressed text doesn't match the original, they can claim it's all *in* the original. They just pull special messages out by numerical revelation.'' Their steadfastness in their beliefs, she added, made them take great risks at times; and made them in some ways dangerous.

Again, Quantrill was silent for a time. Then, ''You think these religious nuts would hurt a little kid?''

She thought of the Church of the Blood of the Lamb, a full generation before; of true believers who would shotgun their kin in a quarrel over dogma. ''No, Ted; certainly not a little girl who won't cast a vote for years to come.'' She met his glance and his smile, and wondered if she were right. There seemed little doubt that somehow, the Granges had met with one of the zealot gangs.

A week later—with all the delays from precincts where ballots were hand-counted, it was on Wednesday afternoon, 6 November,—President-elect Yale Collier delivered his victory speech. Cathy Palma listened morosely, though she had voted for the man. She was more concerned about Quantrill's defection; hadn't known of his delta pass until too late to stop him.

And what could she have done to stop him? The captain of the delta *Schwarz* knew about Quantrill anyway; would hardly have denied him free passage. The *Schwarz* had been the first delta in a month scheduled to College Station via San

Marcos. With either destination, Quantrill's intent seemed clear. Perversely, Palma hoped the kid would break a leg en route to enlist. He was diving headlong, she thought, into the meatgrinder that had devoured his family, his friends, his future. To Palma it seemed a popular form of suicide.

For the dozenth time, she unfolded the page she'd crumpled after reading it. She had found it, in Quantrill's hasty scrawl, on his bunk atop a neatly folded yellow delta coverall. Palma's heart would have leapt if the yellow flight suit had been missing, for then she might have expected to see him again.

Palma did not expect to see him again. *"These should fit somebody,"* he'd written. *"I can't wear a uniform that reminds me of friends. I don't think that's what uniforms are for. Someday we can argue about it. Good luck. Ted Quantrill."*

No, she thought, staring sightlessly at the page. They wouldn't argue; first because he was probably right.

And second because he would very probably be dead in sixty days.

PART II: GUNSELS

Chapter 48

The winter of 1996-7 was a relatively mild one, but a killer nonetheless. In Syracuse and Worcester, without natural gas, neighbors fought over ownership of trees they should have stacked as cordwood months before. In Roanoke and Knoxville, paranthrax crippled essential services until the cities, gasping in their own filth, welcomed December's refrigeration. The rat population leaped, and typhus was not far behind.

On the central Siberian plateau millions died of simple starvation, with the removal of countless trainloads of Evenk beef and Yakut wheat to storage near the Black Sea. The aboriginal Evenk and Yakut people fared well enough on the land by returning to their old ways; but city-dwelling Russians in Mirnyy and Tura starved. The RUS needed rations for the armies that were moving south from Archangelsk to vast training areas in the southern Ukraine. Romania, Hungary, and Bulgaria had declined the honor of hosting the Allied troops, and the RUS could not persuade where once the USSR had commanded.

The RUS did not quarter American troops in the south out of kindness. They did it because advanced training of entire armies could be carried out more or less secretly there. And because thirty divisions of Americans wintering in the Urals would have died like thirty divisions of ants on an ice floe. North of the fiftieth parallel in a Russian winter, winter itself is the enemy.

The SinoInd movement to the west was slowed by the ferocity of Kazakhs, then stopped by the more ferocious ice storms. Only in warmer climes could a war against other men be prosecuted. Chad, for example, was dissuaded by her AIR neighbors from absorbing Libya. If Chad could only wait until the colossi fought to their mutual deaths, an Islamic crescent could become an Islamic world.

Australians and New Zealanders completed their ANZUS
exercises with American marines during a sweltering an-
tipodal summer, making ready for a daring game of trans-
oceanic hopscotch, while Canadian diplomats broached tender topics with Somalia for a bailout procedure, just in case.
Canada's defensive game and her natural resources were
burnishing her image as a major power. Somalia reflected on
the Israeli/Turk agreement and its outcome, and then raised
the ante. But at least she kept quiet.

In Florida, surviving SinoInd irregulars pushed past the
Caloosahatchee River, bypassed the Miami ruins, sacked
Fort Lauderdale and Palm Beach, and advanced on the
Tampa Bay cities. Every Chris-Craft and dinghy in the
American sports-fishing fleet was now armed: night-scoped
AR-18's, heat-seeking SSM, or a self-correcting mortar—
anything to interdict the supply hovercraft that hummed
across from Cuba. There were still enough Harriers north of
Orlando to make a SinoInd air supply route plain suicide. The
average Florida cracker was just as irregular as the invader,
but he fought for his own turf and knew the inlets and
hummocks better. The 'gators fed well. It was thought that
Tampa might hold.

Throughout the Northern Hemisphere and to a lesser degree in the Southern, background radiation was still dangerously high two months after the second-strike nuclear flurries
of October. Among the most essential of US industries,
suddenly, was the scatter of small processing plants for
production of selective chelates.

Years before, the Lawrence Berkeley Labs had created
LICAM- C, the first chemical capable of selectively and
safely removing plutonium ions from living tissue. By now,
other chelates existed which had special affinities for iodine,
cesium, strontium, calcium. Of course, a human body
robbed of its stable iodine and calcium isotopes would not
function for long. The murky suspension of Keylate that
Americans swallowed contained not only the selective chelates, but coated particles of replacement elements which,
like tiny timed-release caps, became available to the body

only after chelates had removed newly-absorbed elements. There were side effects, but temporary nausea was better than cancer of the spleen.

Americans listened to local media and took the recommended doses of Keylate. In the Ukraine, Keylate was in short supply. In San Bernardino, missile plant workers took it every four hours through November. In San Marcos Infantry Training School, Recruit Ted Quantrill took it once a day through December.

Chapter 49

The big man in the dun uniform barked an order in Chinese, jerking the barrel of his assault rifle as if to goad his prisoner. Quantrill grasped the weapon, thrusting its barrel to the side as he swept one leg behind his captor's knee and wheeled. He fell atop the man, one elbow seeking the vulnerable soft flesh just beneath the sternum's bony mass; jerked his head back as his adversary spat in his face; found his throat hooked by the big man's calf, and was hurled backward.

The dun-clad man swung his weapon toward Quantrill without rising, a grim smile across his camouflage-painted face. "Zap, Quantrill, you're dogmeat," he growled, then shouted at the circle of onlookers: "When are you assbreaths gonna learn to follow through? You let go of a Sino's weapon once you snag it, and it's all over!" He waved Quantrill back to the encircling squad of recruits and came to his feet in a practiced backward roll, watching the recruit wipe spittle from his face. The instructor's half-sneer seemed fully permanent. This bunch of green-uniformed recruits, it implied, would *always* be green until the day they saw hand-to-hand combat; that is to say, the day they died.

Sergeant Rafael Sabado could afford to sneer. Though

garbed for the moment as a Sino, his own forest-green
uniform was neatly sewn with small patches that meant more
than some campaign ribbons. Airborne training at Benning;
special combat school at Ord; languages at Monterey; unconventional warfare at Bliss. Now that most troop transportation was hamstrung and Fort Benning no longer existed, the
Army was forced into one-station training with too few
specialists. These poor raw recruits, thought Sabado, would
be funneled straight from Texas to Russia. All but a very,
very few . . .

"Sergeant?" The lettering on the fatigues said it was
Symons; the concern in the lank intelligent face said he
wasn't being a smart-ass. "How can he hold onto a weapon
when a bigger man is hauling him away by the neck?"

Sabado paused, cocking his head, then smiled. "Leverage, Symons. He had it, but he let it go. Come back here, uh,
Quantrill; we'll run through it."

Quantrill, with surprisingly little reluctance for an anglo
kid who couldn't be much over sixteen, moved onto the
practice mats. The green eyes watched Sabado's moves with
flickering interest. He nodded as Sabado showed him how to
hook his arms over the weapon, seemed satisfied with the
other instructions.

"Now I want you to spit in my face," Sabado smiled. 'I'd
castrate you for that ordinarily, but when we're on the mat,
be my guest."

The circle was suddenly silent, the recruits motionless.
"Fair's fair, Quantrill," someone joked.

"Fuck fairness," Sabado said; "Go ahead, recruit. I
won't hurt you."

The Quantrill youth smiled almost shyly, then spat without
seeming to pause for spittle. Sabado's eyes flickered, but his
head did not move a millimeter. Yet even that instant's
involuntary blink hid the beginning of Quantrill's sidelong
ducking roll that carried him to the edge of the mats.

"Very good," Sabado purred. "You don't trust me in this
uniform. But what's more important is that I didn't flinch
from a little spit." He motioned the recruit back with the

others, looked around him. "In personal combat you can't afford to care about little things. Flood, mud, shit or blood, it's all the same: flinch and you're dead."

Into the murmur around him, Sabado inserted his calm Tex-Mex voice of command with a tone his recruits had come to dread. This was something Sabado liked, so it was sure as hell gonna hurt. "Choose a partner; don't choose a buddy. I see any asshole buddies, I get to make 'em my partners. *Move*," he said. Soon, twenty-five pairs of recruits stood toe-to-toe. It was a little exercise their mommies never taught them, Sabado said with relish, though his brother had taught him in a Houston slum. The pairs were to take turns. Every time a man flinched, he lost his turn. If any recruit lost his temper, he'd do laps with a full pack instead of eating chow.

In a way, it was a very simple exercise requiring stainless steel discipline. All the recruits had to do was spit into each other's faces.

Sabado halted the drill after two minutes, affecting not to see the bottled rage in the men; judging to a nicety when they had taken enough. "From now on, every day we run a two-minute spit drill," he said, pausing a beat before adding, "just like screwing a schoolteacher. You got to do it and do it, 'til you get it right." Sabado was good at his work; the laughter took the edge off their outrage and, with luck, some of these recruits would master one more small advantage.

Sabado took them through a few two-on-ones, then some slow practice throws, and lazed watchfully while they continued at it in pairs. He watched the Quantrill kid surreptitiously. A lot of kids, given the order to spit like that, were so scared they could muster no spit at all. Quantrill had tried to sandbag him with that smile—and his side roll had been damned fast. All right then: unbelievably fast. Nobody could be faster than Rafael Sabado, but a very few were almost as fast. The problem was in taking time to hone that natural gift. Sabado knew what the recruits did not: in three weeks they would all be headed past the Canadian border. All but a very, very few . . .

Chapter 50

Two weeks later, Symons and Quantrill were en route to an hour of classroom drill on maintenance of the new Heckler & Koch machine carbine, walking in step as prescribed. Symons sought the source of an aerial whisper overhead, pointed at the drab, newly-camouflaged delta in the distance. "Don't you wish you were crewing one of those," he said, and got a shrug in answer. He persisted: "Rumor says you did, once."

"Don't I wish," Quantrill agreed.

"Jesus, three whole words," Symons grinned, his Dallas drawl bright and animated. "Better watch yourself, Quantrill; people will say we're in love."

"Let 'em. I'm saving myself for a Chinese pederast," said Quantrill.

Laughing: "Tell that to Sergeant Sabado, maybe he'll let up on you."

"It's that obvious, is it?"

"Rumor says the Mex must be into S-M, the way he loves his work. And he sure loves it with you, bubba."

"Tell me something I don't know."

Symons mulled that over. "Well, you don't know the squad's rooting for you. I mean, shit, you aren't giving your friends a chance, man. You could put in a complaint about the way he picks on you. We'd back you one hundred per cent."

Quantrill had to look up to meet Symons's blue-eyed earnest gaze. Somehow he gave the impression that he was looking down. "You're kidding," was all he said.

"Try us."

"The Army's doing that," was the reply. "You notice that parade ground full of kids that came in last week? Still marching in civvies today? Well, guess whose fatigues they'll get when we get out battle gear, Symons. The Army's up against the wall, short on bodies, equipment, training. The more fiendish sonsofbitches they have like Sabado, the better they'll teach us. Anyhow, thanks but no thanks. Somebody told me once, 'Don't say it; it wouldn't help.' She was right.''

They paused under a jury-rigged awning, took off their rain cap covers, shook them in approved fashion. Fallout precautions were ritual now. ''Well, I tried,'' Symons chuckled. ''If you ever need a friend,—''

''I should buy a dog,'' Quantrill finished for him, smiling.

''Right. And there's always me.''

Another shared glance, a guarded offer of friendship met by a plea for apartheid. Quantrill found it hard to concentrate on field-stripping the H&K weapon during the next hour. Until now, he'd thought the special attentions of Sabado had been only in his imagination.

That afternoon during the current hour-a-day stint in the unfiltered outdoors, Quantrill decided otherwise. Calisthenics were no longer a trial in the brisk chill air, but as the recruits went through gradually quickening combat moves he was certain that Sabado stalked him and Symons, watching closely. The swagger of the small hips and big shoulders could not be hidden by Sabado's shapeless Sino fatigues as the instructor, his Toltec eyes glittering, chose first one victim, then another for disarming drills with a machine carbine.

When Sabado had worked his deft lightnings on Fiero, a hundred-kilo hulk from Socorro with a linebacker's disposition, he held the H&K up in one hand while fishing in his pocket with the other. ''A touch of realism,'' he began, and held up a magazine loaded with ammo, ''to sweeten the pot. These are special loads with gel blank tips.'' To prove it, he slapped the magazine in place, handed the stubby weapon to Fiero. Donning polycarbonate goggles he said, ''Set it for semi, Fiero, and see if you can bag me at point-blank range.''

The sullen Fiero peered uncertainly at the magazine, raised the carbine, aimed at the smiling face from five meters. Then he lowered its muzzle; licked his lips.

Someone snickered.

Fiero brought the H&K up and fired, a snap shot that caught Sabado on the cheek. The report was oddly muffled, almost like the pop of a plastic bag, and the gel did not even snap Sabado's head. Another round put a crimson blot on the brown-clad breast. Sabado held up one hand then, staring Fiero down as he advanced and took the murderous little German-developed piece. Fiero quickly moved off the practice mats, his glare a challenge to his peers.

"Now then," Sabado breathed in his special murmur, "it's kickass time. Let's say I'm on night patrol and my image enhancer has a malf. But yours doesn't, you can see me just fine. And you'd like a nice shiny H&K for a souvenir. Anybody takes this off me gets a 'bye all next week—unless he takes a slug from this," he patted the weapon. A long silence greeted him. "Well? Would you rather have a ten-minute spit drill?"

By now the spit drill was no more than a nasty joke; Sabado's flaunting of it was the real goad. The first man to step forward was little Tinker, the wiry black from Amarillo. Tinker donned the goggles while Fiero tied a very unmilitary, very Texan bandanna over Sabado's eyes.

"You never looked so good, Sergeant," said a voice.

"I never forget a voice, Symons," smiled Sabado blindly. "You're next." Laughter.

As Tinker advanced on his sergeant the entire squad backed away, conscious that they were not wearing goggles, fearful that the gel blanks would sting. And blind or not, Sabado made a fearsome foe, especially with the padding sewn into that Sino uniform. Seldom had fifty recruits been so silent as Tinker stalked the big man, first from the rear, then reconsidering.

Tinker made his move from Sabado's right, curling his own right forearm under the weapon as he tried a leg sweep against the back of the big man's knees.

Sabado must have heard the movement of Tinker's clothing; he'd been standing erect but, crouching with his left foot forward, he bent his knees in readiness stance and almost maintained his balance. Still, Tinker levered the weapon half out of his opponent's grasp as they twisted and fell together. Sabado's reflexes were a damnable marvel. He went with the spin, his left upper arm slapping the mat to break his fall while his left hand still held the foregrip of the H&K.

Tinker fell chest downward but hung onto the weapon, now with both hands, his knees flailing against Sabado's kidney pads as he wrenched at the prize. Then Sabado made his roll, coming astride the little recruit with both hands free to twist the H&K. The weapon's butt plate—it couldn't be called a stock—caught Tinker's elbow and in an instant Sabado had pressed the carbine's muzzle into the belly of the valiant little youth.

There was no muffled report. "Thank you, Tinker," said the big man, removing the bandanna and helping the recruit to his feet. He raised his voice, waving Tinker away. "For you smaller guys: in real combat, never go to the mat with somebody twice your size if you can help it—unless you're me. And you aren't. Symons! Front and center."

The bandanna went in place again under Symons's trembling fingers. Symons backed off several paces, took a deep breath in the silence, and sprinted with what he clearly intended to be a flying kick.

The listening Sabado was too quick. At the first sound of rapid footfalls he danced to one side, then back, and loosed several rounds toward the noise on full automatic setting.

Symons had dived, rolled, and was up again before Sabado could fire again at the sound. This time he caught the tall blond recruit in the breast and one arm with crimson gel blanks. "Aaaah, shit," said Symons. "You got me, Sheriff."

"You came on like a herd of turtles," said Sabado, and called for another recruit. No response. This game was altogether too realistic. The sergeant looked around him as if undecided; and Quantrill had seen that innocent-looking survey too many times. "Quantrill," Sabado cooed; "front and center."

Quantrill sighed, stepped forward, took the goggles and

tied the bandanna, crowding up against the big man, the
H&K at port-arms between them. With one hand Quantrill
rearranged the blindfold. "Get your goddam hand off that
safety," Sabado murmured, and Quantrill's first ploy failed.

The sturdy recruit backed away then, removing his belt in
an elaborate stripper's pantomime that brought laughter.
"Ah, haaaa, San Antone," someone mimicked an old Texan
refrain in falsetto, and then the other recruits began to get the
idea. Quantrill took off one brogan and held it like a long-
dead thing. Catcalls, mocking wagers against Quantrill,
other crowd noises masked his stealthy approach as he placed
each foot silently on the mats. His belt was looped through its
buckle, the free end wrapped in his fist, as he planted himself
before the grimly smiling Sabado. The sergeant whirled,
jabbed the weapon's muzzle forward, then back again, prob-
ing to learn if Quantrill was close behind him. The crowd
noises were working.

Quantrill made a slow, obvious, obscene gesture and the
squad renewed its mirth. Then he tossed the brogan to the
mat. The sudden burst of fifteen rounds, fired in a semicircu-
lar sweep, struck the mats five meters away from Sabado but,
as the sergeant pivoted again, Quantrill was ready. The belt
loop dropped over the weapon behind its front sight, the
recruit leaping behind the big man, the muzzle of the H&K
instantly jerked onto Sabado's shoulder as the belt half-
encircled his neck.

Sabado essayed a whirling kick but felt a pair of hands over
his trigger hand, a pair of legs tangled in his. The H&K began
to fire into the air, Sabado unable to prevent pressure on the
trigger, and as he tried to fall on his assailant he felt Quantrill
slide away. Again the vicious wrench at the weapon muzzle;
this time Sabado snatched at the belt, caught it, felt it come
free and without rising he swept the H&K in an arc.

Nothing. The magazine was empty.

Sabado stood up slowly, hauled the blindfold down. After
a moment he found Quantrill standing quietly among the
other recruits—as if he had been there all along. Sabado
stripped away the belt, tossed it to Quantrill, held up the

weapon. "It's still mine," he said. "One pace forward, Quantrill, and turn around."

Quantrill held out his arms, slowly turned for inspection. Sabado grunted. "What's that on your hand?"

"Blood, Sergeant," Quantrill said.

A nod. "Did I zap you?"

"Not with the H&K. I tore a fingernail."

"Doesn't count," said Sabado curtly. "We'll call this one a draw. Put your gear back on, recruit." Speaking for them all to hear: "He used his belt for leverage, and had you nik-niks to cover his noise. And he took his time, and used up all my ammo. And he didn't try me on the mat. Never mind all the things he did wrong; just remember what he did right. Dis-*missed*!"

After a moment of surprise, the squad vented a cheer, some pummeling Quantrill's back before squad leader Fiero herded them into ranks and marched them back to the jammed dormitory building they used as a barracks.

Sabado stood alone, pretending to study the fit of the H&K's magazine until he was certain that the squad could not see. Then and only then did he begin to rub the knot that was already forming on the big trapezius muscle that sloped from neck to shoulder.

Chapter 51

Sandys jurnal Dec. 24 Tus.
We must be near a town, they brout lots of flannel for us kids to make fresh air filtars. I wonder what town. Mistery!! Sombody has licker in the ranch house I thout it was aginst the religin of the church of the sacrifised lamb, they pray lots but they whip you lots more. Glad mom is pregnet, the profets think thats keen and let her alone. She told me remimber your only nine and I remimber. Shana is

*eleven shes one of Profet Jansens wives but Im only a
unfired vessel. I never heard such argumints, the profets
all say the perfect kingdom of god is ours to make but all
want to make it diffrent. If they think some god can make
them agree there sadly mistakin. But Im dumb even for
nine, no body cares much as long as I build good filtars.
Merry Xmas jurnal I wonder if Ted ever misses me.*

If he managed to consume enough beer, thought Quantrill,
he might forget other Christmas eves. He refused to look at
the decorated cedar that winked its tiny chemlamps in one
corner of the enlisted men's club; studied his reflection
behind the beer-only bar instead.

The seven weeks of basic training had seemed endless.
Now that he'd passed through the python of basic, he was
ready to be swallowed by a combat outfit. He couldn't wait to
see where it would shit him out. He'd know damned soon;
nobody stayed long at San Marcos after basic.

Someone had been trying to talk to him on the next stool
but finally gave it up. Someone else eased into the vacancy.
The civilian beertender served him immediately, without
discussion. It was like the rest of the Army, the choice was
beer or no beer.

He wondered suddenly if Cathy Palma was having a beer,
then wondered why he'd thought of her. Well, she was nearly
a friend. Too near. He wondered if Palma had located the
kid, Sandy; thought of the plastic tea set; smiled; found his
eyes misting. He thought then of the Heckler & Koch, and
wondered if he were crazy for itching to get his hands on one.

"So where d'you think they'll send you, Quantrill?" The
soft educated Tex-Mex drawl with its smooth sibilance made
him jerk around. Then he looked at the reflection instead.
Looking at Rafael Sabado through a distant mirror gave
Quantrill a sense of distance that he wanted very much. He
shrugged.

"I'm interested," Sabado went on. "Everybody's got a
theory, or a rumor. A few even have choices," he said,
picking his words carefully.

"Florida. Siberia. Canada. Fuckin' lot I care."

Sabado grunted, swilled half his beer, nodded to himself. "I lost my whole family in Houston—just like that," he said with a fingersnap. "That's why I care a whole *chingada* lot. Why don't you?"

"Why do you hate my guts?" Quantrill said it without thinking it out. It had been flicking at the tip of his mind for days.

"I'll answer that when you've done two things. Have a beer on me—and tell me why you think I hate your guts."

Quantrill had absorbed two beers already; just enough that he felt ready to catalogue all the special little treatments, the physical outrages, he had suffered at the hands of the big Chicano. It took him two minutes, all in a growl. He stared at the bubbles in the fresh beer before him.

"Take a swig," Sabado insisted, nodding at the beer; some intensity went out of his face as he watched Quantrill do it. "First, I never, *never* buy for anyone I hate. A point of honor; in *la raza* we live on those," he grinned ruefully. He glanced back at Quantrill's reflection. "As for hitting on you,—there isn't another man in your squad who gives me a workout. They're *dulces*, fuckin' candy. They lack the killer instinct—and you don't, *cabroncito*. How old are you anyway? No shit now; strictly off the record."

Quantrill shrugged, and told him.

"*Ay de mi,* you remind me of me," Sabado gurgled deep in his throat.

"You trying to say you kicked the shit out of me for seven weeks because you like me?"

A shadow passed across the handsome bronze face. "Close, compadre. But I swore off liking people for the duration. I think you did too. If you played your cards right, you could learn to do everything I do."

Quantrill absorbed this with the beer. "You think I joined up to be an instructor?"

"Not exactly. Something a whole lot worse—or better, if it's killing you like."

A quick darting glance directly at the big man beside him: "Why would I like it?"

The high cheekbones faced him. "Why wouldn't you?"
Then, studying Quantrill, he narrowed his eyes and purred,
"I think maybe you already know. I'd like to think so,
Quantrill. Tell you what; let's go outside and inhale some
fresh fallout. Trust me. I just don' want to go the macho route
with all these assbreaths looking on."

Quantrill decided he would soon be stoop-shouldered from
shrugging, but went outside with Sabado. He considered the
possibility that Sabado intended to pick a fight; shelved the
idea rather than reject it.

Standing beneath the single fluorescent light on the porch,
Sabado faced the youth. "Ever play 'gotcha'? Alias the
handslap game. Put your palms against mine." Sabado's
hands were out, palms up, fingers together.

Quantrill had played the game a few times, but denied it.
He hadn't enjoyed it anyway. No challenge.

But Sabado's right hand was less than a blur as it flicked up
and around to slap the back of Quantrill's left hand. One
instant he felt a cool callused palm against his, and in what
seemed the same instant that palm was elsewhere. "That's a
gotcha," Sabado murmured. "I keep on until I miss."

Quantrill saw that Sabado's slaps, nothing more than gentle taps, implied great control. He found very quickly that the
game could be steeped in psychological nuance. Those big
hands feinted, jittered, crossed over to underline their mas-
tery. Only when the sergeant tried to cross both hands in a
tour de force move did he miss with both.

"Your turn," Sabado smiled, and jerked his hands away
the instant Quantrill touched them. "No, keep your thumbs
in," he said as Quantrill used his left thumb to score.

"You were doing it."

"To spook you," Sabado said easily. "Makes it a cinch.
Your opponent gets fluttery guts and then he's lost."

Quantrill looked away with a headshake as if to some
onlooker. And scored with a double-crossover. He scored
with each hand; sometimes with eyes closed; sometimes
crossing. He did not miss once in fifty moves.

"Okay, game's over," Sabado grunted finally, as if troubled. "For awhile I couldn't figure out how you were doing it. Nobody's quicker than I am."

"You think I'm cheating?"

A snort. "No. I was wrong, that's all; somebody *is* quicker, *compadre*. Not because I was spooked. That's easy enough to prove."

Sabado placed his hands atop Quantrill's again, pointed out that neither of them betrayed hypertension with vibratory tremors. "Yeah, I thought so," Sabado said, lowering his hands. "You're a gunsel, all right."

A gunsel, he said, was an old tag. The Army psychomotor test people had culled it from studies on what they termed the 'gunslinger mystique'. The adrenal medulla produced both adrenalin and noradrenalin in response to stress, heightening the speed and strength of muscle response. In nearly all humans were emotional side effects as well as physical, a shakiness that could interfere with coordination, that could even produce panic or unconsciousness.

But in every million humans were a few who made optimum stress-management responses. Those few, said Sabado, got the advantages of their adrenal glands without the disadvantages. "That's me," he added, "and that's you. In the 1880's we'd've been gunslingers. Nowadays there isn't much call for that. But the Army needs a few gunsels, people who can act alone under special hazards. I'm a referral service for those few."

Quantril checked his lapel dosimeter, relieved to find that they were taking only a fraction of a rad per hour outside. "How do they use those guys, Sergeant: Something like a regimental combat team?"

A long slow smiling headshake. "More effective than that, with lower profile. When I said 'alone' I meant it, Quantrill."

"Doesn't sound like the Army to me."

"Doesn't, does it?" Sabado pursed his lips reflectively. "But let's suppose there was a foreign national, someone who did top-level liaison between the President and, ah, another NATO country. Run it on down with me: suppose this bastard was a mole—a deep-cover SinoInd agent—who was pinpointing our key installations to be nuked on cue. Like the Shenandoah Command Center, or the Grand Island Quartermaster complex.''

Quantrill's eyes widened. Both of those underground centers had been secret until they'd taken consecutive impact nukes, drilling down into bedrock to atomize a President and a supply center. ''I guess the FBI would shoot him on sight,'' he said.

''The feebies don't ice folks on contract these days. Some CIA people do, but not on US soil. Treasury Department sticks to other duties. That leaves military intelligence, *compadre*.'' Sabado's eyes were glimmering slits in the half-light. ''I hear the Army has such an agency. I would imagine they'd have a few gunsels trainable to go anywhere, anytime, to complete an assignment. The question is: *are you interested*?''

''This is crazy, Sergeant. I mean, it can't be this simple—''

''It isn't simple; but this is how it starts. Did you think they'd advertise in the Ft. Worth *Star-Telegram*?''

''No-o-o, but if they did they wouldn't ask for anybody fifteen years old.''

''Don't second-guess the Service. They'd be interested in a toddler if he had your reflexes—but it shit-sure isn't an open sesame, they run you through a heavy wringer before they take you. *If* they take you. I gave somebody your name a week ago; surely you don' think I'd make this pitch unless somebody higher up gave the word. But I've told you everything I can until I get a commitment. *Yes or no*?''

A youth came out the door, affixing his headgear, nodding to the pair who stood near. Quantrill smiled, nodded back, waited until they were alone again. ''When do you need my answer?''

''Right now. I didn't come here tonight because I like green beer. Something else that should go without saying but I'll say it anyhow: whatever you answer, you don' even hint to anybody about our little talk. I'd have to say I lie a lot. I wouldn' like that.''

Quantrill took a long breath; expelled it. ''Okay, I'm still not sure I believe it. But I'll do it. It sure isn't what I had in mind when I joined up, Sergeant. You sure I won't wind up with an assignment like yours?''

He had never heard Sabado laugh and was surprised at the musical gurgle deep in his chest. ''This isn't an assignment, Quantrill; this is what I ask for *between* assignments. I'm not always a sergeant. It depends,'' he added vaguely.

This Sabado was subtly different from the big swaggerer on the practice mats. The difference was unsettling until Quantrill realized it lay in the man's speech patterns. Tonight Sabado was relaxing, letting his Tex-Mex accent have its way. Tonight Rafael Sabado was not bothering with bullshit.

''If he plays a lot of parts, a gunsel must get a lot of ID's,'' said Quantrill.

''Sure. But none to link him with 'T' Section. For what it's worth, a gunsel can't flash an ID if he gets in trouble on assignment. And he's up against people who know some tricks—cosmetic work, false prints, martial arts—so he gets the best training Uncle can provide. What he doesn't get is any promise about tomorrow.''

''At least you're up front about it. I gather a gunsel doesn't take prisoners.''

''If they need the quarry alive, the feebies can handle it. If they don't, somebody in T Section gets the assignment.''

''What does 'T' stand for?''

''Terminate.''

''I hope they terminated the guy who pinpointed Shenandoah.''

''What if I tol' you it was a woman, *compadre*?''

''I dunno. I guess it wouldn't make any difference.''

''It didn't,'' Sabado grunted. ''A gunsel takes what comes.'' Pause; flicker of something unsaid in the face. ''He has to. You'll see. You have to make up your mind that T Section chose you and your assignment for a good reason.

You may never know how much you've shortened the war,
how many lives you save, but," he gave a sly chuckle, "you
get to see results first-hand. More gratifying than lugging
mortar rounds in fucking Siberia."

"Too bad; in a way I was wondering what Siberia's like."

"You might find out if you flunk. Don't. Now get some
sleep. Tomorrow right after rollcall, you make sick call.
Take a book with you. Then ask to see Major Lazarus. That's
all. Now repeat that."

"Uh,—sleep. Sick call after rollcall, ask for Major
Lazarus."

"Take a book, *compadre*."

"Right." Quantrill watched the big man take the stairs
two at a time; wondered if Sabado really did lie a lot;
wondered if there really was a Major Lazarus.

Chapter 52

Perhaps Major Lazarus existed. Quantrill never met him,
but the fact that he became the only occupant of an examina-
tion room told him something. There were very few empty
rooms in San Marcos.

The avuncular white-haired medic who bade him strip was
a captain wearing a cool blue smock and a warm pink smile.
Quantrill found some of the exam, like the prostate probe,
familiar. The elastic straps, fitted as anklet, wristlet, and
headband, placed unfamiliar devices next to his skin. Quantrill guessed they were feeding data to the computer terminal
on the desk while he did calisthenics.

The medic was polite, anonymous, mildly interested in the
bullet wound, more interested in Quantrill's microfiche record. When he asked whether Private Quantrill had ever shot
to kill, Quantrill decided that someone had been to considerable trouble to check his recent past.

"They were shooting at me," he said defensively.

"Just answer the question, son."

"Yes, I did. I think I got him."

"I'm not judging you. And I'll only ask one more question along this line." A brief silence before, "Did you ever kill anyone, or try to, before that night at Oak Ridge?"

"No." The question, he thought, had been phrased nicely. There were more questions: childhood disease, sexual experiences, enduring friendships, special fears. Quantrill answered it all truthfully.

The psychomotor and sensory acuity tests seemed simpler than they were because the equipment was highly refined. The helmet adjusted snugly, especially around his eyes and ears so that he became momentarily blind and, except for the medic's voice in his headphones, deaf. The gloves were thin knit fabric with slender instrumentation wafers bonded to each gauntlet. When the animated displays were focused, Quantrill saw a red dot move, and snapped his fingers the instant the dot touched an edge of the maze it traversed. Then he found that he could guide the dot by moving his right index finger, and enjoyed the game. He heard various tones, tapped when he first heard them. He touched his forefingers together blindly, then tried it when the display showed an animated view of his hands before him. He smiled grimly as he learned to ignore the false information on the display. Finally came the red dot again, this time an animated mosquito that appeared and winked out repeatedly as he tried to catch it between thumb and forefinger.

Then he sat quietly like a young hooded falcon, listening to the faint running monologue in his headphones, unable to see the medic's astonishment at the test results. He accepted the flaccid mouthpiece, drew deep breaths, expelled them, heard the medic compliment him on his lung capacity. When he toppled forward, he did not feel the cradling arms.

Chapter 53

Christmas dinner, for Quantrill, was intravenous. So were all his meals for the following week. He was wholly unaware of his encapsulation and shipment in the McDonnell that snatched up two more capsules in Artesia and Flagstaff. Nor did he awaken during that week, though dimly aware of a dream in which faceless interrogators pried at embedded memories.

Shortly before noon on the third of January, 1997, he awoke slowly, stretched until his joints cracks. He winced at a slight pain low on his right abdomen. He sniffed an aroma, salivated, then eased down from the bed and stopped naked before the big windows to stare in disbelief. His first coherent thought was that he had to be dead, or still asleep.

His view was magnificent. Through the multipaned bay window he could see the tops of great trees, rolling wooded hillocks that fell away to a shoreline a few klicks away. The room was more than sumptuous, its furniture and decorations a collection of many early styles. His bed was a four-poster. Tapestries covered one wall and the window niches in a second wall were lined with some of the most intricate laser carvings he had ever seen—either that, or genuine hand carvings, which would make the room beyond price. He was persuaded that the exprience was real by the growl in his belly and by the study carrel, a gleaming plebeian model of state-of-the-art efficiency that stood against one wall like a Mondrian among El Grecos. Its terminal display was lit, and above the printed lines ran a legend that a more wakeful Quantrill would have spotted instantly: WELCOME TO SAN SIMEON.

The holo keyboard was standard. Assured that brunch awaited him in the adjoining bathroom, he ignored his belly long enough to read more, sitting nude at the carrel. Quantrill was for all practical purposes a civilian restricted within the fenced hilltop of San Simeon, a California State Historical Monument leased by Hunter-Liggett military reservation for the use of T Section.

Whoever had crafted the message had probably worked for a chamber of commerce somewhere. The location and quasi-public nature of this monument, the fabled structures and grounds of Hearst's Castle, provided an ideal ambience for training the men and women of T Section. Mr. Quantrill would be personally welcomed at four PM in his room. Until then he was at liberty to use the carrel, peruse a vintage slick-paper brochure praising the conceit of Citizen Hearst, or stroll the grounds—so long as he did not enter any structure but his own two rooms in the little (seventeen rooms!) guest house below the castle. He might notice others on the broad balconies and paths, but must ignore them. Mr. Quantrill might find it helpful to orient himself to his quarters by noting the twin towers of the castle.

He found a sybarite's meal—juice, coffee, steak and eggs, sourdough bread with garlic butter, and a tantalizing sliver of cheesecake—awaiting him, each in controlled-temperature containers on a shelf in the ornate bathroom. A vague resentment smouldered in him; had he gone through the rigors of basic to be pampered, or to fight?

On impulse he tried the bathwater taps, realized he had not soaked in a tub for months. His irritation dwindled; the steak and the stroll could wait. Bending to test the bathwater, he winced again, touched his abdomen. The appendectomy scar was clean, but it had not been there before. Quantrill wondered how long he had been asleep; he did feel a bit weak.

He luxuriated in the ancient tub until hunger drove him out, then consumed every scrap of his meal, never once consulting a mirror until after he had found the small wardrobe in the bedroom. The expensive supple brown loafers fitted to perfection; he assumed that the joggers would, too. He chose the beltless fawn slacks instead of sweatsuit or denims, a yellow vee-necked pullover from the half-dozen shirts, and grinned to himself almost apologetically as he strapped the wristwatch on en route to the bathroom mirror.

This kind of coddling still seemed a hell of a way to fight a war.

A hell of a way, indeed. The mirror revealed a well-dressed young man of leisure, whose smooth face was understandably perplexed. The face, Quantrill saw, was older. And not quite his own.

Chapter 54

The knock came two minutes early; tentative raps on the massive wooden door. Quantrill opened it intending to be surly, but changed his mind in an instant. She was a stunner.

"You're Ted Quantrill, I'm told. May I come in? Or would you rather explore the grounds?" Her voice was musical, her olive skin flawless; her name, she said, was Marbrye Sanger. Quantrill decided she was the kind of college girl for whom tight slacks had been designed.

"I've, uh, looked around some. Getting chilly out there," he waved toward the evening haze, then stumped to one side, made maladroit by her presence. "C'mon in; it's warm."

She tossed him a preheated smile, but he fumbled it badly. Evidently she had grown accustomed to the setting and to youths who fell before her like conversational saplings. "I bet you haven't found the booze." He hadn't. She showed him the false front in the rococo cabinet, the ice cooler, the vodka and bourbon, the mixers; and then she made them each a drink before folding the long legs beneath her on the bench at the big window.

"Don't let all this put you off," she said, indicating the room. "It came with the lease but for God's sake don't break anything. Unless you're better than I am at asking questions to a library carrel, you must be edgy as a straight razor by now. Any questions?"

He began with the obvious. What the hell had they done to his face, and how? Did Marbrye Sanger have the foggiest idea how this gargantuan dollhouse on a mountaintop could be tied in with pursuing a war, and where the goddam hell was everybody, and when were they going to get on with it, and by the way, what was a girl like her doing in a place like this?

San Simeon, she replied, was a world to itself. Its staff was housed in clapboard bungalows nestled among the slopes below the 'big house', as everyone called the castle, and it had been William Randolph Hearst's royal hostel a half-century before. Then the place became a state monument, with sightseers bussed from a parking lot several klicks away for an hour-long guided tour of the big house and what was left of the vineyard, the zoo, the outrageously lavish mosaic pool, and statuary ranging from the sublime to the plain silly. "It's still open on weekends, war or no war. Now you tell me, what could be a more unlikely place for T Section training than a place with tourists barging around snapping holomatics?"

"Unlikely is dead right. About as unlikely as my face."

She sipped her bourbon, squinted at him in the fading light, cocked her head and let her short chestnut curls fall loose as she studied him. If Marbrye Sanger did not know how delicious she looked, thought Quantrill, she was dumber than she seemed. She took another sip without looking away, licked her lips delicately, said, "Quit bitching, Mr. Q. They did some microsurgery on me, too, but as soon as I quit biting my cheeks I got used to it. You look pretty damn' good to me. Were you even better before?"

His glass was empty, his patience draining away as well. "I was *me* before," he said, heading for the bourbon already a bit light-headed. "How the fuck, 'scuse me, I'm fresh from basic training, how'd they do it so fast? And I'm not 'Mr. Q', I'm Private Ted Quantrill and I wonder when the training starts."

"You're not a private, Ted." The voice was still musical,

but low and earnest. ''Your pay is a three-striper's, same as mine, and you'll have your fill of training before you leave this lotus-land.''

''But there must be somebody I report to.''

''You mean Control? Take it from me,'' she smiled, ''Control doesn't impose any hut-hut stuff unless you need it. You'll find out about that in a class we call 'Cover'; the Army more or less took us apart and rebuilt us before we got here. It's a departure from other intelligence schools, but one of the things they know about you is that you don't need saluting or motivating. Gunsels just don't, I guess. None of us do.''

Quantrill poured himself a generous slug of bourbon. ''What if I motivated myself down the mountain and hitched a ride somewhere?''

''I imagine Control would disappear you—but as far as I know, that's never happened. *They know* what you want, Ted.'' For a moment the brown eyes lit with an odd intensity, the nostrils flared above an aggressive grin. ''You have the right stuff to take direct action; personal action. Once they weed out the crazies—the ones who just get their jollies from icing people in general—they come down to us. We have the natural equipment to face an enemy one-on-one, and we're willing to flog like hell for the chance. I don't think you'd be here if you wanted anything more than you want that.''

Studying the girl, Quantrill sensed her zeal to destroy the destroyers, to hunt the hunters. Evidently he had joined the right club. He smiled and tried to sip without choking.

She watched him drink. ''They say bourbon affects people's sex drive. D'you think it interferes or helps?''

He spilled a little, gulped a little. ''I'm not sure.''

She uncoiled, kicked off her wedgies, a smile of bogus innocence transfixing him as she stepped nearer. Her free hand went under his arm, her cheek nuzzling his. ''We could find out. Actually I have a little coke; they didn't search me for my stash—and guess where I keep mine,'' she giggled.

Too kittenishly. He felt lithe muscle in her casual embrace; sensed a tension, a spring-loaded trigger, in her willingness. His erection died at birth, and he knew she was crowded near enough to notice. "Maybe later," he murmured, patting her shoulder. Jee*zus* but she was tempting; and so was the free alcohol, and for that matter the offer of a free body-search to find forbidden drugs within other delights.

Which made it all clearly a setup. He strode to the cabinet again, filled his glass with mixer. Some small imp made him sway his hips as he moved to the bed and sat down, kicking off his shoes in bald imitation of her, patting the rumpled coverlet. He was uncertain about the twitches on the lovely face, but she sat with him and sipped again. "Now," he said with as much nasal sensuality as he could muster, "tell me about T Section."

Her smile was dazzling this time, her body shaking with repressed mirth. "Don't you like me?"

He stared at her breasts, her high-arched insteps, her mouth. "You are without question a Nobel Prize pussy, Sanger, and I promise to think about you later tonight," he said in open insolence.

Her smile faltered under his scrutiny. There was something of relief and of genuine wistfulness in her, "I'll accept that, Quantrill. It's costing me, but I'll accept it."

"Now about T Section," he prodded.

It was a zero-sum world, she sighed. Every move you made in T Section was a step forward or backward for somebody. If you had minor weaknesses they would be found and expunged. Major weaknesses got you bounced. You were issued recorders, keyboard cassettes, anything within reason for the classes which were held in upper rooms of the big house, far from the tourist route. You could spend as little time as you liked studying. You were smart to study a lot, because Control was anxious to use only the very best candidates. T Section would give you every tool to succeed, every opportunity to fail—and cardinal sin number one was the failure of common sense.

Quantrill stared at his drink. Common sense told him he'd gulped that first glass too quickly; anything that impaired your control had to be an error. "I can't read your mind," he said. "When do I get a list of do's and don'ts?"

"Tomorrow's Saturday," she said as if she thought she were answering his question. "Your carrel will wake you early and someone will come for you. We'll be doing covert weapons work on the range—there's half a county for us to use here—so wear jeans, long-sleeved shirt, and sneakers." She took a deliberate sip of her drink, eyed him. "Are we going to let this nice big bed go to waste?"

Instantly: "Is sex a failure of common sense?"

"Sometimes yes, sometimes no," she shrugged, and used a finger to trace the seam on his pullover. "Mm; nice shoulders."

He stared into her eyes, smiled sadly. "I think I'd like a rain check," he husked.

"It'll be a long time before the rain stops," she said with nonchalance, slipping to the floor, scuffing into her shoes. "I live on the floor below, and I have some cramming to do. See you in class."

He walked with her to the door, suffused with a mixture of relief, desire, and uncertainty. "I'll tell you something, Marbrye Sanger, this has been the damnedest welcome I ever got. I need to sort things out."

"Don't worry about it," she said with the barest hint of pique. "You haven't flunked yet." Her departing footfalls were almost noiseless in the evening gloom.

Quantrill was still standing in the doorway when the carrel chimed for attention. He found that his name was now an input code and the terminal would answer certain queries from typed input; no voice input accepted.

When and where would he find supper? He wouldn't, that night.

What was the status of Marbrie Sanger? Marbrye—the correction was underlined—Sanger was an advanced trainee in T Section; 'Q' clearance, no on-site restriction.

Why had Sanger visited Quantrill? A multiplex enticement-frustration test.

"Shit," he muttered, and typed another question: had he passed? No comment.

The terminal verified Sanger's instructions for the next

day, adding that meals would be provided. As afterthought, he asked what courses he would take. He found the list daunting:

COVER, Unofficial, and Control
CRYPTANALYSIS
INTELLIGENCE, Theory
INVESTIGATION, Methods
LINGUISTICS
PSYCHOLOGY, Criminal
PSYCHOLOGY, Social
SCIENCE, Military, unconventional
SCIENCE, Political, and Indoctrination
SURVEILLANCE, Use and Nullification
TERMINATIONS, Covert, and Pursuit
WEAPONS, Covert and Overt

The terminal would give no coursework details. Quantrill suspected that the Sanger hotsy had already reported the results of her welcome; dimly perceived that T Section might have monitored their brief meeting. It did not yet occur to him that San Simeon might be instrumented in such a way that Marbrye Sanger had no need to report; nor that Control, while testing his responses to uncertainty, had already begun the process of instilling in him a mild and necessary paranoia.

Chapter 55

Within a few days Quantrill learned to accept the bizarre setting in which he might jog five klicks with a half-dozen other trainees to a refurbished barn for a class; or find a *dubok,* a message drop, while alone with memorized instructions. He saw the lissome Sanger only in cryptanalysis class; she ignored him. At no time did any class, either in the big house or outside it, contain more than eight members.

Much of the training pitted trainees against each other; no

one had to be cautioned against forming close friendships. He failed to locate the scalpel tip which little Barbara Zachary had cyanoacrylated to the back of her neck until the 'unconscious' Zachary pressed it to his throat—but he did not repeat that failure. He forgot that a one-time cipher could be generated from a telephone directory, and drew two extra cryptanalysis tasks that took him half a night to complete. The youngest of the trainees, Quantrill forgot a lot of things; but only once.

He would never forget his instructors. Marty Cross was half Cheyenne and all whip leather, a wizened wisp of a man so adept at covert pursuit that he seemed to simply materialize behind the trainee he stalked. It was Cross who taught Quantrill to become utterly still; so inert that he could stand erect in a cluttered room and be unnoticed for vital seconds.

Sean Lasser, whose middle-aged paunch danced when he laughed, always had something to laugh about after submitting to a search. Quantrill exulted the day he identified Lasser's signet ring as a garrotte complete with spring-wound wire.

Seth Howell, heavy-bodied with spidery arms and legs, had a whispery tenor and a gift for phrasing the dullest indoctrination material as though analyzing an invisible cud of tobacco. Craggy of face, prematurely graying, Howell claimed a hitch in the quad-service Rapid Deployment Force—and another in the maximum-security federal prison in Marion, Illinois. Howell's adumbration of the current political mess might not be the whole truth, but it didn't put you to sleep either. He took, for example, the Starlinger-Ahbez hypothesis.

Starlinger, a German, had long ago warned of China's expansive dreams, whatever denials she might make. With her southern borders already overpopulated, China would eventually find it necessary to expand into underpopulated Siberia.

Ahbez, a NATO strategist from Turkey, had added an alternative. China might indeed be able to expand southward if her southern neighbors, for whatever reason, became underpopulated. Ahbez theorized that China might find ways to depopulate India, or the Vietnamese peninsula, without overtly declaring war on them. She might even maintain an outward alliance while draining that ally of people.

"Now, Ahbez is a freak about germ warfare," Howell drawled, his Colorado twang lending him the air of an inspired hick; "and he figgered China might dump a few bugs down south. Well, she didn't; she gave the goddam Injuns the paranthrax they dumped on *us*. Makes sense. China had the technology, and thought she could hamstring us and let India take the heat.

"That explains why China didn't dump paranthrax on the RUS. She wants to avoid retaliation in kind, and depletion of RUS livestock she intends to own later. But if the Allies start an epidemic in India,—well, China's natural borders to the south could protect her long enough to produce a defense. Meanwhile, India would go belly-up.

"We think China's waiting for us to do just that. But guess what we've spotted from orbit." Howell snapped the holo projector on; the display was a map of the SinoInd lands. He spread one big hand like a tarantula, placed fingertips on Cambodia, Laos, and the other Viet republics, and slid the tarantula toward China's heartland, Szechuan. "Viets. More of 'em than you *ever* saw, swarming north like ants as far as the Yangtse River.

"Some are doing winter harvests in Yunnan, feeding others who're training in little groups all over south China. And then a lot are disappearing along the Yangtse. Now, the Yangtse's a muddy bitch; even infrared doesn't tell us what's going on under its surface. Some Viets are going upriver, possibly through pressure locks under the dams that're left. One hell of a lot of Viets are popping up on the Kazakhstan front. *You* guess where all the rest are."

"Spam?" Quantrill could not resist the awful jest.

"That's been discussed," Howell said. "Cold storage, too. But we think they're going underground, trained as factory workers while they mass for a hundred-division offensive. Little factories, lots of 'em; a cottage-industry war. It'd be futile to impact-nuke every square meter of Szechuan. Just maybe, it's time we gave the Sinos a taste of their own medicine in Szechuan.''

Graeme Duff, the bull-necked trainee from Minneapolis: ''How do we send germs down into filtered tunnels?''

''Wouldn't the Sinos like to know?'' Howell's smile was one-sided. ''You can bet they have moles boring around every lab in this country, trying to dope that one out. And that,'' he said, snapping off the projector, ''is where gunsels like you come in.''

''We're supposed to penetrate deep cover?'' Zachary was always thinking two steps ahead, thought Quantrill enviously.

''Other people are trained for that. They finger the mole; you take him—or her—out. Usually you just disappear him. That leaves the other side wondering if we've turned him.

''Chances are, you'd get a different assignment against certain folks in media.'' He waited for the murmur of surprise to abate. ''Do I have to tell you how important our media are in reassuring what's left of this country that we're winning—whether we are or not? Face it: we've lost half our population and the other half needs its daily holo fix! The SinoInds would love to nuke NBN's world of make-believe, if they knew where our production centers are. Damn' few foreign stars or directors know; we can't be absolutely sure of their loyalties.''

''Rivas Paloma,'' said elegant young Goldhaber, with a surgeon's fingersnap. ''Killed in a strafing on location in Mazatlan. Am I right?''

''The Spanish film industry's loss,'' said Howell obliquely, ''may have been NATO's gain.''

''But Paloma got an Oscar for directing an anti-Chinese movie,'' said Goldhaber, frowning. You could depend on the well-born Goldhaber for cultural snippets.

''If he was an assignment—I say *if*—then he was a mole. Depend on it.''

''I guess we have to.''

The thin voice was almost a falsetto whisper: "Oh, yes. You literally bet your life you have to. Media star, bishop or bird colonel: if Control says he goes, he goes.

"Which reminds me." Did Seth Howell betray faint cynicism? Quantrill could not be sure as the instructor continued, "Never doubt for a second that President Collier was a lucky break for this country. The Mormons, and nobody else in the US, were ready for this war. They're going to pull us through if we follow the right path. In a war of survival we can't afford the sedition of every Jew and Catholic who won't accept a moral imperative.

"But the LDS has more splinter groups than a toothpick factory. Some of 'em are just wrong. Others are violently opposed to the administration—and they are *dead* wrong."

Kent Ethridge, the gymnast from Iowa State, spoke as rarely as Quantrill. "In other words," he said slowly, "a war of religious extermination."

"What d'you think the AIR confederacy is doing," asked Howell.

"Threatening Jews," said Goldhaber, not smiling.

"What if Control identified someone in the Jewish Defense League who was trying to assassinate your President," Howell asked.

"Ice him," Goldhaber replied. "No religion is more important than my country."

Howell stared out the window for a long time, then glanced at each of his trainees. "Thanks to the ho-hum outlook most Americans had before last August, one religion *is* your country. That's overstated a mite, but it's closer to the facts every day."

"I'm not exactly wild," said Goldhaber, "about joining the LDS."

"A gunsel," Howell snorted, "is not exactly eligible." The tone of his voice put an end to one unsettling topic, and led Howell to the unsettled problems between the Allies.

Chapter 55

The US, as Howell put it, had a neighbor problem. We needed Mexican oil and were still getting it; but the capitalist, Mormon Collier administration could not entirely satisfy socialist, Catholic Mexico of our continuing good will. One needed only study the bloody clashes between Mormon anglos and Catholic latinos in the American southwest. Already the media were spiking rumors that White House Central might relocate again from its New Mexico warrens.

Canada, too, had a strong gentile distaste for the new turn in our political path, but chose to treat it as a temporary aberration. Canada's gross national product and her technologies had swelled to the point where she no longer needed to feel defensive about her southern sister. Rather, said Howell, she began to feel all too protective. From the remnants of Maine to the desperate survivors freezing in Michigan, Canadian currency was now more readily acceptable than US greenbacks. Because Canada was our conduit to Asian battlefields and a potential source of fossil fuel, the Collier administration kept a discreet silence on the currency question. But—Seth Howell chose his words with great care in describing US/Canadian relations—White House Central had an obvious problem. Quantrill had to check the definition of the key word, 'hegemony'.

Meanwhile, Canada worried about her RUS alliance. It was not just a question of competition for polar resources, but also of a big new semi-capitalist union adjacent to an enormous semi-Marxist union. Canadians never tired of warning that the Russians had learned nothing but caution in their 1985 debacle. After the RUS learned to modernize their own frozen northlands and to fully exploit their resources, she would doubtless covet Canada's.

Doubtless. But all that could be dealt with later; the spectre of a Chinese Siberia frightened the Canadians even more than

Russians did. Canada stretched out her hand to the RUS, and counted her fingers.

If anyone expected the Russians to make a big display of thanks for Canadian aid, he courted disappointment. The official line from Tass maintained that the ice-crusted Kazakhstan front held the key to western survival. The RUS Supreme Council no longer blustered in blunt ideological jargon terms for foreign audiences. The old words could be dusted off again after the war. The RUS relied instead on a partly genuine, partly spurious identification with the west, and backed the claim with a few gestures such as the Frisbees they exported for US deployment. Without question, the Frisbees had been a major factor in limiting the Indian-supplied invasion of Florida. Just as surely, that invasion was doomed anyway by the vulnerability of its supply lines. Its Latin American supply sources evaporated with the 'Libyan' nuke strikes on Latin American ports, and excepting the few supply submersibles India had punched through the gauntlet of Allied hunter-killer teams, the invaders were now on their own. Tampa Bay would hold.

A few nations were still seeking ways to turn a global atrocity into local profit. Neutral Sweden remembered her windfalls in World War II and sought to employ her merchant fleet as a pipeline for refugees. She could rake in the krona by providing safe floating platforms for those who could pay the price. Brazil, whose neutrality leaned toward the SinoInds, listened to the Swedes; thought she might slash her huge external debt by billions of cruzeiros; and magnanimously offered sanctuary to SinoInd refugees—prepaid in precious metal which Indians had in quantity.

But Argentina and Peru bordered Brazil, and had scarifying debts of their own. They promptly offered to accept Allied refugees for so many pesos and sols per head, whether they came by Swedish surface ships or waterwings. Brazil instantly reconsidered her offer. She needed high technology, not a prefabricated war. The Swedes sulked, and went on selling machine tools to both sides.

Yet America's most sharply-felt boundary was internal:

the paranthrax quarantine line which ran up the Mississippi,
then the Ohio, extending to Lake Erie via the Ohio state line.
Early in February of 1997, the long-awaited vaccine was
ready for airdrop, packaged as pressure-fed intramuscular
injection ampoules for the millions of Americans in our
eastern states. The first drops were made in Tampa and
Orlando; the health of our swamp guerrillas was more immediately important than that of miners in West Virginia.

Americans knew, because the holo told them, that the
quarantine would be lifted in time. But even the reassurances
of Eve Simpson could not counter a suspicion that paranthrax
spores might lie dormant for decades. Rumors among the
well-informed suggested that the quarantine would stay in
effect until every mammal in the US was vaccinated. Until
then, it was said, quarantine-runners would be shot on sight.
Even quintessential materiel like titanium from mines in New
York and Virginia was refined and packaged hot, for hot
shipment through Cincinnati. No one needed worry about
any bug surviving a ride on *that* stuff.

The American west and midwest fared as well as could be
expected, as reclamation teams cleared debris from city sites
most vital to the war effort. Bakersfield had been a petroleum
nexus and would be again; the burly oilfield workers learned
new skills while revitalizing the city. Fresno, Lubbock,
Wichita, and Des Moines were rapidly rebuilt into the agrarian centers they had been before. The first rolling stock into
Lubbock's rail yards brought cultivation equipment to plant
more Jojoba and variant Euphorbia than cotton. You could
dress in cowhides if necessary, but you couldn't run the
railroads on cottonseed oil. We did not expect vegetable oils
to become a cheap mainstay. We could only hope they would
fill the gaps in our production of oil from wells and Colorado
shale.

Faced with widespread demolition of energy sources,
President Collier gave a nod of the leonine head to fission
reactors. Americans had learned to accept the pervasiveness
of ionizing radiation; well then, they would learn to accept
fission reactors again. Collier was initially heartened by the

simultaneous revelations of a dozen LDS Apostles, all divinely guided to press for more reactors. God had not told anyone how they could be secretly built on short notice. Nor had the Deity hinted that nuclear reactors might become targets of gentiles who would view fission reactors as a symbol of a repressive theocracy. The President went ahead with a sense of disquiet. In the future, he felt, it might be wiser to keep these multiple revelations out of the eye of the gentile public.

And for that, he would need more control of media.

Chapter 57

"Now you're being testy, Eve," said Rudolf Berg, one of NBN's senior VP's. "Some might even say unpatriotic."

Eve Simpson slid from the exercise machine, mopping her forehead as she glared from Berg to the beach far below. Wind currents from Santa Barbara and Los Angeles had not been kind in March. Eve missed her little outings, and somebody had to pay . . . "Brucie, get me a Drambuie."

"Calories, Eve," he clucked.

She would not look toward the mirror in the exercise room; she knew what it would tell her. Those extra few kilos were showing at her waist and chin. "A joint then," she raged. "A cup of hemlock, Bruce; something! Rudy here has Brigham-friggin' City on his brain!"

"I'm only thinking of the network and your future, Eve," said Berg. "You can't really expect the President to drop everything and come here."

"I'm becoming nothing more than an interviewer," she spat, then inhaled on the proffered filter-tip joint.

Berg met her anger with aplomb, a grey little man with sequined ideas. Even Professor Kelsey praised Berg's sensitivity to the public pulse. "You're playing a vital role as sugar-tit, Eve. Don't knock it. You have more credibility now than you ever had.''

"I have more tit, you mean," she grumbled. ''Is there no such thing as a low-calorie London broil?'' She inhaled again; held it.

"Eat less, chase your young men more.'' Berg scratched his nose to hide his expression. ''I should imagine there are enough studly young priests in Brigham City to please you.''

"Salt Lake City's still hot,'' she accused, exhaling as if Berg himself had dropped the single nuke that exploded over North Temple Street.

"They'll take you around it, as you very well know. And the Gulf of Kutch invasion is *really* hot, Eve. Media hot.'' His tone said that the wheedling phase was over. Her irises said that the marijuana was taking effect. ''It's the biggest positive step in this war, and you can get an exclusive from Yale Collier himself—but it won't wait. You'll have to be on that shuttle in an hour or we go with Lindermann. And the President, I'm told, was looking forward to a chat with you beforehand.''

Berg did know how to pull triggers. Eve despised the upstart Ynga Lindermann with her exotic accent and slender rump, whom NBN was surely grooming as a capital-P Personality. Berg knew, too, that Eve valued her tête-á-têtes with men of great power. She hoped that Berg would never guess how simply and directly that aura of power affected her sexually. Even spindly little Berg, when he was wheeling and dealing, made Evie itch.

Of course the idea of virile, farm-raised young Mormon men gave her a different itch; less deeply psychic, much easier to scratch. Also, the Gulf of Kutch affair was more than just prime time. It was a world series-super bowl-Oscar night parlay, and an exclusive summary with Collier was worth a seventy share of the public's attention. ''Get wardrobe and makeup alerted,'' Eve sighed; ''and remember, you owe me for this one.''

Before she caught the hovership to the Lancaster shuttle, Eve managed a brief video call to her mentor, Kelsey. "You must evince genuine confidence in the church's infallibility," Kelsey counseled in his overblown academese that always made Eve feel like screaming. "Be deferential and dress demurely, and don't hold eye contact with him. The President knows you only as America's sweetheart; don't violate his expectations.

"Drop a few terms about demographics and sub rosa media alliances—just enought to dispel any idea that your youth is equivalent to political naivete. Ah, you might drop my name once. Not twice. Don't argue with anything he says. If the President is convinced you are in thrall to his charisma in your personal private session, this relationship could have an incipient importance far beyond your career at NBN."

"And you could pull strings through me, Doc," she teased. "Just between us, is the Kutch invasion really anything more than a snatch-and-grab raid for morale purposes?"

"Immensely more," he nodded, and switched off.

Eve grabbed the latest microfile on her way to the hovership, scanning press releases from ComCenPac in Hawaii. Kelsey had not exaggerated. An Allied airborne brigade dropped into Gujarat lowlands might, by itself, have been only a sacrifice move like the infamous old Dieppe raid—but not when joined by five American divisions sweeping in from the Arabian Sea, with more on the way.

Chapter 58

Lieutenant Mills fingerprint-signed the latest dispatch and keyed it for transmission to stateside censors, having performed his own deft deletions on messages that referred, however vaguely, to Project Phillipus. Phillip II had fielded an enormous armada in 1588 A.D.; thanks to the upgraded

Israeli weapon, US/RUS Allies now had ghost armadas of any size we liked.

We had used the deception only once before, to disguise our Trident strikes on Latin American ports. This time the SinoInds might know the nature of the ruse, might find ways to penetrate it the next time. But this time Phillipus had sent waves of Indian interceptors eastward into the Bay of Bengal in search of an invasion force that did not exist beyond a token force. The real invasion had proceeded north from Diego Garcia into the Arabian Sea, then under its cloak of electronic invisibility to the Gulf of Kutch on India's western flank.

The thirty transmach transports, each lumbering up from Diego Garcia with upwards of an entire airborne company including weapons, had been the last force to leave the island and the first to cross Indian shores three hours before dawn on Sunday, 9 March. The scores of huge skirted hovercraft, prefabricated in Australia and sub-freighted as nested modules to the island, were even slower; had embarked for India the previous evening with their own attack choppers running as vanguard. Each craft carried its battalion, self-sufficient with antitank weapons, hoverchoppers, and rations for a week. After that it would be two intertwined wars in India; one of motorized infantry, the other of supply and interdiction. The Indians would depend more on eyesight, less on microwaves—and they didn't have to be geniuses to see our strategy.

Between India's heartland and Sulaiman, *nee* Pakistan, stretches the great Indian desert which runs north with the Indus River toward Kashmir. If unchecked, Allied hovercraft could swoop up from the Gulf of Kutch, over the Gujarat marshes, and to the very minarets of Lahore in scarcely five hours. Between Lahore and Kazakhstan lay one of the world's great desolations, an awesome series of snowclad mountain ranges. They had names: Karakoram, Pamir, Ladakh. No despot, no army, no form of life had ever conquered them in a thousand times a million years. Whether the US/RUS speared across passes into Tibet, sought passage through the Afghans to RUS territory, or simply sat tight, SinoInds would be cut off from the supplies they needed from the AIR 'neutrals'.

Supply would depend on air cover, and SinoInd forces had no aircraft that could fly rotor-to-rotor with RUS attack choppers developed after the Afghanistan lesson in the eighties. Even US high-tech loiter aircraft could not maneuver well with a rack of heat-seekers at ten-thousand-meter altitudes. RUS air cover could not conquer the Karakorum range, but it could macerate any large supply line trying to use those fastnesses as a conduit.

Suddenly China's thawing spring offensive in Kazakhstan developed more intensity along its southern boundary. She must wreck the Allied transAsian pincer movement at all costs. Her nuke-carved subterranean cavities in Tibet, full of AIR oil, now seemed less secure.

Given the Starlinger-Ahbez scenario, Chang Wei's response might have been expected. He raised the priority of the Ministry of Transport to speed the repair of routes between Szechuan and Tibet. Those routes would soon be choked with human materiel heading for the Tibetan frontier, for Chang would fight to his last Viet to save those oil reserves.

On Niihau, Boren Mills was both fortunate and canny. He was lucky in being so positioned that he, personally, had a need to know the uses of Kikepa Point as a Phillipus relay and perceiver station. Mills had known the airborne troops were Australians and New Zealanders; the seaborne troops were US Marines. He had known of the abort stations in Somalia, and of the two surface ships we sent to certain destruction in the Bay of Bengal.

Because he was a strategist, Mills began to consider a recurrence of searing headaches and double-vision. The Navy would be sending smart young officers to the coast and islands of the Arabian Sea, and Mills had no desire to place his hide where it could be perforated or irradiated by desperate Indians in what would inevitably become all-out suicide attacks to beggar the legends of Iwo Jima.

If the Gulf of Kutch operation was successful. The invasion was only hours old, and if satellite reports were any omen the Marines would face another kind of sea, a boiling bloody surf of Gujaratis and Rajasthanis, north of the coastal swamps. It would almost be a mirror image of the Florida invasion if several divisions of Allied troops were stopped south of the Indian desert.

One thing Mills could depend on because he knew it from a briefing. The Navy would emplace no Phillipus installations in a region subject to sudden capture by counterattack. And what, Mills asked himself more or less rhetorically, if the invasion faltered? Not a total failure; nothing as disastrous as all that. Something more like a momentarily crippling delay. India had failed to delay the invading Allies at the crucial moments before Aussies secured the Kutch beachhead only because Phillipus worked so well.

But Phillipus worked so well because it had been designed by outrageously creative Israelis, systematically modified by extremely orderly Americans skilled in systems management. The perceivers and relays were triplicated so that if one failed, others went on-line instantly. No, argued the Mills alter ego—rhetorically, of course—a crippling 'accidental' failure of the system could not even be surrogated. A truly systemic failure would have to be so exactly triplicated that, eventually, it would be identified as deliberate. Therefore, anybody who tampered with the Phillipus system should leave a subtle trail that would lead to someone else.

Mills knew how to lie to himself. It was just another hypothetical case for his scholarly managerial mind, he mused; if worst came to worse, he could always suffer a relapse from the Wisconsin burrow-bomb, and spend a few weeks recuperating. Someone else—someone like Jon Fowler, the damned circuit designer who was almost certain to be promoted over Mills because two of Fowler's Phillipus refinements quickened the relay response—someone else would be posted to Diego Garcia, or to Jamnagar.

Four days later, elements of the American Sixth Army pushed beyond the coastal lowlands into Rajasthan despite fiendish resistance by ill-equipped, incredibly tenacious Indian regulars. Our Asian foothold seemed secure.

Mills felt insecure. By the most delicate of discreet inquiries he had learned an unpleasant tactical reality about his project, Phillipus. So crucial was its progress, so secret its existence, that personnel in positions like his came under psychiatric scrutiny as a matter of course. Any failure, or suspicion of it, within his cranium would automatically result in his reposting to some forgotten supply depot in, say, central Australia. That might not have been so bad, but under those circumstances the reposting was tantamount to being permanently passed over; sequestered from any possibility of advancement. Such a stigma usually followed its victim into civilian life.

Mills had already decided that after the final curtain of this war he would perform on corporate stages; knew the importance of an outstanding record in reaching the top echelons where military, industrial, and political officers shared first names and villas. Boren Mills could not afford to avoid an Asiatic duty station by claiming a cross-threaded screw upstairs.

It seemed to Mills as though he might develop other plans.

Chapter 59

Latinos, thought Quantrill, sought variety in their accents. He had flogged his way through Crypto and Psych, Poly Sci and Cover courses by sheer doggedness, but he feared that Linguistics would boil his brains before the end of March.

"No, Quantrill; slur it and slow it," said Karen Smetana, whose fortyish but still evil little body contrived to distract her students. "In Mexico, only urbanites pick up the tempo—but never as upbeat as Puerto Ricans. Try it again—not so crisp on the rolled 'r', please."

And again. And again. "I'm not getting any better, Smetana," he said. "I'd always be spotted by a local."

"You're already better. And you aren't supposed to pass yourself off as a local; you can't develop deep cover on a week-long assignment. Be glad you took high-school Spanish instead of French, idiot! Would you rather spend a week in Cuernavaca sunshine, or Quebec?"

"She's got a point," smiled Goldhaber to the grumbling Quantrill.

"And you've got a long way to go to pass as a *judio* from Ciudad Mejico," Smetana reminded Goldhaber.

"Practiced all my life to outgrow Miami pawnshop intonations, and this *yentzer* wants to give me one from Mexico City."

"You just be glad I don't know what a *yentzer* is," said the linguist primly. "And don't avoid your strengths. Wherever there's a Jewish community," Smetana punctuated it with a fingerwag, "you'll have something going for you that Zachary or Quantrill would need years to learn. In T Section we don't train you all alike. That's one way a good counter-agent might spot you; most agencies leave indelible marks on an agent's behavior. We want each of you unique. No agency pattern, especially linguistic."

"They'd find a pattern damn' fast if they captured us," Goldhaber cracked. Smetana merely shrugged; his insinuation touched a sore spot.

Most trainees quickly accepted appendectomies, dental and cosmetic surgery, and in a few cases glandular adjustments which had been made without their permission prior to their arrival at San Simeon. They found it harder to accept the mastoid-implanted radio, for a variety of reasons. They had not been consulted; it was a foreign entity, an alien presence in one's head; and as long as the implant resided within the porous mastoid cells, its bearer was subject to audio monitoring twenty-four hours a day. No wonder, then, Control hadn't worried that a trainee might go AWOL.

Some trainees, including Quantrill, shrugged the implant off as an unavoidable necessity. Some, like Goldhaber, re-

sented it from the first day they were made aware of it in
Control class. The tiny device was powered by an energy
cell which could be recharged without an incision. The audio
transmitter permitted its owner to hear instructions relayed
from twenty klicks away, but which were wholly inaudible to
a bystander. Its receiver allowed Control to hear every word
uttered by a gunsel. At its current state of the art, the receiver
could not pick up external noises with much fidelity. It had
taken Goldhaber less than a day to 'borrow' an illustrated
dictionary from the musty Hearst library. He knew better
than to ask Smetana or his carrel about the manual alphabet.

By mid-March, most of the trainees could damn an instructor or a weak cup of coffee among themselves in sign language, and kept it secret as a harmless joke on the system.
Lacking instruction in the short-hand forms, they developed
some of their own, including facial movement. Quantrill had
little time for this casual byplay, fighting hard to overcome
several years' disadvantage in schooling—Ethridge, for
example, was a college graduate. But Quantrill found he'd
much rather read the lips of Marbrye Sanger than those of
Simon Goldhaber.

It was Goldhaber, though, who gave their mastoid implant
a label. *"It lets Control criticize you; a critic of the toughest
kind,"* Goldhaber signed one evening as he and Quantrill
jogged an undulating trail two klicks from San Simeon.

Quantrill had trouble reading hands while jogging. "Let's
walk awhile," he said, slowing. *"Who d' you think Control
is? Howell? Smetana?"*

Goldhaber, breathing in time with footfalls, practicing
silent movement: "These damned sweatsuits make too much
noise." Signing: *"I suspect Control is some colonel in Intelligence, maybe at Hunter-Liggett, running us by computer."*

"By himself?"

Aloud, Goldhaber snorted. Signing, he said, *"Not when
we go on solo assignments, stupid. Too many decisions for
one man, and I don' t think they'd let a computer terminate a
gunsel without human endorsement."*

Quantrill stared hard at the lank Goldhaber. They had been

told that, if captured and tortured, a gunsel could ask for instructions on a yet-unspecified means to suicide. Quantrill supposed it involved crushing a subcutaneous capsule; had already checked himself for such an implant, and mistakenly believed that a lymph node in his left armpit was really a termination cap. *"But termination is up to me,"* he signed.

Staring back, one eyebrow lifted: *"Naive. How many grams of TNT do they need in your ear? You don't pull your plug. Control does."*

Quantrill, in forlorn hope: *"But I ask for it first."*

"Grow up, Q. It's the ultimate control—invisible, absolute. Now you know why I hate this goddam critic in my head."

Quantrill began to lope then, avoiding Goldhaber's argumentative hands. By now he knew that his and Sanger's critics had followed their dialogue during their first meeting. So long as he did nothing for which he should feel shame, that omnipresent sexless other voice in his head would be a powerful ally—or so he had decided. He did not thank Goldhaber for suggesting that his implanted critic could kill him out of hand.

Simon Goldhaber's guess had missed only in detail. The plastique encapsulated in his mastoid was a shaped charge which, on command, vaporized the transceiver and was so oriented as to drive a white-hot spike of debris into the brain. The faceless theorists of Control in Ft. Ord did not worry too much that a trainee might desert T Section, nor that a graduate gunsel might be turned to the other side. The critic relay function could be managed by personnel of another agency, or if necessary by an aircraft co-opted by Control. Control could even terminate an agent by satellite, given an approximate location of the agent. The critic was not quite foolproof, but near enough; and no part of a gunsel's training told trainees how to build a Faraday cage.

The two joggers neared the castle promontory with its challenging uphill portion. "For Christ's sake slow down," Goldhaber called ahead. "You think Sanger's watching, or are you just trying to kill us both?"

Stung by this reference to the svelte Sanger, Quantrill forgot himself. "Why not? You said Control might blow me away anyhow," he called back. Then he stopped; turned. Goldhaber stood, eyes wide in horror, breathing hard, both hands pressed over his ears as if to protect him from some lethal signal.

Quantrill's hands gestured helplessly. *"Sorry; sorry,"* they fluttered, as Goldhaber trotted past him with a stony glance. Of course there was no assurance that Control was monitoring, or that a monitor would make anything of Quantrill's angry shout. Quantrill told himself as much a few weeks later after Goldhaber disappeared.

Chapter 60

Mason Reardon was an eminently forgettable figure; medium age, medium height, weight, nondescript face and manner. When you described Reardon you were describing anybody, hence nobody. Old successes in surveillance made Reardon an expert on how to be a Reardon. On April 2 his night class was a class of one.

"You're letter-perfect on your cover, Quantrill," he mused, "and I watched you tail Cross like an old hand through that mob of tourists today. When Marty Cross says you'll do, you're good. So what's eating you? Afraid you'll choke on your first assignment?"

Quantrill said nothing. His face was denial enough.

"Can't be buck fever; your record shows you've iced two or three people already, and even managed to hide some of it 'til you were under sedation. That takes coolth," Reardon said, savoring that last word like a rarely-indulged sweetmeat, and then took away the gas-pen. Quantrill had been turning it over, again and again, in his hands. "Is it this?" Reardon held the innocent little pen up for display. "It really writes. Its pressure cylinder dissolves in a pond or a toilet tank. Lasser tells me you can zap a fly with it. And two minutes after your mark gets a faceful of spray, he'll show no symptoms but classic heart failure. But it's scheduled for Saturday the fifth, which means you leave here tomorrow, and I'm not clearing you 'til I think you're ready.''

"I've memorized the whole campus layout, and the Army annex dorm floor plan. I'm ready.''

"You're not. Look, I've even told you this bastard Fowler was nailed while sabotaging a supply fleet that cost us a lot of men—not once, but twice! Naval Intelligence is dead certain it's Lt. Fowler. The only reason they're not icing him themselves is that Fowler's in Corvallis for a tri-service seminar, and the Army's running it.

"What more do you want for reassurance, Quantrill? I assure you, you won't get nursemaided like this when you graduate.'' Reardon waited in vain for Quantrill to meet his gaze. "I'm tired of guessing—unless you're spooked about your return route.''

"Damn' right,'' Quantrill blurted, the green eyes a sullen flash. "Why didn't Goldhaber get back?''

"Ah. So that's it.'' Reardon handed the little weapon back, sat down facing Quantrill, inspected his own cuticles. "I've heard the rumor. All I know is that he drew an early assignment, and blew it. Maybe he was tortured by those religious fanatics in Flagstaff and asked for termination. Maybe he's still alive; they didn't tell us. You know your implant—what do you guys call it, a critic? Your critic can't help you if you're trussed up in a cave somewhere.''

"So far as I'm concerned,'' Quantrill snapped, "my critic's some guy with a World Almanac and a monorail timetable who won't know shit about what I'm up against or how I'm feeling about it. All I want from you is a promise that Control will leave me the fuck alone as long as I'm doing the job.''

Now Reardon had his anonymous face on: emotionless, impersonal, a system automaton. It occured to Quantrill Reardon might be repeating something he was receiving from a critic of his own. "You have my solemn pledge that Control will not interfere with you unless you ask for it."

"Good enough." Quantrill pocketed the weapon. "Now, where's my ticket to Corvallis?"

Mason Reardon managed a convincing smile, patted his trainee's shoulder, and pronounced himself satisfied now that Quantrill himself seemed satisfied.

The following day, Quantrill flew by Military Airlift Service to Salem, Oregon. Clouds masked much of the desolation below, but he spotted Sacramento through a rift of cumulus. He saw some activity at the docks. For the most part, the city seemed an ages-dead ruin that might have been exposed by shifting dunes that day. What blast effects from the two air bursts had not accomplished, the overlapping firestorms had. The collapsed freeway overpasses had, at least, been cleared. A pattern of faint smudges from survivor hearthfires ringed the rubble-choked city center. It might have been Raleigh, he thought, and steered his mind forward. The Mormons might be able to counter destruction with rebirth; was there any paradox in T Section's development of human weapons, to counter with more destruction?

Quantrill, wearing dark body stain and false gold caps on his teeth, excited no one's interest. His scalp felt tight under the longish tight-fitting black wig. As Vitorio Sanchez, a part-time student and dormitory custodian, he had good reason for the master ID plate in his pocket. He also had an assignment to terminate Lt. Jon Fowler somewhere on the campus of Oregon State University.

'Sanchez' hauled his bulky bag from the Corvallis monorail, located Western Boulevard in a light drizzle, and used one of his tokens on the automated shuttle to the campus, pleased that his briefing had been so thorough. The nearer the shuttle came to the campus, the more variety he saw in foliage—and the more he saw of a familiar color combination. Either Oregon State's colors were orange and black, or Corvallis celebrated Halloween in April.

He walked in gathering dusk beneath huge dripping conifers from Thirtieth to the modular annex dorms, located the

garbage recycling area, trudged behind the dorm annex with
shoulders slumped. His fingertip masks were tight even with
rain trickling down from his wrists. He pulled a tab on the
bag, watched a long jagged rip extend along old seams, drew
the antistatic vacuum cleaner from the bag's remains and
stuffed the bag into a recycling container. No one would be
saving such an article now, even by happenstance.

His entry to the Army dorm annex was merely a matter of
offering his ID plate to the door slot and keeping a lugubrious
face turned toward his brogans as he passed a trio of young
Army officers. The vacuum cleaner unpersoned him, and
provided a stash for his change of identity. He turned toward
the stairwell that would lead to 'his' room—vacated the
previous day by a man in Army Intelligence—and then
continued his lackluster pace beyond it as the two Naval
officers brushed past.

". . . See whether Oregon State coeds are really berserk
over uniforms," the taller one was saying.

The other was compact, aquiline-nosed, with a receding
vee of dark hair and thick dark brows. "Ah, Jon, always the
researcher," he replied softly, glancing at the shabby janitor,
holding the sleeve of his dress whites aloof. The lieutenants
paused at the entrance to curse the rain, and to don filmy
ponchos while Quantrill knelt to pry at an ancient blob of
chewing gum in the carpet. A moment later he heard the
voices attenuate; hurried back down the stairwell and
breathed a long exhalation as his ID plate triggered the door
slider.

The room was still furnished. Under a crucifix, the twin-
sized bed was unmade. Quantrill sat on it, held up one
darkened hand, grinned lamely. The hand wasn't trembling,
but he felt as if it should be. The dapper little man with thicket
eyebrows might pose a problem, because he obviously knew
the tall lantern-jawed officer by name. 'Sanchez' had not
needed to hear that name; he'd recognized Lt. Jon Fowler
instantly.

And craved his death in that instant. It was cruel sport to
meet your enemy the minute you set foot on his turf, like the

flaunting of some trophy, and to find that you could not reach out and take it. Quantrill knew that his quarry had a midnight curfew; knew that he slept alone; knew even the position of the bed in which Fowler would lie. He could not know that in icing Fowler he would be compounding an error of Naval Intelligence.

Nor could Jon Fowler assist in setting the record straight. He had a pristine conscience and no idea that he had been isolated, mistakenly, as the Project Phillipus saboteur. By Navy reckoning Fowler was the only man who could have insinuated the subroutines that had twice allowed SinoInd fighter-bombers to destroy Allied supply ships. The Allied presence in India was still not secure, the Mills strategy still undetected.

Quantrill shook the folds from his change of clothing, reassembled the antistatic cleaner, checked the blackout drapes and switched on the wall holo, his alarm set for One AM. Had he chosen, he could have had an alarm sent directly into his head. Yet he did not want that assistance. He wanted to listen to the rain, and to watch Eve Simpson's nightly cameo.

Mason Reardon's promise haunted him like an echo. Maybe Control would interfere only if a gunsel asked for it—but now Quantrill felt sure the cynical Goldhaber had been right.

There were several ways you could ask for it.

Chapter 61

Quantrill did not sleep. Faint vibrations spoke of late arrivals in the dorm, of spirited military scholars enjoying a brief return to a university campus. The holo spoke and postured of success. Success against paranthrax; in Kazakhstan; in Gujarat; and as always, the heroes of the day were dubbed 'saints'.

Lt. Boren Mills did not sleep either. He had found Oregon coeds with Fowler, but unlike Fowler he'd found them too old, had excused himself early in favor of a cram session in his own room on the floor above Quantrill's. Mills took intellectual delight in applying his notes on linear servo systems to social systems. He paid special attention to the optimal control of human elements in the social circuits of industry.

To Mills, Phillipus was only one step in his progress toward a society of rational control, by the few rational people destined to exert that control. Mills was not disturbed by the deaths he had caused in the Arabian Sea; he viewed one mighty will, his own, as infinitely more valuable than a thousand lesser wills. Had Friedrich Nietzsche not existed, Mills would have invented him.

For a time Mills had studied the structure of Mormonism, certain that his rise to prominence in a postwar economy would proceed best through that circuit. Now he saw it as a subsystem to be controlled from outside if at all. The LDS simply was not constructed to let a late convert rise to pinnacles of prophet or seer. But among the corporate bodies that might exert outside influence on a theocracy, only one had an open channel by which a brilliant manager might float quickly to the top: media.

Mills put away his notes and watched Eve Simpson. He heard Jon Fowler enter the room across the hall and hoped he'd struck out; Fowler had already enjoyed too much success.

An hour later, Mills was roused from nodding by a faint noise; the sound of a door sliding shut. His holo was on. Still half asleep, Mills decided the noise was from the holo.

Quantrill tingled with anticipation as Fowler's door slid open, keyed by his master plate. If Fowler were still awake, Quantrill would peer at the scribble on his note pad, apologize in soft sibilant accents, claim he had a message for Lt. Fowler as he moved near.

The room was dark, but Fowler's sleep was shallow. As the door slid open, Quantrill saw the form sprawled in bed, stepped through the portal, waved it shut again while memorizing placement of the two chairs and the shoes on the floor. Once more in darkness, he moved silently past the built-in carrel to the opposite end of the room. His own clothing was of low-friction fabric and made little sound. But sheets and blankets, suddenly thrust aside, make their own audio signatures.

''Who's'at?'' The light over Fowler's bed winked on, Fowler blinking tousel-headed toward the door. He saw only innocent disarray ahead, did not immediately glance behind him.

The canny Marty Cross had taught Quantrill well. By remaining absolutely still, Quantrill managed to extend the moment to what, subjectively, was almost a geologic era.

Quantrill could not have expressed his need for this first sanctioned kill with words, nor his joy in its approach with song. Here in this moment he could face the spectres of slain parents, of friends murdered by panic and by casual bestiality, without apology for his own survival. Here was irresistible justice come to face immovable evil. In his mind, Quantrill had created deaths of Byzantine complexity to fit crimes beyond understanding—but the teachings of Sabado and Lasser urged a quick, clean kill.

Quantrill could not afford to savor the confrontation longer than it took to make identification certain. When he saw Fowler's face, he would fire the gas pen. In the endless heartbeat before that, he was a silent demon of entropy who waited to unwind the clockspring of Fowler's universe, the better to celebrate its last anechoic tick.

Fowler's head snapped around.

The grey mist met him full in the face, his assailant only a blur that muffled him in his bedclothes before he could shout. Quantrill fought to hold Fowler's wrists through the coverlet, lying atop his writhing quarry to prevent signs of violence, waiting out the first ten seconds of Fowler's death struggle. After that, Lasser had assured him, his problem would be over.

But Lasser had not dwelt overmuch on the mechanism of a

dying human system, and Quantrill was moved to sorrow by
the thin despairing wheeze as the innocent Fowler fought for
oxygen he would never use. To Quantrill it seemed that the
word, 'Why?' punctuated each gasp.

"You know why," Quantrill muttered, and fought his pity
as well.

When the shudder subsided, Quantrill risked a glance at
Fowler's fingernails, saw that they were slate-grey. Then he
scurried to the half-bath, flushed the pressure cylinder away,
remembered Reardon's dictum that every new instant may
bring discovery. A cover story perfect at time one might not
work at time two. Quantrill took the fifty dollar bill from his
pocket, palmed it. He glanced again toward the thing on the
bed, turned out the light, damned his sorrow as weakness,
listened at the door before sliding it open to the hall. He heard
nothing because Mills had slid his own door open while
Fowler's toilet flushed and was still standing there, wondering if Fowler was out after curfew, wondering what use he
might make of the fact.

Quantrill slid the door open, found himself staring into a
familiar face under a vee of short hair with eyes that stared
back unwinking under heavy level brows. He mastered the
impulse to attack, essayed a sad little flash of gold teeth. "He
said he would be nice to me," Quantrill almost whispered,
and let the banknote show as he stuffed it into his pocket.
"But he was not nice. Me, I think he is sick." He waited until
the door slid shut behind him, slouching as if contrite, dropping his eyes, then shuffling away to the stairwell. The
witness had said nothing, but had changed everything. Quantrill knew he must not look back.

Mills almost smiled at the retreating youth. This was a
datum worth remembering, he thought; a slice of Fowler's
life that Mills had never suspected. There had to be a touch of
the sadist in Fowler, too; those had been real tears in the eyes
of the little latino.

Chapter 62

Sandys jurnal Ap 5 Sat.
Mom says no use crying your lucky to be alive, at least you
cant have a baby at your age. Maybe but I hurt down there
a lot. I wish it was right to kill, I woud make Profet Jansen
burn in hell if there is one. I woud do it while he is asleep,
he always fires a little vessel and then sleeps after they raid
a temple of false saints like they did in Roswel today. He
says it is his godgiven rite. He says a lot of dumb things to
make it alright that he is stealing. He tried to give me a
dimond ring to make me stop hurting. Id rather have soap
to wash his smell away. I wish I coud talk with a freind,
somone who likes to make you smile, somone gentle. I
wonder where Ted is tonite.

Chapter 63

Because Quantrill could not know that Mills had bought
the charade, he could not risk staying in the room until dawn.
He ran the wig and custodian's clothing through the vacuum
cleaner's macerator, pried off the gold caps and removed the
contact lenses, washed the pigment from his brows; flushed
the debris away in several stages. He almost forgot to swallow the fingerprint masks and strip away the filmy covers that
had transformed expensive low-quarter shoes into cheap
brogans, but the shredded covers went down the tube as well.
He kept the master ID plate in case he had to flee into some
other campus building.

Ten minutes later, he exited the basement room leaving
only an antistatic vacuum cleaner behind; a sturdy blond

youth whose ready cash took him back to Salem on the two
AM interurban. En route, he delaminated the ID plate and
abraded its card to powder underfoot.

Finally in Salem he allowed himself to contact Control.
"Tau Sector, Tau Sector," he intoned, and waited. The
voiceprint, the staggered frequency, and the key phrase all
had to match.

Somewhere in Salem the freq. pattern triggered a relay.
Somewhere in Ft. Ord the key phrase alerted a sleepy major
in Control. From the unique voiceprint ConCom, the electronic part of Control's gestalt mind, identified the gunsel,
Quantrill. By far the longest part of the process was the
major's yawn before replying.

The major's voice was processed into the epicene contralto
a gunsel was trained to recognize. Implanted critics had been
known to pick up bits of stray messages. No human voice,
not even castrati, sounded quite like Control's, so that no
gunsel would be fooled by accident or countermeasure.

It had not escaped T Section's notice that by reprocessing
every Control voice into the same voice, ConCom further
removed the element of human contact from a gunsel's work.
It was, in several ways, inhuman—which pleased Control
immensely.

"Your program is running," said Control. Always that
acceptance phrase, or back to square one.

"Message delivered, Control. Am I clean?"

"Wait one, Q." The long pause gave the major time to key
vital data on his display, then to query the automatic event
analyzers that monitored military and civilian agencies in
Corvallis, Oregon. There was no homicide bulletin or APB
on anyone matching the description of Ted Quantrill.
"You're clean," Control reported, "and on the carpet." So,
he could fly back to San Luis Obispo. Other key phrases
would have sent the gunsel to a safesite, or to one of the
transient camps that now stretched along railway right-of-
ways near some cities.

Quantrill acknowledged the flying carpet sanction and,
with a mixed bag of passengers, caught a flight from Salem

before noon on Sunday. By that time Lt. Jon Fowler's body had been discovered. His death was attributed to heart failure, possibly induced by an early-hours encounter reported by another Naval officer. Boren Mills felt certain it had been a sexual encounter but craftily refused to say so. He thought it wise to leave room for the inference that Fowler might have harbored other secrets. His young visitor, said Mills, had been a foreigner.

Mills did not waste much time gloating over his good fortune in Fowler's death. During the last days of the seminar Mills grew enthusiastic over its subject, which was the refinement of optimal control theory for Project Phillipus. Mills spent much of his spare time with media theorists across the campus, catching up on the academic fads and jargon that had penetrated their field since his last courses at Annenberg. Mills did not discuss the paper he was preparing for two reasons. First, he did not want anyone else writing scholarly papers on the application of optimal control theory to propaganda. And second because he intended to have his own paper protected by the highest security classification he could wangle. It was Mills's intent to submit his paper to the Navy's Office of Public Information. If he could get all such papers classified, he would not have to cope with many rivals. Wiener, Shannon, and Weaver had failed to protect their pre-eminences in information theory after World War II—that is to say, not one of them became a billionaire. Instead, they had spread their new discipline as broadly as possible.

This, to Mills, was plain foolishness. The longer he could cover his arse in his specialty, the faster he might climb to rarefied regions in media. With keenly intelligent planning and a little luck, Mills might exert more influence over his repostings now. One thing he could never do again was to repeat his cunning Phillipus sabotage which, he was sure, would sooner or later be traced to his dead rival, Fowler. Not only was sabotage a personal risk; Mills also felt a mild patriotic fervor. The US/RUS Allies had to win if Boren Mills was to soar triumphant above American business.

From recent reports, the Allies were having a bitch of a time just holding their own.

Chapter 64

As the Kazakhstan front warmed up in April, it became clearer to Yale Collier's chiefs of staff that RUS troops and supplies would not be forthcoming in western India. Burnt hulks of RUS cargo aircraft dotted the sandy plain of Iran and the sere Afghan mountain ranges, mute testimony that the RUS had made a genuine run at it. Emboldened by American success with Project Phillipus, the Allies had gambled that they could get away with overflights above AIR neutrals that leaned toward the SinoInds. But SinoInd interceptors lay in wait at places like Kabul, Ashkhabad, and Isfahan, relying on visual intercept and Indian pilots flying the colors of Afghanistan, Iran, Turkmenistan. The ill will sown by the pre-1985 USSR had grown into a bitter harvest, urged on by every mullah and tariqat of the AIR.

In Latin America it was the Catholics who stirred up pro-Axis sentiment. We could not maintain military bases in the West Indies any more than we could in Chile, Brazil, or Panama. The genuine neutrality of Argentina, Paraguay, and Bolivia was due largely to the same general factors that caused Africa's western and southern countries to stay neutral. They might resent Industrialized Allied wealth, but they feared the fanaticism of their pro-Axis neighbors.

Mexico and the northwestern countries of South America, at least, remained pro-Allies. Thanks to their oil and other developed resources, they had bought enough arms to quiet their fears. Venezuela might be OPEC, but she was not Islamic.

Indonesia, on the other side of the globe, *was* Islamic—which is why Australian fighter-bombers got big pillowy tires. The sporadic war between Australia and Indonesia was one of air skirmishes, not of nuclear exchanges. Many a port installation was walloped from the air or by naval artillery. Each side could lay its hands on nukes. Both sides knew it. But Australia, unlike the corrugated islands of Indonesia, had millions of square klicks that were ideal as unimproved airstrip, and good for little else.

So the Aussie fighter-bombers grew bulges in their fuselages, fairings to accommodate fat low-pressure tires, and soon those sortie craft were dispersed so widely across northern Australia that no raid could destroy more than a half-dozen aircraft at a site. Those same aircraft showered the relatively few Indonesian airstrips with bomblets, leaving island runways so cratered that, by May 1997, very few Indonesian sorties flew. Meanwhile, Aussies scanned the Timor Sea and awaited an invasion, while they airlifted supplies to the Rajasthan front.

The SinoInds nuked more than one island in the Indian Ocean, though wasting fully ninety per cent of the bombs intended for those crucial waystations. We needed only a few delta dirigibles cruising at six thousand meters with particle beam weapons to pick off most of the ballistic incomings that our Moonkillers and F-23's missed. After all, we knew exactly what targets the SinoInds sought.

Despite the density of our defensive curtain, Diego Garcia was now uninhabitable; Aussies refueled in the Maldives.

In Rajasthan we fought a desert war, protecting our new air bases near Jodhpur. Our strategy was to press on toward Delhi while provoking the remains of India's air force into ruinous engagements. Indian pilots drew top marks for resourcefulness and courage—a necessity since they fought faster Allied craft that boasted longer range and more advanced fire-control systems. By mid-May, our air sorties into Uttar Pradesh again threatened an utterly crucial wheat supply, and India began pulling her interceptors back from their AIR sites to make up for local attrition.

Twice, in the spring, India had followed up on radar anomalies to find Allied supply convoys motoring boldly

toward the Gulf of Kutch. She had dumped a lot of Allied
supplies into the Arabian Sea—so much jet fuel, in fact, that
Indians calculated our support aircraft would no longer be
able to fly cover missions from the Indian desert by June. Our
Aussie-bolstered Sixth and Eighth Armies would then be in
serious trouble.

Prime Minister Casimiro was stunned, then, to learn in
May that New Zealanders were turning SinoInd oil into
Allied jet fuel using modular refinery equipment near the
Indus. Safe in tunnels near Nagpur, Casimiro had been
hopeful until now. "Surely," he said to Minister Chandra,
"our second priority is to destroy those midget refineries."

"Our first—surely?" The warrior Kirpal said it as a question, but wanted it as an order.

"First comes our bread. To fight, our people must eat."
Casimiro was still looking at Chandra, an old man long
familiar with Allied strategems.

"To eat next winter, we must choke off those airfields
now," sighed Chandra, who understood both hunger and
priorities, and did not envy Casimiro his political future.
"We must never forget that the RUS can airlift mountains of
supplies the moment we abandon the AIR corridor to them."

"I knew Russians when they were *our* allies," Casimiro
grumbled, "and I never knew them to export troops while
they were needed at home. *Never!*"

Kirpal, in a soft rumble: "The day they see us depending
on that, they will send a division of Germans to our soil in
Tupolevs. And then one of Poles, one of Bulgarians, one
of—"

"Always assuming they would go," said Chandra, who
knew how quickly the Russians had lost their clout after the
internal defections of '85. "But with Slavs or Yakuts, the
RUS is perfectly capable of finding reinforcements. Perhaps
from the American Fifth Army; as Allah knows, American
reinforcements have begun to roll up the southern edge of the
Kazakhstan front."

"Chang Wei is not Allah," Kirpal replied with narrowed
eyes, "however much he yearns to be. We have little more

than his word that the Americans have turned the tide. His demand for more of our troops would bleed the Madhya Pradesh.''

On that at least, he had agreement from Chandra and Casimiro. The Prime Minister, with a bleak view of postwar elections, agreed to throw his support to an all-out offensive against those Indus refineries. That meant more conscripts from the factories and repair crews of the eastern provinces; more chaos when recruits speaking a dozen languages mixed with seasoned troops who, like as not, spoke English.

In China, Chang Wei had given up negotiations with Guatemala, the only country capable of furnishing the sites China needed. The continental leapfrog operation would have to be one great leap, but here at least Chang's preparations had a boost from an unlikely source: the development labs of the Ministry of Materiel. Indeed, both the source and the product seemed so unlikely that Chang had insisted on an eyewitness demonstration. The device had already been field-tested during the early moments of the war, providing cruise power for a pygmy sub which had been lost. Further development had languished until Chinese intelligence sources revealed that British subtlety, and not Chinese technology, had caused the loss.

Once convinced of the gadget's potential, Chang had demanded vastly larger versions of it—only to be told of its inherent mass limitations. Its output could reach only a certain level, and that level had neared its theoretical maximum. Chang considered the long-range implications of the device, then initiated security precautions that all but strangled its production. Perhaps fifty scientists and engineers understood its functions. A dozen of those suspected that their lives would not extend beyond SinoInd victory.

Now, in May, Chang was satisfied with the production figures. The devices lay stockpiled in final assembly tunnels near the Yangtze, a swift conduit hundreds of meters deep in the mountain regions.

Chang was not satisfied with the news from Tsinghai. Cha Tsuni, thought Chang, had finally found a bug to test his serenity. The conventional high explosives the RUS had rained on Cha's labs had probably been pure accident, one more target of opportunity to disrupt the flow of materiel to Kazakhstan. Chang found himself wishing Cha's operation had been nuked outright; might have called for it himself had he known how quickly the new disease would spread to Huangyuan.

Surviving the RUS bombardment, Cha was now treating himself for the bacillus he had somehow produced. Treatment, he had complained in his most recent dispatch to Chang, was almost as dangerous as the infection—but hardly as repellent. Cha would not, of course, be permitted to leave the quarantine region in Tsinghai. Already the supply trains detoured through Mongolia while Cha's people sought new antibiotics to quell their demon bacillus. Now some of them were fighting it, in the most literal sense, blindly.

Chapter 65

On his second assignment, in May, Quantrill endured temporary silicone pads, subcutaneous cosmetics that gave him an extra chin and cheeks of a cherub to go with the red wig. He looked all of thirteen with his 'baby fat', though quite a large thirteen. He was furnished precisely the right image to emulate a kid scamming in Provo, Utah, during the four days he needed to isolate a newspaper reporter.

Investigative reporting had always been hazardous. It became more hazardous if a reporter stumbled onto traces of a construction project intended to house the secret seat of the American Government. Once the feebies discovered that the reporter had made a microfiche drop to an Irish agent, his days were few. Ireland was too friendly with the SinoInds.

To Quantrill it did not matter how or when Larry Pettet

began to supplement his salary with Hibernian money. If T Section said Pettet was superfluous, he would not live to spend much. Pettet entertained few vices, but he had difficulty with even those few in Provo where a vigorous Mormon majority had outlawed booze. Pettet noted with chagrin that more and more cities were returning to prohibition since the Collier administration took over; noted it, and shrugged. He could always find good whiskey; it was all a matter of paying the price.

Larry Pettet paid in full the day after he bought his half-liter of Johnny Walker from the chubby kid who hung around the motel. The JW was the real stuff, all right, but the stocky red-headed kid refused to bring him anything larger. If Pettet wanted several bottles, he'd have to buy it at the kid's brother's place out Bartholomew Canyon Road.

Listening politely to Pettet's nonstop monologue as the reporter drove eastward into the canyon, Quantrill reflected that one could be pernicious without being mean. Pettet laughed easily, sympathized with a kid trying to make ends meet in such a world, asked shrewd questions about the brother's little booze-running operation. Pettet thought it might make a good story once he was safely back in Bismarck. He was still chortling when he walked into the deserted barn, the redheaded kid at his heels.

Quantrill had chosen the site because the barn contained the putrefying carcass of an old horse. If and when anyone cleaned out the place, they would not wonder at the unpleasant smell.

"Jesus," said Pettet as he started to turn in the doorway, "you know there's a very deceased animal in here?"

"Two," said Quantrill, and shot him dead.

This time, thought Quantrill as he shoved the spy's body under rotting floorboards near the flyblown horse, he'd done a more professional job. It had been quick, crisp, as quiet as a silencer could make it; and he did not feel quite the same sense of loss, perhaps because he had not paused to savor the act.

Quantrill was discovering a fact about himself. By deny-

ing himself that rising tide of savage malevolence beforehand, he spared himself much of the remorse he felt
afterward. Vaguely he understood that his value system
would not haunt him for an act of war as it would for a
personal vendetta. His sleep was still haunted, but no longer
by those he had loved.

As Quantrill changed buses in Fresno, a Japanese trawler
south of Kyushu mooched sluggishly over the surface of the
Philippine Sea. Her sonar said that an incredible trove of
protein was moving out into the Pacific at a pace and depth
that ruled out pursuit by the trawler herself. That was what
the herd subs were for; to sample a potential harvest, and to
drive it by audio signals to the nets. If this enormous migration was not one of fish, it certainly fooled the trawler.

Probably, the skipper guessed, it was a school of sharks.
Never mind that sharks rarely massed in such numbers. The
school, a vast shoal steady at six hundred fathoms, ran too
deep for Sei or Orca. Pacific Squid did not grow to six-meter
length, the apparent dimension of the blips found by sonar.
There was only one good way to find out what they were, and
the herd sub darted away under emergency hydride boost to
take a sample.

The trawler picked up a muffled detonation later and
assumed at first that it was the two-man sub, dispatching one
of her little homing torps against a straggler. The huge shoal
was moving away under an inversion layer, a kilometer
down.

Later the skipper was not so sure about that homing torp.
The sonar record was ambiguous and could be misinter-
preted. Whatever the herd sub found, its crew could not
report from their grave in the primeval ooze of the Nansei
Shoto Trench. The vast stream of life passed implacably on
to the east and presently the phenomenon was forgotten.

Sandys jurnal May 18 Sun.
The truth is babys are all ugly even Child. I dont care.
Mom says she looks like her dady, I try and try but cant
remember how my dady looked. Poor mom is all tit, she
lost wait after Child came but I gess making milk takes it

out of you. Child is helthy at least she has a good yell.

Todays a day of rest, ha ha. Well, the profets dont work us as hard on Sundays. I dont know whos ranch we took but Im sure our convoy passed near Sonora, it even smells like home. One thing about herding sheep it keeps you away from Profet Jansen. They tell us the devil is loose here on Edwards Platow, they sacrifise insides of sheep. Somthing sure eats the guts out on the range, I bet its just a old cyote but I hope it is the devil, theres plenty of folks here hed grab in a minit. If mom was strong we coud lite out cross country but wed never get far with Child and the profets know it so they let me go out alone. They coud care less if the devil gets me. Me neither.

Tonite the radio talked about big quakes under the ocean I dont believe it, I never felt a thing here. If true I pity the Looshans whoever they are.

The great sea quake of May 1997 had been expected, but seismologists could not have foreseen its intensity. Its focus was below the great Mendocino fracture two thousand klicks north of Hawaii. Its first cyclopean pressure wave created a tsunami that thundered onto Hawaiian shores three hours later, obliterating beachfront buildings on the north of Molokai and Oahu. The loss of life was very light, thanks to the seismic alert system. Many lives on Kamchatka and in the Aleutians were saved in the same way—which is not to say that the death toll was small. Until that Sunday morning in May, the great Japanese quake of 1923 reigned in record books as the greatest killer of its type in all human history with one hundred thousand victims.

The record books would not be revised this time, because the Chinese People's Republic was in no rush to acknowledge the magnitude of its ill luck. For that matter, while the great majority of the seaquake victims were Asiatic, few were Chinese. Chang Wei 'lost' many records and arranged a hundred deaths to prevent the disaster from becoming generally known.

Chang wondered occasionally how it was possible that a series of waves could demolish an undersea fleet so com-

pletely. He might have understood had he known how seismic P-waves could kill fish, even trigger demolition devices
affixed to secret weapons. It had been Chang's own design-
ers who, in their zeal to protect a staggering breakthrough,
had converted a rough crossing into an appalling catastrophe
in the deep.

On Niihau, Boren Mills stood at a safe distance and
watched the first tsunami climb, a grey-white wall of water
and coral fragments, onto Kikepa Point. At the time he felt
only mind-numbing awe. Much later he would remember the
event in exultation.

On Santa Rosa Island, Eve Simpson stood with NBN
gawkers behind protecting glass and announced her disappointment. In its long traverse of the Pacific the tsunami had
lost its punch, its capacity to overpower; and so it earned
Eve's scorn.

At San Simeon the beach was several klicks away. Quantrill elected to stay on the mountain rather than make the
cross-country run with other diehards to coastal bluffs, there
to watch the waves thunder in. Quantrill much preferred
Marbrye Sanger's proposition; had seen the slabs of rye
bread oozing with ham and cream cheese as Sanger packed a
meal for two; tried with no success to deny his anticipation of
the outing she'd suggested. Quantrill would have said he
entertained no illusions about Sanger. Any young gunsel
with two flawless kills would have intrigued the hunter in
Sanger. He saw himself as legitimate quarry, not sex object,
and intended to be caught.

Chapter 66

Yale Collier interlaced fingers behind his head, leaned
back, studied the holo display on the wall. "You're asking
me to put our entire west coast in a state of siege merely on
the basis of two Indian overflights?"

"After a thorough analysis, Mr. President, yes," said the General, biting into the issue. He looked at the scatter of soft-faced civilians who shared the war room, wishing Collier's cabinet posts had been filled with more plain soldiers than Christian soldiers. Their very presence was irregular, but the President referred to them as his Chiefs of Civil Staff. And close coordination with civilian agencies had never been more vital than now.

"Those were manned aircraft, experimental Indian recon jobs modified in China to disperse a common flu virus. They were one-way flights, probably sea-launched. That's a hell of—a great deal of trouble, sir, for a non-lethal viral weapon. And if one of the pilots hadn't spotted a nice muddy field near Yuba City, he couldn't have landed alive.

"His aircraft was rigged with explosives and his canopy release had been disconnected. Obviously they intended both planes to disintegrate in midair. One did. The pilot we captured is a suspicious sonofa—gun, lucky for him and for us. So we now have metallurgical analysis and a live pilot to tell us the Chinese, not the Indians, wanted a temporary epidemic along the coast from Coos Bay to San Francisco. That suggests we can expect enemy troops there by the end of the month."

"You're certain the pilot wasn't an Indian who happens to speak Chinese," the President prompted.

"He's about as Indian as a fortune cookie," said the general.

The Chief of Naval Ops: "We've put every hunter-killer team we can muster on intercept sweeps out of Oahu, off the Andreanofs, and in the Guatemala Basin. I don't see how the Sinos could mount such an operation without our detecting it. Frankly, I expect to find 'em sneaking some big troop subs north through the Middle America Trench. We'll be ready."

"You'd better be," said the Secretary of Health. "That flu aerosol is already dispersed. By the twenty-eighth, there won't be an aspirin tab or a roll of toilet paper in Northern California."

"Taking the worst case," said the Secretary of Defense.

"Somehow they hit our beaches around the Oregon border. Do we nuke them or don't we?"

Secretary of State: "I hope to God we can begin civilian evacuation today."

"You talk as though the decision to nuke had already been reached."

"No, sir, I think Health and Interior will agree with me that whatever the decision, we've *got* to pull our civilian population back east of the Coast Range in the next day or two while they're still able to walk—before that virus drops 'em in their tracks."

"Meanwhile," said the general, "we pump flu vaccine into green Fourth Army troops and move our artillery in place around the bays."

"And be ready to lift it again by chopper," nodded the Secretary of Defense. "This whole Sino operation could be a blind."

The CNO: "The Latin-American scenario, Mr. Secretary?"

Defense shrugged. "That or a massive resupply of Florida, which could swamp what's left of Second Army. If the SinoInds have immunized an invasion force against their paranthrax, it could happen. We're not going to overlook anything."

Defense was wrong. We had overlooked the possibility that an invasion force had been so thoroughly destroyed that even its own leaders had no way of knowing whether any of it survived.

Major General Karel Lansky, at the far end of the conference table, sighed and put away his floppy discs. Until now he'd hoped the agenda would get as far as the new developments with First and Third Armies in Kazakhstan, Lansky's own bailiwick. It was too early for conclusions, but damned well time for an opinion: in western Sinkiang, rear echelons of the Chinese People's Army were beginning to panic.

Nothing in satellite or RUS espionage reports suggested an Allied strangulation of supply routes to the CPA, yet the movements of troops and materiel in Sinkiang were in mounting chaos. One RUS brigade had already speared back into Semipalatinsk to find that Sino trucks and ACV's had run short of fuel. Rocket artillery, mortar rounds, fuel, food, everything that qualified as heavy cargo: the CPA was starving for it. The American Third Army had whiplashed under the Sino flank as far as Alma Ata, turning the Sino rear at Lake Balkhash. George Patton would have lanced on into Sinkiang. For once, our hesitation proved wise.

Lansky did not trust the briefings he'd had as liaison with the RUS high command. The Russians ostensibly thought that some civil disturbance—perhaps a full-fledged revolution—was shaping up in western China, though no Chinese radio messages supported such an idea. But, said the Russians, if it had happened to the USSR in 1985 it could happen to anybody!

Lansky gathered evidence and kept silent among the Russians; if his own suspicions were correct, he would be wise to hide them from his Russian friends. Lansky intuited that the CPA was as politically reliable as any military entity in existence. If an internal panic broke out in the rear echelons it was unlikely to have an ideological basis. But there were weapons, both chemical and biological, that could dismember the staunchest warrior cadre.

Lansky knew that the RUS Central Committee had sworn they would unleash no biological warfare weapons without prior agreement among allies. He also knew that the Sinkiang anomaly had all the earmarks of madness, or of plague. Unless the RUS had broken its word by secret dispersal of some terrible weapon in Sinkiang or Tsinghai, Lansky had guessed awry.

He had, and he hadn't. Though a Mikoyan attack bomber had provoked the beginning of the end with conventional smart-bombs against a Tsinghai laboratory, the RUS was for once innocent of intent. Ultimately the Chinese Plague was China's own dragon, come to breathe death on her people.

Chapter 67

June 18, '97

c/o Texas A & M
Research Station
Sonora TX 769502531

My Dear Ted:

By now you probably know we've stalemated paranthrax. It was a team effort and for a time, you were part of that team. I thought it might give you a lift to know you've been a giver of life and not a taker.

You really should have said goodbye; it didn't take a Sherlock to trace you to the San Marcos induction center, and God knows you could pass for sixteen. I kept your note—as an object lesson in male inconsistency, I suppose. Surely you've had enough of uniforms by now! How many stripes on yours? Let me suppose it's one or two, and on that supposition I congratulate you. Better yet, write and tell me. I'm not naive enough to think you're still in San Marcos but optimist that I am, I dare hope this will reach you—wherever.

I'm not in Sonora now, either. I can't tell you where. Let's just say I volunteered elsewhere. Incidentally, there's reason to hope that Louise and Sandra Grange are alive and well. Aggie Station resounded with rumors about some of the survivor groups, though they weren't the most law-abiding sects I might mention. But I digress . . .

My current work is with something by the jawbreaking monicker of *Staphylococcus rosacea*, alias Keratophagic Staph, and we can thank God it's still confined to Asia. I'm assuming you've heard about it; it's in the news here. On the other hand: if you're anywhere in its vicinity, burn used hankies, keep your resistance up and your hands away from your eyes. It wouldn't hurt to use goggles. Need I insist that you take any antibiotics you're issued *religiously*? If I have a religion left, perhaps that's it. As long as all religions have their side effects, I may as well pray to Novobiocin as to anything else. Meanwhile, we of the priesthood are busily crafting new gods—the better to counter dat ol' debbil Staph. Wish us Godspeed—or should I say antibioticspeed?

I saw a holo interview last night between the Sec. of Defense and Everyman's hotsy, Eve Simpson. Sorry to say she's getting downright chubby; no doubt you mourn that too, too-solid flesh more than I do. As I was saying, the gov't now admits that our transient camps in the San Joaquin Valley weren't just for agribiz. We expected the little invasion that wasn't there. Why tell you about it? Well, for all I know you're in some engineering battalion out there. So is my daughter, Cathy Palma, Jr., and it's just possible that you may run into each other. If so, tell her Mama says you don't have to salute!

Must get some sleep. I have to keep my resistance up, too. Think of me now and then as I do of you and, if the spirit strikes, write. When all this is over, don't hesitate to use me for a reference, Ted. By then it may be all I'm good for.

                                        As ever,
                                        Catherine Palma

Quantrill read the letter with an aching sadness that became anger on second reading. Damn Palma! Her letter needed ten days to reach him and ten seconds to breach his defenses. The last thing a gunsel needed was a reminder that there were still kind and loving people out there, taking terrible chances without rage or vengeance to prod them.

He scanned the passage on survivor groups a third time, dredging up wry amusement to counter his ire. For damned sure they weren't law-abiding sects; according to Seth Howell they were the chief reason why West Texas and much of New Mexico were justifying the label of Wild Country.

Neither Howell nor Reardon had said so, but Quantrill felt sure his next assignment would be into wild country. Two of

the new gunsels, Desmond Quinn and Maxim Pelletier, were
sitting in on his cram sessions—but so was Sanger. Maybe
Howell was right: to stop a bunch of crazies you'd have to ice
them all or pinpoint the leaders first. Isolating leaders meant
infiltration, and to minimax the operation it would be best to
let gunsels, for once, do the prelim work usually reserved for
the FBI or other agencies.

Of course that meant T Section's charter was thereby
broadened. The Collier administration seemed reluctant to
delegate death contracts to agencies which were themselves
becoming Mormon in sympathy. T Section had no Mormons
and no sympathies. It had one recent casualty whose Chicano
background should have been good cover for an infiltrator in
wild country. That cover had bought him a shallow grave on
the banks of the Pecos River. Quantrill could not yet fully
believe that some religious nut had bagged Rafael Sabado
but, taking it at face value, he could endorse the notion of
sending gunsels into the region in teams.

He glanced at the Palma letter again, acutely aware that
Control would have read it first. "Palma, you soft-hearted
loser," he snarled, and tossed the letter into the carrel shred-
der. It wouldn't hurt, he thought, to let his mastoid critic
transmit a scorn he did not feel.

He checked the time: a half-hour before dark. Maybe
Sanger would feel like a 'little jog', their own code phrase for
twenty minutes of cross-country run and ten minutes of
clean, piping-hot undiluted lust somewhere on the hillside
below the big house. With Marbrye Sanger, he felt, you
knew where you stood; knew that her needs were on honest
display; could depend on a quid pro quo without emotional
aftershocks.

On one level Quantrill admitted his use of sexuality to
salve a psychic wound. On another he assumed that Sanger
was all surface, uncomplicated, beyond the need for friendship.

His was an assumption that Control endorsed. Had Control
found any evidence that Marbrye Sanger ached for dearer
sharing with Quantrill, the pairing would have been dis-

solved by 'coincidence', and permanently. But Sanger was subtle, and regularly chose partners other than Quantrill—and was more vocal in her enjoyment of them. Control, for all its vigilance, did not ask whether Marbrye Sanger invested all her external encounters with the same inner valence.

Sanger rejoiced at Quantrill's syncopated knock. She was not fool enough to show it; if anything, Sanger overestimated Control and her critic; preserved the cool grace that characterized her. She agreed to the little jog, careful to avoid primping, mindful of the video unit that might squat behind her mirror.

Each time she was alone with Quantrill, Sanger sought new insights behind those troubled green eyes; touchstones into the character of a youth she must never claim as friend. She could provoke him into stories of his past, titillate him, ravish him, goad him to take her in the same way. But she knew that she must never befriend him.

Sanger told herself that what she had was enough.

Chapter 68

Liang Chen had taken more than enough. Accustomed from infancy to the security of his social unit, he'd been quite willing to leave his lakeside village unit in Hunan to join the biggest military unit on earth: The Chinese People's Army. Unit within unit, the huge CPA bureaucracy churned its human molecules into motorized infantry, armored, engineering, quartermaster units with all deliberate speed—i.e., slowly. Liang was quick to learn, stalwart under pressure, good with math; the right recipe for an antitank fire controller.

Even when the RUS brought in the fast-scudding armored ACV's to change the rules on him, young Liang reacted quickly, bagged an even dozen. His new conversion tables accommodated the quick lateral capability of an ACV, permitted his battalion to survive the RUS onslaught where others failed, added a deferential note to his unit's phrase 'Xiao Liang'—young Liang. Now, for the first time, he wondered if he would live to be called 'Lao Liang', old Liang. Liang counted the remaining HEAT warheads, wondering when he would see more.

It wasn't just the ferocity of the previous winter, though frostbite had scalloped Liang's ears. Nor the long desperate footsore march to meet the American Fifth Army which had been hurled against the southern face of the Kazakhstan front in the spring. Even the dwindling of supplies and the rumors of a hellish disease to the rear had not, in themselves, sapped the patriotic juices that once surged through Liang Chen. What drained him most was unitary breakdown.

Liang was feeling the surface of a tumor in the military corpus of China. When the supply of antitank missiles was exhausted, Liang's unit melded with a mortar company. When the food ran out, the forty per cent of his company who could still fight managed to attach themselves to a retreating regimental supply group near Birlik, fighting off American air sorties with small arms fire and a few shoulder-fired SAM's.

And when the first of the infected front-line officers began to don dark glasses to hide the signs of that infection, Liang shrugged it off. The CPA would take care of its own, he thought. But units could not prosper when unitary leaders spread horror.

For it was the field-grade officers who first brought plague to the front, men whose duties required round-trips far back into Tsinghai and Sinkiang, men whose necessary contacts meant contact with what Allied medics had labeled Keratophagic Staph. The disease progressed in a human host, and spread to others, with ghastly dispatch.

Liang Chen's devotion to battle kept him from early contact with the ravages of plague. Not until he heeded the call for retreat north of Alma Ata did Liang, gripping his perch on an ancient halftrack, see undeniable evidence that all units, on every level, were breaking down in panic. He saw a red-eyed captain submachinegunned by his own men who cowered more fearful of his corpse than he had been of their weapons. He saw others refuse to join new units, terrified that new unitary contact might chew their faces away. Finally he ripped a patch from a discarded battle jacket, affixed it to his own, and carried off his imposture as a corporal of a Political Solidarity detachment. No one cared much to fraternize with those zealots, and Liang could face down a major with his sham. Meanwhile he made his way back toward Sinkiang alone to find some unit worthy of membership.

The farther he went eastward past Ining, the more desolation he found. Not death, but desolation. Units were becoming crowds of blind men, led to food and shelter by sighted men who might not be sighted for long.

Liang knew intellectually how vast the world was. He knew in his guts that somewhere in it lay safety, and he knew positively that he was developing a cold. Or something. Liang turned north and set Mongolia as his goal. With no unit, no challenge by frightened guards as he pedaled his stolen bicycle toward Ara Tam, Liang blew roadside dust from his nostrils, wiped a sleeve across his nose. Presently a command car hurtled past, going in his direction; probably, he thought, with the same goal. Liang cursed the dust of its passage, blinked, wiped his sleeve across his eyes.

That night Liang Chen holed up far off the road where the bike would not tempt others. He had no food and he worried about that. His fever was worse and his eyes itched so that he found himself rubbing them; but this did not worry him much.

What worried Liang more was the sight of his fingernails, late the next day, as he pedaled near exhaustion toward a deserted village. He allowed himself to coast, stared at his left thumbnail, saw its edge receding from the cuticle as though eaten by some subtle acid. Truly, it did not hurt much. Neither did his eyes. The damnable pounding headache and the blurred vision bothered him more.

And then he passed the abandoned truck, saw for an instant the face of a soldier with scarlet eyes and runnels of pus down his cheeks; a face not of the dying, but of the damned. The truck had been deserted; he had glanced into a rearview mirror. Liang Chen sat down by the road and waited for the unending dark.

Some of Minister Cha Tsuni's records went up with his lab; others were deliberately erased. We may never know whether *Staphylococcus rosacea* was a DNA-tailored bacillus, a spontaneous strain, or one induced by radiation. Like *S. aureus*, *S. rosacea* thrived asymptomatically in the human nose, so human carriers spread the stuff with every exhalation. But also like other staph, *S. rosacea* was not fastidious and could live in a wide range of temperatures, with or without oxygen. Thus the bug could live on airborne dust motes and wait to invade lungs, blood, organs. The best defense was solitude; *S. rosacea* did not travel well without a host.

Once entrenched in a host, the new bacillus released toxins that could lead to pneumonia, meningitis, huge suppurating carbuncles, and septicemia—all potentially lethal if untreated. But *S. rosacea* set itself apart from older staph varieties in two ways. It was highly resistant even to the potent, problematical vancomycin. And it had a horrifying affinity for keratinous tissue, especially the saline-washed transparent anterior covering of the eye. In plain language, while inflaming surrounding tissue it consumed the cornea, characteristically staining the victim's cheeks with a stain of yellow pus as it prospered and devoured.

Typically a victim would breathe the bacilli, or airborne staph might invade an open wound. While the disease progressed into pneumonia or a toxin-filled bloodstream the victim became listless, often feverish. He would almost certainly place contaminated hands near his eyes, or walk through his own exhalations.

Either way, the eyes had it. *S. rosacea* flourished in the salt tears, eating away the cornea and, to lesser effect, into the nails of fingers and toes. Treatment was at first a matter of administering exactly enough of a powerful antibiotic to quell the bug without generating serious side effects, e.g., renal failure, to kill the patient. This knife-edged balance required constant monitoring and considerable skill by trained medics and, given that edge, only thirty per cent of *S. rosacea* victims died. But *ninety* per cent of the survivors would be sightless after the disease had run its full course.

The demoralizing effect of a disease that turned one's eyes into pus receptacles and was highly communicable, would be hard to overestimate. Faced with the spectre of a future full of blind men, even sighted survivors often chose desertion or suicide.

The Chinese plague was over a month old before the Allies realized its full pandemic potential and sought a true cure as a blue ribbon top priority. Its horrifying symptoms generated panic far greater than paranthrax ever had, and China thought to share that panic with her enemies. She arranged to cloister a few victims, all palpably learned technical people, in a setting where they would be captured. Since it takes a scientist to adequately interview a scientist, Chang Wei hoped that those few victims might pass the epidemic along from the top.

But those were prisoners the Allies did not choose to take. Horrifying problems engender horrifying solutions; the RUS pulled back, detonated one last Wall of Lenin that demarcated a zone of lifelessness. While fifty thousand SinoInd troops perished in the neutron spray, so did ten thousand of ours, including a Canadian armored regiment and two battalions of American infantry. The Fifth US Army bitterly resented this misuse of 'friendly fire', but did not retaliate. Canada reserved her retaliation.

Then came a signal of utter determination that Chang and Casimiro could not ignore. In an unprecedented burst of candor, the US/RUS Allies sent an open message to the SinoInd Axis listing over fifty locations. At the first sign of deliberate dispersal of the hideous *S. rosacea,* we would hit those locations with our cultures of the same stuff, and more.

The Allies roamed orbital space at will now. The threat
was highly public, and stupefying. The locations list covered
all of the most highly populated regions of the SinoInd Axis:
sites in eastern Szechuan, Kiang Su, Hopeh; in Kerala, West
Bengal, Punjab, Bangladesh; in the Red and Mekong deltas;
near Surabaja and Makasar.

Because the Allies were better stocked with antibiotics and
medical staff, and because their civilian populations were
better equipped to take their own hygienic measures, the
SinoInd pundits abandoned their plans to mount a global
series of dispersal raids. Instead, they turned their attention
to defensive measures.

Chapter 69

On receipt of the scholarly paper of Lt. Boren Mills, the
Navy's Office of Public Information automatically granted it
a 'Confidential' classification. Mills instantly pointed out to
Naval Intelligence that the paper had been misclassified, and
earned himself a ten-minute interview with a bored commander on Oahu whose eyes were not so sleepy two minutes
into the discussion. "You can optimize a persuasive message
to an Arms Appropriations Committee," Mills pointed out,
"just as you can to the public."

The commander took Mills to lunch that balmy day in June
and, when affixing his endorsement to the 'Top Secret'
reclassification, phrased his recommendations carefully. His
phrasing implied that he, the commander, had immediately
seen applications of the Mills paper that Mills himself
had—perhaps—missed. While achievement is nontransfer-
able, the image of achievement can be transferred. This is the
one towering secret of management, and the commander
managed nicely.

It was while Mills awaited notice from higher echelons

that the tiny submarine washed into the coral off Lehua. The islet of Lehua lies in plain sight of Niihau, one of the many small jewels of the Hawaiian chain that most *haoles* ignore. Mills had seen it many times. It did not seem likely to offer much in the way of entertainment and, when two Radiomen Third Class returned from a fishing jaunt with the news, Mills tended at first to ignore it.

But the stubby little craft bore Chinese markings, the two ratings insisted, and had all the earmarks of an unexamined derelict. Mills had seen the orders pertaining to the strange assortment of debris that had been washing ashore in Hawaii during the past month. He grumbled. And then he organized the small patrol that was to change his life.

Mills and four ratings brought their inflatable ACV to the site of the beached sub at low tide, circling twice before making fast to a hatch fairing hardly larger than a manhole cover. The polymer hull showed bright coral gashes through gray-green paint.

Radioman Kimball Norton, without much enthusiasm, opened the hatch while one of his fellows stood by with a carbine. Mills, his knuckles white on his carbine, caught the faint smell of decay as Norton stepped back with a grimace. "Anyone alive?"

"Doesn't smell like it, Sir," Norton called back.

"Lob a pacifier grenade in," Mills ordered. "It'll clear the air for you down there."

Norton caught the implication. Mills was perfectly sanguine about ordering a man down that black hole and if he was going to have to do it anyhow, Kim Norton would rather not flaunt his reluctance. He jerked the poptop from the grenade and tossed it down the hole.

The only response was the paper-bag 'thwock' of the grenade. After ten minutes, Norton saw the lieutenant's eye stray to his watch. "Permission to go below, Sir?"

"Granted," said Mills. Norton was the kind of man who understood the chain of command, and his status as flail at the end of it; and this, Mills appreciated. Perhaps he would do something for Norton.

They all heard the "*Jee-*zus," and the clang of a dropped chemlamp, and two ratings took Norton under the arms to quicken his already sprightly exit. There was nobody alive down there, said Norton, coughing. There were over a dozen deaders there in plastic capsules, though. They were in uniform and looked oriental.

Mills waited longer for the finely-divided grenade solids to precipitate; donned SCUBA gear with a prayer of thanks to reservist training he had once cursed; made an external survey of the little Chinese sub.

It had the look of an enormous toy, cheaply mass-produced, and it had no propeller at all. The thing had evidently been powered by the tiny reaction engine at its rear. Though no engineer, Boren Mills knew that this was an unlikely candidate for propulsion. Before surfacing, Mills was aware that this minuscule warship held important information.

He changed again into his uniform, replenished by its authority, and took a second chemlamp. By now the grenade's chemicals were only a tickle in his nostrils. Mills, alone with instruments and tool kit, toured the little sub.

The thing held a cargo of human bodies, twenty of them, in plastic cocoons. They wore CPA uniforms; one was a noncom. Umbilicals ran to the cocoons, suggestive of life-support systems for catatonics—but Mills knew putrefaction when he saw it, even through a polycarbonate bubble. There wasn't room in the narrow walkway for twenty men, or even ten; and he found no evidence of battle stations, steering apparatus, or control console. The sub had not been intended for sorties, then.

Mills recalled the Mendocino Seaquake, cudgeled his memory for connections, and found them. An entire army of Viets had gone to earth near the Yangtze months before—or rather, he corrected himself, *had gone to sea*. He wondered where the rest would turn up, then wondered why none at all had, before this. Between his sneezes, Mills was smiling.

The weapons storage near the bow clarified a lot. The biggest items in storage were fifteen-cm. shoulder-fired

SSM's and, laid down like cordwood, bangalore torps. Munitions for land warfare, for maximum mobility; for a tiny unit living off the land while traversing it. The assault rifles boasted folding stocks. There must have been at least a hundred thousand rounds of 9-mm. ammo in beltpacs. How many other tiny subs had accompanied this one? Mills guessed perhaps a thousand, and missed by an order of magnitude.

Mills searched for air and food storage tanks. He was pressed inexorably toward the conclusion that, additives and concentrates aside, most of the food and all breathing oxygen were provided by the same subsystem. While he pondered, the young officer traced lines and circuits.

From his SCUBA survey Mills knew that the sub was propelled, incredibly, by a reaction engine. At great depth it would generate a hiss undecipherable by sonar. The problem, of course, was that the sub would require vast amounts of propellant. Unless the craft were staged with huge jettisonable tanks, it made no sense to Mills. A missing piece of puzzle nudged the elbow of his mind, was thrust aside. *Ridiculous*.

His instruments pinpointed a local source of radiation and, for a long hideous moment, Mills pondered the possibility that he stood before a fused fission device. But this part of the system was obviously linked to umbilicals for food, oxygen, and for—something else. Lines leading to small collector tanks, which fed the reaction engine.

Ridiculous, he thought again. But the evidence was overwhelming; despite the gloomy predictions of the best western minds, Mills thought, he stood beside a plug-in unit that provided endless quantities of oxygen, hydrogen, simple sugars, to permit a small troop-carrying submarine to cross the Pacific without surfacing.

The key device was not a bomb—unless it was a social bomb. It was small enough to carry under his arm—and it used sea water as input mass. Mills stood before a *fusion* device; and it synthesized. Endlessly.

Boren Mills began to perspire.

During the disassembly, Mills found five occasions to apply quick-setting cyanoacrylate paste. These were occasions when mechanical detents seemed likely to spring up or down. He was to learn that only three of those detents were destruct mechanisms, and that the one electrical booby trap he did not find, had corroded harmlessly. At length he was sure that the tiny cornucopia lay disconnected. No, not quite sure. In any case, he could not haul it up from the little sub without being seen. Mills affixed a USN proprietary tag to the unit and, stowing tools in his beltpac, emerged from the craft.

"Let's get back to quarters," he said to the men. "Each of you will write a full report and, until our reports are in, this is absolutely Q-clearance stuff. Kim, you can help me word my input. You were down there first."

Kim Norton was the nearest thing to a friend that Mills could claim among the enlisted men. The others puzzled alone over their reports that night, confined to quarters, while Norton sat uncomfortable in officer country, alone with Mills.

"If this satisfies you, Sir, it does me," Norton said when their draft was complete. "I wasn't down in that tub for more than a few seconds anyhow."

"Why don't we drop the 'sir' crap for now," said Mills, knowing he sounded less than genuine. His smile didn't add much. He rushed on, crowning the moment with still another lie. "The truth is, I wish you *had* been down there. I tagged a piece of equipment to bring back—hell, Kim, I mentioned it in the report!"

"I wondered about that. How big?"

"Size of a small suitcase. I—just forgot. Can you imagine anything so stupid?"

Norton juggled the notion of stupidity in Mills, and dropped it with a shrug. "We can get it tomorrow," he offered.

"Of course, of course," Mills muttered, "but something just occurred to me." *While staring at those detents*.

When Norton failed to nibble at the bait, Mills arose and

walked to the percolator at the far end of the room. He poured two cups, unobtrusively flicked on his pocket 'corder, and laid it near the percolator. Then he continued their talk. Presently Mills asked, "Did you see much down in the sub?"

"How could I, coughing my head off in the dark? No, Sir."

"My name is 'Boren', Kim. Relax. So you don't even recall the piece of equipment I tagged?"

"I told you before, uh, Boren: *no*," Norton said with a trace of irritation.

Now that he had something he needed, the Mills smile was genuine. He sat companionably near Norton on the table's edge. "Do you think you could recognize it if you saw it tonight?"

Norton was not happy with the idea until Mills hinted at a citation. But reassured that the officer would make the trip worth his while, Norton agreed to the midnight requisition.

When the rating had gone, Mills strode to the percolator and began to toy with the 'corder. It was only a few klicks from Kikepa Point to the derelict sub. What if there *was* an honest-to-God fission device, after all, connected to the fusion synthesizer? Well, at least Bonham Base on Kauai would suffer little damage. Mills indulged in this small patriotism, sipped coffee, and avoided looking toward the west. If he could not become a rich man, at least he could avoid blindness.

Two hours later, the synthesizer sat on the desk before Mills. It looked a bit like a cipher machine from an earlier war, fitted for intravenous feeding.

"Nothing to it, eh?" Mills extended his hand. "When all this is over, Kim, you'll be remembered." He swore Norton to secrecy and dismissed him. Then Mills generated a new report that made no mention of the synthesizer. He sealed the device in a desiccant-filled bag, placed that in another bag, then buried the treasure near the access road.

The next morning, Mills and his crew were again at the sub, ostensibly to take exact measurements and photographs for the salvage teams. Mills put two men to work examining the keel, stationed a third on deck to keep the forced-air unit cramming fresh air into the sub, then shifted his big shoulder-bag and went below. He took Kim Norton with him.

While Norton obediently listed loose personal articles in the crew compartment, Mills selected a package in his bag and placed it in the weapons storage locker. He then took the forage hatchet from his bag and carefully brained Kim Norton from behind. He returned to the storage locker to recheck the setting of the timer, then laid his pocket 'corder near the bangalore torpedoes and checked his watch as he flicked the 'corder switch.

Mills climbed outside empty-handed. "I forgot my fast film," he called down the hatch. "We'll have to get it from the cache on shore." While the three crewmen scurried to the small ACV moored by the hatch, he checked the time again, temporized by inspecting the forced-air unit, then called down the hatch again. "Taking the rest of the crew, Kim. We'll be gone fifteen minutes. Sure you don't want to go?"

There was the briefest of pauses before, "I told you before, uh, Boren, *no*," said Norton's recorded voice with a trace of irritation.

"Suit yourself, love," Mills forced himself to say, choosing a phrase least likely to sound premeditated. "But keep your damned hands off those munitions." Then Lieutenant Boren Mills leaped into the ACV. They were nearly to their equipment cache when the submarine disintegrated with two distinct explosions.

Mills was absolved by the board of inquiry, though he assumed blame for leaving Radioman Second Class Norton behind. Fragments of the Chinese vessel were recovered, some of them quite large, none of them in condition to answer the Navy's most vexing questions. In time, fragments of similar vessels turned up.

The Navy file characterized the doomed fleet as an official curiosity, but opined that the craft must have had a huge tender, a mother ship. There was never any serious suggestion that the tiny craft were capable of running submerged from a thousand klicks up the Yangtze to the Oregon coast. The only evidence of that lay buried near Kikepa Point.

During the next two weeks, Mills found a suspicion confirmed: interservice rivalries could not match the complex intimacies of rivalry within the Department of the Navy. During the series of conferences provoked by his scholarship, Mills watched the maneuvering between his superiors in the Office of Naval Intelligence, the Public Information pundits of OPI, and the crusty staff of CNO who only wanted, as one rear admiral said, to cut the crap and convert some senators.

Day by day, hobnobbing with few ranks below full commander, Mills expounded on the persuasive uses of his new discipline and stressed the need for experimental work to prove his ideas. If transferred directly to the CNO staff he would chafe under the control of old men in Naval Ops. If he stayed in Intelligence, he might be hamstrung by their passion for watching the watchers. But the OPI was an aggregate, the Public Information career officers rattling and clanging against men who had been civilian media men a year previous, who would be civilians again a year or so hence. Here in media lay priceless connections and worthless bullshit; expertises so vague, so multifariously counterfeit, that a legitimate media theorist could help himself to a pretty piece of territory among them.

Mills maintained his studious mien, implied a 'natural' preference for his existing Intelligence connections, and steadily built a case for testing optimal control theory on segments of the public. He permitted himself to be persuaded that the best way to test his ideas lay with the feedback techniques already in use by the OPI. Besides, the OPI was fundamentally a service available to both Intelligence and Operations, both of which could profit from Mills's work as media control segued into social control.

By mid-July, Lt. Commander Boren Mills had seen the orders posting him to Sound Stage West. His floppy cassettes, his notes, even old textbooks were accorded special security and Mills made certain that his personal effects were packed in the same containers. In one container lay a souvenir for which he had a less than compelling cover story. It was hardly larger than a breadbox. He hoped he would not have to claim he had found it among the personal effects of Radioman Second Class Kimball Norton.

Chapter 70

The revenues of Schleicher County, Texas were not wasted on air-conditioning the Eldorado jail. Quantrill had sweated off two kilos after three days in his shared cell. "Man's got a right to be with his helpmeet," he yelled, shaking the bars, the concrete walls mocking him with echoes.

"If you was a man," chuckled the husky scarred specimen who lay on the lower bunk, "you wouldn't'a let no halfpint deputy bust you both."

"God's curse on 'em," Quantrill spat, then railed again at the bars. "God's curse on the gentile bastards!"

"I've had about enough of your noise," said his cellmate. "You and that hightits bitch in the women's wing—what's her name? Delight?"

"Delight," Quantrill yelled, his shoulder-length hair flying as he gripped the bars again. "Pray for deliverance, darlin'!"

From the opposite wing came an answering cry; a pitiable hopeless wail of female anguish. Sanger's voice, maintaining the guise of a young woman easily led.

The open-handed slap drove Quantrill's head against steel bars. "I'll give you deliverance if you don't shut up," said the man, fists on hips, no longer good-humored. "Them gentiles won't care if I beat some true religion into you."

Quantrill, huddling on his knees, hid his face and surreptitiously watched the man's feet. A reasonable amount of abuse, he could handle; but he could not pursue an assignment in the field with broken ribs. Snuffling, wishing he had the knack of weeping real tears on demand: "You sound like my pa."

"Maybe I am your pa," said the man, pleased with himself. "Your ma ever mention a Mitch Beasley?" Beasley eased himself back on his bunk.

"My ma didn't talk about men," said the youth querulously. "She was a good God-fearin' vessel—like my Delight." He let the silence spread; turned and wiped his nose on his sleeve; let his eyes grow wide and full of ersatz trust. "You really do remind me of my pa," he said. "But pa wasn't no gentile. He was kind of a prophet."

"The hell you say," Beasley murmured.

"We liberated a lot of folks, pa and me," Quantrill insisted. "And a lot of wordly treasure, too. Why, the stuff we buried near Ozona would buy salvation for a dozen sinners."

Beasley, after a long thoughtful pause: "I might just want to meet your pa."

"Gone to his reward," Quantrill said, biting his lip, looking away.

Locusts buzzed in the hackberry tree outside the cell. Beasley's bunk creaked. After an endless thirty seconds: "What if I was to tell you they call me Prophet Beasley?"

Contact. Quantrill had begun to think he'd wasted three more days on another false lead. He made his eyes wide again, came up to a kneeling position, his mouth slightly open. "I didn't think no jail could hold a true prophet," he said.

"Not in the fullness of time," Beasley intoned, studying the muscles of his heavy forearms as he stretched. The deep-chested voice lowered to accommodate the topic: "Maybe it was God's will brought us together, boy. You ever think about that?"

Quantrill gave a tentative nod, then clasped his hands and bowed over them. "Before you decide to leave, will you bless the union of me and my helpmeet?"

"It don't always work that way," Beasley said.

"Maybe—just *maybe,* God sent me as your earthly salvation."

Time to set the hook. "I'd have to think on it, pray on it. One thing sure, whatever happens me and Delight already said our vows before God."

"You sayin' you're purely stuck on that little hightits I seen joggin' around the exercise yard?"

Quantrill, head bowed: "We said our vows. I can't change that now."

"We'll see," said Beasley, and began to whistle a border tune through the gap in his front teeth. The youth retreated to the far corner of the cell, palms together, speaking in a near-whisper unintelligible from Beasley's bunk.

Quantrill had promised to pray for guidance. In a way he was doing precisely that. "Tau Sector, Tau Sector," he narrowcast, and waited for his critic to reply. Control had set them onto cold trails twice; this one felt warmer by the second.

Sandys jurnal Jul 18 Fri.

Mom says their going to librate profet Beasly soon as profet Jansen and his men get back from trading up north. They make lots of hooraw about revlashuns but there afraid to say boo without Jansen. Mom says sooner or later theyll come back with a possy on their tails. Dont you wait for nothing me or Child either Sandy, she says, you hitail it. These dam profets wont let us be took alive.

Chapter 71

Though it had been dark for three hours, Quantrill was still perspiring as he lay on his sodden upper bunk cursing a week of inactivity and Beasley's body odor. An insomniac locust still sizzled outside, endorsing the summer heat. He heard the faint squeal of brakes in the distance, then only night sounds. Presently he heard a murmur beyond the lockup; someone talking with the lone deputy. Quantrill would never know how the deputy had been taken out, but knew from the muffled commotion outside the window that someone outside was not too worried about discovery.

"Gadianton," said a male voice somewhere outside their window. In the front office, an alarm quavered, tripped by perimeter sensors.

Beasley rolled to his feet, chinned himself to the high window ledge. Quantrill noted the man's swift physical power. "Lamanites," Beasley hissed the countersign. "Here; and hurry up, I got acolytes."

A cargo hook grated on the ledge, linked to a steel beam that Beasley laid across inside the bars. Beasley was obviously experienced at demolition. From his upper bunk, Quantrill could see gloved hands arranging a one-cm. glass rope that stretched away into darkness. "We got maybe five minutes," said the man outside; "Jansen's got a reg'lar Saturday-night ruckus goin' in a roadhouse up north. But he didn't say nothin' about nobody else."

"I got reasons he'll understand," Beasley insisted. "Now, haul away!"

"On yore head be it—and you better get under somethin', don't forget that roof collapse in Roswell." Racing footsteps dopplered away.

A diesel coughed to life, steadied, clamored in the dark. At the window was only a keening scrape of protest while the cellmates lay curled beneath thin musty mattresses. Then a screech of metal, a shambling clatter of concrete and a puff of dust into the cell.

The hole started waist-high and extended to the ceiling. Beasley went through it with careful questing feet, backward, then was in urgent argument with others outside. Quantrill saw Beasley in the spread of half-light, now armed with a machine pistol. "I've told you what betrayal means, boy," he said. "Among the prophets, I'm the only friend you got."

"I want Delight," Quantrill whined, scrambling through the hole, one eye closed as Marty Cross had taught him. If you kept one eye closed in the light, that eye would have better night vision.

"Ever'body wants delight," an unfamiliar voice snickered. Faintly they could still hear the alarm; Quantrill felt sure it was patched into a radio alert.

"We got a little hightits vessel to get yet," Beasley warned, scooping up the beam and glass rope.

"You get her yourself," was the reply over receding steps of two men. Beasley stopped, indecisive.

"Go on," Quantrill said, taking a chance. "I'll find a way to get her out tomorrow."

"Tomorrow, shit, you don't know much! There ain't time; leave her!"

"I dunno where pa buried the stuff, and she does," Quantrill said, playing his hole card.

More cursing. A small vehicle thundered away without lights and Mitch Beasley sprinted to the larger vehicle. "Find the bitch so I can line up the truck," he called, tossing the cable into a cargo bay.

Quantrill knew Sanger's location; knew also that Control had arranged the transfer of other prisoners. He warned Sanger to get under a mattress, then resumed his monotonic transmission to Control. If law enforcement people reacted too quickly, he warned, they might blow the whole operation.

Beasley backed the terratired vehicle furiously toward the far end of the lockup; rushed to aid Quantrill at the high window. "Don't be scared, darlin'," Quantrill crooned through the window. "The kingdom of God almighty is at hand," and then the truck was lurching away, the glass cable humming as it came taut. The embedded windowframe came free this time, and a moment later Marbrye Sanger was wriggling past rough concrete. He grabbed her, felt the slide of lithe flesh, tasted the dusty, musty flavor of her mouth. Even in a jailbreak at midnight, he thought admiringly, Sanger gave award performances.

The cable and beam stowed, Beasley gestured Quantrill into the open cargo section and waved Sanger into the cab with him. When Beasley gestured now, he did it with a gun barrel. The truck sped away, going to battery mode for stealth, the hum of terratires and windsong muffling the electrics. The break had taken all of three minutes.

Alone, Quantrill spent the next ten minutes in an urgent dialogue with Control. "If Sanger acts too vulnerable to his religious doubletalk," he warned, "this Beasley character may decide to ice me and then sweet-talk her into showing him the stash. Tell her now, Control. He's quick; don't underestimate him."

"We don't," was the impersonal reply. "Beasley's thumbprint was on Sabado's belt buckle. We will brief Sanger as soon as she can acknowledge transmission."

Quantrill filed this for future reference. Sanger did not have to acknowledge a transmission, but inside that cab she was mostly surrounded by steel. Perhaps, after all, Control's own transmissions were more affected by a steel cage than T Section would like to admit. Quantrill reported that they were heading south on a secondary road, then cutting a trail to the east.

Beasley's helmsmanship was savage but unerring, the treadless terratires making a smooth spoor hard to follow. In an hour the truck, low beams flashing on when necessary, had covered fifty klicks of open country showing few and distant lights.

Quantrill roused himself as the truck stopped; saw the rhythmic flash of Beasley's lights, saw answering flashes from afar. Somewhere in the wild country on open range-land, T Section was about to enter the sacred sanctum of the Church of The Sacrificed Lamb.

Chapter 72

By the last week in July, media broadcasts had done what SinoInd troops could not: US/RUS forces were pulling back on two fronts in fear of Chinese Plague. India's Parliament initiated a massive withdrawal of her expeditionary troops from Kazakhstan and repositioned them in an arc north of the Indian desert, on recommendation of the sly Kirpal. Everyone knew that a few of those troops had plague but, by isolating all transferred units, India kept ANZUS invaders guessing. China no longer needed those Indian reinforcements because the American Fifth Army had pulled out, taking up new positions in the Irkutsk region north of Mongolia. The Allies no longer feared a coordinated breakout from Mongolia but, perhaps inevitably, Russian troops had run short of antipersonnel mines and Frisbees before retreating.

The Russians knew of Chinese Plague from their radios, and those who placed little faith in protective CBW gear (i.e., most RUS troops) feared that they faced an enemy more than human. A Siberian salient already bulged up across the Amur, chiefly of harmless tribesmen seeking abandoned riches, becoming less harmless as plague spread into the tribes. Our Fifth Army made good use of RUS railways, racing to new positions above the Siberian salient. Thanks to excellent medical aid and frequent injections of half-truths in briefings, the morale of US troops was still good.

Keratophagic staph, our troops were told, depended largely on transmission from host to host, unlike windborne paranthrax. If you were young and well-fed, and if you stayed well clear of infiltrating locals, you might not be in danger. The CBW masks and envelopes would protect you in plague spots. The advance of the enemy—assuming he could rally for any advance—had been taken into account by the countless millions of antipersonnel minelets left by our retreating armies which we could trigger by microwave, or an enemy footfall could do it. The RUS still employed their interdicting Frisbees while backing away from the Sinkiang border. The westward retreat of our First and Third Armies was orderly.

The US Sixth and Eighth Armies still protected sortie bases in India, devastating that country's efforts to harvest a crop—*any* crop. The Viets were clamoring to know the whereabouts of some twenty divisions of troops they had sent into Szechuan. Allied media were only too happy to suggest a numbing truth (which we did not for a moment believe), namely that entire Viet divisions littered the floor of the Pacific in small defunct submarines. All this, our officers made clear to our troops. From several quarters, Allied troops were repeating an old phrase: home by Christmas.

In short, our troops got only the news.

Non-news: neutral Mexico, though pro-Allies, permitted a few well-heeled SinoInd refugees to take refuge in the State of Nayarit in June before she identified at least one case of plague among them. Removed offshore to the Islas Marias, they posed no threat beyond that of rumor.

Non-news: the rumor of Chinese Plague in Mexico was itself a news-vectored plague, gaining early credence through a few initial holo and radio broadcasts in our southern border cities. Our subsequent denials were fruitless appeals to frightened householders in Tucson and San Diego suburbs. While admitting that 'a few' Americans were needlessly evacuating, we did not add that in three days' time no US Customs people remained at Mexican border posts. Well-supplied by Pemex, Mexicans lost little time in streaming across the border. If gringos were fleeing from shadows, an enterprising campesino could help himself to what they left behind. Within a week, Pemex fuel was sloshing in Mexican trucks that plied the roads north of Mexicali, Nogales, Ciudad Juárez, in entrepreneurial support of this casual invasion. For the first time, America was learning what Germans had experienced in the final months of World War II.

Non-news: the US Fourth Army was thinly spread on the
west coast and depended on Mexico for half of its refined fuel
since most of our refineries were in ruins. When Mexican
tankers began to produce passengers as well as diesel fuel
from San Diego to San Pedro, we had the choice of accepting
both or neither. The Mexicans would not listen to schemes
that kept their citizens offshore. This disrespect for US law
was directly proportional to our loss of clout in Mexican
eyes. Since the 1980's, Mexico's petroleum traffic had expanded her wealth greatly, but the US had lost half her
population and ninety per cent of her industrial potential in
the first week of the war. We were still capable of defying
Mexico, but running on our reserves. It was a forthright case
of a healthy neighbor leaning on a sick one, and only the
politically naive were surprised. We had done exactly the
same to Mexico, twice upon a time. Power politics is the only
kind there is.

Non-news: our Second Army had all it could do to enforce
the continental quarantine and to guard our eastern shores. It
was a sympathetic army of occupation, committed to an
endless fight against paranthrax in a battle that required great
courage and stamina, but conferred little glory.

Non-news: White House Central abandoned its Sandia
Mountain warrens for a safer residence in the Wasatch Mountains east of Salt Lake City. White House Deseret was a
phrase, and a concept, deeply satisfying to many men in the
Collier administration. The citizens of Utah, largely Latter-
Day Saints, were among the staunchest patriots and most
unquestioning followers America had ever produced. In this
climate of Mormon hope for a devout America, only one
internal problem had grown larger: the guerrilla groups.
Outlaw bands continued to borrow the trappings of Godliness
to support their claims to plunder.

Yale Collier's days were focused increasingly on items in
the non-news—not a very encouraging sign. He could not
afford to threaten Mexico, a major energy supplier, with
force against her lackadaisical occupation of our soil. The
Mexicans ignored our borders from the wild country of

southwest Texas to the coast of central California. It had been a mistake to build tanker facilities at Lompoc and Monterey because Mexicans leaving those tankers triggered widespread evacuation in those coastal regions south of San Francisco. It did little good to broadcast subtle hints that a foreign pilgrim could not spread disease after his burial. It did no good at all to insist that Mexicans were not carriers of the plague that was blinding China.

Collier studied holo maps with the commanding general of Fourth Army, and prayed for guidance. At bottom, Collier believed in the goodness of humankind, and mourned the necessity to wage an undeclared guerrilla war on Mexican emigrants. But already El Paso, Las Cruces, Tucson, and the California coast above San Francisco were ruins in which Mexicans, not US citizens, sifted the detritus and reclaimed the land. If it was to be war, it would *have* to be low-key, and defensive. We did not have the troops to pursue it far, and Canada rejected our suggestions that Canadian troops might help us. For that matter, we were none too keen to give Canada more influence on our soil than she already had.

After a forty-eight-hour search of his soul, President Collier accepted the plan of Fourth Army strategists. Our fuel reserves would support redeployment of infantry on the western side of the San Joaquin Valley, thence in a thin khaki line south of the Mojave to Phoenix and Roswell. While giving up (temporarily, Collier told himself; only temporarily) valuable anchorages, we still had access to the Pacific from Point Arena northward. Our Navy still owned the continental shelf. Oil fields near Bakersfield and the fecund farms of the San Joaquin would still be ours, protected by the Fourth Army. In effect, we had leased some of our soil to Mexico in exchange for fuel.

Unofficially, the Mexican Government was understanding. If by some miracle the SinoInds managed a west coast invasion, the Mexican fuel would help us reclaim what latinos now called Alta Mexico. Officially, we permitted Mexican squatters while warning that we could not assure their safety.

Collier dared to hope that a persistent CIA abstract from
Canada was more than rumor, though Canada was equally
persistent in her confidential denials to White House Deseret.
Moreover, said the Canadian ambassador, any open rumor
that Canadians had beaten keratophagic staph would only
exacerbate troubled relations between Canada and the RUS;
the beleaguered Russians would instantly demand the secret.
A secret (the ambassador repeated) which did not exist. After
all: if Canada had found a cure, would she not already be
distributing it?

The implied answer was 'yes'. The correct answer was
'no'. Canada needed time to produce her breakthrough
against *S. rosacea* in quantity, and to distribute it selectively.

Chapter 73

"Selah," intoned the Prophet Jansen.

Quantrill responded like the others, got to his feet, willed
the pins and needles to leave his feet after an hour on his
knees in a sweltering barn with fifty others. Rituals of the
Church of The Sacrificed Lamb owed little to Mormonism,
much to enthusiasm. Once again Seth Howell's briefings
were verified in the field; the zealot gangs borrowed just
enough from the LDS to attract some unstable Mormon
rejects. Whatever crimes they committed would ultimately
be placed, by gentiles, at the feet of the LDS. No wonder,
then, that the Collier administration entrusted its remedy to T
Section . . .

"I see you got the grease out of your hair in time for
devotionals, Brother Stone," said Prophet Monroe, a
sallow-haired little man in a suit that had once been expensive. Monroe kept the financial books for the church, but had
also helped with an engine change the day before. Barring his
religious views, he seemed a reasonable sort.

Quantrill, alias 'Lendal Stone', nodded; watched Jansen's approach from the corner of his eye. "Clean hands and a pure heart, Prophet Monroe, like you told me," said Quantrill. "Didn't want to be unseemly first time I showed up in church."

"Plenty of wives and little vessels cuttin' their eyes at you," Monroe grinned; winked. "If they had votes, you'd be Prophet Stone already." Quantrill did not comment on Monroe's fantasy. Most of the women and children seemed dull-eyed captives with all the personality of so many ears of corn in a crib.

"Brother Monroe." The little man jumped, made a show of facing Jansen as an equal. Jansen went on, "Could you spare an acolyte for awhile?"

Quantrill had been watching the man—had studied them all—for three days. Jansen stood tall and tanned in a suit of black, with a formal white shirt and black string tie. His dark gray Stetson and low-quarter black boots fitted well; lent authenticity to his leadership in the devotionals. But every afternoon, Monroe had said, a different prophet performed that solemn office. This was Quantrill's first gathering with the faithful, and it seemed to be an occasion for formal attire. Earlier in the day Jansen had worn work clothes, the tendons in his arms marking him as one familiar with hard work. But always he wore that stern look of command, and his flat twanging baritone implied that it was used to obedience.

"Glad to oblige, Brother." *And scared not to,* Monroe's tone said. Since Quantrill was Monroe's only helper, the subtlety was shallow. Monroe formally presented Acolyte Lendal Stone to Prophet Jansen, excused himself, and hurried from the barn to seek the warm Texas breeze.

Quantrill gazed up at the commanding face with a polite smile, waiting. Gradually the lines in Jansen's face grew more stern, the eyes more piercing, until Quantrill's smile became quizzical. Then, "Oh," said the youth, and dropped his gaze.

"Oh," Jansen mocked him. "That's better, boy. Insolent eyes aren't fitten in the young. Remember that."

"Yessir, I will."

"Yes, *Prophet Jansen*."

Quantrill made his voice very small: "Yes, Prophet Jansen."

Pleased, the baritone lifted a bit. "Prophet Beasley testified on your behalf Sunday morning. Some were in favor of consigning you and your vessel to perdition, but Prophet Beasley thought you might be worthy of the kingdom of God. I heard all about your pa and his ways and your pilgrimage back from Modesto." He paused, rocking slightly on the balls of his feet. The next moment his voice was almost singsong, as if murmuring to himself: "That's all a pack of lies, of course."

Still looking down at his feet, Quantrill shook his head ever so slightly. "I know better'n to lie to a prophet, as God is my witness," he mumbled.

"No you don't," said Jansen, enjoying himself. "I know Modesto like the back of my hand. Where was your pa's cafe?"

If this was true, Quantrill had only seconds to make some decisions. Control could not hear Jansen; only Quantrill himself. Scuffing his feet in the dust, scanning his memory furiously for details of his cover, he said, "Out Route one-thirty-two on the right-hand side of the road, east of the shopping center. We had snooker tables and shuffleboard." Surely, Control would recognize this as an interrogation, but his critic lay silent.

Judicious silence, then a chuckle from Jansen: "More of a roadhouse than a cafe." More silence, then suddenly: "What was your under-the-counter beer?"

"Coors," said Quantrill, blessing Mason Reardon's thoroughness in the cover sessions. "But the black-and-whites knowed it; wasn't no secret."

"I just bet it wasn't," Jansen chuckled again. "Well, you pass muster on that score—so you tell me why your pa would *hide his treasures from his own seed*, but trusts the secret to a vessel that isn't even family!"

In a crystalline burst of insight, Quantrill realized that a man like Jansen was simply incapable of believing such a thing, true or not. He spoke huskily, adding a touch of nasality; tried to recover the lost credibility. ''Pa showed us both, Prophet Jansen. It was down the road from a kilometer post, but I ain't that good at numbers. Delight, she's real good, why she—anyhow,'' he feared overdoing it, ''I can't recall five-ninety-two or two-ninety-five, so what I told Prophet Beasley ain't really a lie. Not *really*,'' he whined.

''And besides, you'd say anything to get your little hotsy out of the jug. Right?''

''We made a vow. And I ain't seen her at all today,'' Quantrill said, not missing the practiced ease with which Jansen was removing his broad leather belt.

''A half-lie deserves half-punishment,'' said Jansen, and began to swing the belt.

If this was half-punishment, Quantrill thought, cringing in the dust, he hoped to be spared the whole article. Jansen had the knack of flicking the belt's tip, and of picking his spot. He picked a dozen spots on Quantrill's naked flesh; wrists, ears, the back of his neck. The young gunsel groaned and writhed face down, hands protecting his head. Quantrill's tears were real, half from pain and half from suppressed rage.

''That wasn't for lyin' to Beasley,'' Jansen said when he had begun to reinsert his belt through its loops, breathing hard but speaking pleasantly. ''That was for askin' Almighty God to bear false witness to your half-lie. All the prophets are equal in the sight of the Lord, Acolyte Stone; but I ask you in all loving kindness to be careful which one you talk to about your pa's stash on the Ozona Road.

''Now I don't like to say things twice, so listen. We're missin' three vessels—missed 'em ever since the night you came, some fool thought Beasley was a posse and gave the alarm and off they went. A mother with a nine-year-old and a sucklin' babe. We got men out that you ain't—haven't—met yet, still lookin', since they were in charge when the three got away. It's fitten. If they make it to a highway, we might have to pull up stakes. Your vessel, Delight, is on a sweep with prophets right now. You're goin' with others to cover another area. Bring me a body. Mother, girl, or babe, where one is the others are—and that'll be the Lord's sign you're worthy of us.''

Quantrill got to his feet slowly, dusting himself off, disgusted with his own genuine fear of this cool merciless fanatic. ''Yessir—Prophet Jansen. You want me to shoot on sight? I don't know what they look like; maybe I should bring 'em in for questioning.''

''Mother's skinny, short gray hair; hell, they'll look like strangers, Stone, that's all you need to go on. And you won't have a gun, but I don't need them three for questions. I have all the answers, all I need is bodies. Let it be a challenge to you.'' The black eyes flickered in glacial amusement: ''God put plenty of rocks out there to be used in His service.'' With that, the Prophet Jansen straightened his severe black suit, polished the tips of his boots before striding from the barn into God's own brightly-polished, midsummer wild-country sun.

A half-hour later, Quantrill stood empty-handed in jeans and canvas work shirt and watched morosely as the terratired vehicle bobbed from sight over the toasted-meringue tints of Texas rangeland. He knew exactly where he was; had known it from the morning when he saw the way that barn listed like some shiplapped drunkard lost on broken limestone soil. He was on the Willard place, without the Willards. There were enough predators on two legs and four to dishearten the most hard-bitten of small ranchers. He had alerted Control, seeking confirmation that he was again in Sutton County east of Sonora with a raging case of *déjá vu*.

Another man hopped down from the distant vehicle and waved. They paced each other in a slow march to the north, a red sun over their left shoulders, and Quantrill murmured his prayer to the great god Tau Sector.

''We have an interesting sanction, Q,'' said the sexless Control as Quantrill moved down a gully in search of the escapees. He intended to ignore them unless they shot first, but could not afford to blow the assignment on behalf of some poor human flotsam. Control continued, ''Pelletier and

Quinn are reassigned to counter intrusions by Mexican nationals to the south. Their team will not, repeat not, be available to you.''

"That's interesting, all right. Doesn't help us much here," Quantrill replied.

"Neg, Q; *your* new sanction is interesting. S has met two more prophets on picket duty to the south. She reports sexual harassment but stands ready when you are." Something almost humorous, rare in Control: "Even *more* than you are. From your team reports I make it twelve male prophets, seventeen adult females, ten immature females. No immature males; we doubt they intend to keep you long."

"Figures," Quantrill .murmured, staring down at damp sand in a dry-wash. He knelt to study the hoofprints, thinking at first they had been made by deer. The split print was huge; a handwidth long, almost as wide, trailed by small secondary marks. "Control, patch me to CenCom research."

"Patching," then a voice indistinguishable from Control's: "CenCom research on standby." CenCom's site was never far from the soul of government. Now it was near Ogden, Utah.

"I have a hoofprint in wet sand," Quantrill mused, "and I want to know what made it. Uh—identify an animal track, CenCom."

"Please lay out a graphic plot," said CenCom, as if he had all the time in the world.

"Neg. Work from oral description, CenCom. Ah, give me a human auditor."

Somewhere an electronic mind was passing the buck without reluctance. CenCom could not care less, or more. Or at all.

"Research auditor on-line for Tau Sector," said the same voice, no longer the same mind.

"I have an animal track and need you to identify it." He was walking again, aware that he might be drawing the curiosity of the man on his flank, speaking now from memory. "Split hoof like a deer but a very wide splay in front. Bullet-shaped marks behind, the diameter of my finger and pointing outward. Width of print eight or nine centimeters, length ten or more.''

"Location?"

"Oh; open range in Sutton County, Texas."

"Searching," said the voice. Every five seconds it said, 'searching' again. Finally, "No Olympic elk your area. Swine a possibility, but no known variety with prints those dimensions."

"Check on Russian boar," he said, licking dry lips. Suddenly Quantrill wished very much that he had a weapon; and if possible, one much larger than a thirty-caliber brush gun.

"Neg. Repeat, neg. Subject would mass four to five hundred kilos or more, the size of a Montana grizzly. A definite possibility if you downsize your figures."

"Try upsizing yours," Quantrill snorted. "Thank you, CenCom; patch me back to Tau Sector Control." He advised Control of his suspicion that a red-eyed satan of five-hundred kilo mass was not far away. Then, "Now, about my interesting new sanction—"

"Take all males; repeat, your team sanctioned to take all males. Do you copy?"

"*All* the prophets? Good God, first you tell me Pelletier can't make a weapons drop, and next you call for a massacre!"

Control's tone did not threaten. No threat was necessary in its, "You're aborting, Q?"

"Neg. Maybe we can pick 'em off gradually. Listen, some of these guys are just harmless weirdos. Do I rate an explanation?"

He had never heard a voder translate a sigh before. "Fourth Army can't spare troops into wild country for Mexican incursions. There are more vital things to protect further west. Civilian agencies are swamped and every one of those crazies is a potential nucleus of another group. They're just too good at what they do. Wait one, Q." Pause; a long one. Quantrill saw the man on his flank angling in his direction. Control again: "S has just reported that a Prophet Ryerson has killed a woman escapee. Now your sanction priority reads Jansen, Coates, Beasley, Ryerson, Contreras. The rest are secondary.''

''I don't know Coates or Ryerson.''

''Your partner does. Intimately,'' said Control. ''They took their frustrations out on her.''

Quantrill quenched a rise of fury, coded out, squinting at a rock overhang swept clear in a recent freshet. Protected from the midday sun by the ledge, a shallow stagnant pool gleamed in late reflections. Quantrill spotted the tracks in gritty sand, hurried near, squatted by the puddle and ran his fingers over the deep prints. The hackles of his forearms were at attention.

''What'cha got?'' Striding up with his small arsenal was Contreras, the only latino prophet, who made no secret of his distaste for young 'Stone'.

Quantrill stood up, stepped forward, planted a foot squarely on the print he had been studying. ''Aw, shit,'' he mumbled and made a gesture of hopeless cloddishness. ''Well, you c'n still see 'em. Biggest deer in these parts, I reckon.''

Contreras blanched, crossed himself, realized what he was doing and ended by scratching his right breast. ''Come away from there. That's the devil's waterhole.''

Quantrill went quickly, glad that Contreras did not want a closer inspection. ''The real devil, Prophet Contreras? Honest?''

A gulp and nod. ''I saw him once,'' Contreras said, gruff and matter-of-fact, climbing up a prominence in search of the truck. Quantrill knew he could take Contreras with or without weapons; but he was none too sure of the return route. Better to wait until he and Sanger could cover each other's flanks.

''You seen the *devil*?'' Tell me about it,'' Quantrill pursued, because it seemed to put Contreras on edge.

''Folks who used to own this spread told us he was here,'' Contreras said, scanning the brush in half-light. ''Prophet Jansen, he said it was devil worship to set out sacrifices. He put three of us out as sentries ever' night. Then one mornin' we found a prophet tore all to pieces. His gun had been fired once. We seen the same prints you seen. We spread out and went after him afoot thinkin' it was just some ol' boar hog. It was after dark when I sat down for a breather, waitin' for the moon to show me the way home. Pretty soon I hear a snuffle. Looked around, but all I seen was this boulder on the rise above me.

"And then I seen the boulder *move,*" Contreras breathed. "It sort of growed, big as a chickenhouse, and he was lookin' down on me and I seen his horns and I didn't wait to see no more."

Horns? Quantrill wondered if moon-silhouetted ears or tusks would serve up such a horrific vision. "Why didn't you try and shoot," he asked.

"Shoot the devil? Shoot Ba'al? It's been tried, fool. I value my hide too much," said Contreras, staring toward the headlights that bobbed toward them in dusk, clicking his chemlamp in reply.

The driver, Monroe, had already picked up Beasley, whose elation balanced Monroe's dejection. "They found the Grange woman," Beasley said, clapping a hand on the shoulder of Contreras. "She nearly made it to the Roosevelt Road."

At the name, Quantrill forced his pulse to diminish. Not once, until now, had anyone mentioned the names of the fugitives. It was the third one, the baby, that had diverted Quantrill's suspicion—and hope.

Contreras: "She lead 'em to the others?"

Monroe: "She might have, if Ryerson wasn't so trigger-happy. Jansen figures we'll find the kids around there tomorrow."

"No point snoopin' around out here in Ba'al's back yard anymore," Contreras said in plain relief.

"You see him again?" Beasley's religion was in his ammo clips. He fingered the safety of his carbine.

"Just his prints. The acolyte here seen 'em first at a water hole. Why shit, he didn' know *what* he seen."

The others laughed uneasily. Quantrill nodded as if the

joke were on himself. In a way, it was. At first he had known only that a child's sandal had made a single print in the sand, later marred by the great deep incisions of a demonic hoof. Quantrill's foot had erased the datum. Probably, he thought in sympathetic dread, that grizzly-sized brute had already tracked the child; had sought his kill many klicks from any possible help. But now he was certain that the sandal had been worn by little Sandy Grange. How long ago had she made that print?

Quantrill felt gooseflesh at his nape, arms, calves. The superstitious awe in these murdering fanatics was affecting him, he decided. He'd give a year of his life to be left alone out there with a night-scoped H & K—but the little truck was taking him away, toward a danger he understood, and to Marbrye Sanger whom he thought he understood. Unable to contact Control in such close quarters he sat sullen, silent, listening to Beasley exult over the murder of an exhausted woman; promising himself that Beasley's ledger would balance before long.

Chapter 73

Decanting from the truck between the Willard house and barn, Quantrill peered at moving figures, seeking Sanger. The dark earth was splashed with parallelograms of light from the house and, as always, the women and children cowered anonymously hoping to be overlooked. Near the husky terratired truck was a group of prophets, variously armed. At their feet lay a pitiful handful of rags. "Delight?" He'd almost shouted her real name.

"Lendal," Sanger answered in a whine, and he saw that she was restrained by two unfamiliar males.

Quantrill hurried toward her, crooning endearments, and was felled by a backhand from Jansen. "Control your lusts,

acolyte,'' said the big man without heat. ''You'll be with
your vessel soon enough. Stand over there in the light,'' he
ordered, and Quantrill scrambled up to comply. With his
body illuminated, face in shadow, he could use Control as
go-between to Sanger.

The huddled body on the ground was pitifully thin, a
gray-haired husk of a woman that Quantrill saw had been
Louise Grange. Jansen stood above the corpse. ''Brothers,
you know what'll happen if the gentiles find we're here. We
have four trucks; not enough for everybody. It has been
revealed to me,'' he said, his voice rising, peaking on *'revealed'* in a liturgical rhythm long-practiced in many a pul-
pit, ''It has been revealed to me that we must stand ready to
flee again, yes I say *flee*, into the wilderness. The devil's
seed is still at large. If we find her not tomorrow, we must
repair—to another place.''

Jansen had the knack of the old phrasing; could bind
credulous minds with his spell that was more music than
words.

Quantrill spoke with Control; asked to be patched directly
to Sanger who stood between two men and could not be
expected to answer. To Sanger he said, ''Jansen's warning
'em they'll have to travel light. That may mean killing a few
people, Sanger. They'll start with me or you, so don't get
separated. Uh—if you have a weapon, cough.''

Sanger didn't cough; moved her head sideways instead.
Quantrill noticed that Jansen had now ripped away the veneer
of equality and fraternity from his orders and was apportion-
ing men to cruise the roads until dawn. The little Grange
vessel, with or without a baby in her arms, might try to flag
down a vehicle if she had not already collapsed from thirst or
exposure. It had been revealed to him, Jansen boasted, that
the girl was not far from where her mother had been gunned
down. Quantrill's smile at this was grim and short-lived; if
Sandy Grange was where he thought she was, she and the
baby were between two devils.

Grumbling, trotting away for quick meals and canteen
refills, the men hurried to do Jansen's bidding. ''Now then,''

said the mollified Jansen to the youth, "while our brothers toil in the Lord's service, you can bring some worldly goods into the fold, Acolyte Stone. Prophet Monroe, we'll need you to drive."

"I've felt a callin'," growled Beasley, now pressing an old police revolver into Sanger's side, thrusting her forward. "It's fell to me to do the drivin', dear brothers."

Jansen was silent for two heartbeats, then replied in pleasant tautology, "Revelations always reveal. Prophet Monroe can help guard the females of the flock in your stead."

Jansen moved away, incisive with command, checking on fuel, weapons, a sufficiency of guards whose heartlessness he trusted if more of the flock tried to stray. Quantrill suspected that Jansen did not put much trust in Monroe or Contreras where murder was concerned. But Ryerson had shot down an exhausted mother that day, and Ryerson would again help guard the flock while others pressed their search. As Jansen conferred with Monroe and Ryerson, three of their four vehicles rolled away in convoy, running lights taped, the lead truck using one headlamp. From a distance it might have been a single motorcycle.

Beasley motioned Sanger and Quantrill toward the four-passenger pickup, muttering. "Thinks I dunno what he's up to," he grated, and, "figgers that assbreath Monroe wouldn't insist on his cut," he snarled, and, "all we'd get is a hard luck story."

In the dim light of the pickup's instrument cluster, the two gunsels exchanged glances; if Jansen was expected to lie about buried treasures, his young guides were to be silenced. Quantrill was neither surprised nor dismayed; he wanted isolation from the ranks as much as Jansen did, and for the same reason.

Jansen returned in minutes with carbine and sidearm, checked the pickup for pick and shovel, then shoved into the rear seat with Sanger and stowed a recent-model assault rifle at his feet. A moment later Beasley had the vehicle jouncing in the direction the other vehicles had taken while Jansen, cool and cordial, prompted their captives to recall a number.

"It's a little away from post five-ninety-two," Sanger said truthfully. She and Quantrill had buried the marked bills and bits of jewelry themselves before beginning their charade in the Eldorado jail. "I'll find the spot when we get near it. Prophet Jansen, you gonna treat us nice after we share with you?"

"Of course," he said, stroking the chestnut tresses, not putting his automatic pistol away. Then his free hand moved toward her breasts, as one might idly fondle a stray cat.

"You make me feel cared for," she said, letting her head slide onto his chest.

"A good shepherd cares for his flock," Jansen said.

"And we care for our shepherd," Sanger went on, her voice becoming muffled as her head slid steadily downward.

Quantrill heard the hiss of a zipper; peered hard through the windshield, willing himself above anxiety and dull rage, watching Beasley with care. Beasley grinned to himself. By now they were four or five klicks from the ranch. Quantrill felt a tug at his seat back. Jansen was gripping it with one hand.

The report was a thunderclap in the rear seat. Sanger's, "Beasley's yours," came a split second before the second and third explosions. Jansen's scream was only quasi-human.

Beasley slammed the brakes, reaching for the long-barreled revolver under his left thigh. But Beasley was not left-handed and, in any case, Quantrill was braced and ready.

The howling wheezes of Jansen, gutshot three times at point-blank range, carried too much vitality. Sanger fought hard for the automatic now, one elbow jamming into his throat as she sought the trigger again. But the fourth and fifth rounds went through the pickup's roof.

For Quantrill the scene unfolded in slow motion. Facing Beasley, feet braced against floorboards, he swung the edge of his left hand upward, catching Beasley above the lip in a driving slam to the base of the nose. His next slash was against Beasley's throat, but now the driver had relinquished the steering wheel and hammered at Quantrill with a rope-corded right forearm. Then the revolver came into view, and at the same instant the pickup began to tilt as it spun sideways into deep ruts. Quantrill harbored a healthy respect for Beasley's superior physical strength, but more still for the heavy slugs. The gunsel's right hand slammed the hand with the revolver against the window frame while he butted upward into Beasley's face.

The revolver went out the window as the pickup tilted onto its right side, Quantrill pivoting his legs to drive them into Beasley's ribcage when the larger man tumbled toward him. The pickup continued its roll, the windshield shattering into the myriad tiny cubes typical of automotive glass. Quantrill planted his head into the safety of Beasley's midriff while he waited for the world to quit its headlong tumble.

Beasley felt himself flung halfway out the windshield opening and, as the vehicle came to rest on its wheels, was conscious enough to try crawling free. But one leg was still inside the cab when the phenomenon of Quantrill's reflexes came into play. The gunsel ducked away from the man's flailing brogan, caught it with both hands, wrenched it more than halfway around and held on.

The grinding snap was audible over Beasley's cry; he tried kicking once more as Quantrill gripped his trousers, screamed as the raw edge of a fractured fibula scraped, then lay across the hood of the vehicle, pounding an impotent fist on the plastic, whinnying with rage and pain.

The driver's door was open, the interior light revealing Sanger with teeth bared, both legs locked around one of Jansen's arms as she pinioned him and waited out his final struggle holding his right arm in a double arm-bar. Jansen's head was visible, pressed against the seat back; his eyes open, his face a terrible cyanotic blue-gray. Quantrill twisted a good grip on Beasley's trouser cuff with one hand, stretched back with the heel of his free hand and triphammered Jansen's face until the prophet went limp.

When Sanger glanced toward him, Quantrill hand-signed for a weapon. Sanger found Jansen's automatic in the seat, passed it forward, then felt at Jansen's throat for a pulse.

Quantrill knew she was checking on the evanescence of the human soul, but he was an observer, too. He saw her eyes searching, the play of tiny muscles in the high cheeks, her tonguetip serious and prominent between pursed lips. He thought then that he had never seen Marbrye Sanger looking lovelier than that moment, as she hovered over a man she had destroyed in mortal combat.

When he felt the youth release his leg, Beasley tried instantly to escape. He tumbled from hood to road, blinded by the headlights that still glared at the horizon, gobbling with pain. He managed to stand, testing his weight on the traitor ankle, then jerked himself off-balance as he saw the despised acolyte striding into the cones of light holding a fifteen-round automatic. For six or eight hundred milliseconds, Beasley was the picture of a beaten man.

Then, because he depended upon the naivete of youth, Beasley was something else. Several times in his blood-spattered career, Beasley had indulged in a tactic that had always succeeded by its very strangeness. Literally, he had a fit.

Throwing a fit is not all that difficult. One must simply be willing to short-circuit *all* of the shame constraints learned from infancy onward. 'This or that you must not do; this shames you, that makes others feel shame.' Urination, tearing at one's own hair, speaking gibberish as though in (foreign) tongues, groveling and capering in the dirt—all public behaviors forbidden to most adults to such a degree that 'speaking in tongues' is a legitimate topic of psycholinguistic study.

''*Don't touch me, don'ttouchmedon'ttouchme*,'' Beasley shrieked, flopping down in fair imitation of a chimpanzee, arms slapping past his head to strike the opposite shoulders. Beasley's voice rose gradually to falsetto, ululating like an alarm, then spewing flecks of spittle with syllables crammed together in bizarre combination. He pounded the ground, screamed at the sky, cursed in tongues and in good old Texas American, and all the while he writhed closer to a stone at the edge of the road. But Beasley had to know where his enemy was, the little bastard, standing there without a word as if he knew what he was doing with that Browning in his hand; one good fling with that rock and *then* we'll see who's so fuggin' calm; and then Beasley paused for that necessary instant to get his bearings as he located the enemy.

The single round, fired from two meters away, was still applauded by its echoes when Quantrill murmured, "Nice try," in compliment to a dead man.

With Sanger's help, Quantrill tumbled the body into the rear seat, arranged next to Jansen so that a casual glance would reveal nothing. Sanger, always fastidious, used a canteen to wash the blood from her hands and blouse as Quantrill steered the pickup toward the ranch.

Sanger kissed Quantrill under the ear before advising Control of their tally. "If we can secure their command post," she went on, "we can pick them off as they return."

Control asked a question on Sanger's frequency.

"An Army-issue M-27 and a new Browning auto with, um, eight rounds left. I propose circling around on foot with the carbine so Quantrill can draw them out in the open with some wild story. There's three of 'em; should be a turkey shoot."

Quantrill doused the lights before the gleam of the ranch house showed on their horizon, heard Control's reply in his own critic. "Q qualified better with Army-issue weapons, S, and you'd be less threatening bait. Swap roles and pursue your assignment."

Quantrill stopped the vehicle a kilometer from their goal, spent the next fifteen minutes crossing the broken plain on foot, informed Control that two of the three guards were strolling about and clearly lit from the ranch house. Only little Monroe was unaccounted for; doubtless he would emerge when the pickup churned into view.

Presently the pickup raced in, horn tooting, obviously much worse for recent wear. Quantrill waited until he saw Monroe hurry from the barn, then slipped to the rear of the ramshackle ranch house. Its rear door had been nailed shut and inside he heard female voices raised in consternation at what they saw from the front windows.

"From what S is saying, they're not buying her story," said Control. "They've taken her weapon."

Quantrill could see that much. Monroe stared motionless at the carnage in the back seat, but Contreras held a sidearm on Sanger and was too near her for a safe shot at fifty meters, much less a three-round burst from the M-27. A beefy young gorilla stood by with a pump shotgun. From Sanger's description he'd be the murderer-rapist, Ryerson.

Quantrill ducked behind the house, smashed a window with the butt of his carbine, heard screams from within. "Lights out," he hissed at them, then broke the other window at the back of the house and wriggled forward along the foundation line.

The lights did not go out, but two dozen wails went up from within. It was just as well for Quantrill; the light gave him a good view as the heavy-set Ryerson abandoned Sanger to race toward what he imagined was a prison break. Ryerson fired one blast from his shotgun as he ran, evidently not caring what he hit so long as the sound carried authority.

Now some of the brutalized sheep of the Church of the Sacrificed Lamb were battering at the remaining shards of windowglass as Quantrill held his finger motionless on the trigger. He lay still, in full view of anyone who happened to glance at the porch foundation. Ryerson pounded nearer, heading for the rear of the house. And *still* Sanger did not make a move to get clear of Contreras.

To Quantrill's intense relief, Ryerson disappeared around the other side of the house. Then a chorus of screams as Ryerson punctuated the roar of his voice with the shotgun's exclamation. Contreras whirled in Quantrill's direction, Sanger's unerring kick sent him spinning, and with two three-round bursts Quantrill left Contreras dying. Sanger dived for the sidearm of Contreras, rolled out of the light, then followed Monroe who had run bleating into the scrub.

Quantrill stood and darted a quick look, aghast as he saw through the front window into bedlam. The parlor partition had been removed so that one side of the house was a long dormitory of squalid pallets. Slumped in the ruined back window was a ruined human being gunned down while athwart the ledge. Two dozen women and children lay on the floor screaming, some trying to protect their small wards as another blast lanced in, blowing a hat-sized hole in the roof not far from where Quantrill stood. Quantrill did not know whether his enemy had correctly interpreted the burps of the M-27 until he saw the hulking Ryerson move into view, peering past his victim who lay in the window.

Ryerson was grinning fiercely as he recycled the pump, but the grin flicked to something else as he glanced down the length of the room and saw what faced him outside the front window, ten meters away. Quantrill, knees flexed, his fire selector set on 'full auto', stared impassively over his front sight into the eyes of Prophet Ryerson. It was the last thing Ryerson ever saw.

Chapter 74

Control had an excellent suggestion which Quantrill followed when at last the female captives could listen to him. They trooped to the barn, there to stay until dawn unless they spied familiar vehicles returning. In that case, Quantrill advised, their best course was to fade as fast and silently as possible into the open range—and not all in one bunch. Three of the women had husbands among the prophets, but none were thinking in any terms but plain desertion by now.

Sanger returned as Quantrill was questioning one of the women. According to Sanger, Monroe had been too slow and too loud. "The score," she said, counting the remaining half-dozen rounds in her clip, "is five to zip. Control tells me we should be setting out the pickup as bait if we're still operational."

Quantrill did not expect the prophets until dawn but, as

Control pointed out, the enemy would be haggard, sleepless.
The T Section pair could sleep in relays and would have both
cover and surprise on their side. They broke into the pantry
cum weapons cache in the house, loaded the half-dozen
weapons and all the ammunition into the pickup before
returning to the rutted road.

At midnight the pickup stood across the ruts in a depression where it could be seen from only fifty meters away.
Beasley's massive form slumped behind the wheel as if
asleep. Jansen sat erect in the back seat, held up by a pick
handle under his chin. Empty weapons, each barrel and
receiver filled with dirt, lay strewn widely where a questing
prophet would have to expose himself to fire from two
quadrants.

From Sanger's description of the setup, Control was
pleased. If the prophet vehicles returned one at a time there
should be no problem. If they returned in convoy, the gunsels
were ordered to be sure no vehicle was left operational, and
to be ready for a day-long siege while awaiting help.

Their fire positions established by chemlamp, they huddled together for warmth in the starflecked night, Sanger
taking first watch because she could not, as her partner could,
shrug off the effects of violence and drop off quickly into
slumber. Marbrye Sanger held her sleeping youth close,
gently massaged his back and shoulders, watched for moving
lights, and now and then silently kissed the unresponsive
lips. Quantrill, normally a light sleeper, could have made no
greater demonstration of trust than to abandon care in her
arms; and Sanger's silent tears were of purest contentment.

Control advised Sanger, at three AM, to turn her watch
over to her partner. She roused him, found that sleep came
easily to her now, and smiled to herself as she felt his hand
glide gently along her arms. Perhaps, she thought, he even
returned her affection in some small way.

When Sanger's breathing steadied into sleep rhythms,
Quantrill eased out of his jacket and spread it over her. He
was tempted to rouse her with subtle caresses but knew that
she needed sleep more than he needed active love-making.

He made himself content to feel her warmth and her implied faith. He steadfastly refused to dwell on the possible meanings of their mutual accommodation to one another, for in that direction lay acknowledged friendship; love; vulnerability. Had Sanger given him reason to suspect her yearning Quantrill would have been shocked and, to a degree, disappointed. Gunsels knew better than that, he told himself: the only viable response to tenderness was retreat.

He found it easier to think about Sandy Grange, but not much easier. From the women of the prophets he had learned that Louise Grange had been near the end of her strength even before her escape. Little Sandy had taken her tiny sister and her prized backpack, and had fled shortly before Quantrill's first arrival, her mother stumbling away into the dark not knowing which way the two had gone, Coates and Ryerson too far in arrears to find them.

It was patently ridiculous to be worrying about two small lives at risk in the wild country when his quarry was still capable of razing whole townships. But there it was: given a choice, Quantrill would cheerfully abandon his assignment in hopes of finding Sandy before some stupendous predator did. But the choice was not his. He was rigidly bound by Control—more accurately, by his growing suspicion that his implanted critic might levy the ultimate criticism upon him if he abandoned an assignment.

He thought on the problem for an hour before contacting Control, speaking softly to avoid waking Sanger. "If those captive women and children run loose tomorrow, they could wind up in another band of crazies. Or feeding some really nasty predators out here. I recommend a sweep of the whole area, Control."

The answer was prompt. "Neg; we can pass that on to the locals, but we need you to hold the lines against Mexicans north of Alamogordo. The situation is deteriorating all along the border."

"Since when is that T Section business?"

"Since you volunteered, Q."

"I never volunteered for a personal destruct mechanism."

"You *are* a personal destruct mechanism, Q. It doesn't have to be a self-destruct. You still have free will to choose."

"Like Simon Goldhaber did?"

"If suicide is your choice. That would gain no one anything."

"Sounds like we're all losing, doesn't it?"

"It sounds from here as if you need a rest. Some of your decisions tonight have been amateurish."

"For instance?"

"You attacked two armed men while they were in control of a moving vehicle, in terrain you did not choose."

Privately, Quantrill had already cursed Sanger for that but, "You weren't here and we were. It worked," he observed drily. "If your situation is going to hell, why not give us a longer leash?"

"The news from Asia is good, Q. We're having setbacks here but nothing we can't handle. I recommend you defer your objections until debriefing. T Section has now relocated from San Simeon to Santa Fe. If all goes well, you will be apprised of the big picture there." The unspoken warning was clear enough: if you slip up, you won't be around for debriefing.

"Thank you, Control." Quantrill coded out, frowning into the false dawn, planning hs disobedience with care.

Dawn swelled through a golden haze and Quantrill listened to a lark's *a capella* welcome of the light for long minutes. He saw an insolent jackrabbit stand erect, ears turned to the south, then spring away. The lark fell silent. "Okay, Sanger," he grunted, "company's coming."

Quantrill had rolled his M-27 into a blanket forty meters from Sanger's bower. He ran to it, swung its bipod into place, lay prone in the protection of a stone outcrop. He placed his spare magazines where they could not be spattered by a ricochet. The curl of the road would hide the battered pickup until an approaching vehicle was past, below his and Sanger's hidden positions. They would each have the advantage of enfilade.

But they had forgotten the choking dust that would prompt

a second vehicle to stay well behind. With the first arc of sun came two vehicles, trailing dust clouds, a hundred meters apart.

The terratired vehicle squalled to a stop thirty meters from the pickup. One short-sleeved man exited running, turned to shout to the driver who pulled a sporting rifle from the floor. Sanger's first burst tattooed the truck, the driver turning in time to receive her next burst. He seemed to leap backward as if jerked on a wire, the rifle spinning like a majorette's baton. The second man was unarmed. Quantrill watched him snatch up one of the weapons Sanger had placed at the verge, and smiled. If it would shoot gravel, Sanger might have a problem.

The driver of the second vehicle must have seen dust spurt from the jacket of the first driver. The all-terrain pickup swung hard out of the ruts and began a desperate U-turn, throwing gouts of dust and gravel as it veered toward Quantrill, chips of paint flying as Sanger poured automatic fire into its rear quarter panel.

Quantrill saw the shirt-sleeved man hunkered behind his truck away from Sanger, frantically shaking his useless trophy, an absurdly easy target from the nearside. Then, in one long easy burst, Quantrill perforated the windshield of the moving vehicle from edge to edge, watched the rider plummet to the ground, the pickup bucking and snorting as it slowed to a stop a hundred meters distant, the driver hanging half out of the cab.

"Down, Sanger," he shouted, and sent two singles moaning high over her nest. He put a round into the dust at the feet of the lone survivor, grinned at the man's impromptu leap. "Tell Sanger to stay the hell down," he muttered to Control as Mr. Shirtsleeves scrambled into his truck. The next few seconds would be critical. Quantrill drew breath and held it, his sights on a man who seemed to be fighting an invisible brushfire at the wheel.

The truck roared, lurched. Quantrill disintegrated its windshield, punctured both rear tires, and then emptied an entire fresh magazine into the other vehicle for effect.

"Permission to pursue, Control," he said, and called Sanger down on the double. He was shaking with silent laughter as he dragged Beasley's body from the pickup, and hand-signed silence to Sanger whose glance at her partner was furious. The pickup was cold, but not for long.

Quantrill steered directly across a wide arc in the trail, gesturing for Sanger to withhold her fire at the fleeing prophet. Her face was a scowl of mimed protest until she saw their quarry lurch away from the trail on flat tires. Only then did she realize that Quantrill was registering joy as he herded the man away from the ranch house.

"Subject is heading north in open country at his best speed, Control," Quantrill said, grinning at Sanger. "I propose to close on him after we pass the ranch, to avoid witnesses. We have a deader in the back seat. We can disappear him out here."

Sanger shook her head in disgust, aware that Quantrill was playing Control's game for reasons of his own. Control could not possibly know how many witnesses had identified the T Section team, and gave the sanction for the delayed kill.

Cutting his speed, hand-signing his explanation to Sanger as best he could, Quantrill paced their quarry for twenty minutes. He was wondering how much farther he dared go when the pickup faltered. "Bag him," he shouted, and braked savagely. The pickup was out of fuel.

Sanger fired through the dust pall. The fleeing truck lurched, began to circle. Quantrill fumbled for his own M-27, added his short bursts to Sanger's, saw their quarry grind to a stop a hundred meters away.

"Got him," Sanger cried.

"He's on fire," Quantrill said, gesturing for Sanger's silence. *"He will be in a minute,"* said his hands.

Hands on hips, Sanger watched as Quantrill carried Jansen's body to their most recent target. He managed to set the pock-marked truck afire with matches. Now they were afoot, he advised Control, and would head back toward the ranch to intercept the one vehicle that had not shown up at their ambush. Control agreed.

By now Sanger had had time to fume over the fact that they

were searching for a small blonde girl with a tiny baby. For a time, they pondered a thin vertical smudge to the north, then decided it was a dust-devil.

"*You deliberately shanghaied us here, and abandoned those poor devils at the ranch,*" Sanger's hands accused as they turned eastward.

"*I don't think that last pair of prophets will go any farther than the ambush,*" he replied manually.

"*Two dozen hostages against two,*" Sanger insisted.

"*But one of those is my,*" he began, and could not make the sign for *friend*. "*I knew that kid,*" he signaled.

Sanger rolled her eyes toward heaven, squelched a smile, then pointed a finger in warning and added, "*Don't you ever put me in the middle like this again. Clear?*"

His sheepish nod was almost that of innocence, and disarmed her wrath into inaudible chuckles.

Together, Quantrill and Sanger covered several sections of land before resting, at noon, beneath a lone scrub oak. He admitted via signs to Sanger that he hadn't really expected to cut a fresh trail from Sandy Grange.

"*But you had to try,*" she signed.

A shrug.

"*Would you do as much for me?*"

Dust-covered, sweat-stained, he could not help grinning. "*For you I do other things.*"

"*Promises, promises,*" she signed, licking cracked lips, fully aware that she was a dust-caked travesty of herself at the moment. She found that he did not care about the dust; warned herself that Quantrill's unusually gentle and deliberate love-making was only a ploy to keep their breathing quiet—one more way to allay the suspicions of Control.

At midafternoon they set out again, this time quartering toward the ranch, and found it at last. Control meted out a small punishment then, insisting that they head straight for the south. The last pair of prophets had been intercepted by a civil patrol outside the town of Menard. Was there any reason why the team could not buy a ride and rendezvous with others north of Del Rio?

Quantrill and Sanger spat cottony fluff, accepted their new

assignment, and trudged toward the highway. Sanger signed
once, as they waited coins in hand to buy a ride just before
dark: *"Don't feel bad. You risked your head for the kid, when
we both know she's probably been iced days ago."*

Quantrill nodded. He made no other reply then or later; it
was not the first time he had exiled a memory.

Sandys jurnal 30 Jul. Wens.

*Im the black sheep, yessir yessir 3 bagsful. When these
bags of formla is gone I dont know what Child will
drink, but I bet she can live on sheep milk if I can do it
right like mom but I wisht I knew where mom is. I try to
chew food for Child but she just spits it up and grins. She
dont know nothing.*

*When I saw my freind Sunday my legs about gave way. I
tried to keep still but Child fijited and there wasnt no
place to run and this poor litle knife in my napsack didnt
scare him none and maybe it was right to cry.*

*My freind sniffed me and Child a long time then shoved
us toward this old dugout shack. I heard that ants keep
bugs and rats keep mice but my dady never told me big
animals keep sheep, he just said Rusian bores was
devils. I gess even my dady didnt know everthing.*

*My freind likes getting scrached on top high as I can
reach and I think it tikles him to give me and Child rides
but he dont like grownups. Today I thout hed go after
them 2 with the guns but I scrached him and we kept hid.
Jurnal I swear the man looked like sombody I knew once
but no, his hair and face was a little diffrent. Besides
Ted was nice but this man did bad things with the
woman unless they was maried. One thing sure, he
wasnt no profet to judje from what they did to them
devils in the burnt truck if it was them, I dont know. I
gess Child and me will stay here long as I can feed her.
This is your last page jurnal and I dont have no more
paper just when Im having crazy ideas with words. Like*

> *Knifetooth*
> *Hammerhoof*
> *Windswift*

Treetoptall.
Enemy of my enemy
Is my freind.
O well, paper or no paper I have Child and I have my
freind and thats enouf. I know folks call him Bale but hes
freind to Child and me. Thats good, boy Id sure hate to
have him for a enemy!!
Almost had a fire going today but too much smoke, next
time will try at nite. We sure dont need blankets when my
freind is here in the dugout, what we need is earplugs. I
never knew hogs snored but ever day you learn somthing
new. Keep your pages dry jurnal ha ha.

         Love Sandy

Chapter 76

Eve Simpson had expected to find some careworn drudge in a closet-sized office in a forgotten corner of Sound Stage West. Her first astonishment was that Commander Boren Mills rated office and apartment space nearly as large as her own. It did not sweeten her mood much.

"You know damned well who I am," she flashed at the female rating who screened Mills's callers. "And your inky-fingered censor is about to find out who my friends are if I don't see him *right now.*"

The heavy door behind the secretary slid back. The harried rating flushed as she turned. "I'm sorry, sir," she said, "I was about to—"

"It's okay—ah, as you were," Mills said easily. "I think I know—"

"It's not okay," Eve stormed, stalking around the desk. "I came to beard this old bastard Mills in his den. *No*body chops up an interview of mine like that, mister."

"The old bastard is in," said the young commander with a rapid wink at the rating. "Let's beard him together."

Eve swept past the young officer, determined to maintain the fine edge on her anger, glaring about her in search of a third party in the inner office. She thought the young officer's handshake would be perfunctory until he kissed her hand.

"Where is Mills?"

"Praying for forgiveness," he murmured, "and holding your hand."

She jerked back, made an open-palmed gesture, then dropped both hands to her ample hips. "Shit oh dear," said the rosebud mouth, fighting a smile. "I suppose you think I haven't been charmed by experts."

"You deserve nothing less," he said, meaning it. Now buxom to the point of pudginess, Eve no longer provoked dry mouths and itchy fingers in most young men—except on video, where NBN's image enhancement magic made her appear merely a bit plumpish. To Boren Mills, she was a classic by Titian, a haughty nymph with the mouth of a cruel Cupid; intelligence to match her arrogance; perfection itself.

Eve did not have to trust a man to enjoy him. This cool natty customer with the widow's peak and the smooth line just might be susceptible to her young-old charm if not to her threats. Besides, she thought with a tingly rush, he swung a heavy stick around NBN for such a young guy. Probably a pal of Brucie's. But oh, well, whatthehell . . . "What I really deserve," she said musically, "is freedom of the press."

Mills poured her a Cointreau, sat with her on a well-lighted couch, listened to her argument. Her interview with an English-speaking Chinese refugee in Mexico, she insisted, was just what the American public wanted: a dirge for a dying China. "That stuff about the little matter synthesizer was pure dynamite," she added, "even if it was just rumor."

"And could blow up in our faces," Mills replied. "If you weren't who you are, I wouldn't be discussing it. But obviously you have the need to know. Forget about what Americans believe, for the moment. What if the RUS believed—and I happen to know it couldn't be true—that the chromium and platinum they trade us might not be key minerals if someone could synthesize them? Even a rumor like that could damage relations with them."

Eve fumed, invoked a name in White House Deseret. Mills, undaunted, countered with optimal control theory and the awe in which it was held by the Secretary of State—not to mention the White House Press Secretary. The message optimization program, he said, had shown that no rumor about matter synthesizers should be offered to credulous Americans. Mills did not add that he controlled the numerical biases of that computer program.

"Anyhow," said Eve, her formidable curiosity abubble, "what makes you so sure matter synthesis isn't possible?"

"It *is* possible," he said; "it's been done. But at incredible cost, using big experimental facilities. The clincher lies in the idea that any government as rigidly controlled as China *would* mass-produce a small gadget like that, even if it *could*. Give a few million Chinese their own personal synthesizers, and the government's control would vanish overnight. Think about it."

While she sipped and thought, Mills wondered whether any girl Eve's age could possibly juggle the subtleties of the problem. It had never occurred to him that her intellect might rival his own.

"Seems to me that would be true everywhere. Chinese, us, the RUS, the Canadians,—any government that thrives on central control," she reflected.

He said, "Uh—to some degree you may be right." She was precisely, preternaturally right, he thought, elevating his opinion of this morsel—no, this banquet!

But Mills was a patient man, and managed to avoid figuratively licking his chops. He had already been tempted by dizzying offers for his civilian services; knew the day would come soon when he could pick his banquets, even without the synthesizer. But *with* it? He could rule a country as Rothschilds and Rockefellers never had. As Eve dallied with the scenario he had suggested, Mills was wondering if the Chinese had scaled up the device, and whether copies still existed other than his own. He must set up a research team

and somehow compel their loyalties—but all in good time.
Sooner or later, scaled up or merely mass-produced as it was,
the synthesizer could make an economy dependent on Mills.

Because, of course, Boren Mills did not intend ever to sell,
lease, or license it. He would only sell its products, and grow
rich beyond imagining. His eyes refocused on the face of Eve
Simpson.

"So the rumor is a problem in domestic policy as well as
foreign policy," she was saying as though he were not there.
"The Chinese would've been crazy to produce such a thing;
and whether it exists or not, Americans would be howling for
one in every garage."

Mills, startled: "Not in the kitchen?"

"I was thinking of fuel," she said.

"Might as well think of beef or heroin," he said, to
channel her thinking toward the bizarre.

Judiciously: "Very complex molecules."

"Jesus Christ; what *don't* you know?"

Titillated by the power she sensed in him, Eve gazed at
him through lowered lashes. "I don't know if you fool
around."

It was one way to deflect this brilliant wanton from pursuing a secret that Mills had thus far protected. It was also the
exact question he had been pondering about Eve Simpson;
and her question was his answer. "I should probably play
coy," he said, seeking cues to her appetites.

"I didn't know men with clout knew how," she lied,
watching the advance of his manicured forefinger on her
thigh.

"Men with clout are kinky," he purred, his tongue showing through the smile, deliberate in his choice of feminine
nuance.

"It's a small world," she said huskily, undressing him,
"—but I see that some things are larger than others."

He laughed, letting her set the pace. Later he could study
the holotape of this first encounter, the better to consolidate
this essential alliance. But it was to be weeks before he
focused on something she said while nodding, nodding,

nodding above him. "Even with," she said dreamily, "free synthesis,—there should be—ways to—make them—sweat."

There were: superstition, media, implanted fears both emotional and physical. Mills was expert with emotional implants, and had learned a few things about the physical kind. There was that bunch of brutes attached to Army Intelligence, for instance . . .

Chapter 77

Once she had tooled up to produce the oral vaccine for keratophagic staph, Canada knew she had won her war. The vaccine was processed from polysaccharide components of the dried *S. rosacea* organism in factories isolated by permafrost and wilderness. While firmly denying her breakthrough, Canada managed to distribute the vaccine in her antiradiation chelate doses to virtually her entire population.

Soon, more of the vaccine was secretly dispensed in military rations to Canadian and US troops in Asia. An infantry man who traded every chocolate bar away was trading his immunity, though he could not know it; a confirmed chocoholic who ate too much of it suffered from something similar to influenza. Some Canadian chocolate was distributed to RUS troops, too—but if the wrapper said *shukulaht* in Cyrillic, it provided no immunity.

Sooner or later, there would be enough oral vaccine to eradicate Chinese Plague throughout Asia, but Canada took the long view. The RUS would get it later, rather than sooner.

By the second week in August, 1997, Allied forces in Asia celebrated the war's anniversary in defensive consolidations—their weasel-phrase for a brisk retreat. ANZUS forces in India no longer sought the spearhead that

would have met our Fifth Army on the western edge of
SinoInd territory; for one thing, the US First and Fifth Armies had largely completed their redeployment north of
Manchuria, into Siberia. RUS strategists growled as the
Americans moved ever eastward, ever farther from defense
of Russian population centers and nearer to the Bering Strait.
The RUS were pulling their own armies back, intending to
wall off European Russia using the Urals as a buffer, and still
had the US Third Army to help.

Konieff, who still chaired the anxiety-ridden Supreme
Council, argued that it was better to have the rest of the
Americans in Siberia, for however short a time, than to let the
region be overrun immediately by surviving SinoInds. Besides, the Americans had left an entire army, with English
and Canadian assault brigades, in Central Asia. Some members of the Council warned of duplicity here. Fearing that the
foreign army might turn hostile on the banks of the Volga, the
RUS worked out an accommodation. The Americans and
their English-speaking friends could retreat through a corridor south of the Caspian Sea toward Turkey. Only the Irani-
ans would protest this, and Iran had long since bled herself
powerless with childish purges.

Konieff did not know that the US Joint Chiefs had placed
our Third Army at such risk only after top-level meetings
with the Canadians. Canada pledged to protect the escape
corridor for our armies in Siberia, if we would lend our
battle-wise Third Army to the Turks—who had a bit of a
problem.

Turkey's problem began in 1992 when she contracted with
Israel for desalinization plants on the shores of the Tuz Golu,
a huge brackish lake in Turkey's central Anatolian plateau.
The Israelis had tapped geothermal energy in nearby volcanic
highlands by 1994, and knew better than the Turks that the
central plateau offered an excellent, if not quite ideal, staging
area for a project that would take a decade to complete. Israel
envisioned nothing less than a fabrication and launch complex by which Israelis could begin their escape from Earth.

Not that this scheme had the blessings of every member of

the Knesset. The premise had stuck like raw pork in the gullet
of many a traditional Zionist. But the odds against Israel's
tomorrows mounted every year, and the only thing more
unthinkable than an orbital New Israel was an Israel that
could survive its present neighbors where it was.

With the Turkish connection, Israel would gain freedom of
movement to build and launch the seed ships to harvest
asteroids to build vast habitats in Lagrangian orbits. Turkey
would gain a newly fertile highland near Ankara, and rapid
industrialization using Israeli and Canadian engineering.
Canada would gain from favorable trade with New Israel's
spacefaring factories, and harbored the conviction that this
solution would rinse away, once and for all, the trouble spot
of old Israel. Canada well knew that worldwide objections
would be raised against an orbital New Israel. She also knew
that no corporate state on Earth had been in the past, or ever
would be in the future, likely to bring such single-minded
dedication and ability to the establishment of space colonies.

Canada found that Egypt, Arabia, Iraq, and other AIR
countries would willingly help finance the extraterrestrializa-
tion of Israel. In 1995, major powers would have intervened.
By 2010, some major power might again intervene. But this
odd consortium of Canadians, Islamics, and Israelis saw the
next few years as a launch window in time.

Turkey, nominally a democratic Islamic moderate, had
already permitted many Israelis to relocate from Cyprus to
the Tuz Golu region, but knew that in transforming her
central plateau to an Israeli staging area she would risk
opposition from inside and out. Internally, the nomadic
Kurds were raiding advance Israeli camps. Externally, Turkey feared that the RUS might retain enough clout to mount
an expeditionary force to prevent Israel from developing her
orbital habitats.

Turkey's problem, then, was simply that she needed an
army of janissaries for a few years. Canada was the broker for
these services. She knew that the US was in no position to
withhold our Third Army, now that we depended on Canada
for aid.

Ultimately, White House Deseret viewed the 'Ellfive Solution' with cautious optimism. The Apostles—the ruling
committee of the LDS—felt that the official Mormon ac-
counts of world history would, in time, greatly benefit by a
general Jewish exodus from the planet. They reasoned
(simplistically) that Jews everywhere would clamor for
berths on Ellfive shuttle ships, so that Mormon America
would be rid of one highly visible religious minority. The
truth was that most American Jews had lived urban lives, and
died urban deaths, a year before. More Jews survived in
Europe than in America. Like Japan, Europe was rich in
industry, poor in natural resources. There was good reason to
expect that New Israel could have her pick of emigrants to a
new industrial frontier.

The long purposeful retreat of the US Third Army was
applauded by Allies and SinoInds alike for varied reasons.
Iran and Kurdistan mounted token opposition, but feared
contamination by plague more than they feared the passage
of the infidel. Thanks to Canadian chocolate, very few cases
of plague assailed our troops in Asia and by early September,
our Third Army reached Eastern Turkey. The First and Fifth
US Armies were streaming toward the Bering Strait while the
weather held.

We had historical precedents in Dunkirk and Cyprus for
the massive crossing from the Chukchi Peninsula to Alaska.
We believed that the SinoInds, like the Russians, were too
weak to mount serious opposition to our crossing. But just in
case, the US and Canadian fleets assembled in the Chukchi
and Bering Seas.

Chapter 78

The Bering Shoot was a misnomer coined by media; it
should have been called the Chukchi Nukes. Before dawn on
Thursday, September 11, a covey of ballistic birds sailed

over from the Sea of Okhotsk to pound the Chukchi Peninsula where over one million US troops were staging to cross the strait.

Most of our naval forces stayed submerged and could not affect the outcome of the SinoInd attack. It was the big delta dirigibles, refitted by the US Navy after their success in the Maldives, that intercepted most of the nukes with particle-beam weapons. Inevitably, shock waves from airbursts blew seven of our fifteen deltas out of the skies over Chukchi. Our few orbital weapons salvoed every warhead they could muster against the SinoInd craft in the Sea of Okhotsk, and no second strike came from that quarter or any other.

In all, the Bering Shoot accounted for two hundred thousand US casualties. Without the antimissile delta squadron it would have been over a million. In the two weeks after the Bering Shoot, naval and commercial craft shepherded all but the rearguard of our Fifth Army across the strait. The rearguard was, man for man, probably the most heavily armed and mechanized military group ever assembled. Sampling each fuel dump before razing it, chiefly with crews of no more than two to each armored ACV, the rearguard met no strong opposition. In this respect, they fared better than their comrades who had reached Alaskan soil.

Opposition to the returning US armies came from the last quarter they had expected: White House Deseret.

One of the most signal failures of American media was its failure to reassure our civilian population on the subject of plague. Everyone knew that any influx from Asia would bring keratophagic staph and blindness—and no facts to the contrary had much effect. When Yale Collier announced an 'overnight, God-sent miracle cure' from Canada, only Mormons and the RUS believed him. The public outcry in the US amounted to an instant plebescite which Collier dared not ignore. In the face of several resignations by general officers, the President insisted that our First and Fifth Armies hold fast in Alaska—at least until the message optimizers in our media could turn the public from its panic.

To pragmatic veterans this implied a winter in Alaska and

many of them said The Hell With It. While fuel dumps still
burned in Chukchi, entire divisions were moving toward the
states of Washington and Oregon in open defiance of their
Commander-in-Chief. America had never faced such widespread military defection, perhaps because America had
never been in such disorder.

Once again Canada found a compromise, and urged it on
our deserters without much concern for Collier's approval.
Obviously, she pointed out to the deserters, they did not carry
plague—for which they could thank Canadians. Just as obviously, Canada was emerging from the war as one of the few
winners. American deserters could apply for Canadian citi-
zenship immediately, so long as they did *not* continue their
headlong rush beyond the regions where Canada's hegemony
reached.

Canadian money was now preferred in most of the US
northwest. The Royal Canadian Mounted Police and their
frequently summary courts were already maintaining order
from Portland to Duluth, sanctioned by the US Government
which worried more about its southern borders than its north.
There was, bluntly, not enough US Government to go around
anymore.

It became clear to the Collier administration that we could
keep Alaska and Hawaii but we would—temporarily of
course—lose Washington, Oregon, Montana, most of Idaho,
North Dakota, and so on to the shrewdly sympathetic Canadians. But there was hope for future reparations because, for
one thing, Mormonism had a solid toehold in western Canada.

It was equally clear to the RUS that the Union of Soviets
was dying of Chinese Plague and Canadian neglect. On
September 23 the RUS made their demand on Canada: vaccine or war.

No one—not Canada, not the US, not even Chairman
Konieff—knew whether remaining RUS weapons could deal
serious blows past Canadian defenses. Canada's Parliament
quickly replied that shipments of oral vaccine were being

readied for the Russians and, meanwhile, the US Third Army in Turkey could help by sending its stocks of Canadian chocolate to the Ukraine and Azerbaijan, across the Turkish borders.

The RUS, naturally, wanted distribution to begin in the Urals and the heartlands around Novgorod, Gorkiy, Volgograd. It was transparently clear to the Supreme Council that Canada was more interested in saving rebellious Ukrainians than in protecting the central RUS nervous system.

Less than fifty hours after acceding to the RUS demand, Canada began her airlift of vaccine-laden chocolate. Ironically, the distribution could have been faster if the vaccine had been by gel capsule, but Russians knew by now that immunity came in *shukulaht*; so chocolate it must be.

A few cases of plague had turned up in Leningrad, Grodno, and Baku, cities on the edge of RUS dominion. Tens of thousands of cases were being treated in the heartlands. Naturally, predictably, the Canadian airdrops began in Estonia, Byelorussia, Azerbaijan. Canada wisely asked UN observers to help, and to vouch for the fact that enough vaccine had been dropped onto Russian soil to immunize a hundred million people. All the RUS needed to do was complete the distribution. Any country powerful enough to threaten war on Canada was surely capable of passing out chocolate—and, Canada added, she would not send aircrews of slow transport craft two thousand klicks into the heartlands of a country which *had* just threatened war against her.

Boren Mills could not have optimized messages better than the Canadians. Millions of RUS citizens—Russians, Tatars, Bashkirs, all those who heard the news through RUS jamming and feared the plague more than they feared the Supreme Council—made pathetic attempts to reach the vaccine dropsites. Few RUS citizens owned private vehicles, so most of the travelers went by government-owned mass transit, which required faked permits, outright bribes, or stowaway status. The result of the peripheral airdrop by Canada was almost complete clogging of RUS mass transit. This failure of the RUS circulatory system destroyed the remaining confidence Russians had in their leaders—gangrene throughout the body politic.

Chairman Konieff's last success, in a stormy session of the Supreme Council, was in preventing Field Marshal Zenkovitch and his faction from countering civilian panic with bullets. Zenkovitch was after all, said Konieff, a Ukrainian who perhaps thought real Russians should not obtain their chocolate immunity.

Taras Zenkovitch removed his belt with its empty holster and placed it, breathing deeply, on the table. "If that is what you believe," he said to them all, "you leave me no alternative to resignation."

"I spoke in anger with a troubled soul," said Konieff. "We are not Dzugashvilii, Stalins who would destroy our people to save an idea. Please, comrade Zenkovitch, accept my public apology."

Second Minister Vyacheslov, a gaunt Byelorussian, patted the trembling arm of Zenkovitch and said in his vodka tenor, "Taras Zenkovitch, your army might serve best by trying to keep the transit system running. At the same time, surely each of us retains enough personal charm to obtain a few cartons of vaccine from local officials."

"Begging from party hacks in Estonia," growled Zenkovitch; "is that what we are reduced to?"

"We could be further reduced," said Vyacheslov, placing a hand over his own eyes in a gesture that now signified plague.

Vyacheslov, a great believer in hands-on charisma, carried the day. Both Zenkovitch and the absent Suslov had been assured by field officers that any orders to a military unit that included forcible removal of vaccine from a dropsite would mean almost certain mutiny, supported by the local officials. Marshal Zenkovitch huddled with his staff to expedite civilian travel while Konieff and others made ready to visit known dropsites. Each committeeman carried a pocketful of small elegant cases, and in each case was a large elegant medal. It was the only coin in which they hoped to pay party hacks.

Though Vyacheslov and several others returned with vaccine, Konieff's two-place jet vanished over the Caspian Sea. It was believed that he fell victim to Iranian or friendly fire. In any case, Konieff would not have returned to find a functioning Supreme Council near Perm; the transportation riots had already begun, and the food riots would not be long in coming.

China's fragmentation was well advanced, more profoundly than in RUS states because Chang's Central Committee had depended even more on the acceptance of central control. With the unitary breakdown in the CPA came a fast reshuffle into China's ancient standby, the feudal warlord system. The best that could be said for Chang's government was that, until early October, it still controlled Shansi Province with remnants of the Third CPA manning parapets of the Great Wall against plague-infected deserters returning from the western provinces.

Then Jung Hsia, Third Army Marshal, discovered that Chang was dickering with Canadians for plague vaccine in a transaction which would amount to surrender. Supposedly, Chang hoped to buy immunity from prosecution with microcoded specifications for some secret device, no doubt a weapon. Jung reflected that Chang's own death squad had removed a number of top technical people during the past fortnight; and Jung further reflected that he knew a few folk whose unpleasant arts might unlock Chang's tongue. But art sometimes fails in its purpose, and Jung did not learn what kind of weapon had been worth so many assassinations. Chang Wei died of multiple injuries in the night, and Jung became a warlord until Chang sympathizers offered Jung Hsia to Canada as 'earnest money' for a transaction they needed urgently.

India's Casimiro, taken alive near Nagpur by New Zealanders, was released on October 3, disappearing again into Madhya Pradesh with a Turkish delegate from the UN. It took Casimiro two weeks to assemble something that might be called a Parliamentary quorum, with a few members voting arguable proxies. The chaos of India was hardly more chaotic than it had been a decade, or two or three, before.

In some ways Indians stood to gain; many US troops in western India were to remain as an army of occupation. For the first time in Indian history, hungry Indians had reasonable hopes that surpluses in certain regions would be diverted in the interests of full bellies instead of mountainous bribes.

Still, angry Moslem tribesmen sniped at the garrisoned infidels and were targeted in turn. It had always been thus. It might always be thus. The winter of 1997-8 would see as many deaths throughout moribund Asia as had been suffered in the opening weeks of the war.

Chapter 79

Blanton Young, Vice President of the United States, stood and stared out the window of the Presidential suite toward the dusting of November snow atop the Uinta Peaks east of Provo. His hands were pressed to his ears as if to guard against more bad news. Finally he turned, blinking back tears, shoved hands into the pockets of his jacket. "Six months, Mr. President? And just when we'll need you most! These are tears of self-pity," he added wryly.

Yale Collier draped an arm over the broad shoulders of his friend, felt the physical strength and forgave, as always, the internal weaknesses. "Six months at the least," he reminded Young. "I might still be around to nominate *you* three years from now, if this chemotherapy works."

"But—Yale, I know my limitations," blurted Young, and pointed toward the fax folders on the desk across the room. "Do you honestly think I can handle all that?"

"You'll have help, just as I do. You'll make mistakes, and

you'll learn from them. Don't underestimate our strengths; the Church has never been stronger, Blanton, and——" a wan smile, "God's work may be much easier with the 'Streamlined America' package."

At the phrase, Blanton Young smiled too. It was a common ploy of any government to phrase weakness in terms of strength. Using semantic differential programs managed by a brilliant young naval officer, Collier's savants had obtained the new catchphrase, a 'Streamlined America', and hoped that the verbal mask would hide some unpleasant restructuring beneath that slick surface.

US boundaries had been streamlined into a broad, roughedged diamond with apexes near Cleveland, Houston, Eureka, and Pollock, South Dakota. The secession of the eastern states had been bloodless—even amicable, once it became clear that the quarantine line was necessary and would be maintained indefinitely. White House Deseret had suggested a protectorate status for the eastern seaboard, but the Old South preferred to confederate on its own.

Alta Mexico now extended its hazy borders from the Texas 'Big Bend' country to the central California coast. Canada, perhaps with more politesse than was really necessary, had 'provisionally' accepted most of our northern states as territories. Despite returning troops—a mixed blessing—the plain fact was that the US could not maintain civil order in regions where illegal immigrants, paranthrax, deserters, and armed zealot groups abounded. The physical streamlining of the US, by November 1997, had finally stabilized.

Internal streamlining had scarcely begun but, with the help of far-sighted industrialists, Collier's administration was taking the necessary steps.

The President, seemingly as healthy as ever, placed his cancer-ridden body at the work carrel of his desk; waved Blanton Young to the seat beside him. "Take the reform of the Federal Communications Commission," he said, selecting a fax sheet. "With lifetime appointments, we can count on a majority of good conservatives for decades to come."

"The FCC is the least of our troubles," moaned Young.

"How very right you are," Yale Collier said softly.
"Blanton, with full unrestricted control of network holovision in this country, we can remake it into the true Zion. How
beautiful upon the mountains," he murmured, glancing out
the window.

For the past six weeks, the Vice President had been im-
mersed in the process of nationalizing our fossil fuel sources;
had only skimmed daily briefs on other topics. "Print media
will be tougher," he hazarded.

"What print media? The price of newsprint and Polypaper
are forcing the dailies to offer subscription by holo—which
we can influence in several ways. The outlaw media can be
dealt with by—law enforcement," he said vaguely. "And I
hardly need tell you how much more effective American
business can be under the control of new conglomerates like
International Entertainment & Electronics. Look," he
urged, turning to his carrel display.

The President keyed an instruction, smiled at the mul-
tihued organization chart that swept across the big holoscreen. IEE was little more than a set of interlocked intentions so far, and had provoked liberal outcries when those
intentions reached the Securities Exchange Commission. But
the nation still reeled from its war losses: we had failed to
obtain full reparation in the peace so recently negotiated by
Canada, Brazil, and Arabia between the allies and SinoInds.
The war had begun over the price of oil, and impoverished
America now found the stuff dearer than ever. Islam had not
really fought the war, but had won it nevertheless.

The United States needed efficient reconstruction, did not
want it from outside, and could not obtain it from inside
without 'streamlining' a few checks against repressive
monopolies. This kind of cooperation between government
and industry had fertilized the Union Pacific and Standard
Oil, and it could boost the growth of International Entertainment & Electronics.

IEE was a set of commercial broadcast networks, interlaced with the Holo Corporation of America, tied to Loring
Aircraft, engaged to Entertainment Talent Associates, in bed

with Deseret Pacific Industries, romantically linked to Latter-Day Shale. It would have to tread carefully around a few other surviving consortia and necessary evils such as organized labor—but tread, it would.

Blanton Young asked the pivotal question: "And how much of all this is in the hands of devout stockholders?"

"Enough to assure us," said the President, 'of the very most cordial relations. This country must never allow the identities of Church and State to merge," he said, the great voice rolling across the room, "but in Zion I foresee that both government and business will serve God."

"A magnificent vision," Young murmured as Collier wiped the display. "I presume the Apostolic Council will recommend men for key positions in IEE. You'd be surprised how many shale company executives forgot they were Latter-Day Saints the day we confiscated their present-day mineral leases."

"Regrettable—but predictable in sight of so many heretic groups. That's one job IEE will undertake early: to lead our strays back to righteousness through media. As it happens," Collier went on, "I have in mind a certain young man for IEE's Chief Executive Officer—who is not even a member of the Church."

"You always have your reasons; I'm waiting," said Young, always most comfortable when working under supervision.

"Commander Mills is a decorated war hero, a media genius, and a great organizer. No liberal rabble-rouser can show he's one of us."

"Then how do you know he is?"

"By their works shall ye know them," said Collier, "and Mills is working for a vision of Zion that is very like our own." The smile he turned on Young now was one of sadness, but not of self-pity: "It will be your task to preserve that vision; to win more hearts; to keep the hearts we've won. In all loving kindness, Blanton, I offer you this warning: you have a tendency to persuade more by punishment than by reward. If this nation is to regain its old glory, it will be by the same old path of reward, with less emphasis on retribution. That is partly what I had in mind with the establishment of a Search and Rescue bureau,'' he said, tapping another fax-sheet.

"Yes, Mr. President,'' said Blanton Young, using the full title to suggest agreement with a philosophy he could never espouse. Raised in a strict household, Young respected punishment. His father had often said it: ''An ass will use up bushels of carrots, but you only need one stick.''

"I'd like you to get back to work on this S & R bureau so the media people can give it exposure,'' said Collier, renewing an old topic shelved during the secession months. The big hands flew over the keyboard, the voice resonant and vital as ever. It seemed implausible to Young that his chief was a dying man as Collier outlined a favorite scheme, a small arm of government that would come to represent the best any administration could offer.

Search & Rescue squads, chiefly underpaid paramedics, had long been on a few county payrolls and enjoyed enviable reputations. Now, living in ruins and short on dedicated paramedics, many Americans needed S & R teams more than ever. It was Yale Collier's dream to organize a federal cadre who would search out the lost; rescue the imperiled; and would do it on camera with panache, a reminder to Americans that a Godly administration would go anywhere in support of its people. Smart uniforms, the latest equipment, the sharpest personnel, the best training. Such was the vision of President Yale Collier.

The Vice President questioned, advised, concurred, silently filed away some thoughts for further study. An S & R bureau might achieve great things with sparse funding, he saw, and said as much; but he cautioned that some rescues would inevitably involve victims of the paramilitary bands that defied the central government.

Collier tended to gloss over this facet of the S & R charter; yes, yes, certainly an S & R team should be capable of handling a few armed outlaws on occasion, but it was impor-

tant that S & R build an image more of rescue team than
SWAT team.

Thus was oral agreement reached without a meeting of
minds. As he sat beside his old friend and made notes on
organization details, Blanton Young again mulled over the
sort of recruits he might prefer. It was certain that some of the
clear-eyed young S & R men—and women, of course, for
show—would be confronted by brutish, bewhiskered ruf-
fians who swaggered up to spit into the eye of Authority. The
kind of rebels now termed by the LDS as 'Gadianton rob-
bers'.

And how should God's judgments be meted out to the
wicked? Young was in no doubt here; he knew the passage
well from the Book of Mormon, iv, 5:

> ". . . the judgments of God will overtake the wicked;
> and it is by the wicked that the wicked are
> punished. . . ."

Young was pleased with the neatness of his secret solution. Forty years before, an American administration had
recruited the wartime wicked of the OSS into an ostensibly
peaceable CIA. Surely, the armed forces still harbored a few
young cutthroats who would not look out of place among the
clear-eyed exemplars of Streamlined America . . .

Chapter 80

". . . and in the coming months we'll be seeing a lot of
these special, dedicated people," hummed the voice of Eve
Simpson. On the big holo screen of T Section's briefing room
near Santa Fe, a powerfully built young man winched himself to the portal of an open elevator shaft carrying a limp and
lovely girl to safety. The voice-over continued on the slickly
made documentary, but no one was listening anymore.

"Ethridge, you let 'em pluck your eyebrows," crowed
Barb Zachary, glancing from the screen to the blushing Kent
Ethridge. The gunsel, Ethridge, was one of perhaps two
dozen in the room. T Section survivors; a small elite assembly.

"We made a deal; they let me pluck the blonde," Ethridge
replied. Actually, Ethridge had played the part only on orders, after a computer search cited his gymnastic grace, and
after Eve Simpson saw him on an old holotape.

Max Pelletier, tiny and dark and lethal as a Brown Re-
cluse: "You should've held out for the Simpson hotsy,
Kent."

"Fat as a pig," Ethridge protested. "I don't know how
they hid that on the holo."

"I can see this isn't holding you spellbound," said the
disgusted instructor Seth Howell, flicking on the room lights
and freezing the holo frame. Howell wore a uniform identi-
cal to the one Ethridge had worn in the holotape: flare-leg
black synthosuedes, long-sleeved black blouse with
turned-back cuffs and deep vee collar, set off by a brilliant
yellow side-tie neckerchief. On his left shoulder was a yellow sunflower patch with centered, stylized *S & R* in black;
soft black moccasins completed the outfit. Howell was a big
man, heavy in the trunk with a bony neck and long slender
limbs. For all their sarcasms, the gunsels could see that the
exquisite cut of the S & R dress uniforms enhanced the image
of the wearer.

"Of course they hyped it—even stuck Ethridge in a dress
uniform. On assignment you'd wear a mottled two-piece
coverall and overlap-closure boots."

"Always assuming you could make the grade," put in
Marty Cross, who'd been harping all morning on the difference between the simple requirements of T Section and the
broad-spectrum charter of the Search & Rescue people.
Cross was in civvies—but boasted a tiny sunflower emblem
on a neck chain.

"Hype, hype, hype, hype," chanted Des Quinn, as if
counting cadence. "I joined up for the duration. The war's

over, gentlemen, and I say fuck it, all I want is out. And they can start by taking *this* out," he said, tapping himself ominously behind the ear.

Quantrill exchanged a glance with Sanger, several seats away. Her eyebrow lift was cynical reply to Quinn.

"I'll say it once more," sighed the portly Sean Lasser with good humor; "when your implant energy cell runs down, that's the end of it. There's always the chance they could trigger the terminator or cause infection when taking it out, and there's no danger in leaving it in there, so—"

"I don't buy that," said Quinn. "That goddam cell could be energized again by accident or maybe on purpose for all we know. Am I gonna have to find a surgeon myself?"

"Anyone but a T Section surgeon would almost certainly set it off, Quinn, even after the energy cell is kaput. The Army did not intend those things to come out," said Lasser softly. "*Ever.*"

A three-beat silence. You could always gain rapt attention by telling a man more about the time bomb in his head. "I could file suit," said Quinn, looking around for support but finding ambiguity—the ambiguity he might have expected from T Section survivors, who had not survived by forthright honesty.

"Right now you're begging for court-martial," rasped Howell, then caught himself and shrugged. " 'Course I'm just an interested spectator now, recruiting for a strict-ly civ-il-yun agency. Got my discharge over the Christmas holidays."

"I just bet you did," from Quinn.

"I can vouch for it," said the laconic Cross. "He buggered an ape in a tree." Cross surveyed the pained expressions, gave it up. Cheyenne humor seemed lost on this bunch.

"You two may be civilians," Lasser waved at Cross and Howell, "but I'm still on duty." Turning to his gunsel audience, he went on. "T Section's cutting orders for you, but I'll summarize them and then dismiss you.

"You've all got thirty-day compassionate leave with pay,

beginning zero-eight-hundred tomorrow, 13 January. We don't want to see you around Santa Fe for a month. Bum around solo, look for work, see how rough it's going to be on the outside,—whatever. Use your covers; you know better than to talk about T Section. No buddying up; solo means just that.

"Don't stray beyond, ah, streamlined America—but that's in your orders, too. You'll probably be seeing more about Search & Rescue. Think about it. For the record, I wish I weren't too old for it; it'll be a snappy elite bunch and the pay will be good." A pause, an old reflective grin: "A lot of young starry-eyed Mormons will be competing against you for S & R; it offers medical training, airborne and mountain survival stuff, urban disaster work,—you name it." He saw Quantrill's hand rise lazily, nodded toward him.

"That's not where we specialize," said Quantrill. "I mean,—I'd stick out like a bullet in a box of bonbons, Lasser." Murmurs from Pelletier and Zachary; a nod from Sanger. "All day you and Howell and Cross have been dropping hints about needing us for what we do."

"Yeah; tell us what you can't tell us," prompted Graeme Duff.

Lasser's raised brow and lopsided smile implied, *fair enough*. He stroked his chin, looked thoughtfully at his old colleague Howell, saw that the responsibility was properly his own. "It's all innuendo," he admitted, "so I'm guessing why certain people might want to see you apply for S & R. It takes a certain kind of dedication to put your arse on the line for some idiot who's caught in a collapsed building. That's the image of Search & Rescue, to save the lost sheep.

"But if I read the signs right, there'll be times when S & R will need muscle—a sprinkle of gunsels, maybe. How many stray nuclear warheads are in the hands of private citizens now? How much binary nerve gas? Maybe S & R will have to deal with those questions. Simply put: there may be occasions when they'll need to search out *treason* and rescue the *system*. It's a system in shock, and first aid may hurt a little. I say 'maybe' about all this, because I wasn't told.'' He darted another quick look at Howell.

The big man stood with folded arms, resplendent in black synthosuede, and said nothing. The twitch at the corner of his mouth said, *you got it, Lasser*.

Quantrill again: ''Why can't I apply today and avoid the rush?''

''Officially? Because you're still in the army, fool,'' Lasser said, scowling in mock irritation. ''Still off the record, I don't know. All I do know is, they *don't* want any of you for a few months yet—not even your applications.'' He surveyed the gunsels he had trained, palms out; a friendly little fellow who, as they all knew, could be hiding two dozen deadly weapons on his person. ''Any more questions?''

Sanger was yawning. Pelletier muttered a joke to Quinn. ''Dis-*missed*.'' said Lasser.

Chapter 81

Cedar Rapids and Dayton would be knee-deep in snow this time of year; Quantrill scratched them from his mental list. The port of Eureka was a boomtown, perhaps not too cold for a few days of desultory job-hunting. Bakersfield and Odessa would be warm, if you didn't mind the brawling and the sidearms. Maybe in a week or so . . .

He snorted at his attempts at doublethink, turned up the fleece collar of his denim jacket against a cold breeze that scudded across Route 84 on the outskirts of Clovis, New Mexico. He knew damned well where he was going first, and if it took the full thirty days to make sure, he would spend them. Palma, back at her old post, would be glad to see him; might even find him a job or at least a cot and a computer carrel. In mid-February he'd be back in Santa Fe for muster-

ing out and, almost certainly, a set of black synthosuedes
with the sunflower patch.

He placed two five-dollar pieces between gloved fingers of
his right hand, ready for the casual wave that might negotiate
a ride as far as Lubbock or San Angelo. With his left hand he
fumbled for the folded note Sanger had slipped him; read it
again in the hard chill light of a winter sun.

> *You're right, of course. Control would know we were
> together & we need to keep our noses clean. Good luck in
> wild country, I know where you're going even if you don't!*
>
> *I also know in my bones what Quinn will be up to. Can't
> wait to see if he makes it back. Interesting problem for us
> all–how to call your soul your own. Funny, when we were
> out for a little jog I always felt mine was my own. Call it
> therapy. Just wanted you to know in case I don't see you in
> Santa Fe.*
>
> *S.*

Not 'Marbrye', but 'Sanger'. No affectionate terminal
phrases, no promises or complaints or worrisome strategies
to enmesh him. Just the sort of note he had drafted for her, but
had given it up when it said too much. He told himself it was
stupid to wish she had said more; no one with a mastoid critic
could afford that.

Slowly, he abraded the note to shreds under his hiking
boot, then squinted toward the faint cough of a diesel in the
distance. He tucked the camera out of sight because he did
not want to answer questions about that telephoto lens. The
thirty-mm. self-propelled warhead might not penetrate heavy
armor, but it would stop a truck—or anything on four legs.

Quantrill could not bring back the dead, but he could
avenge them. Smiling, waving, he sought his ride into wild
country.